Priceless Changes

by

Alexandria May Ausman

Copyright © 2025 by Alexandria May Ausman

Book cover illustration by Alexandria May Ausman
Editor: Jon M. Ausman

Library of Congress Control Number: 2025902564

ISBN: 978-1-963335-36-1 (ebook)
ISBN: 978-1-963335-35-4 (paperback)

Published By:
Ausman & Cousins LLC
1700 North Monroe Street
Suite 11, Box 284
Tallahassee, Florida 32303-0501

For author interviews: ausman@embarqmail.com

Das Kaiser Haus Series

The Collar King Series

The Most Brutal Man in Europe Series

Claus's Revelations (Chapters 1 to 8)
Priceless Changes (Chapters 9 to 17)
Silver Well (Chapters 18 to 25)

The Psycho Series

Cemetery Kid (Chapters 1 to 20)
Stop Calling Me Psycho (Chapters 21 to 33)
Motor-Psycho (Chapters 34 to 44)
Delusion of the Collar and the Key (Chapters 45 to 53)
Brutality's Prisoner (Chapters 54 to 64)
Aesthetic Akathisia (Chapters 65 to 74)
Metallic Burden (Chapters 75 to 83)

27 Masters Series

Anita the Benevolent (Chapters 1 to 7)
The Beast and the Witch (Chapters 8 to 16)
High Priestess of Schizophrenia (Chapters 17 to 24)
The Professional Dominatrix (Coming soon)

Stand Alone Books

The Grannybat's Weird Tales & Gothic Stories Volume 1

Book 2 Characters: Priceless Changes

Agnette Krauss: the mother of Christian Axel, daughter of Gregor and Ingrid

Alice: a Haus Voter

Almut: a son of a black collar door guard

Amos Altergott: a deceased Fur King, succeeded Felicity

Anna Altergott:

Annika: spouse of Gregor

Attila, Doctor: the Haus physician

Awiwa Krauss: daughter of Ingred and Gregor

Barnim: a Haus Voter

Bartram: a former Haus Dominant

Bernt Schmidt: brother of Xavier

Birgit: a black collar maid, lover of Xaiver, sister of Viviana

Bladrick Reinhardt: cousin of Keifer

Bren: a former Haus Dominant

Britton: a Haus doctor

Byron Schmidt: a Haus Dominant, a Voting Council member, son of Xavier and Birgit

Cary: the Shadow King

Casper: a deceased Haus Dominant working for Gretta.

Christian: the anger and lust shard

Christian Axel: a Haus Dominant, the Priceless, son of Xavier

Christoph: a Haus Voter

Claus Albrecht: an Elder of the Haus

Cora Reinhardt: a Haus Fur Queen

Dämonen: the Demon sharing the shard Maximillian

Der Goldene Hund: the Voice or the Boss shard; the Conscious shard

Derbeck Schmidt: brother of Xavier, father of Oliver and Rolf

Die Brutale: three shards melded together; Mad Max, Max, and Christian

Dina Krauss: deceased sister of Malfred

Drexel Reinhardt: half-brother to Bladrick

Ebba A. Albrecht: spouse of Gerard Albrecht

Emmerick: Peter and Rachel's son

Eric: a Haus Dominant

Evelyn: a Haus black collar kitchen worker

Felicity: the Mother Lamb, a shard

Felicity Albrecht: mother of Claus, the Fur Queena

Felix: Peter' black collar Dark Bonded

Florian Schmidt: the first Priceless, deceased

Freidrick Schmidt: a Haus Voter, son of Bernt

Fritz Finck: a Haus Dominant

Gerard Albrecht: a deceased sadistic step-father of Christian Axel

Gregor Krauss: grandfather of Meine Liebe, Fur King of the Danish House

Gretta Albrecht: a Haus FemDom, the Silk Queen

Hans: a Haus Voter

Heidi Schmidt: a Dungeon Mistress

Helga Schmidt: a Dungeon Mistress, sister of Xavier

Heidi Schmidt: a Dungeon Mistress

Hemmel Krauss: a deceased Haus Dominant, a Dane
Ingrid Reinhardt: spouse of Xavier, ally of Claus, sister of Keifer
Ivan: captain of the Russian Guard
Jacob Wagoner: a Haus Dominant
Johannes: a Haus Voter
Jonas Weiss: an Elder of the Haus. Spouse of Christian Axel
Joseph Schmidt: an original Founder of the Haus
Justus Schmidt: son of Bernt and Ingrid, half-brother to Christian Axel
Karl Krauss: brother of Malfred, a Haus Dominant
Karsten: a Haus FemDom
Kay: a Haus Dominant, co-founder of FBL
Keifer Reinhardt: spouse of Claus, cousin of Kristian, great uncle to Christian Axel
Kilian Altergott: a Haus Fur King
Kloe: a deceased Black collar
Kristian Reinhardt: cousin of Keifer, great uncle of Christian Axel
Leo Albrecht: an Elder of the Haus, cousin of Claus
Liam: a rural German firefighter
Liliam: a faux Haus silver collar, a Dominant working for Gretta
Lucus: a Haus Dominant, a royal
Ludwig: a Haus Elder
Mad Max: the sadistic shard of Maximillian, aka the Heart and Judgment
Mad Maxx: husband of Meine Liebe; a Haus Dominant

Mad Maxx: the masochistic shard, also the Brain and Guilt
Mad Maxximillian die Brutal: the most brutal man in Europe
Magnus: a Haus Dominant, member of the Wolf Pack
Malfred Krauss: a Haus Elder
Marc: a deceased Black collar
Maus Albrecht: sister of Leo
Max: the Soul shard
Max: cousin to Keifer, great uncle of Christian Axel
Maximillian Keifer Schmidt: the twin brother of Christian Axel
Maximillian: the seductive shard, aka the Libido
Maxximillian: the shard controlling the wheel
Meine Liebe: submissive and spouse of Mad Maxx
Mueller, Doctor: physician that healed the deeply injured boy that escaped Gerard
Nestor: a deceased Russian Guard
Noah: a Dungeon Master, son of Bladrick Reinhardt.
Noethan: a deceased Haus physician
Olaf: a deceased black collar door guard, son of Bladrick Reinhardt.
Oliver Schmidt: brother of Rolf, son of Derbeck
Peter Schmidt: a Dominant of Der Kaiser Haus; uncle of Christian Axel, son of Bernt
Rachel: an American, known as Meine Liebe, designated wife of Christian Axel
Rachel Krauss: spouse of Peter Schmidt, first cousin to Malfred and Karl, a Haus Voter
Rolf Schmidt: a Haus voter, son of Derbeck

Roselina: a Haus black collar, spouse of Cary

Rudolph: a Haus Stable Master

Ruslan: Captain of the Russian Guard

Sabastain: a deceased Dungeon Master

Sasha: a Russian Guard

Squirrel: a faux black collar assigned to Jonas, known as Eichhörnchen

Tadeas: a deceased Dungeon Master

Tamina: a silver Pleasure submissive, loved by Malfred

Taube: a Ram, Taube in German is "Dove"

Valitin: a Haus dominant, a member of the Wolf Pack

Viviana: a Haus FemDom, sister of Birgit

Wilber: a Haus black collar, partner with Olaf

Wolf Krauss: a Haus Dominant

Xavier Schmidt: deceased Fur King, father of Justus, Byron and Christian, brother of Derbeck and Bernt, known as the "Child Killer"

Preface

The Elder Claus, the oldest Elder of Das Kaiser Haus and born in 1890, shares with Christian Axel many of the secrets of the Haus. The Haus, nearly three hundred years old, is both a place of pleasure and of death. Starting in the 1930s and onward the Haus was under the constant scrutiny and use by the Gestapo, the SS, the KGB, and the Stasi.

To survive the members of the Haus complied with the agents of the police states. They also, at times, hid hunted members of society that were sought by state agents. The deaths far exceeded the lives saved.

Christian Axel, born in 1957, is five months shy of his approaching his eighteenth birthday. He was trained to be the ultimate pleasure submissive known as the Priceless. He is adept at providing the greatest of sexual pleasures as well as putting to death a list of persons given to him by a mysterious cabal of Haus leaders. As a consequence he is sought out by those seeking to use his sexual prowess as well as by those who want to rise to the top through the elimination of their competitors.

As Mortar King, Christian Axel, will be incarcerated in the "Palace" located way below in a subterranean cell located deep in the foundation of Haus. Before then Christian Axel has to win the loyalty through fear of his subjects.

He also must name a Regent that will serve as his Voice while he is locked down below. There is heavy competition for the post that includes an abandoned Royal named Lucus, an Elder who thinks he is a Vampire named Jonas who is also married under Haus law to Christian, a sexual sadist and half-brother named Byron, and the Silk Queen named Gretta who is under a death sentence once her pregnancy comes to an end. There are others, currently unknown, who also want to be the Voice.

The competitors are ready to go for control of the Haus. Others, who may not succeed in their quest, think killing Christian Axel is a solution to their failed efforts.

Language in italics is a conversation between the adult male Master Mad Maxx and his female submissive Meine Liebe. The editor is related to both.

Chapter 9: The Last Dance of Santa Claus
Maxx and submissive Meine Liebe

I looked at the old man lying there weeping silently over the traumatic memories of his distant past. For a brief moment in time, I felt a twinge of pain for Claus. The idea of having to speak with one you love in the effort to send them to the place you and their kin can never be together again, well that tore at my black heart. I had assumed I couldn't feel anything for anyone. Not anymore, but I was wrong.

I reached over without thinking and caressed his hallow cheek. "You did what had to be done for Keifer. There wasn't any other option and as you say he was dying either way. At least you were able to say all the things to him you never could to your beloved mother, ja?"

Claus smiled bitterly and nodded. "Ja. Keifer went to the other side knowing that my love for him was secure. That will provide a bid of comfort in the coming hard weeks after we laid him low. However, with Bladrick down in the dungeons, and Ingrid on the run then Kristian and Max, oh those poor boys. There death was horrible. Only their cousin Keifer suffered slightly more."

I winced at the memory of lighting up a few fires myself only a week past. "I'm surprised no one in the Haus raised hell over Kilian and Xavier sending them to the hill, Claus. I thought you said they're popular like your Mann had been."

He groaned and sat up in the bed as he replied, "They had been that's truth. You must understand, the atmosphere had changed. None of us from Keifer to Max noticed the growing discontent among the residents. Hitler had come to power, and his words were like poison in the ears of Germany. He stroked their fears and fueled their hatred for anyone that wasn't of the Aryan decent or at least looked like they were of such a pedigree. It didn't matter that Max and Kristian were blond and blue eyed. They were unmarried and always viewed together. Me and Keifer were open about our nature as the proud schwulers but those boys' sexuality were the enigma. Privately, I was aware both fellows were fooling around with a pretty black collar maid. That sort of affair wasn't legal even back then. So, Kristian and Max kept their attempts to woe her quiet. That girl wasn't stupid. She realized the attentions of the powerful Voters was in her favor. The lady kept her suitors guessing as to which man she preferred. It was always a shock to me that the brothers never once took the other as a rival that needed to be vanquished. I suppose their friendly attitudes despite their shared interest only speaks of their rare, good +qualities. I must tell you, in all my long years, I never met finer men than your Great Uncles Keifer, Kristian and Max. I confess this hell hole destroyed them. I lost all faith in humanity. Especially when these rats that live here kill the beautiful and cleave the evil Xavier to their damned souls."

I took a deep breath and looked to my lap. "So, their names, which is where my names comes from. I am named after all three of the men. Agnette named me Christian Axel.

Then after falsely claiming me dead, talked Peter into calling me Maximillian Keifer? Why would they do that?"

Claus broke out in wild laughter, which startled me for a moment, and after recomposing himself replied, "Nein. Agnette and Peter didn't have a fucking thing to do with what you or your brother were called. Ingrid was the one that honored her lost brother and cousins by giving the Princes of Das Kaiser Haus a version of their names. She wished to give a gift to Max and Kristian because had they not sacrificed their lives, Agnette wouldn't been born. She then mingled her beloved brother Keifer Axel's name between you both. It was her deepest wish that none of these great men died in vain. She did have to hide Kiefer's name in the middle to keep your honest ties with the Reinhardt secret."

I narrowed meine eyes. "Huh? I don't understand Claus. Peter is the one that forced that name Maximillian on me. I never knew till this moment there was a middle name. As for Agnette, once again I refuse to believe the fantasy that I had a twin brother. I see no need for you to continue to push that agenda. Tell me something old man, have I ever failed you? Nein, therefore creating gruesome illusions is a cruelty I would expect of anyone but you."

The Elder grimaced and leaned toward my face as he said in the whisper, "What color are my eyes my love?"

I startled over the question. "What? I'm not sure Claus. Maybe grey or light blue? The same as the marble pillars in the Great Hall I think."

5

He chuckled hard. "You always say that. Let me speak with Christian Axel or maybe Der Hund."

I growled angrily. "Christ, are you demented or something? How many Gott damned times must I tell you old man, Christian cannot come to the wheel and Der Hund, that coward ran off. You talk with me, Maxximillian, or you can go jag off motherfucker."

The Elder frowned. "You are quite rude Maxximillian. Your manners seem to have degraded since last we spoke. I suppose that's to be expected when a submissive is no longer held in check by the silver collar. However, I must insist you mind your voice tone or I will be forced to send you below for correction. Is that clear?"

With an expression of disbelief on my face I responded, "How dare you call me a fucking submissive. I'm Maxximillian Die Brutale. That pussy pleasure submissive got himself shattered awhile back. Threaten me again and I will be happy to help you comprehend that I'm not a Max brother to be fooling with."

Claus sucked in his wind slightly and narrowed his eyes as if suspicious. "A Max brother? You call yourself this as if there are more than one Max in there with you?"

I nodded with a snort. "Well duh. There is Mad Max, Mad Maxx, Max, and me Maxximillian. We aren't really brothers, more like uncles and son, father and shit like that. I'm not about to go through the Max family tree here, Claus. Give me some more candy. I don't even care if it is drugged. I'm starving and the lambs haven't eaten yet."

The Elder smiled widely and pulled back from my face. "Four Max but only one Christian and a single Der Hund, who is actually the fifth Max brother. This is interesting."

That caused me great irritation when he said that. "So what? I like the name Max. It's beautiful and that bitch Christian isn't worth a shit. In all the boy's life he never has been able to prevent a fucking bit of trouble. When the chips fall, it's always the brothers Max that manage to haul us out of the fire. What does Christian do? I'll tell you. He screams, flails, fumes, gnashes his teeth and his eyes burn with flames but if he is permitted to run the wheel. Well, if he had his way we would all be destroyed."

Claus's eyes twinkled with sudden delight as he replied, "Ah. Now, just so we are clear and I am sure I am understanding you correctly, Maxximillian, you're saying this Christian is the mindless anger with suicidal intent but otherwise not useful. Tell me something, does he pick a lock?"

I snorted with a giggle. "Him?! Hell nein. The only thing that idiot does is pick his nose. Well, he cannot do that anymore either. The fool cut off his hand awhile back. I believe that will slow the prick up a bid. Hahaha. Awrooo. Look at him. He is stuck to that creepy Max thing. I know that's got to be the bitch. Serves him right. Ha!"

He suddenly grabbed my chin with a boney claw. "Enough, you will calm yourself immediately, Maxximillian. If you continue to behave the brute I won't give you any more chocolate. You listening to me?"

I nodded with a frown. "Ja, I hear you Claus. Give me the candy please?" I batted my eyes and made the pouty face. The that move of mine that always works on the old bastard.

Claus gasped and led go of my face. "My Gott. How the fuck could I have missed this? All these years and the answer was there. Oh Ingrid, honey, our boy, I've discovered which one returned and the poor baby that's only the delusion." He looked up at the ceiling as if speaking to the heavens.

I sneered at the old buzzard. "You left your speakers on Claus. Better be careful doing that. The others around here get pretty upset when they can hear what you are thinking."

He nodded and returned his steely gaze to mine own. "Okay, so Christian is attached to Max, Der Hund is missing. Felicity is in your pocket but without Der Hund you cannot speak with her."

I interrupted him. "I didn't say I couldn't speak with her, Claus. I said I couldn't trust Taube's interpretations of what she says. Max, Christian and Mad Max are stuck together not just the two of dem. The dumbasses tried to take up the wheel in triplicate. That's forbidden. Only two at a time can run the boy. They knew the rules and now they pay the price for being stupid."

The Elder's eyes went vide and he peered hard into mine as if trying to see into the wheelroom you know. "A rule that says only two can be in command at the same time. Another clue I completely missed. Okay, let's see, that is Mad Max, Max, Christian, and Der Hund accounted for. This Taube is he in there with you too and what about the other Max brother. Where is he. Mad Maxx you called him?"

I rolled mine eyes and blew mine breath into his face. "Taube is a dirty lamb raper. He used to be in here but he shattered. Then that motherfucker Der Hund brought him back in the flesh of the male lamb. Foolish thing to do if you ask me, but there it is. Mad Maxx, my father, is here with me sleeping. Those Stasi's nearly busted his horns right off his head."

Claus's mouth near dropped to the mattress. "Horns? Are you saying he is a lamb like this Taube. Can I see him, the Ram?"

I groaned but pulled the dirty lamb rapist from my pocket. The Elder smiled widely and held out his hand motioning me to give Taube to him. I felt the Ram trembling as I minded the Fur King without hesitation. Claus looked him over with a furrowed brow, but still grinning ear to ear.

He cleared his throat then glanced up at me. "Wake Mad Maxx up. I wish to speak with him please."

That caused me to sputter. "Hu…huh? Why would you desire to bother my father? He's earned his rest, Claus. Leave him be."

Claus held out his hand. "Don't argue with Maxximillian. Wake Mad Maxx and hand over Felicity. I wish to speak with the three of them since you refuse to allow me counsel with my boy Christian."

9

With a deep glare of fury I kicked the beast Mad Maxx as hard as I could. "Get up pops. This fool wants to break words with you." I reached into the coat pocket and gently handed the brave Felicity over. I was unable to resist Claus's demands for some weird reason.

I yawned and with some effort took up the wheel unsure what the fuck was going on. "Claus? What's wrong? Did Maxximillian fail to meet your desires? Do I need to correct the shard? Did he bite during oral services or complain of your mount?" I stretched and rubbed the boy's eyes.

The Elder stared at me appearing dumbfounded for a moment then shook his head slightly. "Nein, nothing like that. Mad Maxx I presume?"

I nodded and elbowed Maxximillian that was hoovering too close to the wheel. "Ja, you are correct. I ask with respect, what is the problem Master."

He sat there seeming almost too stunned to respond. "Uhm, no problem Mad Maxx. I was just asking Maxximillian a few questions and he claims not to be aware of the answers. Perhaps you can aid me better?"

I suddenly became aware he was holding on to my lambs. "As you wish, Claus. Can I please have my lambs back? They are not a threat, I swear it. I will put them back up and you need not be bothered by their constant bleating if that's caused you frustration."

Claus pulled the lambs to his chest and cuddled them in a childlike fashion. "I adore the lambs, Mad Maxx. How could they ever be annoying to anyone? So, this boy you're running, what is his name?"

That caused me to pause. "I'm not sure what you mean Claus. The boy?"

He nodded and then gently stroked Felicity and Taube as he repeated, "I want you to tell me Mad Maxx what they called this boy before he become a prisoner of the Dungeons? Not the name Peter gave to him, nor the one he answered to when Master Noah trained him to function. Who is the boy, Christian Axel or Maximillian Keifer? Which brother pulled the skeleton across Gerard's field after their escape from the shallow grave?"

With a loud wail I replied, "I cannot breath, brother. Help me dig. Please mother, help. The dirt, I taste it in my mouth."

Claus whispered, "You made the hole to the air, calm yourself my beauty. You pulled yourself out after a rest. Where are you?"

The room morphed into the rugged outdoors. I glanced up and saw the huge mountain ranges covered in the snow. Under me the damp ground was green with the fresh grass of spring. The wind blew through my mud encrusted hair. I took many deep breaths and spit out mouthfuls of earth.

I whimpered as the sun beat down upon my pale skin. The sight of the light was upsetting. I hadn't seen that yellow orb in two years. My weak eyes had trouble adjusting to the brightness of it. The boy's bladder led loose it's water. I groaned and shivered unsure what to do. The chain was still buried in the hole. The skeleton had been put in the grave first, and the flesh on top.

Maximillian told Christian their mother would be able to put the skin back on my brother. Der Hund agreed. They decided to dig up the bones. Then we'd travel together and find mother. The boy remembered the hounds and foxes in the picture books. The canines would use their paws to move the dirt. I ignored the agony of the flesh and began to mimic these clever animals.

Maximillian let out the howls, Christian wept, and Der Hund kept a look out for Gerard. This task was tiresome. The boy had to rest many times. Each handful their pulled out the earth, more fell into the void left behind. After much time, it seemed the impossible task.

No matter how hard the brothers begged the skeleton. He wouldn't help them get him out of the hole. The work was too much for the ravaged flesh. The brothers were forced to give up freeing him this way. Der Hund suggested we pull on the chain with all the boy's strength.

We gritted our teeth and crawled away from the hole. For a moment, this seemed to work. The skeleton's head come up from below. Then his arm and shoulder pulled out of the grave, but then something went wrong. A loud snapping sound cut through the air. The boy was thrown face first into the grass.

The skeleton's bones had broken. Only part of him wanted to come to find mother with the boy. Maximillian and Christian were upset that they been unable to convince him to travel in completion. At least some of him wanted to come. We decided this would have to do, because all of us understood Gerard might come back and discover we'd escaped his hold.

Slowly, the boy crawled on his hands and knees across the green fields. The baby lambs called to him from the distance. He wanted to pet them but there wasn't time for it. Maximillian and Christian were looking for the truck. Gerard brought them there in that vehicle. The brothers assumed it would know the way home. All they had to do is get back inside it and ask it to return them to her.

The bright sun began to sink into the mountain side. Soon the light wasn't so brilliant and the shadows grew larger. Maximillian and Christian felt the icy fingers of the night air caressing the boy. He trembled and wept but kept crawling. Pain from the many wounds and stiffness from the years of being unable to run or play made moving even a single inch almost impossible.

Darkness was descending upon the land as the boy made it to the end of the tall grass of the green fields. There before his very eyes was the old farm house he recognized from the night Gerard brought the frightened brothers to this hellish place. He halted his agonizing journey and lay still in the weeds listening.

He feared Gerard was lurking about. If he saw the brothers there the results would be far worse than he already done to dem. Barely able to pull in a full breath the boy and skeleton waited patiently. The rest was much appreciated. They had crawled all day and the flesh's muscles were well worn.

The darkness overtook the world, and the boy made ready to continue his bid for freedom. He pulled his heavy weight across the yard of the farmhouse unable to find the strength to stand. It took all he had to hold back the wail as the agony of his bloody gashes tormented him. With deliberate but slow movements, he managed to reach a hiding spot under the front room window.

He listened as the voices of Gerard's soman, Ebba wafted thru the air, "What will we do, Gerard? When you tell Agnette you killed both the boys, she's is going to hit the roof."

The gruff response of the man we hated the most growled out, "Shut up Ebba. I need time to think without the constant nagging of your stupid sounds. I'm fuckin aware Agnetta won't be pleased. I believe the best thing for us to do is just leave. We can head for the border and take our chances in Denmark, or maybe Poland. I have a few contacts that maybe led us stay with them in either country."

Ebba groaned. "Are you serious? You really wish to waste two years of our lives only to end up fleeing like rats empty handed? How are we to survive without the money promised by Ingrid or anything but the clothes on our backs? Fuck this. I say we meet with Agnette and say nothing of the accident. Once she arrives, I can distract her while you can sneak up on the bitch. We kill her, take the cash, and then flee Germany, ja?"

Gerard took a moment then responded, "Agnette said Ingrid won't turn over the ransom until she sees the Princes."

Ebba led out a frustrated shout, "That's bullshit. I bet that witch has the money already. She's full of crap and you know it."

Gerard blew out his breath. "Nein. Trust me Ebba, if Agnette had the money she'd not bother to demand we bring that brat to her. She'd already be gone. You and me would be left to do what has already been done. Face it baby, we are screwed. That fucking little monster ended any shot we had at getting a taste of the good life. Like it or not, we must get away while we still kin. I'm assuming that Agnette will tell Ingrid we killed her grandsons. When that happens, I'd rather not know what lengths that crazy bitch will go to in her need to see us punished for it."

Ebba sighed loudly, "Fine, we do it your way but I want you to know the second I find a man with a heavy purse, then I'm leaving you for him. Then I will turn you in for murder. I'll contact Ingrid and offer to stand as witness at your trial. I bet she'd pay good money to see you hanged."

Gerard chuckled with a bitter tone. "For starters no self-respecting fellow would caste you a second glance. You're stuck with me and me with you. As for turning me over to the cops. Let me remind you of something sweetheart. I killed one of the boys and you were there when I did it. If the authorities find me, they're sure as hell going to know

15

about you also. Maybe I call Ingrid and offer her the same deal you just come up with, ja?"

Ebba growled and the sound of something crashing into the wall startled the boy. "Fuck you, Gerard. If I were you I'd sleep with one eye open, motherfucker. I'm going to be rid of you one way or another. Wait and see."

He laughed wildly. "You turn me on when you're angry baby. Get over yourself and come to bed. We need to leave before the sun comes up. Agnette will surely be headed out this way after she realizes we are not showing up with her sons. The more kilometers we kin put between her and us the better."

Ebba snorted. "Okay, that will solve the issue with Agnette and Ingrid, but what of the German authorities? Sooner or later, some nosy farmer may find that shallow grave. What will prevent the neighbors from identifying that they saw you or me in this area for many months prior to a couple corpses turning up? I don't desire to spend the rest of my days looking over my shoulder waiting to be arrested over the likes of that trash rotting in the field, Gerard."

He laughed hard then responded, "Good thing you and me never had any children, eh Ebba? A tenderhearted mother you certainly are not. Well, calm your fears darling. I have a tank of petrol on the front porch. Before we leave I'll dig up the evidence, toss a match and poof, no one will ever know they were here or anywhere for that matter."

Their hound began to bark. He must have smelled the boys' blood or perhaps he could hear his labored breathing.

The brothers' heart raced and he looked about trying to discover another place to hide. Ebba and Gerard halted dare dark discussion. The boy heard heavy footsteps approaching the window above him.

Gerard's voice rang out, "What is it boy? I don't see anything. Why are you barking like the German army is coming? Shit, you nearly caused me to have the heart attack. Shut the fuck up." The dog led out a yelp, apparently the mean bastard kicked the hound for doing what dogs do.

Despite that 'light tap' the hound continued to call out the intruder alarm. Gerard grumbled and Ebba complained of the noise. The sounds of a mild struggle were heard. Then suddenly the front screen door flew open. The boy pulled up tightly in a ball, trying to shrink small as possible. He watched the big man come barreling out of the farmhouse.

Gerard was dragging the struggling hound by his collar behind him. He didn't seem to notice the nearly broken little boy hidden behind the sparce shrub brush by the porch. The huge man continued to pull the dog along, all the while cursing the animal.

To the boys' shock Gerard was headed for the old barn. It then dawned on the brothers, that the man was intending to lock the beast in the old holding cell. His cruelly locking the animal away was intended to keep him from annoying the evil couple with his sounds of distress.

This was a stroke of luck for the brothers. Without the hound in the farmhouse to alert his Master and Mistress of their presence, the chance of discovery went down substantially. They watched the burly brute rush by them without noticing their hiding spot.

Not long after Gerard returned he went back inside after locking up his guardian hound. Then the lights in the lower level went out. Maximillian and Christian saw a dim lantern illuminating the tiny loft room at the top of the rickety old haus. The couple were preparing to catch a few hours of sleep before trying to flee from their crimes.

The brothers waited in the bushes until at last one of the monsters blew out their candle. Fury filled the flesh, as he recalled all the months of torture at the hands of these people. Neither boy ever did a damned thing to deserve any of it, nor could their understand the reasons.

Despite the ravages of Gerard's cruel treatment and the many wounds, an inner strength filled the boy. He managed to take to his bare feet. Using the sides of the farmhouse to aid him in balancing, he slowly crept around to the back door.

This took a painfully long time to accomplish. His muscles were weak with atrophy. His clothing was threadbare and rotten. The cold night air did all it could to chill his skin, causing further strain in his daunting tasks.

However, he managed to arrive at his destination without making a sound. The boy spotted a wooden board, laying discarded in the backyard. He carefully propped it to block the back door. His job accomplished; he retraced his steps back to the front porch.

Once there he quickly retrieved the tank of petrol Gerard intended to use to burn him and the skeleton with. He removed the cap with some difficulty and then turned it to its side. The highly flammable contents spilled across the dry wooden platform. A wicked smile crossed his face as he watched the flood force itself under the crack of the front door.

Not a bid of hesitation come over him while he took up the lighter left by Gerard's smoking ashtray. He'd seen the brute flick this instrument hundreds of times before lighting up his cigarettes. Gerard's laughter at using the boy's skin to put them out during hours of ceaseless torment filled his mind.

He looked up at the tiny window of the loft for a moment. Maximillian, Christian and Der Hund struck up the flame. This time it would be the boys thrilling at the screams of pain caused by the torture of deep burns. The flesh dropped the zippo into the fluid. A flash of brilliance blinded the boy as the fire greedily sped across the accelerants surface.

Almost by instinct he fled away from the fast moving inferno. His stiff joints, injured right knee from that straight razor attack, the skeleton and heavy chain hampered an easy escape from the heat. He clumsily tripped, falling face first from the engulfed porch.

A loud thump cracked thru the air as my head collided with the parched earth. I rolled to his back and vailed from the agony of it. My heart pounded in terror over making the loud noise. I knew Gerard heard that. I held his breath waiting for the brute to appear and beat the stuffing out of me like he always did.

However, to my shock, the huge man didn't come rushing out the door to bash him. In fact, Gerard couldn't have, even if he had been alerted to the boy's presence. The gasoline had prevented anyone from getting out of that house, at least from the front or back door.

Awe overcame the boy as he witnessed the licking flames devouring the bottom of that shack with breathtaking speed. He glanced up at the tiny loft window. His air stalled in his chest. Gerard was there peering back at him, a look of stun on his face.

The brute appeared unable to believe the evidence his eyes reported to his brain. It was apparent Gerard honestly thought the boy had died. He stood there staring as if in a trace through the window. He didn't attempt to try to push his huge carcass out of it.

The look of horror on his face told the tale. Gerard realized, too late, that the arsonist had cleverly trapped him and his woman. They were doomed. Neither could escaping the burning building. The boy heard Ebba scream that the fire had blocked the ladder. She was begging for help.

A loud crash was heard, and red ash filled the air as the part of the roof collapsed. Ebba's cries of desperation were suddenly silenced. Gerard continued to stand there unable to tear his fury filled gaze from the frightened boy's eyes.

Then another deafening boom shook the earth. The old home crumpled into ruin taken the brutal Gerard to hell with it. Maximillian and Christian laid there too shocked to move. The roar of the hungry fire filled his ears and warmed his aching flesh.

A sudden emotional burst overcame the boy. Tears of relief, grief, and agony leaked out him in rivers. He found it hard to fathom that the monster Gerard and his cruel Frau were no longer able to hurt him.

Thanks to the hours of stressing, fatigue filled the flesh. Unconsciousness came for the boy, allowing him a much needed rest from his troubles. He closed his eyes and welcomed the quiet of the void.

Sounds of unrecognized voices rousted him from that deep slumbering. The boy opened his lids. There above him was the face of a bearded man. He was wearing a strange hat and yellow jacket. This fellow's expression was that of fear. Maximillian and Christian startled to full alertness at the sight of him.

This man looked at the boy and said, "Leicht, Kleiner. Ich bin nicht hier, um dir zu schaden. Kannst du mir deinen Namen sagen? Wie bist du hierher gekommen? Wer hat dir diese schreckliche Sache angetan?" (Easy, Kid. I'm not here to hurt you. Can you tell me your name? How did you get here? Who did this terrible thing to you?") His worried gaze turned toward the piece of skeleton that had come with the brothers seeking revenge.

I shook my head. "Mor. Mor. Grrrr. Baaaa, baaaa. Woof, woof, Hjælp Mor. Awrooh."

The fellow frowned as he replied, "Ich verstehe deine Sprache nicht, Kleiner. Sprichst du Deutsch? Liam. Hierher. Weißt du, was der Junge sagt?" (I don't understand your language, kid. Do you speak German? Liam. Come here. Do you know what the boy is saying?") He looked to his left.

I followed his sight and led out a loud gasp. It was then I noticed I was surrounded by several large males. All of them were dressed like the man speaking to me. I didn't understand his words, nor had I seen any of them before. This scared the hell out of me. I assumed they had come to beat me for daring to try to escaping from Gerard.

With a loud vail, I rolled to my face. I scrambled in the crab crawl fast as my tiny legs could carry me. I had to get back to that grave and rescue the rest of the skeleton. Without every part, mother couldn't fix him. If that happened my brother couldn't ever go home again.

The men backed away while I tore past them in the blind panic. They shot each other confused glances, but didn't attempt to prevent my departure. This strange behavior didn't halt me in the attempt to return to that hole in the ground Gerard dug.

I wanted to take to my feet. That wasn't possible. Gerard's blade cut deep in the back of my right knee. As the hours had passed, the muscles in that leg had become stiff and nearly useless. I was forced to remain on all fours. I was so frightened I barely noticed the terrible agony that screamed out from almost every nerve ending.

It became apparent the men were following me at a safe distance. This was scary to realize but I couldn't do anything about it. That journey back to the shallow grave seemed far shorter than I recalled. I arrived at its edge quickly. I was driven to a mad pace by the intense fear that my pursuers were planning to take my brother away and do only Gott knows what to me.

I plunged both bloody hands into the cool earth. A wail from the pain escaping my throat before I could stop it. The crowd of males approached and fanned out into a circle. The sight of their arrival further fueled my terror. I tried to dig into the ground faster, while making the dog growls to warn them to stay away.

They weren't detoured by my sounds of threat. One of these strangers came toward me. He moved with speed and grabbed me around the waist. I led out wails of terror and anger over his touching. Without hesitation I turned in his grip and bit him as hard as I could. He screamed and let go immediately.

I scrambled back to the hole and continued trying to reach the skeleton. Another man shouted something to the one I attacked. He then rushed forward and snatched my head by the hair. I screamed, clawed and kicked at him. This guy was smarter than his buddy. He held me tightly at arm's length. This prevented me from landing a single blow on my subduer.

He held me like this until I found myself beginning to wear down. This man patiently waited for my fit to show signs of slowing. When he observed I was panting heavily and my lashing out weakened, he pounced.

I was so tired I could barely muster up the whimper while he forced me to the ground face first. The man rapidly pulled my arms behind me and yelled out something I couldn't comprehend. A second fella come running up with a piece of rope. Together they tied my wrists tightly to prevent any further disagreement from me.

I watched helplessly as the attackers produced a shovel and finished what I'd desperately been trying to do. I didn't know what they were going to do to me or my brother's skeleton. I began to weep heavily in the understanding that I was their prisoner.

In no time their managed to pulled all the bones from the grave. Then one of the men produced a blanket. I watched in stunned silence as their laid it over him with tears in their eyes. Several of them caste pity filled glances toward me as their did this weird thing.

A screaming noise echoed in the distance. It had been growing louder with each passing moment. No doubt whatever was making the sound, it was getting closer. I strained my neck hard trying to get a look at the creature that spoke in the scary wailing. To my shock a large truck that resembled Gerard's, only this one was painted white, cam speeding in our direction.

I shot a terrified glance at the many men surrounding me. Most were shaking their head, wiping their eyes or staring at me with expressions of wonder. I was ready to demand to be told what they intended to do with my skeleton and me.

With all the bravery I could collect I opened my mouth and yelled, "Mor, mor. Grrrr. Caw caw. Ah, woof, woof. Ah, mor." I thought for sure this would demonstrate I wasn't the man to fool around with.

The man that tied me up winced then said, "Lieber Gott, das is ein verdammter Albtraum. Dieser Junge hat gerade in die Hose gepinkelt und nach them Geruch von ihm zu urteilen, is dies nicht das erste oder sogar das tausendste Mal. Liam. Nehmen Sie die Bolzenschneider vom LKW. Diese Kette muss sich lösen. Die Polizei braucht das ganze tote Kind, würde ich denken. Pass auf, wenn du die Überreste freigibst. Dieser kleine Junge hat einen ziemlichen Biss. Das arme thing is verrückt geworden. Nicht, dass ich weniger erwarten würde. Himmel. Beeil dich, Mann. Der Krankenwagen is fast da. Dieses Kind braucht ärztliche Hilfe und ein starkes Beruhigungsmittel." (Dear God, this is a fucking nightmare. This boy just peed in his pants and judging by the smell of him, this is not the first or even the thousandth time. Liam. Take the bolt cutters from the truck. This chain must come loose. The police need the whole dead child, I would think. Watch out when you release the remains. This little boy has quite a bite. The poor thing went crazy. Not that I would expect less. Heavens. Hurry up, man. The ambulance is almost here. This child needs medical attention and a strong sedative."

25

I saw this man called Liam run back toward the smoldering farm house. I turned my anxious attentions toward the fella that spoke to him. He kept his eyes on me while he motioned another of his buddies to approach us. I wailed in fear as the two of them rolled me to my back.

They used their knees to keep me pinned to the ground. I growled and gnashed my teeth in the vicious threats but neither man paid me any mind. That white truck come flying thru the green fields. It slid across the slippery earth as the driver slammed on the breaks only a few feet away from me, the men and the covered skeleton.

Two men got out of that truck. Both were wearing the white coats. I saw one hurry to the back of the vehicle. A couple of the men wearing the yellow jackets rushed off to join this man. The other guy come toward me and my pair of kidnappers in the quick steps.

I whimpered and struggled under the weight of the men. "Naaa, baaa, mor, mor, awrooh, ah." The man halted his approach and shot my attackers a look of distress.

The one that tied my hands groaned and said, "Worüber zögern Sie, Doktor? Siehst du nicht, dass dieser Junge Hilfe braucht? Mach dir keine Sorgen um die Geräusche, die er macht. Wir werden ihn festhalten. Beeil dich und bring ein Beruhigungsmittel für dieses Kind und einen Leichensack für das andere." (What are you hesitating about, doctor? Don't you see that this boy needs help? Do not worry about the sounds he makes. We're going to hold him. Hurry up and bring a sedative for this child and a body bag for the other.")

This man in white gasped and responded, "Was zum Teufel is hier los? Warum is das Kind in Bänder geschnitten and trägt einen Kragen and eine Kette...und um Himmels willen. Was is es, das an ihn gekettet ist? Oh mein Gott. Das is ein Schädel. Hast du die Polizei gerufen? Ich darf nichts anfassen, bis die Polizei grünes Licht gibt. Dies is sicherlich ein Tatort." (What the hell is going on here? Why is the child cut into ribbons and wears a collar and a chain. And for heaven's sake. What is it that is chained to him? Oh, my God. That's a skull. Did you call the police? I'm not allowed to touch anything until the police give the green light. This is certainly a crime scene.")

The man shook his head and growled back, "Die verdammten Bullen sind unterwegs. Schau dir diese arme Kreatur an. Dieser Junge braucht Hilfe, and er wird nicht auf Verfahrensbürokratie warten können. Es is ein Wunder, dass er nicht bereits verblutet oder an einem Schock gestorben ist. Entweder mach deinen verdammten Job oder ich werde ein paar Anrufe tätigen, um dir zu versichern, dass du arbeitslos bist." (The fucking cops are on their way. Look at this poor creature. This boy needs help, and he will not be able to wait for procedural bureaucracy. It's a miracle that he has not already bled to death or died of shock. Either do your fucking job or I'll make some calls to assure you that you're unemployed.")

"I see the man in the white coat coming for me. He holds the needle in his hand. There is the board with a white blanket. They want to put me in that truck. Stop them please. This man Liam has brought the bolt cutters. Nein, he is going to take the skeleton away from us. No one loves him. Do you hear me? He is mine. Leave us alone. Get away from me, you monsters. Let go of my skeleton. Mother, help us. Ah, Maximillian, no." A loud slap and the burning of my check woke me from the nightmare dreaming.

I blinked several times and the wizened face of the Fur King come into focus. His gaunt face wore the expression of concern. He frowned deeply and gently caressed my stinging face. I realized he'd backhanded me once again.

I sneered at the old man. "Why do you keep hitting me, Claus? I don't desire to sit here and endure your repeated abuse. Tell me what you want and I do it. Then release me so I can get back to tolerating the beating and raping by my expected tormentors." I pushed his fawning hand away from me.

Claus's eyes became watery as he replied, "Mad Maxx, I don't torture you. Your memories do. I'm trying to help you face your trauma in the effort to see you finally overcome it. I think for the moment though, we both can use a break, ja?"

I shook my head. "I'm not Mad Maxx. You are speaking to Maxximillian, dammit. Didn't you hear my father call for my help? If you didn't than I must wonder if you are going deaf as well as demented, old man."

The Elder startled. "Maxximillian you say? I thought that was Christian calling for his brother Maximillian as their cut him from the chains."

I interrupted with a scoff. "There was no fucking twin, Claus. Gott damn, you are the nag. I know you're trying to get into my head. Mad Maxx was sleeping and didn't realize your games. I pushed him from the wheel to keep any misunderstandings from occurring. Now, get to commanding your special service rights and back my lambs. I've had enough of your bullshit." I tried to snatch Felicity and Taube from his cuddle.

The Fur King glared at me with barely veiled fury. "You keep your hands to yourself young Maxximillian. I will release these lambs to your care after I've examined them a bit. Settle down. I mean it."

I blew out my breath in frustration and crossed my arms angrily. "You have no right to take them from me, Claus. They are my lambs."

Claus chuckled bitterly and then held up the Ram to look at him closely. "I am not taking them. I am borrowing them for a minute. Ah, this one is Taube? Well, he is a handsome Ram isn't he? I can see why Felicity was seduced by this young stud, ja?"

Taube shot me a prideful grin as the Elder examined him with an adoring expression on his face. That pissed me off more than you can know.

With a growl low in my throat I replied, "He is a rapist. Felicity didn't grant consent. She was misled by that cad."

The Elder turned to stare at me appearing stunned. "You honestly think Felicity so weak of character she would fall for the manipulations of this Ram easily? Come now Maxximillian. That's an insult to the mother lamb. Not to mention giving this fellow far more power than I believe he possesses." He held Taube out at me.

I snatched the ram from his ancient claws with speed. Then without a word or hesitation threw the Ram across the room. Taube led out a loud scream that was silenced the second he collided with the wall. He bounced off the wooden barrier and was hurled helplessly to the floor.

Claus was shocked to stupid as he watched the Ram's unwilling flight and crash. After Taube's violent trip come to the end the Elder turned to me appearing bewildered. I glared at him defiantly while his wet eyes searched my own.

He cleared his throat and said, "That wasn't very nice Maxximillian. Why would you be mean to Felicity's lover? Are you jealous of the attention she gives to him. Or perhaps it's because Der Hund gives Taube a new body but forces you to continue to share yours with your brother, ja?"

That accusation the old man made stirred me into a fury. "What is this you say? Nein, this is my Haus, Claus. Just like those are my lambs. I do with them and this flesh as I please without interference from you, the residents of Das Kaiser Haus, Christian, or that coward Der Hund."

The Elder furrowed his brow. "There is no need to raise your voice to me, boy. You will end this insolent behavior or I make you very sorry for it. Go pick up your pet Ram. While you doing that, calm down. Then you will return to my bedside with a meeker attitude. I won't entertain any arguments in the matter. I mean it."

I glared at him for a moment, calculating the chances he would make good on his threats. Finally, with a sigh of frustration I got up and did as he told me to. I decided this wasn't worth fighting about. After all, he was right. He'd be dead soon enough. I'd be shut of him and his nasty touching for the rest of my life. All I had to do is keep from blowing my top for a bit longer.

Taube sniffled loudly as I gathered him from his place in the floor. "Felicity will punish you for taking out your aggressions on me, Maxximillian. Claus is a wise man. You're just jealous of the mother's affections for me."

I held him to my face. "Shut up rapist. Say another word and I will tear out your stuffing, fool."

Claus bellowed out from the bed behind me, "Enough Maxximillian. Get back over here and leave that Ram alone."

Taube grinned at me victoriously as I begrudgingly did as ordered. I made the mental note to kick his wooly ass later as soon as the Elder wasn't around to protect the rude bastard.

Claus shot me a glance of caution and took Taube back from me as he said, "Let's get back to my story and allow you to cool off a bit. I don't wish for my final memories of this life to be of my beautiful boy abusing his helpless wards."

I shrugged as I made myself as comfortable as possible next to him. "Talk all you want, Claus. I'm happy to sit here tolerating you molesting my ears rather than my backside. I confess it's a nice chance of pace."

He chuckled bitterly as he gently petted Felicity and Taube. "Oh, I'm glad to hear you don't mind me working my tongue for a while longer. However, you know how it is. Service for service my boy. Shortly, I will be expecting you to engage me with that pretty mouth of yours." He winked at me and I groaned under my breath.

With a smile coming over his haggard face he began his tale anew.

"So, there I was that horrible summer of 1935. Keifer, Kristian, Max, and Ingrid gone. Bladrick trapped in the Dungeon, and me held hostage on the fifth floor on the fifth throne. I was helpless to prevent Xavier from raisin his brothers Derbeck and Bernt to fill the seats he'd cruelly vacated for them.

It wasn't a bit of surprise when only a week later the two Wagner Silk Princes suddenly took ill and died. No one dared to question the suspiciousness of the fit men's strange sicknesses. Most assumed Xavier had threatened the Haus doctor to ensure he declared their deaths were from 'natural causes.' Everyone knew better.

Rumors swept through the halls that the Silk King removed his opposition by poisoning them. Of course, this gossiping got louder because the Silk King filled the newly open slots with Barnim and Drexel.

Not even a fortnight had passed since Keifer, Kristian and Max's murders and Xavier had managed to fill the Silk thrones with men loyal only to him, except me. Xavier and the others weren't too concerned about silly old schwuler fifth Prince Claus.

The other Voters realized I didn't give a shit about the politics of the Haus. I barely looked up from my boots and wouldn't dare to raise a voice of discontent to anything their wanted during Council meetings with the Elders. They knew I was overwhelmed by the grief of losing my Mann and all my friends. Xavier and his men believed I wasn't a threat to their authority. I was far too weak of mind and flesh to be taken seriously in any regard.

That is what everyone thought, that is what I wanted everyone to thing. But in reality, it was anything but the truth of it...

I understood that the days of living as the honest man were over the minute that needle ended Keifer's pain. The world he and I had fought to create was buried with him and lay smoldering in the ashes of his cousins on the Hill. If I'd had any ideas that I could somehow survive without them and not compromise all that we'd believed it that was quickly dashed by the Silk King himself.

Xavier approached me the very afternoon Keifer was laid to rest. He callously informed me from that moment forward I was forbidden to be seen wearing the trappings of the Frau. That bastard stated that if I didn't desire to find myself incarcerated in the Dungeon cell I'd best get used to sporting men's suits. The Silk King went further to insist I lock away, actually he said throw out, all the beautiful gowns my beloved Keifer bought for me over the years.

Then he rubbed salt into the wound. Xavier told me that I was to never be spotted engaging in any activity associated with the gay man. In other words, he expected me to behave as if I were straight. He suggested I get a girlfriend with speed and forget my true nature of interest in the male of our species.

I normally would have assumed the man was funning me, but I knew better. His preposterous demands weren't actually coming from his personal bias towards my sexual preference. Xavier, believe it or not, was trying to prevent my arrest and eventual destruction. He had been made aware that the SS und/or Gestapo would be paying Das Kaiser Haus a visit in the near future.

It wasn't a secret that the ruling Nazi government despised and outlawed homosexuality. Any union that didn't result in many Aryan 'pure breed' German sons to serve in Hitler's army was viewed as useless, unnatural and therefore it was a crime.

Without quarrel I told Xavier that I would do as he ordered. I left Keifer's graveside and returned to my apartment on the fifth floor. Most of my and his things were still packed in the boxes. I'd been forced out of our home with speed if you recall. I stood over the ones marked 'Claus's dresses' and wept for several hours.

I know that sounds silly and looking back on those hard moments I cannot deny it might have been. I'd been cross dressing for years by that time. I did enjoy wearing the pretty gowns but it was for my Mann's satisfaction more than anything else. Putting them in a closet, locking the door and throwing away the key wasn't as hard as Xavier thought it would be.

Without the joy of seeing the sparkle in Keifer's eyes over the sight of me in a lovely dress, I lost my desire to wear them. There they would stay, hidden, nearly forgotten for many years. Then one day a beautiful young boy was leashed to me by his Master, Peter. With a vicious swing of his cane, and the twinkle reminiscent of his Uncles's icy gaze, he reawakened the sleeping giant, but I need not get into that story. You were there and I thank you for the mercy of it.

Anyway, I let go of all the things that had brought me to Das Kaiser Haus in the first place. I bought the three piece suits and turned away every offer I received from the many suitors that come calling. That last part was far easier a task then storing away my fancy wardrobe. It was disgusting how the gay men of the Haus flocked to my door like buzzards. Most before my beloved husband was even cold in his grave.

I cannot say these fella's were attempting to court me because I was the handsome man. Hell, I wasn't the young or rich man either. I believe my sudden popularity was because of my status as the fifth Silk Prince. Nothing like power to make anyone the artificially sexy beast, ja?

Truth is I wasn't interested in dating or bonding with any of them. My heart belonged exclusively to Keifer, and no one could hope to take his place. I was the accomplished self-stimulator despite years of being the happily married fella. I didn't need a partner in my bed, nor did I desire to have someone around to witness my other private behaviors, you know, like enacting revenge plots. Oh ja, above all things I was hell bent to make the people responsible for making me a widow pay with their lives.

I know this may come as the surprise, but Keifer managed to communicate at least one of the men responsible for his death. He told me all he saw and figured out before I called the doctor in to grant him mercy. It took a bit since his lack of a tongue reduced us to hit and miss reading of lips.

He said he was ambushed in the Fur King's apartment the second he arrived for the meeting with Kilian. Someone hit him in the back of the head and he was knocked unconscious. When my beloved returned to alert status, he found himself bound in a chair in the center of Kilian's living area.

The Elder stood over him with a knife in his hand, but Keifer could heard the sounds of several boots behind him. He tried to turn his head to get a look at his other attackers but the room was too dark to get a clear view. The Fur King demanded to know why I wasn't with him, and where I could be found.

Of course, Keifer refused to answer any of that sonofabitch's questions. He was aware the Fur King intended to kill him. His only hope was that somehow I would escape his wrath, figure out the identity of his killer and then avenge him. Well, unfortunately, Kilian was thinking the very same thing and he worried that would be the case.

When the Elder couldn't get the Silk King to talk, he grew angry. He took the knife and cut out Keifer's eyes. This was done to punish him for refusing to comply but also to prevent him from getting a look at anyone else involved in the upcoming brutal, mortal assault.

You see, Kilian had secretly hated Keifer with a passion. My Mann had become popular among the residents, and had single handedly saved Das Kaiser Haus from ruin after the Great War. The constant praise and adoration lavished upon the Silk King by a grateful population dug under the Fur King's thin skin. He'd been desirous of seeing Keifer die a slow, agonizing death for several years before he finally decided to make his wishes come true.

So, Kilian took turns with five other people torturing and humiliating my beloved Keifer. The group of criminals ended their brutality upon his flesh only after he was beyond repair. He was then dumped in the hallway by two of his assailants blind, castrated, gutted, and slowly dying in hellish agony.

He'd resolved himself to endure his torment until I reached his side. My Mann feared I was in great danger. Keifer relayed the tale of Kilian's treasury and begged me to swear I wouldn't join him in the grave till that fucker paid for what he'd done to us.

I need not tell you, my beloved didn't have to ask me twice. The second Kilian dared to harm a hair on my precious Mann's head he was dead. At least he was going to wish it many times before I allowed him the peace of it.

So, I spent the thirty days after Keifer's death in respectful mourning. I ignored all attempts from the residents to offer condolences and their attempts to ask me on dates, yuck. I stayed in my apartment most of the time and when I did come out I often broke down in tears.

I won't lie. This public display of grieving was maybe the last thing I did that was more honest than fake. My weeping for Keifer was real as anything in this life can be but allowing everyone to see the weakness of it. Well that was part of my plans to extract revenge on the Fur King.

I'd hoped my observably sullen behavior would lead Kilian to believe I was unaware of his guilt. To my great relief, it turned out he was as stupid as he was lazy. His initial intentions of dispatching me to join with my husband would never come to pass. Either he decided I wasn't a threat to him with my husband gone, or he hesitated too long. Whatever the reason he allowed me to survived, I wasn't about to allow him time to regret this lack of tying up a dangerous loose end.

On the thirty second day after Keifer's death, I noticed a flurry of activity among my brother Voters and the sitting Elders. It didn't take long for word to reach my ears the Nazi government had sent a few top officers to speak with the Kings. I knew with such important men visiting, Kilian would be far too occupied to taking notice I was sneaking up to end his reign on Earth.

That morning I made sure many eyes witnessed my emotional state of deep grieving as I sat down for breakfast in the Great Hall. I barely picked at the meal in front of me and openly wept without saying a single word to anyone.

My actin job was so believable that Derbeck became concerned enough to beg me to visit with the Haus doctor. He was sure that sawbones could give me a pill that would alleviate some if not all my paralyzing heartbreaking.

I didn't verbally respond to the Voter's suggestion. I merely nodded and kept my wet eyes on the floor. The grumbling of the other Silk Princes was that I was the kill joy to be around caused me a bit of secret thrill. I was glad to know I was making them miserable. I suppose even before I had good evidence I knew a few, if not all, of them were balls deep in the plot with Kilian.

When they announced they were headed off to attend their daily duties, I whispered to Derbeck I was willing to take his advice. He smiled and patted me on the back softly, then hurried to catch up with the other Voters. With my alibi in place, I too rushed from the table, only not to visit with the doctor.

I went towards the clinic but detoured at the last minute and headed to the back staircase. Quick as lightening I headed up the steps, careful to avoid detection of any prying eyes. This was my only chance to sneak to the sixth floor without witnesses. All the leaders were headed to the front door to greet the visiting government officers. None of them would notice their lowest ranking Prince was missing and if their did, Derbeck would offer up my understandable excuses, ja?

Without any trouble I managed to slip into the corridor and hide under the seventh floor stairwell. I knew it could be hours of waiting before my target returned to his apartment. That didn't phase me a bit. For the chance to taking out my fury on the man that killed my beautiful Keifer, well shit, I was happy to wait as long as necessary.

To my shock, I barely got myself situated in a somewhat comfortable spot when I heard Kilian's voice ring out. From what I could gather he was in a conversation with one, maybe two other males. At first, I couldn't decern anyone but the Fur King's sounds. That all changed very quickly. I didn't have to see their faces to recognize Xavier, Drexel and Barnim were tagging along with my prey.

I held my breath, hoping none of the approaching fellows would discover my hide out. I nearly had the heart attack the second they halted their journey at the bottom of the steps. They were so close to me at that point, I nearly could reach out and punch them. It seemed inevitable that one or more of the group would notice my eavesdropping.

However, much to my relief and stun none of the men saw me. I listened intently as the four demons argued amongst themselves.

Xavier blew out his breath and said, "Kilian, you motherfucker. How dare you deny me this reasonable request? You owe me, Gott dammit."

Kilian replied in the huff, "Like hell I do. You wanted to be Silk King and you got it. That's far more than you deserved given the job you did wasn't only far too easy but I dare say you enjoyed it."

Drexel whined out, "Come on fellas. This fighting over a woman is stupid. Xavier, why not just divorced that bitch and marry Birgit?"

Xavier bellowed, "Birgit is the black collar maid fool. Why the hell would I mess around with low trash like that?"

Barnim laughed in the cruel sounding tone, "Ja brother. Xavier only fucks the help. He'd never stoop low enough to cut off her metal and call her honorable wife."

Kilian scoffed, "Xavier, what the hell are they speaking about? You better not be sleeping with any of the Haus submissives. You know the law."

Xavier growled in reply, "Drexel is being the comic, your Majesty. I don't know any submissives silver or black. Now, as I said, my wife? A letter from you to King Gregor surely will force him to send Ingrid back where she belongs."

Kilian spit in the floor then yelled backed in response, "The day I correspond with that false King of the Denmark Haus is the day I die. I believe you forget your place, your Majesty. Now I have many important things to be considering at the moment. All of you are dismissed. Do not bother me again with your petty complaints or Xavier, you will have far more in common with your late predecessor other than his sister. Good day, gentlemen." I heard Kilian stomp up the stairs leaving his companions behind to grumble amongst themselves.

I held my breath as Xavier mumbled, "Fuckin ingrate. I suppose I will be forced to use my outside connections to bring that bitch to heel. You boys best brace yourselves. That SS officer wasn't kidding you know. The Haus better find a way to pay their price or they will take it from everyone's carcasses."

Drexel snorted. "It's highway robbery plain and simple. No one around here can meet their demands. I have no more intention to handing them over my future fortune any more than I intend to start producing children for their use."

Barnim chuckled. "They aren't interested in your plastic sons anyway, Drexel. What I wish to know is why Xavier is made the Silk King but all the rest of us are treated like paupers. Me, you, the Schmidts, shit we all got our hands bloody. I think it only fair we all have get a taste of the riches for our parts in it. Kilian behaves as if we were nothing but gum on his boots."

Xavier moved with speed and grabbed Barnim by his collar as he growled, "You shut up idiot. What if someone were to hear you confessing to killing Keifer? If Claus or Bladrick were to find out, or hell that brutal Frau of mine, we'd have to murder all of them too."

Drexel sniveled, "Maybe Bladrick or Ingrid sure, but Claus? Come on Xavier. Surely you're not afraid of that Queen. If you honestly are, then why the fuck did you put him fifth instead of Heidi or Helga? I vote we send the three of them to be reunited with that pussy cousin of ours. Then we can be shut of the entire mess."

Xavier led go of the grinning Barnim with a sigh, "You Reinhardts are a brutal lot. Especially to your own people. Nein. Claus isn't my real concern, but Ingrid is. Without her I'm unable to create a legitimate Prince of the Haus. If I am to grant Justus that crown, I need to be sure of his loyalty to me, his father. I dare say killing his mother isn't likely to win his affection."

Barnim snarled out, "So that's what you're planning is it? Well, thank you for enlightening us Xavier. You're a fucking fool. What makes you think me and Drexel or hell any of us won't simply murder you, Justus and Ingrid to keep any of the tree from assuming the mantel of power?"

Xavier chuckled with a diabolical sound, "Go ahead and try it you bastards. The second I'm named as the abused corpse, my connections on the outside are ordered to start killing every name on my list. Do you wish to bet your name is not on there somewhere? I promise you, you'll never see your assassin coming. If you think what we all did to Keifer was horrific, wait till my brutes come to give each of you a taste of their dark skills. If I were you boys, I'd share that information I just give to you with everyone that aided in sending the Silk Queen to his grave. Best for all of you fuckers to shut your mouths and do as you are told. Be grateful you are going to be rich men or you will be the poor dead ones."

Barnim and Drexel gasped then both men took off in the huff. Xavier stood there a few more minutes, then he joined them in their retreat. I didn't move a muscle as the words they said wrapped around my brain. I now had three more names to annihilate, but Xavier's discussion made it seem clear there were even more involved.

I took a deep breath to brace my resolve. I come out of the shadows and stood at the bottom of the staircase. I knew this was the perfect time to strike. In our final moments together I'd made a vow to my beloved Keifer. I was sobbing hard as I swore to him no matter how long it took I would torture and kill all those responsible for taking him from my loving arms.

I didn't feel a bid of fear, remorse nor pity as my boots pulled me toward the Fur King's door. Kilian was all alone. I'd come prepared to make the useless bastard empathic for his victim the Silk King. I closed my eyes for a moment and when I opened them I knew the submissive cross dresser had gone to sleep and the killer Queen had awakened. I took the small hunting knife from my belt and crept up the steps, quiet as death.

Chapter 10: Which Twin Survived?
Master Mad Maxx and submissive Meine Liebe

I crept up the stairs and stood at the door for several moments. I was unsure if I could find the courage to do all that had to be done to see Keifer avenged. With a deep breath I braced and knocked softly. As I expected Kilian's loyal black collar answered almost immediately. The look on his face told me that no matter what my reasons, he wasn't about to allow me to visit with the Fur King.

Before I had time to think about it, I plunged that knife deep into his throat. The poor bastard desperately tried to push me off but it was too late for him. My blow was mortal. Within seconds, his struggling against me came to the abrupt end. His eyes rolled back into his head, just as he fell forward. I prevented his collision with the floor and mouthed an apology for this necessary cruelty into his deaf ear.

You must understand, I didn't desire to kill this innocent fellow. I had no choice in the matter. Had I permitted him to survive, he'd been able to identify Kilian's murderer. Plus this man was loyal unto death to the Fur King.

Back in those days, the sitting monarchs selected special 'Kings men' from among the most skilled Haus submissives. These black collars took oaths to serve all their Master's needs. Most even followed them to the grave.

I gently propped the dead submissive against the inner wall. Then quiet as a mouse I entered the seventh-floor suite, bolting the door tightly behind me. To my relief, Kilian wasn't immediately spotted in that big apartment. I moved with stealth through the many room searching for the motherfucker. Until at last I found him asleep in his bed taking the afternoon nap most old men engage in.

A huge smile crossed my lips when I realized there wasn't any need to hurry this dark task. I admit, I intended to taking my time making Kilian wish he'd never laid a hand on Keifer. To be sure I wasn't disturbed during my bloody work, I took a moment to disconnect all his phones. This way there wasn't a chance he could call for aid.

With the door blocked, his protector gone, and lines of communication disabled, I returned to his bedroom. I'm sure he thought it a nightmare to open his eyes and find me standing over him. He opened his mouth to let out a cry for help. I ended that noise with speed by pushing my knife to his throat and threating to cut it if he dared to attempt any loud sounds of distress.

His eyes were wide with terror as he whimpered, "Claus? Surely whatever it is you upset about can be settled peacefully between us. Name your price and I will see you compensated if you let me live."

I chuckled bitterly and pushed the blade harshly as I replied, "I'm glad you eager to pay what you owe me, old man. Not that I care if you willing or not. Get out of bed Kilian. I don't wish to soil these fine silk sheets or that feather mattress with the blood of the Silk King's murderer." Of course, he immediately fell into the tears of false claims of innocence.

You are aware, I didn't entertain a word he said, nor did his pleas slow up my actions. When he refused to mind my command, I jerked him from the bed. The beast within me reared its ugly head while I dragged that useless bag of bones across his room. I made sure that he wasn't able to complain of my rough treatment by gagging him with a pair of his own boxers (hahaha).

I hauled him thru the hallway and didn't end my hurried journey till we arrived at the end of it. I bet you recall the color of the door located there. Don't you my beautiful boy?"

I swallowed hard and nodded at Claus. That red door of Xavier's personal torturing chamber still haunts my dreams to this day.

He frowned. "Well that horrible room was created by Kilian's predecessor Amos. Mother Felicity wouldn't have dreamed of such abomination. The brutal men that followed her benevolent reign seemed to grow more demonic with each succession. Amos was rumored to have conceived of that nightmare when he grew too feeble to travel downstairs easily. Apparently, his diminished capacity to walk didn't weaken his twisted interest in watching helpless victims enduring torture. Anyway, I've no idea why Kilian didn't eliminate it when he took over the apartment. However, Keifer told me his abusers ripped him apart in the confines of that room. It seemed fitting that Kilian would gain a little empathy for my beloved Mann by suffering the same hellish fate in there."

I felt a shiver travel up my spine. "Did you, uhm, or maybe Cora redecorate the seventh floor? Or is the set up still the same as it was during Xavier, Kilian's and Amos's time?"

Claus sighed. "Sadly, I was far too ill to be thinking of remodeling the Fur Palace, Maxx. You wisely had the Elder Princes move me down here closer to the Haus doctor on the first floor. I've waited all my life to gain the chance to make that apartment all my own. Only to fail most miserably the second I finally achieved the honor of it."

I winced. "Oh ja. I suppose you did have far more important things on your mind than that terrible torture chamber. It must've been difficult to step a foot in there with the hard memories of terrible things your loved one suffered while in the Fur Palace."

He nodded and took on the serious expression. "A truer statement you couldn't make, my beauty. I confess the first night I found no rest. I kept thinking I heard Mother Felicity calling out for me to help her off the floor and I swear Keifer's screams of terror as the men mutilated him echoed off the walls. By the morning, I thought seriously about consulting Doctor Atilla to ask him to give me a strong sedative."

But you have managed to interrupt my story yet again Maxx. I'm gonna warn you once more to be still. Next time, I'll have to punish you. I'm not only too old for so many distractions, but as I've said, our time is short. Do you hear me, boy?"

I nodded with a scoff. "Ja, there is no need for threats, Claus. I'm listening like you told me to. In fact, take all the time you wish to blabber about people I never met and don't matter to me. The longer you our waste time together, the more likely I will escape your nasty lusting for the week."

He grinned at me wickedly and squeezed the lambs tightly to his chest as he replied, "I assure you Maxx I'm keeping an eye on the clock. If my tale runs too much longer, I'll insist you provide oral services while I continue talking. If you were hoping to escaping your duty to me, may as well get that out of your pretty head right this minute."

I groaned. "Come on Claus. Christ man. You about to meet your maker and still you will force me to give you the special services? Fuck, just so I can prepare myself for the nightmare possibility, there isn't anything in your will that demands I endure your copulation before they nail your coffin shut, right?"

That caused the Elder to break out into humored laughter for several moments. "Oh my Gott, you always could making me laugh Maxx. Nein. It's true I cannot stand the idea of never being inside you again, but if you seriously worried that our contract still exists after I taking my final breaths. Well, you can calm that fear immediately. The idea of necrophilia gives me the willies, even if it were my corpse that would be your lucky partner in it. Now, silence. Where was I in the story? Oh ja, I'd hauled Kilian's sorry ass into the room with the red door…

I made it clear from the beginning it would go easier for him if he answered my questions. I swore to be merciful. All he had to do is say the names of everyone that had a hand in the destruction of my Mann.

However, Kilian turned out to be as useless in granting information as he'd been in wielding power correctly. No matter how painful the punishment, his lips remained sealed. Looking back on it, his understanding that Keifer somehow told me about his role in the murder caused him to realize I wasn't planning to stop till he was dead.

No doubt, the Fur King decided his only recourse to gain a little more revenge on me was to refuse to speak. Even if it meant dying knowing his co-conspirators maybe would get away clean. This final cruelty he tried pissed me off beyond reason.

At first, I attempted to keep my wrath under control a bit. I'd hung him in chains, to hold him still for my interrogation. But in short order I found myself cutting, burning, sawing, gouging, and skinning that old buzzard while nearly insane from a rage driven fit.

I admit. I didn't feel a damned bit of pity for him as I slowly removed his eyes, testicles, cock, nipples, fingers, toes and eventually, since he continued to refuse to speak, his worthless tongue.

I must say it was a lucky thing for me that Kilian was so unpopular among the residents. I was able to subject him leisurely to tortures most foul for hours. No one come to check on the fool the entire time even though his screams of agony were loud enough to wake the dead.

When his cries of pain grew weak and I couldn't find another inch of uncorrupted skin. I committed my worst acts of revenge upon him. I forced all the parts of him I'd removed up his anus. Then with experienced skills taught to me by Mother Felicity, I sewed the hole shut. I didn't really need to do another brutal thing to him at that point. He was already beyond saving and I dare say not desirous of living on as the human stump. That said, I still wasn't satisfied that this murderous coward had suffered enough.

I leaned into his ear and whispered, "I don't know if there is a Heaven or a Hell you asshole. I suppose soon you will find out. However, I'm not going to allow you to serve at the cloven hooves of your Dark Lord as quickly as you'd like. My beloved Keifer never considered harming a single hair on your head Kilian. Yet you did horrible things to him, or had other do them simply because of your jealousy. His kind, loving heart outshined your wicked, cold one. It didn't have to be this way. If you'd asked me or him to step down from the Silk throne, we would have without quarrel. Killing him was only necessary because you feared as long as he lived the people would always love him and hate you. Well, I know I should want to see you die for what you've done, but I honestly don't. Instead, I pray you live a long, long, time." With that I stuck my blade into his belly and emptied the contents of it onto his floor.

The Fur King screamed until he was hoarse and writhed wildly in the chains. I stood there admiring the gruesome artwork I'd made of his flesh for many minutes. Then I hurried from the scene of the crime leaving Kilian to expire very slowly. I returned to the living area and moved several heavy pieces of furniture to double bar the door.

I did this to assure if anyone did come seeking the whereabouts of the Fur King, they couldn't enter easily. I made damned sure Kilian wouldn't be granted the mercy of a quick end. That honor, I believed, should be reserved for those that earned it. This bastard had behaved like a brute. I decided he should die like one.

The seventh-floor apartment was not only built to be the most comfortable in all the Haus. It also possesses a secret passage. This was created by the founding families in case the Fur monarch needed to escaping unseen from any enemies. Mother Felicity had shown me where in the home to find this useful way out of the suite.

I've always kicked myself for not taking one more gander at the mortally wounded Kilian. It would've been of great solace over the next many years to know that he hadn't succumb quickly. As it is, I must rely on the gossiping I heard in the hallways regarding the details of the condition he was discovered in.

The rumor was Kilian didn't die right away, but how long only he and Gott knows. Everyone was confused that his killer or killers were able to escaping from the scene without exiting through the front door. I left it barricaded, remember?

Only the man or woman that was granted the silver crown was privy to the secret way out of the Palace. Not even the Fur Princes were aware one existed. So, for many years, the gruesome business was whispered to be the work of a demon or perhaps Ghost.

It was left to Xavier the Silk King to launch an investigation into the murder of the Fur monarch. He, of course, knew it wasn't a supernatural occurrence. The Voter did his best to piece together the facts of the case. For a change, he wasn't able to figure out the culprit with ease. I think this really pissed him off, but I cannot be sure of it since he never openly said so.

I honestly thought that bastard would suspect I was behind the brutal crime. Xavier did act a little strange around me for the next few weeks. In the end, I have to assume he scratched me from his list because he never knew Queen Felicity was truly my mother. She'd kept the secret of our relationship quiet, leaving it up to me as to who I wished to share the information with. I wisely only told Keifer and Ingrid about it. That, for a change, was a smart move on my part. Xavier thought I couldn't have known about the way to sneak out without being seen.

For a minute, I believe Xavier did wonder if Hemmel was behind the mess. Lucky for the boy, or unlucky depending on how you look at it, his ability to remain of importance to Bladrick took the spotlight off him. The Dungeon Master stood up for his unwilling sex partner. He gave the young man a strong alibi and Xavier was forced to seek his answers elsewhere.

As the weeks turned into months, the trail to find the murderer kept running into the wall. Xavier finally gave up looking. It seems to me he shouldn't have bothered in the first place. It turned out I'd done that man a great favor by taking out the useless Kilian. Without a Fur King on the throne, the Silk monarch ran the Haus exclusively.

Normally, the sitting Fur Princes would've voted in a new leader quickly, but in the years leading up to the second World War things inside Das Kaiser Haus had become dangerous and unstable. None of the old buggers wished to taking on the responsibility of the head of the Haus. That's because by fall of 1936 the Gestapo and SS were breathing down the collars of every living soul within the walls.

As I told you, Xavier come to me the day I buried Keifer to tell me to hide my homosexuality and cross dressing fetish. Well, the entire Haus population was called to a meeting in the Great Hall by their Silk King only days before the discovery of Kilian's mutilated corpse.

It was standing room only as Xavier and the rest of us Princes of the Silk and Fur took center stage. To everyone's shock, their acting leader announced due to new government rules, things around the Haus were to change.

For starters, all sex other than the kind to procreate was banned. This fellow Hitler had outlawed homosexuality, deviant fetishes, and carnal acts with any child under the age of sixteen. Anyone caught engaging in 'illegal lustful acts' were to be severely punished. Though he didn't say it specifically, we all knew he meant killed.

He went on to inform the men and women of Das Kaiser Haus that their country expected them to fulfil their duty to making children for Hitler's army. Every married FemDom was ordered to become pregnant immediately. If the lady was unmarried and of age, she was commanded to accept the hand of a suitor with speed.

If the person was too old to sire or birth young, he or she was expected to making welcome any and all guests of the SS or Gestapo. The Dungeons were to house enemies of the country. If the male was under forty and desired to leave the Haus, he was invited to sign up to become a soldier for the glory of Germany.

Xavier ended his frightening diatribe with the cryptic words, "The Haus has been too soft for too long. It's time we all braced ourselves for a future of purging the useless, so that only the strong survive." He went on to make it clear that all the residents were expected to do their part to help their Führer.

It didn't taking the genius to realize this news Xavier was sharing with us was a notice of our impending doom. No one doubted any longer that the angry little man Hitler was about to drag Germany right to hell. Everyone believed him insane over his selfish bid for world domination, but few stood up against him. Those that did found themselves rooming with Keifer, Kristian, Max and Kilian very quickly. Yikes.

My own desires to see the promise for vengeance I'd made to my Mann had to be put on hold. Xavier, Barnim and

Drexel plus whoever else I needed to eliminate, were deeply entrenched with the suddenly ever-present SS and Gestapo officers of high rank. Touching any of them wasn't only impossible, it would have been suicidal.

Like it or not, I was forced to spend the next many years watching Keifer's killers thrive and grow more powerful by the day. Without aid of any kind there wasn't a damned thing I could do about it. I wasn't the youngster anymore though. During the lonely night with a cold bed, I consoled myself by remembering nothing lasts forever. All wars come to an end. Hitler couldn't live forever, right?

So, I did as Xavier and the ruling government demanded me to. At least on the surface anyway. Finding a Frau to sport around on my notoriously gay arm was more difficult than I imagined. The first several months I was in desperate danger of being identified as the unrelenting schwuler.

Then just before the Yuletide celebrations I was informed that my troubles, at least this one, was coming to an end. Bladrick called me from his cell in the Dungeon to ask a favor. His late wife's sister had found herself widowed. She and her Mann had a single kid between them, a daughter. This young woman was over the usual age expected for marriage by this time but there was a problem. The girl was a die-hard Lesbian.

His sister-in-law feared her girl would be picked up if not given a place to hide soon. To be discovered gay, male or female, assured you'd be sent to one of the numerous concentration camps that were springing up across the countryside. Rumors flew within and outside the Haus wall of what was going on in those prison camps. Everyone knew being hauled off to one meant death, and not a merciful one either.

Bladrick still felt adoration for his lost Frau's family. He begged me to taking this young lady under my wing and pretend we were the smitten couple. I of course was relieved to be offered this opportunity to play the false lover. Especially to a female that wouldn't ever misunderstand this was a game and was never going to be a reality.

And so the day after Christmas, Cora moved in to my apartment on the fifth floor. Don't give me that look boy. I didn't know at the time she was the snake in the grass. I did what I had to do to live to see another day just like everyone else in the motherland did during the years of Hitler's madness.

As it was, back den, Cora was the quiet roommate. She kept to herself and I did the same. The only time we even spoke was when making the public appearance to have meals in the Great Hall. Then we would carry on like a straight couple was expected to do. Other than that, our courtship was cooler than the German winter.

Despite all that, most residents, and more importantly the Gestapo, came to believe the twenty year young girl and me were truly together. Our acting job saved our lives, and I believed at that time this was for the best. I did wish to join with my lost Keifer on the daily basis, but I was hell bent to not return to his arms as a man that didn't keep his word.

Unknown to any of us at that time, off in Denmark, Ingrid was about to become your grandmother. The Fur King Gregor fell head over heels with the still very beautiful woman the second she showed up in his Haus. The two of them, according to Ingrid's accounts, had one hot love affair for the entire five years she was separated from her husband Xavier.

She told me almost a decade later (the reason she held on to the secret so long I will discuss soon) the Haus doctors had been dead wrong. The Silk Queen wasn't barren at all. Gregor's lusty antics quickly seeded her womb. A daughter was born almost exactly nine months to the day from their first copulation. They named the love child, Agnette.

I glared at Claus angrily. "Ah, I've been waiting to hear the bullshit story you'd come up with to claim Ingrid my honest grandmother. I applaud your clever thinking, but it's too bad for you it's not quick enough to fool even this idiot. There is no fucking way I'm believing Malfred and Karl's father just happened to sleeping with my father's wife. The result of which is my cruel mother coming into being. Come on Claus. You surely can do a better job of lying. I thought you said you're the Master of illusions."

The Fur King's face took on the expression of irritation as he replied, "I'm not telling you a false story boy. Ingrid is Agnette's biological mother. She and Gregor did have the torrid affair in the Danish Haus from 1935 until Xavier forced Ingrid back into his brutal grip in 1940."

That made me scoff. "Okay, say I were to buy what you're selling. Why did Agnette and Peter tell me that her mother's name is Annika? I won't deny I've discovered the proof that Malfred and Karl share the same father with that vile woman but that's the end of it. I accept that I am the evil offspring of the Schmidt/Krauss union, but I refuse to add insult to that injury. I will never believe there is horsey faced, statue fucking, hook torturing, limp dicked Reinhardt blood in my veins as well. Hell, nein." I spit onto his floor with those words.

Claus looked me over for a moment then with a deep breath said, "Cora isn't a Reinhardt. Her relationship to Bladrick, Drexel and Barnim was through marriage only. As for those nasty fellows, they were half Reinhardt, not pure bloods like my Keifer, Ingrid, Kristian, Max and Bladrick were. That said, I find it interesting you don't hesitate to claim the kinship with child killing Hemmel, the slut Helga & Heidi twins, the rapist Malfred, his brother Karl, Peter, Byron, Friedrick and that horrible murdering bastard Xavier. Yet you refuse to acknowledge and find no pride in your kindhearted Great Uncles Keifer, Max and Kristian?"

I shrugged. "I guess that's because I never met any of them. I'm glad of it too. Knowing the way these perverts are around here, if the three had lived, they'd have fucked me like the rest of you did and still do."

The Elder frowned deeply. "I'm going to let that insult slide for the moment. Hand me the phone will you?"

I startled. "Huh? What the hell do you need that for? I'm sitting right here, Claus. Tell me what you desire fetched and I will go get it for you."

He furrowed his brow and glared at me with barely contained fury. "You are the thing I was about to have picked up boy. I told you to stop interrupting my story and you persist in ignoring my commands. Give me the phone so that I may call Noah. He's the man I trust to get my Priceless under control. In all the years I've dealt with Bladrick's son, he never let me down, unlike that brute brother of his, that useless interfering fucker Olaf."

I led out a yelp of shock before I could stop myself. "Huh? Did you say Olaf was Bladrick's son also? That's bullshit. Olaf wore the black collar because his mother was that criminal bitch Evelyn. If his daddy really was the infamous Dungeon Master, Elder Bladrick, he'd been a Dominant like Noah is."

Claus chuckled bitterly and responded, "Ah but Olaf was a Dominant like his younger brother Noah until he crossed Ingrid. You see, prior to Xavier taking control of the Haus in 1935, the Dungeon Masters and Mistresses were not permitted much interaction with anyone above ground. Your wicked father changed all that. Bladrick continued to subject Hemmel to his unwanted lusting but he also took a secret lover. The black collar kitchen maid Evelyn.

In 1937, she gave birth to their first son. The man you knew as the door guard Olaf. Then soon after in 1940, she produced their second and final kid, Noah. Bladrick couldn't

60

openly admit the boys were his own, but it was common knowledge these bastards were of Dungeon Master decent. Xavier turned a blind eye to his Headmaster's illicit and illegal) affair with the lady, but he made sure neither of them would become a threat to his power.

He made a deal with Bladrick and Evelyn that the moment their sons turned sixteen, they would both be sent below. There they would be enslaved as Dungeon Masters themselves until the last sitting Voter of that time found the grave.

Bladrick was thrilled to be offered a chance to be the kind of father to his boys. Without hesitation he signed an agreement contract with the Silk King on it. Well, the years pass quickly as you surely know. When the their come for Olaf to leave his comfortable place on the first floors of the Haus to go below he wasn't going without a fight.

That idiot honestly thought he was savvy enough to put one over on the clever Silk Queen but he didn't get the chance to rethink his error. I will get to that story when it happened. All you need to know at the moment is Olaf's punishment for breaking the contract was forced lifelong submission to the Haus. He was held down by his own father and the dark metal locked around his throat.

Noah saw what happened to his big brother. When his time came to go down the stone steps, like a good boy he complied. It wasn't a surprise to hear he'd done what was expected of him without giving anyone argument. Noah and Olaf were as different as night is from the day. But you already knew that, since you killed Olaf and call Noah your friend since you first arrived in the Haus.

I started to dispute what the old man said about Noah, but I saw him glance at the phone. It took all I had, but I managed it, to hold my tongue and remain silent. I wasn't in a hurry to meet up with Noah to ask him about the truthfulness of Claus's story. Nor did I want to visit with the Headmaster's skillful whip. Yikes.

Claus noticed my struggle to remain composed. He watched me suspiciously for a moment. Then apparently, he decided not to press the matter further. After clearing his throat, and a weak cough, he went back to his seemingly never-ending tale.

"Well, Bladrick was busy minding the orders of Hitler to making many sons for Germany, but he wasn't the only fellow. All over the Haus, FemDom's waistlines grew larger. It was as if everyone had the baby fever. The first family to boast theirs were 'good Germans' were the shrunken clan Altergott.

The last patriarch of Sirin age and his Frau welcomed their son Reece into the world in 1936. They're were quite prolific in their rush to repopulate the Haus with tiny Altergotts. Reece's birth was followed by another in 1938. This son the pair named Kilian, after his late, not so great grandfather, ja the one I sent on to hell.

The couples third attempt to produce offspring resulted in a daughter their call they Anna. Her arrival marked the end of the clan's expansion in 1940. I think the two of them would've kept trying to rebuild their Altergott empire, but the war, and Germany's eventual defeat stopped them from it. Thankfully, thought Maxximillian, since the Earth will be a better place if no more of that blood line were to be conceived.

While the nearly extinct Altergotts worked their fertility magic, the Schmidts did all their could to compete. Bernt and Derbeck barely came up from the Dungeon hell before both the men were chasing females left and right.

Bernt managed to fool some poor FemDom of no worth into bearing him two sons. Peter was their first born, well second actually since you know Justus is also his kin. He entered this story in 1937, followed in 1939 by the simple minded Friedrick.

Derbeck, wasn't gonna stand to be outdone by his bully brother. He also snagged a pretty FemDom and managed in 1937 to produce Oliver who was only two months younger than Peter. Rolf was born in 1939. His woman also give him two daughters to go with his fine sons. The girls were born in 1941 and the last one 1943. Derbeck never met that one because he found his grave before discovering he'd seeded his mate a fourth time. Again, I will get to that story shortly.

Then there was the last Wagoner. He'd managed to graduate from a good medical school, but like all loyal Germans he didn't let his professional life interfere with his bid to fallow Hitler's orders. He and his wife produced the boy you know as Jacob in 1939.

Sadly, this was to be the couples only kid. Jacob's mother passed away about five years after his birth. Her death was of a suspicious nature, and old doctor Wagner blamed the Haus for his lose. Before Xavier could talk him out of it, Doctor Wagoner packed up and left Das Kaiser Haus forever while leaving his little boy behind. The circumstances of his abandonment of the good natured Jacob I'm not completely aware of.

All I can say for sure is Doctor Wagoner apparently did intend to send for his boy just as soon as he was established a solid home in Stuttgart over in western Germany. The Iron Curtain come down on the East before he could do this with ease. To this day, the old man and his son are not on good terms because of Doctor Wagoner's perceived abandonment of him.

The Altergotts also decided to seek their fortunes elsewhere. They joined with Doctor Wagoner in Stuttgart and were forced to leave their three youngsters behind until they could afford to retrieve them. They, unlike the good doctor, did manage to collect the funds to send for their children and rather quickly too.

However, by the time the couple extended their invitation to their brood, only Reece was willing to leave the Haus culture. Kilian opted to remain behind with his broken hearted lover Jacob, and Anna chosen to stay with her younger brother. The family clan Altergott, unlike Wagnor, remained on friendly terms until the day they buried that old buzzard patriarch of theirs.

With all that in mind. That leaves only the one Schmidt's history left to discuss. This fellow I believe you've had many rough dealings with. If you haven't yet, you sure as will shit at some point. He's perhaps more dangerous than Peter or Xavier ever hoped to be in their most perverted fantasies. Of course, I speak of that shady bastard son of Xavier's called Byron.

His birth was one that should've never happened, but alas it did. Xavier had been working tirelessly to regain possession of Ingrid. During the interim of her absence, he'd been fooling around with his beautiful black collar maid, Birgit.

It wasn't that the girl had much of a choice in the matter. Once Xavier set his eyes upon her flesh, denying him his desires would've been deadly. I wish to believe that kindhearted woman never honestly fell for Xavier's false charms, but I'd be lying if I said I knew for sure she was merely being compliant. It's just as possible the ignorant submissive was smitten with him and because of that blinded to his brutal nature.

Whatever the truth of it, Xavier managed to fill the young woman's womb with the fruit of his aging loins. Byron was born in the summer of 1939, healthy, strong and the spitting image of his Uncle Bernt. This odd physical similarity to Xavier's most hated brother, caused many tongues to wag.

Xavier was more than a bit furious over the rumors that Birgit cuckolded the Silk King with Bernt. He was often seen in the hallways, pushing the frail Haus maid around demanding she confess to the crime she didn't commit. More than once, that poor girl showed up to work on the Voter's floor looking more like the black eyed panda than an admired lover of the Silk Monarch.

Anyway, this baby booming led to a new set of problems for the Haus residents. Until this time, all children of the Dominant/FemDom classes were made to leave at the age of eight. Any kid that didn't fallow this rule, was forced into the Dungeon and put into the collar selection.

As you know, High borns would serve as the silver until their fifteenth birthday. Then they would break their metal by tradition and become the low-born first floor Dominant or FemDom. The ones that didn't wish to be submitted could return and apply for membership at age sixteen. That is how it'd always been since anyone could remember.

As the Second World War broke out Germany's enemies grew in number. Xavier decided the practice of sending away their sons and daughters was outdated and possibly dangerous for the continued survival of the Haus.

In the Summer of 1941 just as the United States began to enter the var, the Silk King set down a new law. He commanded that special cottage be built on the grounds. This was to become the nurseries to all the youngsters of Haus members in good standing.

He announced that a High-born child wouldn't be expelled at age eight from that moment on. Xavier went further and invited all the families to enroll their babies in his new program. He sweetened the deal by assuring that all children that graduated from the nursery at age sixteen would automatically claim the status of their parents. You know, instead of having to start from the bottom and work their way up as they had done in the past.

Well I need not tell you his idea was received with a standing ovation. There wasn't a single parent within the place that didn't want to keep their babies close by war or not. I stood in the back of the Great Hall watching the long line of happy mothers and fathers signing away their children's chance at a future free of that hell haus.

There wasn't a thing I could do to talk any of them out of it. None of them could fathom that their boy or girl would've been better off living anywhere else, even a ditch, rather than rotting away within the hall confines. I guess I shouldn't judge the parents of the war babies too harshly. Most of them were frightened of the obvious signs that Germany had once again gotten deeply involved in the losing battle.

If bearing little ones for Keifer had been possible I know damned well I would have done whatever necessary to keep our kid with me. That said, perhaps instead of signing him or her into the ultimate care of Xavier, I'd have likely run as far from this Gott forsaken country as I could.

So, all the children I mentioned were put into the nursery cottages. Peter, Oliver, Friedrick, Rolf, Reece, Kilian, Anna, Byron, Noah and Olaf all grew up together under the same roof with the same teachers and similar environments. These boys and that girl were thick as thieves, and I dare say the best of friends with each other.

As you are well aware, a few were even involved with their fellow brothers intimately. Kilian courted and captured Jacob's heart before either boy could grow the proper beard. Byron and Friedrick were also inseparable.

Even after Byron was sent to the Dungeons, his ever-loyal buddy made the daily trips to visit with him. Eventually, they became an item, like Kilian and Jacob, at least for a while that is. These four fellows paired up, but Peter, Oliver, Rolf, Reece, Anna, Noah and Olaf fell under the spell of the 'Free Love' generation.

I will get to the story of their many famous conquests in time. Believe me, I think you'd be hard pressed to find a man or woman between the ages of fifteen and sixty-five that lived in this Haus during these kids' teens that one or more of them didn't sleep with at least one. Yikes!

So that five years after Keifer was murdered were maybe the toughest in my entire life. they surely were the loneliest. Even worse than after my mother was sent away. I visited my beloved's grave daily, but thanks to the hyper repressive Nazi run environment, I had to do it in secret. It's sad that I was forbidden to open grieve for the man that made my life worth living simply because he was male.

Hitler thought all homosexuals were debauched perverts. That's ironic since that motherfucker was a far bigger monster than any other human could claim. I became aware, around the summer of 1938 that the Dungeons of Das

Kaiser Haus were filling up, and more rapidly emptying, with the poor souls deemed unfit by the Nazis.

At night when I snuck out to the grave yard to visit Keifer, I saw the huge fires lit near the Hill. The smell in the air was horrifically familiar to me. The scent of burning corpses told the tale of the role Das Kaiser Haus was playing in Hitler's war efforts.

The Jewish people, gypsies, middle easterners, Asians, political dissidents, Russians, the mentally incompetent and the chronically weak or ill were being brought for private elimination by the scores. I cringed at the thought of being forced to end the lives of so many innocent folks.

I confess that I was thankful that this time I wasn't stuck below and forced to face the grim realities of Germany's insanity. That didn't save me from becoming freshly haunted by dark nightmares from my past deplorable behaviors. It seemed to me, 1939 forward was a repeat of 1919. Only this time, there wasn't a loving husband to help sooth my tortured soul.

I found myself spending more time in bed than was healthy. In the desperate attempt to pull myself out of the oncoming depression, in the Spring of 1940, I faced my fears and headed down below to visit with Bladrick. It was my hope that his company, no matter how brief, could rekindle my resolve to hang in there until I got an open shot at ending Barnim, Drexel and Xavier's lives.

I found the Headmaster loudly berating and backhanding the badly treated Hemmel. Bladrick didn't immediately notice my arrival nor did he realize I was witness to his cruelty. From my place in the shadows I watched Keifer's favored cousin bully the poor boy until he was on his knees begging for mercy. I started to leave the two of them to working out their differences but stopped cold in my tracks. Bladrick was unsheathing his cock and demanding Hemmel blow him right there in that public place.

I couldn't believe the audacity of Bladrick to dare such dangerous humiliation tactics in an environment rife with tattle tales. I rushed from my hiding spot and demanded Bladrick release the sobbing Hemmel from his vicious hold.

Bladrick grinned the second he recognized the face of the man that was calling him to heel. "Ah. Claus, you old dog. It's so good to see you brother. You need not concern yourself with the likes of this little bitch. Hemmel, you worthless worm. Thank this man for his providence to you and do it fast. You are released for now but keep that pretty ass of yours handy. I will finish what we started after I spend some quality time with the quality. Now get the fuck out of my sight." He pushed the Krauss boy harshly as he yelled dat.

Hemmel didn't look up from the floor as he took to his boots and literally ran from our presence. I felt another twinge of remorse for the unfortunate fellow, but it was far weaker than it had been the first time I witnessed his abuse. My lack of strong sympathy for Hemmel wasn't because I'd become a cold hearted bastard.

70

By this time rumors of his brutality against helpless females had started to circulate. No one could prove him guilty, yet. But I'd been around the Haus long enough to know such gossiping wasn't without at least a kernel of truth to it. There was no doubt in my mind that Hemmel had become a ruthless serial rapist and killer.

I shook my head with pity as I watched Hemmel scurry off into the shadows, "Bladrick, it's none of my business, I know. However, I think you better lay off that Krauss a bit. I've heard some disturbing tales about his, uhm, anger fits. Perhaps you should give him some space and also keep a closer eye on his movements. I say this as your friend, brother. I'd be remise to break words with you and not mention this small issue. Best to nip it in the bud before the idle talking manages to stroke the wrong ears, ja?"

Bladrick chuckled with a diabolical tone then slapped me on the back heartily as he said, "Alright, I hear what you saying, Claus. I thank you for the wise advice. Surely you didn't making the trip down into this hell hole merely to thump me over my treatment of my plaything. Don't leave me in the dark, brother. To what do I owe this unexpected and much appreciated pleasure?"

I shrugged and glance around to making sure no one was listening in. "Oh, you know me, Bladrick. I'm forever the romantic soul. I was missing Keifer this morning and thought to visit with his favored cousin may cheer up my gloom. If you're busy, then I can come back another time."

Bladrick shook his head but kept smiling. "Nein. nothing is so pressing I cannot spare a moment for an old buddy. Gosh Claus, you are looking old these days. If the good looking young man like you can appear worn by father time, I think I'd better avoid all mirrors at any cost." He shot me a mischievous glance.

I snorted at his attempt to rile me up. "They won't allow me to cover up my ugly mug with makeup anymore is all. That girl you saw so long ago was only the glamor illusion."

The Headmaster roared out in hearty laughter, "You are still the fucking riot, Claus. Gott damned have I ever missed you and that sweet cousin of mine too. If I ever find out the names of the rat bastards that stole him from us, well Heaven help the sonsofabitches because I'm willing to do worse to them than that fellow did to old Kilian."

I startled when he said that. "Oh, I'd forgotten about that, uhm, gruesome business. Guess they will never catch the crook that murdered that Fur King. Luckily the pervert seems to have moved on. No other killings like that has happened since."

Bladrick winked and shot me a knowing smile as he replied, "Maybe he moved on or maybe he hasn't. I'm willing to bet he's still around the Haus somewhere waiting for the right opportunity to release his inner beast. Then again, perhaps he hasn't repeated his skillful attack because Kilian had personally offended the killer, but no one else been dumb enough to."

I stood there gawking at the man unsure what to read into his playful demure. He continued to stare back, unblinking, and grinning like the cat with a rat in his paws.

Finally, I broke from the stun and said, "With all this despairing surrounding you brother, I would think you'd prefer to discuss more peaceful topics and avoid the bloody ones."

He nodded with a twinkle still lighting up his dark eyes. "Sounds good. Anything in particular you wish to speak of?"

I shrugged. "W ell, I was kind of hopeful that you'd be willing to reminisce with me about Keifer. Maybe swap a story or two?"

Bladrick slapped his knee and laughed. "Sure thing, Claus. What story about him would you desire to hear? I have several."

That caused my own face to break out in the smiling. "Would it be too much to ask to hear all of them? I thank you for the mercy of it."

Bladrick's face suddenly fell into the frown as he replied, "Claus, I think it only fair, I mean I thought you were merely fooling with me, but you seriously are still hurting over losing Keifer, aren't you?"

I was quite confused by his strangely heartless question. "Uhm, ja I'm still broken hearted, Bladrick. Who the fuck wouldn't be? I never am going to be able to hold that beautiful man in my arms again in this life. I'm lonely without his light to guide me through each day and night."

The Headmaster clicked his tongue and looked down at his feet as he said in the near whisper, "Claus, Keifer he, uhm, it was his job to, you know, seduce you. Mother Felicity promised our family membership in the Haus If we could find a way to bring you to Das Kaiser Haus. Keifer was the correct age for the task so he was chosen to do it."

I groaned over his admission. "Bladrick, I know all about that. Felicity told me the day I joined the Haus. There is no reason for you to worry I'd be hurt by the knowledge of it. Keifer may have become my friend because he was ordered to by his family, but his loving me was independent of that arrangement."

Bladrick glanced up at me appearing surprised by my response. "Is that what she told you? Or did Keifer say this?"

I was more than puzzled by this point. "Bladrick, what is it you trying to say to me? Both of them said Keifer's affection for me was real. He was only supposed to become my best buddy. Becoming the lovers wasn't part of the bargain but it happened. Hell, Keifer wasn't even aware I was schwuler till the day he confessed he wanted me for his own."

Bladrick snorted and then stared at me coldly as he replied, "That's what you believe, ja? So old Keifer just happened to be gay and somehow he knew you were also. Pretty damned lucky don't you think?"

I felt my heartbeat speeding up from both fear of what he intended to say and the intense fury over it. "I think it might be best if I head back up the steps. It's been a pleasure seeing you, Bladrick, but I just recalled I do have a pressing matter that must be attended immediately. Perhaps we can enjoy each other's company again real soon. I see you later." I started to haul ass in the opposite direction before he had the chance to destroy my beautiful delusions of perfection.

Bladrick called out behind me, "He was told to make you his lover at any cost Claus. I should know since I was the one that ordered him to do it. Felicity knew your nature. She fed Keifer information through the years to make sure he adjusted his personality to suit your tastes. Our family sacrificed him in the hope it would improve our fortunes. Keifer was a good sport about it, but he did understand he was signing up to be a prisoner to your whims for all his, or you, life. His family still adores him for caring about all of us enough to give up his future so that we could have the chance to thrive. But he is gone now Claus. I always liked you and I thank you for treating my little cousin with great kindness. You've done so much for me, and our family. You even took in my late wife's hard luck daughter. Look, it was wrong of me to wait so long to return your generosity by releasing you from the payment you never owed. I offer my sincerest apologies for being the gutless sonofabitch for all this time while you suffered needlessly. I pray you will find it in your heart to forgive me and still call me brother for truth despite it all."

I turned around nearly blinded by the hot tears in my eyes as I shouted back at him, "Fuck you, Bladrick. Kiefer did love me for truth. You are lying. He wasn't sacrificing his happiness to advance the status of his family. No one can fake the feelings he expressed to me daily for almost forty years. I thought you were my friend, but now I must wonder if I ever knew you? I ask myself why Keifer favored you? Clearly you aren't worth wasting a single moment on. I suppose the answer is obvious. Keifer was the baby when he left your family hovel to live next door to me. He met the fellow you wanted him to see. You always hid from him the cruel bastard you really are." I ran from the Dungeon nearly tripping over the Masters, and Mistresses that rushed about the hallways doing their jobs."

I sucked in my breath then whispered. "Bladrick was a real monster to say such awful things to you Claus. I mean, I know he lied to me several times to get his way. But why would he say that shit to you about Keifer? Did he get some sadistic thrill by hurting you? Like he did when he raped Hemmel, ja?"

Claus sniffed loudly, as if about to cry as he replied, "Oh Maxx, my beauty. Bladrick wasn't trying to get a sick kick that day. He was telling me the truth, at least the one he understood."

I gasped in shock over his response. "What? I thought you said Keifer loved you and you loved him. Bladrick was being mean for no fucking reason. Why do you defend him when to do so sullies the memory of your Mann? I don't understand."

The Elder nodded and pursed his lips. "You see Maxx, I already knew the truth long before Bladrick said it out loud. Felicity told me she hired the Reinhardts to bring me home to her, remember? I also said that I believed her story that

76

Keifer fell for me naturally without any prior knowledge of my sexual preference because I needed to believe it. Just because I chose to buy into the lie, it becomes the reality. Deep inside, I knew she'd been guiding his every move all those years."

That caused me to startle. "So, Keifer's adoration was false then? He was only faking interest in you the entire time? He would have left you in a second if he thought he could is what you are saying? Christ, that is horrible." I didn't know if I should try to console the grieving Elder or leave immediately before the pain of such a betrayal sunk into my brain too far.

Claus surprised me with a weak smile through his erupting tears. "Calm down boy. I didn't say Keifer's words of love to me were empty. I merely tell you that Bladrick wasn't lying, but my mother, she did lie. I believe that Keifer initially was with me because it was the path he was forced into. However, over the years, he learned to care for me. Then eventually he did love me with all his heart. That's what I believe anyway. Only Keifer can honestly answer if I'm correct or completely misled. He's not here to defend himself. I do know that actions speak much louder than pretty words. No matter what the motives were behind his playing my loyal husband, when he lay there dying it was my presence he desired. He even held off the reaper till I could get there to hold him in my embrace one last time. That, my beloved, is a fact no one can muddy up with details of triviality."

I shook my head in disbelief. "So, you basically are saying that even after hearing the truth, knowing Keifer was faking being your buddy and then your lover, it's okay because he eventually fell in love with you. Or should I say, when he was on his deathbed he waited till you arrived before taking the doctor's mercy. Claus, you do realize he maybe only hung around so that he could making sure he would be avenged, ja? If that's the case, you realize that's not love, Claus. That's a final kick in your teeth."

Claus laughed hard but his tears continued to flow as he said, "Damn, just when I think I couldn't adore you more than I already do, you say something that touches my dark soul. Maxx honey, if you are lucky enough to live the long life like me, you'll come to accept that reality is what you want it to be. The world is a loud, noisy place full of lies, half-truths, and mysteries. A man could go insane trying to fully comprehend even a fraction of the tiny space he occupies. That doesn't include understanding the private thoughts or secret motives of his fellow human beings. In the end, you'll figure out if you wish to exist with any hope of happiness. It's best you learn to taking command of your destiny and leave the rest of the population to attend to their own gardens. Belief is personal, and the only thing you honestly have some control over. If what you wish to accept as truth makes you smile and it's not hurting anyone else, then no one has the right to steal that from you."

I guffawed loudly then replied, "That is the stupidest thing I believe I've been told in a while, Claus. Reality is not something you can bargain with. Keifer either loved you or he played you. Choosing to buy into his lies, that, well, that caused you great pain. Look at you. After he died you didn't take another lover. A life of loneliness is sure as hell not a happy one, was it?"

The Elder sat up in his bed and stared into my face. "Tell me something, Maxx. What color are my eyes?"

I stammered suddenly full of fear as I responded, "Uhm, didn't you just ask me this already? They are maybe grey or light blue? The same as the marble pillars in the Great Hall I think."

Claus nodded. "Ja, that's the correct answer my boy. Tell me, is your reality sound or have you chosen to bend or ignore some facts in the effort to gain peace?"

I shrugged. "I don't know what you mean, Claus. I never hide that truth from myself if that's what you are asking."

The Elder snickered then covered his mouth to stifle the sound as he said, "You are lying to yourself right now, little Maxximillian. I would dare to say in all my many years I've yet to meet anyone that can twist the truth more skillfully than you do."

I shook my head and felt a trance coming over me that I was helpless to prevent. "It's not purposeful, Claus. I wasn't given the choice. Somone stole my memories, then they hijacked my will and replaced my history with one they thought I could live with."

He smiled as he nodded. "Ah now, you are stepping closer to reality at last. Come out of the shadows my pretty

79

boy. Where are you at this moment. Tell me about Doctor Mueller."

I closed my eyes and took a deep breath. When I opened them the apartment had vanished. It was replaced by walls made of white padding. I glanced around this odd room. There wasn't anything else in there with me. The door to the place wasn't easily noticed. It seemed to be perfectly camouflaged in the uniformed appearance with the borders of the area.

I gasped in shock. A tremble of fear caused my flesh to quiver slightly. With caution I attempted to taking to my feet. A stabbing sensation, followed by an aching sting rushed through the boy's nervous system. The pain forced a wail from my throat.

A man's voice called out in the soothing tone from beside me, "Easy there, little one. I apologize for that. The cut was deeper than many of the others. I thought the anesthetic would prevent you from feeling the needle but as I said, the cut is a pretty nasty one. Tell you what, let's try to keep you occupied on other things. I don't believe you have told me what they call you. Can you tell me your name son?"

The word 'son' caught my attention. I turned my head and saw a man in his middle ages sitting next to me in a chair. I suddenly noticed I was laying on my back on a weird table apparatus. My arms and legs were held to this table, that I assumed was a torturing device, by the use of soft leather cuffs.

Panic filled my senses the second I understood I was this fellow's prisoner. With all my strength I attempted to pull free of the restraints. The man that spoke to me, backed away a bit but didn't leave or release me. I howled, neighed and bleated for several minutes, nearly insane with terror.

This man never took his deep brown eyes from my flailing flesh. As I began to weaken from the useless battle, I stole another glance at him. To my confusion he was wearing a white coat. I'd seen another guy dressed like this one, just before the men wearing yellow jackets stole my skeleton from me.

I remembered they put the skeleton on a slab of wood. Then they covered him with a blanket to keep him warm. The idea that this white coat could tell me where to find my brother worked to settle down my terrible fear reactions.

The man saw that I was trying to be the brave boy. He smiled at me and was careful to avoid making the aggressive eye contact. I quickly decided this behavior indicated he wasn't looking to fight with me. I knew escaping his bondage wasn't going to happen unless I could convince him to leave the room or loosen his restraints.

It seemed my only hope was to go silent and still. This game of pretending to be the stone statue was one me and Maximillian had perfected over the last couple years. It'd been quite effective at ending Gerard's agonizing blows or his cigarette burning.

I focused on the ceiling of the white room and put out the lights of my mind. This effectively turned off the outward signs that the boy was alert or even alive. The flesh didn't move a muscle with my breath coming almost too slow to see without careful observation.

The man in the white coat sat there staring at me for several moments. He seemed quite interested to know if I was faking death. When I refused to relent this state of nothingness, he moved forward to examine me closer. I held my stance without wavering, though I was very frightened of him and of the torturing I was certain he intended to do to us.

I could see his clean shaven chin hovering above my sightline. He reached out and gently pushed my face. I allowed it to fall unhampered in the direction he desired it to go. He sucked in his air and grabbed my forehead. I offered no resistance as he manipulated my head till it was maneuvered to be staring directly into his eyes.

His trembling hands fumbled in the pocket of his doctor's jacket. He pulled out a thing that resembled a writing pencil. To my shock, he made it click and a bright light came pouring out the end of it.

The man held my lids open wide while he shined that intense brilliance into the boy's eyes. I wanted to yelp from the discomfort but I held fast. I was nearly blind before he appeared satisfied his torture device wasn't going to work. I nearly messed up and grinned as he cursed under his breath, while putting his tool away.

Denying him the sadistic pleasure of knowing he was injuring my flesh wasn't helping me escape him, but I hoped it would make him lose interest in hurting me.

To my dismay he returned to his seat close to the boy. I held the noise of frustration and did my best to brace for whatever nightmare he had in store next. He took up a stiff piece of paper. Curiosity filled me as I watched him scribbling something on it.

I wanted badly to taking that stuff from him. I could remember mother would give me and my brother the coloring pencils to making pretty pictures with. I missed her and him bad. I thought maybe if the man went to get other tools to cut me up with, I might steal that pencil and his paper.

The thought of entertaining Maximillian and Der Hund with my drawing skills kept me distracted for a bit. The voice of that white coat man called me back from the dreaming of showing off my talents.

He'd picked up a threaded needle and started sewing shut a cut on my arm as he said, "Well, I suppose it was rude of me to expect you to speak with a stranger, ja? I bet your mother told you never to break words with one. She's a wise woman if she did. I guess I need not tell you about the bad people in the world looking to hurt a sweet little child like you, poor baby. So, I will introduce myself first, okay? My name is Doctor Mueller. I fix broken little boys and girls and make them good as new. See here? Your skin will heal up in no time. There will only be the painless scars, but don't let that bother you. Scars prove a man is brave. I must tell you, my man, the girls will gaze upon you and know you are a warrior most rare. If you have any question your abilities, tell them to come and ask me. I will tell them my boy is tougher than old Alexander the Great. He may be marked up a bit, but holy cow, they should see the other guy. Hahaha, ja?"

I blinked my eyes and turned to look at this man that sounded friendly. Something about him reminded me of mother. He saw me gazing at him. Doctor Mueller flashed a warm smile and I mimicked it back to him. This seemed to please him which confused the hell out of me. Normally if I demonstrated anything but fear toward Gerard, he hit me.

Doctor Mueller rubbed his cheek and calmly said, "Hello little one. Do you wish to tell me your name? If you do that for me, I bet I can find a piece of candy as the reward for your kindness to me."

I gasped at the idea of having a sweet. "Mor. Mor. Ah, woof, woof. Hahaha. Baa, Baa." I looked around wildly hoping that he'd produce the candy he'd promised.

To my dismay, he leaned back in his chair with an expression of distress on his face, "You say Mor. I wish I could get your Mor for you but sadly no one knows her name. If you tell me who you are, perhaps the police could help track her down. You want to go home, ja? Please help us help you. Tell me your name sweetheart. I give you a pound of candy if you do."

That nearly drove me insane with desire for both mother and the candy. I struggled hard against the cuffs but they wouldn't budge an inch. Sweat began to pour off my brow as I opened my mouth and tried to form the words he was asking me to give to him.

I could see the air turn black with the oily rot as the sounds poured out my mouth, "Hold mund. Stop med at græde som fissebaby. Hvis du laver en anden støj, sætter jeg dig ind i de grønne marker. Fortæl mig noget møgunge. Vil du være død som det skelet ved siden af dig? Hvis du ikke stopper kampen, vil du være. Hej. Hører du det? Lammene efterlyser frisk græs. Jeg vedder på, at du er grim will fodre them godt, ja? Hold nu stille dammit. Åbn munden. Spyt det ud denne gang eller forsøg at bide mig, og de lam bliver fede denne vinter."

Doctor Mueller's face twisted into the expression of pure shock as he replied, "So did you, uhm, spit it out or bite him when he, uhm, put what in your mouth? You can tell me. I'm here to make sure no one hurts you ever again. Do you know your name?"

I whimpered and then screamed at the top of my lungs, "Maximillian. Kristen. Hjælp ham. Vær venlig at redde ham. Mor kan ikke tage hans hud på, fordi de stjal hans skelet. Lad ham ikke røre ved mig. Det gør ondt. Lad ham ikke dø. Han skriger. få det til at stoppe. Christian holder Maximillians hånd, som mor lærte os. Ah, baa, baa. Vi ønsker ikke at fodre lammene i de grønne feilder. Følg lammene. De kender vejen hjem."

Doctor Mueller's eyes turned wet as he replied in the soft tone, "Hush, Maximillian. Kristian is safe now. I will let the police know where to start looking for your mother. I promise, if it's the last thing I ever do, I'm will help you feel better. And I swear on my life I will never let another fiend touch you in the painful ways ever again. Maximillian, that's a regal name you possess, little one. I like it very much. It suits you too. It's quite the mouthful. Can I call you Max for short?"

I shook my head. "Ah, woof, woof. Awrooo. Hahaha. Mor. Mor."

The doctor shook his head and stood up just as the walls melted away and the stark white was replaced by the color of stone. My leather cuffs turned into the silver collar held by a chain in the rock wall. The huge man in the black chest harness yelled out…

Gott dammit Maximillian. Eat the fucking porridge with the spoon and stop behaving like the wild animal. What the hell. What a fucking idiot you are. I cannot believe you have managed to spill it again. Too bad for you. I'll be damned if I'm getting you more to feed the rats. I swear I'm gonna beat the stuffing out of you for trying to sup like a fucking hound. You know what, never mind, stay dare on all fours like a mindless beast. That's probably the only thing you will ever be any good for anyway. You insane little creep. Wait a second.

Come to think of it your benefactors aren't due for their daily visit for another hour and a half. That's plenty of time for you to give me a little payback for all the trouble you've caused me these last few months. Come here boy. Open that big mouth of yours wide. Time for a new lesson boy

Your cousin Noah is going to teach you how to eat your supper like the proper pleasure submissive. You better not bit or spit it out, you little beasty, or I swear to Gott I will kill you and bury your bones in the yard."

Chapter 11: Noah and Olaf
Mad Maxx and submissive Meine Liebe

QUICK RECAP: We shall pick up where we left off. Maximillian has survived Gretta's assassination attempt through both Bartram and the Stasi. Our dark hero, badly beaten and broken hearted has buried his lost fiancé and tiny adopted son. During his turbulent recuperation in the "cock bed" under Mad Lucus's watchful eye, Maximillian had a disturbing dream, he fears might be more real than fantasy. Once recovered enough to walk unaided, he has sought out the one man in the Haus that can answer his burning question regarding a memory of hooded figures, drugged candy bars and a picture of Felicity his trusty mother lamb. As Elder Claus lay slowly dying of pancreatic cancer, he finally unburdens his tormented soul with the many dark secrets he has kept for nearly sixty years.

Maximillian is faced with a dilemma. Should he trust Claus's story or is the Elder merely using his last moments on Earth to mislead him one last time? Is he really the twin Prince of the Haus to survive a horror so unbelievable that insanity would be the ultimate outcome? Was there a time that the Haus was a place where all the classes, submissive and Dominant treated each other with respect? Is Ingrid really his maternal grandmother and the person he had mistakenly recalled as his mother in his memories? Was the Great Silk King Keifer his uncle and is he his namesake? Was Noah really the man he had to thank for bringing him back from the brink of madness? And more importantly who is he, really? Christian Axel or Maximillan Keifer?

So, let's go back to that darkened room on the first floor in the Fur King's temporary apartment back in the Spring of 1977. Maximillian will turn 18 in June, and as the Morter King, he will be forced to name a regent just before he is incarcerated for life in the Morter Palace as is Haus law. He has six months left above ground to do all he can to protect himself from a repeat of the months he suffered there with Florian just as he turned seventeen. With a strange DJ following him around in the walls, a vampire coven stalking him, a sadistic half-brother blackmailing him, a love crazed husband trying to control him, a royal blooded Master hounding him, a disgruntled Silk Queen trying to destroy him, physical damage caused him by his Stasi encounter so extreme his ability to use his seductive skill have been compromised, and the Haus population afraid of him, he has plenty to be worried about.

But maybe every answer he needs to find his way out the front door to freedom is laying right there in front of him at last, if only he could believe the source.

Maximillian is recalling his past as an eight year old boy in the dungeon just days after being dragged to the Haus, while under a deep trance brought on by Fur King Claus, and drugged candy.

I trembled as the big man with the leather harness come toward me. He grabbed the boy by his hair and pulled him from the dog position to his knees. With a sneer he leaned down into my face.

"Pick up the spoon and open your mouth I said." He shook me like the rag doll.

I felt my bladder let loose as I wailed out, "Ah, vha, vha. Mor, mor. Ah." I didn't understand what he wanted of me.

The man frowned and growled in response, "Gott dammit. All you do is piss and scream. What the fuck does my father think? I cannot train an animal to behave like the human. Fuck me." He reached out and took up the strange tool with the round end and forced it into my hand.

With all the strength I had I attempted to wiggle out of his hold on my mane. "Ah, ha-ha. Woof, woof. Baa, baa," I yelled at the top of the boy's lungs.

He slapped my face with force. "Shut that gibberish up. Hold the spoon. I will break your hand and tape the spoon onto the busted flesh if you let it go. Do you understand me, boy?"

His big hand surrounded my tiny one. He squeezed the fingers till I howled in agony. Then he forced my arm to scoop up the some of the spilled porridge off the dirty dungeon floor. There wasn't a thing I could do to stop him from pushing that nasty mess into my face.

The man made me repeat this action like the puppet on his string. I continued to make the sounds of distress, despite a quickly filling mouth. Once he believed no more could fit into me, he led go of my hand to snatch me by the chin. He

90

held my jaws together. The gritty contents and his restraint blocked my ability to yell in terror. I nearly choked before recognizing I could swallow the food and thus end this torture.

When he realized I'd dispatched the gruel, he laughed out loud. "Ah, well, you may die on my watch yet, but it won't be of starvation. Now, try to do this without my help, ja?" He released my chin while pointing at the remaining porridge scattered about in the straw.

With my tongue free at last I let out a loud wail, "Ah, Maximillian. Mor. Skelet. Uh, ha." My bladder led go of its contents into my heavily soiled breeches once again.

This seemed to send the man into a fury. He let out a shout of his own and shook me till I nearly fainted from the pressure of it. I suppose he recognized he nearly killed me with that move. His mood suddenly shifted from overtly murderous to what appeared to be desperation.

He jerked me into the air by use of my hair, until I was staring at him face to face. "Are you purposely trying to get me killed? Is there even a brain in the pretty head of yours? Where the fuck did you come from? You don't speak an intelligible world. You wallow in your own filth, and you're not capable of understanding if you don't eat you will expire. These cuts all over you, did your last owner tire of the constant strain of trying to care for you, ja? Well, obviously his cruel attempts to get through to you didn't work. You respond no better for me no matter how brutal I am. Perhaps I should think outside of the box. Ja, maybe a bit of kindness is the way to gain your compliance? Shit. At this point, I'm willing to try anything." He lowered me back to the sitting position at his feet.

I stared at him too frightened to move as he dropped to the kneel in front of me. "Okay, so let's start over. Hello little one. My name is Noah. I'm the Dungeon Master that's assigned to train you in the arts of the pleasure submissive. It's an honor to serve you." He held out his hand and smiled at me as he said this in a friendly sounding tone.

I whimpered and backed away, "Ah, caw, caw. Baa."

The man's face didn't change expression as he said, "You don't understand German, do you? I don't speak your language either. Alright, that's a problem but I bet we can solve the language barrier together. Watch me, and you do as I do, ja?" I cowered as he stood up and walked over to the wooden privy.

He turned around and began to undo his breeches' buttons. "This is the proper way to eliminate your water boy. I do this first. Then you do the same." I kept a baleful eye on the man as he pulled his penis free and began to urinate into the hole.

This strange action was of interest to watch. I wondered if this was a game I could play also. With a great deal of curiosity I looked down at the breeches that clung to the boy. I saw that I had buttons too. This made me giggle. I'd never noticed them before. My sounds of humor caught the man's attention.

He put his manhood back into his leather pants and come toward me appearing surprised. "Did you just laugh? I don't believe I've ever heard you do anything but cry or scream since you arrived. Surely that was merely wishful thinking on my part."

I couldn't taking my eyes off his crotch as I whispered, "Brrr. Baaa. Noah. Noah. Ah."

The man startled. "Did you just say, ja, you did. You said my name. Holy hell, there is a light still on in that mangled brain of yours. Hahaha. I will be damned. Okay, give me your hand. I will help you make the water like a man instead of peeing in your pants like the baby. Come on little one. I won't hurt you, Noah swears it." He held out his hand once again.

I stared at his appendage for a moment then slowly reached toward it. I almost had taken his offer for aid when the door to the cell swung open with suddenness. I let out a wail of terror just as a man covered in wrinkles with a mean face come storming into the room.

The man called Noah fell to his knees and dropped his face to the floor. "Your Majesty, how can your worthless servant be of use to you?"

This evil looking fellow glared at me as he replied, "So this thing has been leveled Priceless. Not much to it is there? A bit small. How old is it Noah?"

Noah sucked in his air and responded, "Your Majesty, I wouldn't know anything about this silver's level. I've only

93

been told he is the selected pleasure submissive and around the age of eight. He will grow larger in time like all children do that survive the training that is."

With a frown the old man crossed his arms. "Oh, this little bit of nothing better not find the grave before I have a taste of his skills, Noah. If he does, you will quickly follow him. Stop pretending your ignorant of the importance of this little beast. I'm aware you have been warned he is special. I must say, despite his lack of presence, I'm glad to finally set eyes upon it. There hasn't been a Priceless in the Haus since World War Two. Bladrick and that bitch wife of mine tried to keep its existence from my knowledge, but like you they should've known better than to attempt fooling Xavier."

Noah shot me a glance of wonder. "I wouldn't presume, I mean I honestly didn't know anything, your Majesty. Though it certainly explains a few things."

The man called Xavier laughed hard. "Like?" His sudden loud noise caused me to back up toward the wall slowly.

My trainer looked up at Xavier and said, "I thought him merely poorly treated prior to his manacle purchase, but deep madness certainly could account for his lack of comprehending the simplest of personal functions."

Xavier nodded with a wicked grin spreading across his wizened face. "You are a shitty liar, Noah. Normally I would see you whipped to death for daring to play me the fool. However, I'm aware that a son's loyalty to his father isn't something that should be counted as a punishable offense.

Bladrick surely is a proud man to claim such a fine son. So, I forgive you this time but test me in the future and you'll find me less compassionate. Now, collect that thing and bring it to me. I wish to examine it more closely."

Noah gasped anxiously but didn't hesitate to come at me with speed. I scrambled trying uselessly to avoid the Dungeon Master's capture. He easily cornered me, then took me into his huge arms. I struggled wildly but his hold wasn't going to be denied.

Noah didn't break a sweat as he hauled me across the cell. I couldn't do anything but whimper and tremble, while he dropped me at Xavier's feet. I was restrained on my knees before that mean fellow by the tight hold of my abductor.

The old Fur King looked me over from head to toe with an expression of thrill on his face. "It's an attractive creature, I'll give it that. Too bad its beauty is marred by the wounds of its lost battles, ja? Agnette told me the kid's handsome features were tarnished a bit, but as usual, that woman attempts to diminish the truth of it. Tell me Noah, is there worse damage hidden from my sight? Or is what I see the nastiest of the scarring?" He leaned down to gaze into my panicked eyes.

Noah cleared his throat and responded, "Uhm, sadly, the boy's skin was mistreated without restraint your Majesty."

Xavier startled and glanced at Noah. "Every bit of this thing is marked like this is what you are saying?"

95

The Dungeon Master nodded but kept his eyes to the floor. "Ja, only his backside, palms of his feet and hands along with his male parts were spared. The physician that attended the wounds before the boy was brought here did a remarkable job minimizing the signs of abuse. But there was so much of it. No one could've done more to preserve his beauty than has been done."

The Fur King winced then stood up tall as he barked out, "Strip him down. I wish to get a sneak peek at this Priceless thing."

Noah sucked in his wind. "Your Majesty, I uhm if you wish to, uhm, test his purity, there is no need. I can see the boy's virginity is intact. His abuse appears to be of the physical nature. He seems quite innocent of the pleasures of the flesh. I was told the intake Masters qualified he's unsoiled. You can ask them yourself."

Xavier put his hand up and frowned as he interrupted him. "I didn't fucking ask you to give me a report on his virginity, Noah. Strip this Gott damned thing like I ordered. Disobey me again and find yourself fired." The Dungeon Master didn't have to be told a third time.

I kicked and bucked as Noah pulled my foul clothing from the boy. Within only a few moments I was pushed back to my dirty, bruised knees shivering from the cold air naked as the day I was born. Xavier's face lit up with a nasty smile while he watched this humiliating show.

With a whistle low in his throat he said, "Wow, this thing is lucky to be alive isn't it? Quite a piece of art to boot.

Hell, I can understand why it's leveled Priceless before it can barely walk. Seeing it just now makes me feel like the young stud ready for the rut. And it's skills not even honed to the most miniscule ability yet. I suppose you better cover it back up. The temptation to have it for a quick thrill is too difficult to resist for long. It would be a real shame to pluck it before it's ripe, ja?"

Noah nodded and quickly forced me to hold still as he attempted to cover up my nakedness. "It would indeed, your Majesty. I wasn't aware the boy belongs to the great Fur King himself. I shall remember to use extra caution and train him to be worthy of such a lofty Master," he said this with his head bowed low.

Xavier scoffed and recrossed his arms. "You misunderstand, Noah. I've not formally purchased its metal. That doesn't mean it's not mine though. Agnette tells me this creature is the fruit of my own loins. I thought her funning me but now that I've laid eyes on it, there isn't any question. The resemblance is undeniable. It's a pity, you know, that the thing survived whoever did this rearranging of his features. He won't be as lucky when I add a bit of my own brush strokes to his brutalized canvas. That will be sublime pleasure I most eagerly await. Unlike my ancestor Joseph, I won't allow the Haus to murder my son like he did his beloved Florian. That pleasure will be mine exclusively. I warn you Noah. Tell no one of this visit I make here today or anything I've said of this creatures true identity. If I find out you speak tales out of school, need I say more?"

Noah shook his head slowly. "Nein, I hear and seen nothing out of the ordinary today, your Majesty. In fact, I already have forgotten everything from the moment I got out of my cot this morning till I return to it tonight."

Xavier reached out and patted Noah's bowed head. "There you go. You always were a good boy, Noah. Keep on proving your loyalty to me, and one day soon you will be the blessed man for it. As for you my little bastard son…" he quickly moved his hand to stroke my hair as he done the Dungeon Master.

I opened my mouth wide. "Ah. Baaa, baaa. Mor. Mor." With the speed of a cat I latched my teeth into his approaching fingers.

Xavier screamed bloody murder, "Holy hell. Get it off me. Ah, shit, fuck, ouch." Noah grabbed me by the back of the head and forced me to release my toothy hold on the old man.

The Fur King pulled his bleeding hand to his chest and with a grunt kicked me in the stomach. The air flew from the boy's lungs. Without a sound I hit the floor writhing in agony from his blow. Noah snatched my flailing flesh from the straw and without a moment to spare dragged me across the cell. He tossed me into the wall with light force. I collided with the stone, bounced and landed nearly unconscious onto the ground.

The Fur King growled, "You better teach that thing proper manners, Noah. Do not fail me or else." With those cryptic words the cruel old man stormed from the cell, slamming the stony door behind him.

Claus's shout of surprise shook me from that strange trancing behavior as he yelled, "What? You surely are remembering this incorrectly, Maxx. Noah never told me, Ingrid nor Bladrick of a visit from Xavier while you were held in the dungeons."

I rubbed my eyes and took a deep breathe. "Huh? I don't understand your meaning, Claus. You're the one putting these lies into my mind. None of it is real. I never barked like the dog nor peed my breeches like the baby while old enough to wear the silver manacle. You better stop fucking with my head, dammit." I glared at him angrily.

Claus fell back onto his pillow appearing frustrated. "Gott dammit. I've always wondered when exactly that bitch Agnette turned on Ingrid for the second time. That asshole Noah kept that little meeting a secret from all of us. Had we known your mother had sought out Xavier's aid to betray us so quickly, perhaps we'd have been capable of predicting her turning to Peter when that plan failed. The stupid woman honestly thought the child murdering Fur King was about to reward her for admitting she'd bore his son? I knew she was a dipshit but holy hell, there are no words."

I chuckled bitterly. "Well, at least you finally are saying something truthful. I don't know why you bothering to fool with me about Xavier's knowledge of his relationship to me or how he found that out. None of that matters. I killed that motherfucker, and I didn't need to know he was my father to

99

feel justified in doing it either. Unless the memories of his raping and brutalizing me in public are falsehoods you fed to me also that is. As for Agnette telling that man about his paternity, that only adds more disgust to an already horrific truth. I suppose you are aware she made great sport of watching the show as she guided his raping me when I was only the boy of thirteen." I grimaced as the scene of my mother cheering that monster on while he brutally fucked me ran across the wheel room screen.

Claus frown and said, "Ja, Agnette bragged to me after Xavier's death of her little family get together with you and that nasty bastard. Maxx, there isn't anything I can say to make that trauma less brutal, so I won't insult you by bothering. I just wish I'd discovered this bit of information about that early visit sooner. Maybe, if we'd known, things would've gone easier for you."

I shrugged. "You're capable of creating nightmares for me at will. Seems to me if you can fill my memory with darkness, it shouldn't be too much trouble to replace them with happiness, ja? I'm waiting. Go ahead and making me believe I had the perfect childhood and all you perverts are really gentle, loving uncles."

The Fur King startled. "Maxx, I know nothing I say will convince you, but I swear I'm not behind this flood of recall you are experiencing. Okay other than helping you lift the repression of them that is. Giving you the beautiful lie would be a waste of time, and frankly dangerous as hell. Sooner or later you will have to face the tragedies you spend all your energy trying to forget. I don't enjoy watching the boy I love more than life itself suffering. That's not my kink unlike so many around here. There isn't a thing I can do to erase the past no matter how much I wish I could."

I snorted. "Whatever you say, Claus. Are you satisfied with this weird service call yet? I want more of that candy, and I've got pressing things to attend." I glanced around the room hoping to spy a sweet wrapper that I hadn't emptied already.

Claus sighed. "Nein, I'm not finished visiting. I will let you know when you're released, dammit. The dogs of this Haus waiting on you for their cruel games can remain at bay a bit longer. As for your interest in the chocolate, you haven't done a thing to earn more of it."

That caused me to gasp as I cried out, "Come on, Claus. I've patiently sat here as you assault my ears with your boring old man recollections of you youthful perversions for hours already. That's a fair trade for more of the candy. If not, then name a price and I will pay it. The lambs are starving you know."

Claus sat up with suddenness and grabbed me by the wrist. "I think you would do well to recall your manners, boy. Didn't that bitch mother of yours or your evil father teach you anything but how to scream and beg for mercy? Oh and speaking of monsters of the female species, I wonder something. Have you seen Agnette recently?"

I startled both from his latching on to me and over that weird question as I said, "Huh? Agnette? Nein. I've not laid eyes on her since she betrayed me by marrying that nasty bat Jonas and turning my guardianship over to him."

The Elder released my wrist and pushed me slightly with a low chuckling erupting from his throat. "Is that so? For possessing an epic reputation for seduction and manipulations, you sure are a horrible liar my boy. I'm the biggest fool in the Haus, but yet I am catching you in fibs several times in only a few hours."

I narrowed my eyes at him as a said in the suspicious tone, "I don't know what you mean, Claus. I'm not telling a false tale. I will say that it's a lucky thing Agnette made herself scarce. Personally, I've wondered if after all the deviltry she'd pulled over the years, she finally realized running into me wouldn't be good for her health."

He grinned from ear to ear as he said, "Interestingly, what you just said works to verify the rumor I've heard. Birgit told me that the family reunion Agnette attempted with her disturbed son left the evil mother with one hell of a headache. She swears to me that the Mortar King's Palace privy is lined with the putrefying noggin of our Stone monarch's mother. Birgit claims that she knows this to be truth because she was charged by the Priceless himself to place Agnette's remains in there with her moldering mouth propped open to assure it's filled with the piss and shit of her dearest son for the rest of eternity."

I gasped and interrupted his disgusting accusation with a yelp as I said, "What? Birgit said that? Why would the Head Dungeon Mistress make such slanderous statements against her King. I tell you Claus, I don't keep Agnette's skull nor any ones boney head in the Mortar Palace toilet."

Claus nodded but kept smiling as he replied, "Shut the fuck up, Maxx. Don't even attempt to deny Birgit's allegations. I believe that honest lady over the man with motivation to keep her story quiet. As far as I'm concerned, the fate you handed out to Agnette was far too gentle despite the reported brutality of her bloody end. I more than anyone in this Haus am aware of the damage she's done to you, your brother, your grandmother, all the submissives, the Haus, and believe it or not, yours truly. Xavier was a brute, and many other cold hearted men have called Das Kaiser Haus home during my and your time here. However, none of them can hold a candle to the pure evil that woman is guilty of. It's of no consequence how she found her end, nor what dishonor her remains suffered or will suffer. All I care is that she is no longer a threat to you or anybody else. I only mentioned the things Birgit reported to check if she was mistaken. I clearly see in your expression and reaction she's not. You killed your cruel mother, father and my sorry brother Gerard too. I tell you, they deserved it Maxx, all of them. I'm fucking proud of you for doing what none of the rest of us ever could. I wish I could tell you to lay down your arms, retire to the life of the peaceful man and forget about the nightmares that come before this moment. That's not possible, not yet anyway. I dare say that list your grandmother gave to you still has many names left to scratch out, ja?"

I glared at him hatefully as I spit out through clenched teeth. "I have no idea what list you're babbling about Claus.

I'd better call down to the Great Hall and tell Sergie to get back here. You need your medication for the dementia and hallucinations that the dying sometimes do."

He snorted. "Stop playing coy, Maxx. You know damned well I'm referring to the mission. I'm aware it's not completed. Until it is, you are condemned to play the executioner several more times. Now you ready to hear the rest of my story or would you rather get on with your oral services to me?"

I sputtered as I attempted to back away a bit. "Oh, uhm. you should continue with the story, Claus. I'm absolutely riveted by the details of your, uhm, journey through life. I thank you for the mercy of your wisdom." I cleared my throat and glanced nervously at the bedroom door.

He sneered at me then rolled his eyes as he responded, "You've sucked my cock how many times Maxx and still you behave as if it's abhorrent to you. Seriously? How dare you attempt to shirk your duty to me, while insisting on insulting me with chronic bad manners. This will never do. I'm forced to make you pay double. On your knees. Get to it boy." He put my lambs onto his nightstand then threw the blanket off his thin frame.

I groaned as he I watched him struggle to pull down his pajama bottoms. "Okay, I do as you wish Claus, but can I have some chocolate after?"

Claus shot me a look of shock. "I must be hallucinating as you said I am. I didn't just hear you attempt to bargain with me over a deal that has long since been agreed upon, did I? I hope not. You know better. If I must repeat my command a second time, you know the penalty as you're no novice."

I blew out my breath and crawled across the bed to taken a place between his gnarled legs. Doing my best to hide the fury, disgust, and humiliation this sex act always causes me as I took his member into my mouth.

I assumed it would be nothing worse than the usual gross mechanics of blowing the elderly man. There was a bid of surprise on my end when Claus proved his threat to punish me for the perceived insolence to the reality. Before I could protest his claws grabbed both sides of my head by the hair. He used all the strength within his power to force me down on him. He held me there blocking off my airway with his withered cock for what seemed like forever. I swear to Gott I was turning blue by the time he allowed me to come up for air.

The old bastard refused to relent his hold on my mane. I barely filled my lungs and he pulled me down into the deep throating once again. This violent oral service continued till he found his apex. My eyes were bulging and filled with tears, from both his rough action and the emotional upheaval that caused within me, as he emptied his foul seed into my head.

With a loud moan of pleasure he finally let go of my hair and yelled, "Gott dammit, that was amazing. Holy hell, I needed that. Hey, Maxx, don't forget. Don't swallow. Spit that shit out. Hurry the fuck up." He didn't have to repeat that order twice.

Without leaving my position in his lap, I leaned my ravaged head over the side of his bed. I loudly retched the disgusting contents of my mouth onto the floor. While I dispatched his cum, Claus emitted a satisfied sounding chuckle and petted my back.

The Elder sucked in his air loudly then said, "I've always hated to discipline you boy, but I dare say this time wasn't the burden I thought it would be. Act the ass again and next time I won't be the easy touch with your punishment." He watched me lift back up from the barfing position.

I wiped the wetness from my eyes, "I thank you for the mercy Claus. Uhm, though I don't plan to anger you further. I think you should know I'm forbidden by the doctor's order to engage in the penetration services. I thought you may wish to know that." I trembled slightly as Claus ran his wizened hands down my breeches clad thighs.

His wandering fingers halted as he shot a glance of surprise at me and yelled out, "Stop that crying. I never could stand to see you weep. You must believe me a real fiend if you felt the need to warn me of your fragile condition after what I can only imagine those Stasi pigs did to you. Damn Maxx, I would never punish you that cruelty. I'm fucking aware of the horrific situation you endured. I swear I won't ask for such luxury as the penetration until you've had plenty of time to heal."

I led out my breath feeling immediately relieved as I nearly whispered back, "Oh, I must thank you for the mercy of your understanding." I shuddered and sniffed loudly in the attempt to end my unmanly display of tears.

Claus frowned and motioned me to 'get off him' as he pulled up his pants, "I suppose you are still the King of manipulation, Maxx. You're bad behavior required correction but somehow you making me feel like the brute for doing it. Okay, I will now call to get you that chocolate you want, but if I let you have it you must be still for the remainder of my story. This you understand, ja?"

I nodded and wiped my eyes as I replied, "I swear I give you no further reason to use the heavy hand."

The Elder chuckled low and took up the phone. "Stop the lying Maxx, it's getting real old, you know. Be still and let me finish this call to get you some candy. Then we shall continue the story where we left off."

I listened to the old Fur King tell the Black collar attendant to bring him more of his special batch candy stash without moving a muscle. Instead I focused my attentions on Felicity and Taube sitting on the coffee table next to Claus's bed. The lambs stared back at me appearing curious as to the reasons behind this elaborate acting job Claus was pulling on us. We all had to wonder what the end result he was hopping would be if he could get me to believe even half of the bullshit he was spewing. It simply made no sense to any of us at all. I silently told the lambs to be still and patient.

Surely at some point if we allowed this old liar to keep yapping he would fuck up and let the cat out of the bag.

Quietly I munched on the delicious candy feeling that strange trancing thing happening to me while at last the Elder Claus went back to his attempts to twist my mind.

"So, I rushed back up to the first floor with the sour words of Bladrick ringing in my ears. I wasn't the youngster any longer. The many years of hard living from the wars, the killing, the grieving, well, old Claus could no longer hide away from the ghosts crying out from his past. I rushed to ma apartment on the Voter's floor barely able to get into the safety of seclusion before I fell into a deep weeping of the most epic proportions.

I likely released enough fluid that afternoon to dehydrate the normal man. I didn't believe I would ever reach the end of my torment, but just as suddenly as that mourning overtook me, it released my heart. With a numbness I finally took back to my feet and left the confines of my bedroom. I didn't have much time to question the remarkable lack of emotionality though, because as I walked into the living area, to my shock my eyes laid upon the long lost Ingrid.

I had to do the double take to be assured I wasn't hallucinating. Yet, there was no tricks of the mind. Ingrid was there in my house, with tears streaming down her checks as copiously as my own had been only moments earlier.

She sniffed loudly as she said, "Dearest Claus, do you not offer a kind welcome to your sister-in-law? Surely, you haven't also become the brute all these others in the Haus seem to be."

I cannot lie, Ingrid's return to Das Kaiser Haus was the Godsend I needed at that moment, even if there was no doubt she didn't feel the same.

With much eagerness I replied, "Oh my Gott. What are you doing here, love? I don't mean to sound unappreciative of a visit from an old and great friend, but I thought, I mean, did you find no better fortune outside the Haus walls than you endured while within them?"

Ingrid shook her head as she took a seat on my couch. "Nein, Claus. I found great happiness having left this accursed Haus. My return to this hellhole was not of my own design. Xavier threatened King Gregor that if his Haus didn't return to him his wife, he would set the SS upon their heads."

I sucked in my breath and took the seat across from her as I replied, "And Gregor believed Xavier had such sway with those Nazi bastards? Surely he knew it was the empty bluff."

She sighed as her weeping grew slightly heavier, "Xavier does have that kind of power, dearest brother. Gregor was willing to fight to keep me at his side, but I couldn't allow my beloved to risk all the innocent population of the Denmark Haus nor the life of our precious daughter."

Without realizing it I gasped loudly and clutched my chest as I cried out, "Nein, you and Gregor produced issue? Oh Ingrid, which is wonderful but I think it would be safer to take your chances with the SS. Bringing a kid that isn't Xavier's here where he could harm her, what the hell are you going to do?"

Ingrid growled back in response, "Do you think me that stupid, Claus? I would never allow that monster Xavier the chance to touching a hair on my daughter's head. This is why I cry. I was forced to return to protect Gregor, and the Denmark Haus, but Xavier doesn't have knowledge of Agnette. If he were to find out, I would know exactly who to come seeking to kill, this you understand, ja?" She glared at me with fire in her sky-blue eyes as she said that.

There was no hesitation as I swore my eternal silence regarding her most dangerous secret. She already knew she could trust me, but no doubt it made the grieving mother feel better to hear me say it anyway. We spent that afternoon catching up on all the happenings since she had fled the Haus and away from Xavier's cruel grip.

I hated more than I can say having to be the one to deepen her sadness as I recounted the execution of Max and Christian, as well as the horrible new rules Xavier had imposed upon all the residents. Ingrid's normally strong composure appeared to melt as each terrible report fell from my lips. When at last, I could find no further bad news to give her I went silent, again feeling that weird numbness overtaken me.

She sat there seeming stunned for several moments, then I swear to the Gotts, I watched that incredible woman dry her tears, and puff out her chest as she said, "Well, then I think we both know what must be. Xavier, Drexel, Barnam, and even Bladrick, if it be discovered he is with them will all have to die. I will murder each bastard with my own hand if it comes down to it and damn the consequences. Claus, I've made so many mistakes in my cursed life, but the fates have decided to given me a second chance to fix what we all had a part in breaking."

I stared at her unsure of her meaning as I replied, "Fix what we broken? I don't understand Ingrid. I mean I agree we must murder the men responsible for killing Keifer, Max and Christian but are you saying that you wish to do more than punish the guilty?"

Ingrid smiled bitterly as she said, "You know exactly what I'm saying, Claus. Stop playing with me. I tell you I intend to overtaken both the Fur and the Silk thrones by force. In fact, it would be my darkest pleasure to destroy Xavier and his men slowly and as painfully as possible."

With much fear I rushed to my door and locked it while I whispered back, "Be careful of your words, dearest sister. The walls have ears, and what you are suggesting is impossible anyway. I don't fear dying but I don't wish to join my beloved without the blood of his killers on my hands. Besides, Xavier is many things, but a fool he isn't. That bastard will be expecting you to retaliate. I bet he is filing for annulment of your marriage vows as we speak or perhaps he will be seeking to see you put to the stake like your cousins."

Ingrid laughed loudly and replied, "Are you blind Claus? Xavier wouldn't let me go even when I ran away to Denmark far from his sights. I know that man better than anyone other than himself. With him, it's always about appearances. He believes I belong to him, and he will never let me go willingly, even if he no longer desires me. I am of the coveted Reinhardt blood line, and he shares his only legitimate son with me. To lose such a connection would make him look bad in the eyes of the residents of Das Kaiser Haus. Xavier is too vain to allow that to happen, trust me. That is the weakness that I intend to exploit to the fullest. I don't know yet how to go about bringing him down, but believe me, I've nothing but time to consider a fool proof plan."

I returned to my seat across from the determined lady and said, "Okay, I suppose if the truth be told, you and I have the same desires. You can count Claus your honest ally in whatever plot you come up with. Just promise me that if I don't survive our plans, you will lay my bones to rest next to my beloved Keifer, wearing the dress I married him in. You recall the one, ja? The one Felicity made with her own loving hands."

Ingrid swore on her life she would do this for me and in her promise I finally found the first bit of peace I had known since the last day I had rested in Keifer's loving arms.

"Claus, God damn it, will you stop farting around and get to the point? At this rate I will be an older man than you before you finish this fucking story," I yelled out at the Elder feeling a tinge of nervousness that he was wasting precious time I simply didn't have.

Claus glared at me as he replied, "See that promise you made earlier to be still didn't last even thirty minutes did it? I would think with all the painful training you've endured your patience should be further advanced. I swear, Maximillian, you always were the headstrong kid. Tell me Christian, did you learn this rudeness from your brother before he was killed by Gerard, or is it guilt that makes you take on his traits?"

I startled at his statement as I stammered out, "Huh? Are we going to play this game again? Okay, fine then. Uh ja, Christian taken on his brothers traits, and sure Maximillian was the pushy kid. Whatever you want me to say, I can and will, Claus. Now, are you about done with this story or what?"

Claus snorted and said, "Christian Axel. Ja, you heard me boy. I tell you that I've discovered your identity at last. You are the first son of Agnette, daughter of the Fur Queen, and Fur King Xavier. Because you were born while your first degree relatives sat on the Elder's throne that makes you the truthful King of the all the thrones of Das Kaiser Haus. Your poor little brother Maximillian was the second son, not the heir but the spare. Ingrid's plan to secretly fulfil Xavier's plan to bare a legitimate Prince of the Haus has been successful. You are the child every Monarch of the Fur has tried to create since the birth of this place. All had failed, until the birth of you and you brother that is. Too bad Ingrid couldn't find out you were indeed the precious Christian

Axel before death prevented her from completing her plot of having you take control of the entire ruling classes."

That made me laugh hard as I barely squeaked out, "Oh you are a funny guy, Claus. You should have been the comedian. Stop the games already. I don't need to be this fancy made up Prince of the Thrones to taken over this hell hole anyway. I am the Mortar King, the Collar King, and now thanks to the rat Noah, the Dungeon Master Supreme. This means I took over the Haus ruling class without the inventive fantasy you're spewing. I am, however, offended that you give the credit to this woman Ingrid for my hard won victory. She may have had some hairbrained plot as you're saying, but I did all I did without a fucking bit of advice, help nor use of any made up pedigree of the Reinhardt. Nein, I used my clever wit, brute force, and unfortunately my ass-ets."

Claus chuckled as he replied, "Ah, well we shouldn't discount those ass-ets should we? Christian Axel, I've had enough of your interruptions. Look at me boy. Tell me something, what color are my eyes?"

I glared at him angrily as I replied, "I already told you this like a million times, Claus, they are brown. Because you are so full of shit."

The Elder's voice seemed to echo off the walls as he yelled out, "You will never find the green fields if you don't follow the lamb. Look there, Felicity and her flock are waiting for you. Where is the skeleton boy? How can mother fix him if you leave him behind to grow the grass for the baby sheep?"

The walls melted away and I felt the cold, damp floor of the dungeon under me. I gasped and glanced around the moldy cell. The silver chain clank as I whimpered and rushed to the farthest corner away from the stone door. I knew it was time for the man called Noah to come bringing me my rations for the day.

I watched with fear rushing up and down my spine as the entry slowly creaked open. The young Dungeon Master stepped inside carrying the tray of gruel and bread with a smile on his face. Despite my intense hunger I did the best I could to cower behind the fort I'd built of straw.

"Come here little one. Noah has your dinner. I know you must be famished. Be the good boy and maybe I given you the candy for behaving, ja?" He closed the door and began to approach me appearing cautious.

I shook my tiny head and yelled out, "Nein. Go away Noah. Brrr. Caw, caw. Mor, mor. Help."

He chuckled lightly but didn't stop his approach as he replied, "Ah, your German is improving. I understand some of your words. Very good, little one. Maybe soon, you will speak like the proper human, ja?"

There was no escaping him. I trembled as the big man reached my hiding spot and snatched me from the corner. I closed my eyes and trembled as he forced me to my knees in front of him. The tray of food was put down where I could reach it, but Noah stood over me like a giant refusing to give me space for my dining.

"Well? Take the spoon like I taught you, boy. Eat this and do it without making a mess or you know what will happen, ja?" He pointed at the tray of food.

I kept my frightened eyes on him as my baby fingers took up the utensil. I quickly and quietly shoved the tasteless mess into the boy's mouth, barely chewing before swallowing. My stomach purred loudly with each spoonful as it slowly filled my nearly empty space inside.

Noah heard my tummy growling and said, "I bet that feels better, doesn't it? See this ritual of ours need not be such a display of drama each day. I bring you the luxuries that make you comfortable and you return the favor by giving old Noah a bit of relief too."

I couldn't understand all of his words but I already knew this man wasn't there to merely see to my baser needs. Nein, he wanted to fulfill a few of his own at my expense.

The second the last bite touching my tongue, I threw the spoon across the cell and took off running back for the corner. Noah knew that I was going to make the move though. He moved with the speed of the cat and grabbed me by the back of my threadbare shirt before I barely made it a few steps in retreat.

"Where you off to, little boy? Are you that stupid to believe you can escape me? Look around. There is no way out of this cell and you are chained to the wall to boot. Ah, whoever cut you up must have kicked you in the head. That's got to be the answer to this silly belief you can run away. You got the soft brain, ja?" He forced me to my face on the straw strewn floor as he said this.

I wept loudly as I called out, "Nein, help me. More, more. Bahaha." The weight of the huge Dungeon Master laying down over the top of me crushed my sounds of distress from my lungs.

Noah leaned into my ear and whispered, "Be still and stop the crying, little one. I'm not going to harm you, I swear it. This thing we do isn't a violation of your maidenhood. I only wish to touch you a bit, and then I swear I leave you as innocent as I found you." with those words I felt the man begin to rhythmically grind himself against my clothed flesh in the mock mounting.

I was helpless to stop him as he used me in this integral sex act. My childish mind couldn't understand the truthful meaning of this behavior but instinctually I knew it wasn't a good thing to have to endure. Despite several warnings given by Noah for me to be quiet, I continued to wail and protest.

Eventually, he covered my mouth with his hand to end the racket I was making while he said, "I think you are the prettiest thing I've ever seen but all that beauty is marred the second you start wagging your tongue. I cannot fantasize the sexy thoughts of you with all this noise. When will you figure out this will go a lot faster if you stop fighting me?"

I wriggled and attempted to bite his hand, but it was no use. Noah had me trapped until he found his apex and that was always the way this situation would go until they came to fetch me to hand me over to Peter. This revelation of Noah's mild breach of the strict orders to leave me alone was a shock to Claus, but the next thing that I recalled happened at this particular time nearly sent him into a rage.

Noah led out a moan that I'd learned by then meant he was about to let me go. I readied myself to flee the second his grip loosened on me, as it usually did after he made that weird noise, when suddenly the door of the cell flew open.

There stood the man that I would come to know as Olaf with a wicked grin on his face. I was still stuck under the recently relieved Noah, but even with all that Dungeon Master crowding me, I could see this evil man's face clearly.

Olaf led out a loud guffaw and said, "Christ brother. Is this the best you can do? Dry humping some little nothing down here in this hellhole. Oh what a life you have made for yourself. Why the hell don't you just fuck that brat proper and be a real man?"

Noah took to his feet and released me as if I were on fire as he stammered back, "It's not what it looks like Olaf. Listen, you better keep this between us, you hear me? If dad were to hear of this, oh I don't even want to think of it." He brushed himself off while keeping his eye on me while I rushed to my corner with speed.

Olaf shook his head and replied, "What the fuck would dad care? He knows what it's like down here. Gott knows he spent many years rotting in this place himself. Hey, tell you what. Grab that submissive and I will go first. That way you can claim innocent if by any chance our father did give a shit that a worthless silver got soiled." He started to come toward me.

I yelled out in terror, "Nein, more. Help, go away. Skelet Maximillian, help." I grabbed my tiny legs and tried to hide behind them from the approaching man.

Olaf stopped in his tracks. "Wait a second. Noah brother, look at his eyes. They are the same color as that bitch Ingrid. Oh, now I'm really going to hurt this little motherfucker. I'll pretend he is the Fur Queen, that unfairly put this black collar on me. Then tonight while I serve at the feet of that cunt and her bastard husband I will find a tiny bit of peace over it. I tell you brother, I thank you for this mercy." With that he rushed forward and grabbed me.

I screamed, flailed and kicked with all my might while Olaf dragged me to the center of the cell. Noah, that at first seemed stunned to stupid, seemed to realize that he had to intervene or I was good as dead.

"Nein. put that boy down Olaf. Laying even a finger on his flesh is forbidden I told you already. Not just by dad but by the Fur King and Queen themselves. If you harm him, they will send me to the stake, and I swear to you before they light my pyre I will sing your name so that you join me." Noah came at Olaf swiftly, punching him right in the face when the brute didn't immediately release me as he commanded him to do.

Olaf rubbed his red jaw as he watched Noah gently help me back to my feet. "Seriously Noah? You would threaten to see me killed over this bit of fluff the King and Queen find thrill in?"

Noah nodded as he replied, "You are a fool, Olaf. I would think after Ingrid forced that collar on your neck for defying her once, you'd have learned not to anger her or Xavier." I took off running for the corner once more as the Dungeon Master dressed down his Black collared brother.

The brute snorted angrily. "Always the good son aren't you, Noah?" Olaf glanced around the cell. "How's that working for you? You mind those idiots that call themselves leaders and are stuck with false rewards and false pleasures too. Well, no matter to me. If Xavier does have interest in this thing, I will get the chance to have a little revenge soon enough. He will make sport of him till he tires of the game, then I swear to you I'm gonna poke out his eyes and dry fuck the empty socket left behind. Stupid blue-eyed son of a bitch is what he is." He spit onto the floor as he said that.

Noah grimaced and replied, "So be it then. Once this kid is taken above, his welfare is no longer my concern. However, as long as he is in my care, you won't be touching even a hair on his head. Now, why are you here? Surely you didn't walk down the stone steps merely to insult me. Come on, out with it. What the hell do you want?"

Olaf glared at Noah as he responded, "Evelyn wishes to speak with you about something. She sent me down because father wouldn't led her get a pass to leave the kitchen to see you."

The Dungeon Master rolled his eyes as he said, "Gott damn them both. When the fuck is Bladrick gonna stop playing games with mother, or her with him, or hell with us for that matter. It isn't Ingrid or Xavier you should be wishing dead brother. It is him. This nightmare you and I endure is all his fault. What good is he when as the Prince of the Fur one brother suffers in the Dungeon and the other is cursed to the Black."

Olaf shook his head and sighed as he headed back for the door to leave. "Suck it up, pussy. This is the way illegal half breeds are treated in the Haus. There isn't a thing we can do about it without risking warming the Russians with our corpses. Isn't that what you told me only moments ago? Anyway, go see our mother. She says it's important. Oh, and next time you want to play pretend stud to the playthings of the Monarchs, lock the fucking door will you?" With that he took off slamming the stone slab behind him.

With Olaf gone, Noah turned his attention back to me, "Well, you heard him boy. One day Xavier will come to collect what is his. When that happens watch out for my brother Olaf. He's got a lot of resentment in him and, baby, he has locked his hatred on you. If you do manage to survive that killer King of ours, Olaf will do his best to making sure that victory is short lived."

Claus led out a loud cry of fury, "Fucking Noah. I'm going to kill that secret keeping son of a bitch. To think I trusted him."

I startled from my trancing. "What the hell is wrong with you, Claus? You keep scaring me with these random outbursts. I tell you I may die of the heart attack, and it will be a wasted death too. After all these things are all falsehoods. You already know what I'm going to say cause you decided what to making me recall. So, stop the dramatics. I'm still not falling for your lies."

The Elder closed his eyes and led out his breath slowly then said, "Evelyn was involved in that kidnapping of you and your brother. Ingrid and me always suspected Bladrick was ultimately involved somehow but managed to keep us from finding evidence of his part in the plot. I always believed part of the reason Ingrid put Noah in the Dungeon and Olaf in the black collar was to punish Bladrick without openly admitting that was what she was doing. After all, the boys were half Dominant and there father a Fur Prince. I never understood her hatred of those boys but now I think though I intended to give you closure, you gave me a some in return." He smiled weakly.

I shrugged and replied, "So, if I brought you some relief telling you things you already know then return the favor and release me Claus. I'm already behind, you know. I've a Haus to run."

Claus opened his eyes and set them on me as he said in the irritated tone, "I'm tempted to send you off without the answers you will need to survive. However, if you go now, you will never hear the story of your precious Leo, nor of Jacob."

My eyes went wide as I replied, "What about Leo and Jacob? Claus, I'm warning you. If you intend to besmirch either of those fine men in my presence, I swear I will send you to your beloved Keifer's hold before mother nature calls for you on her own."

The Elder laughed hardily as he said, "My Gott are you sexy when you are annoyed. I'm not afraid of you Christian Axel, even if you are the most dangerous person I've ever known. Given the list of despotic creatures I've met, that's saying something. That said, I've no intention of bad mouthing either the honorable Leo nor the sweet but misled Jacob. Are you willing to be still and listen or not?"

With a groan of frustration I replied, "Fine, go ahead Claus. Enjoy this little mercy because I swear I will give you no more of it if you are lying yet again."

Claus really howled over my empty threat then once he got a hold of himself he began his story anew.

"As the war of the worlds part two raged on, the Dominants of the Haus followed Hitler's orders to the letter. Children were crying out there first breaths almost hourly. At first, from all accounts, our country was doing as well in the battle for supremacy as our Haus males were at producing sons and daughters for the third Reich.

Xavier's little nursery for these children was soon bursting at the seams. Down in the Dungeons, Bladrick and Hemmel worked around the clock helping to cleanse Germany's blood of the unpure, the unwanted and the foreigners. On the seventh floor, Ingrid did her very best to appear the subdued, dutiful wife to the King of all the Haus. The Silk throne remained empty, but no one dared to question the authority of Xavier. He'd become so powerful most in the Haus lived in constant terror that he would notice them.

That's because, it wasn't only the gypsies and Jewish people that were keeping the night bright with their cremation fires. One by one, Xavier found reason to execute all that did so much as utter an unkind word about him or his rule.

No one was safe when it came to the cranky nature of your father. Not even his own kinsmen. Bernt, that had always been a thorn in his side, was the first of his brothers to find crossing that cruel man was a deadly mistake. I can still recall the day the bitter Bernt fatally fell down the stairs. Cora and I had just left the Great Hall after doing our ritual fake spouse breakfast when the news of the death of the first Fur Prince rang through the halls like the fire alarms.

Though his death was ruled officially as an accident, everyone realized he'd managed to do it with a bullet hole in the back of his head. Ja, the Haus doctor Britton, told everyone that it wasn't really a gun wound, but the damage caused by falling down seven flights of stairs. It is interesting that Bernt just happened to take a trip on the first step after leaving his brother the Fur King's apartment. Ha!

Well to be honest, no one, especially me, was too upset that gruff old Bernt was gone. That sentiment didn't hold though when Xavier's good natured and generally liked brother Derbeck also found an untimely death. This time, the doctor didn't bother to attempt a lie. Derbeck had been found decapitated in the pool room. There was no question the kindest of the Schmidt brothers demise wasn't an accident.

However, no one ever was suspected of his murder. I say that with bitterness because everyone knew the name of his killer. It was without any doubt old Xavier himself that laid Rolf and Oliver's daddy low. The reasons for it are the only thing that remain a mystery to this day. Though I believe, Xavier killed them both to assure neither of them got any ideas of holding the Fur or Silk throne for themselves.

Now the reason these deaths were important to this story I tell you is because with Bernt in particular, his death was partly responsible for some of your own worst pain many years later.

I scoffed loudly and said, "Oh? And how is that Claus? Are you trying to tell me if Bernt hadn't been killed, he'd have ended Xavier before I had to? Well if that's what you got to say, save it. Xavier was only half my problem, and not even close to the first one."

Claus snorted then replied, "Exactly boy. Let me finish will you? You need to understand had Xavier allowed Bernt to live it wasn't just his overly jealous brother he had to fear. You know damned well that any sitting Fur Monarch's throne can be passed to a sibling of the correct age with five years served in the dungeon. That in mind, if Bernt had managed to get rid of Xavier he was the next in line to become the King, but more than that his sons Peter and Friedrick then by law would be the Princes of Das Kaiser Haus.

I nearly choked as I said, "Really? So, you are telling me that Peter got that close to being the King of all thrones? Oh my Gott. Does he know this?"

The Elder chuckled as he nodded, "Fucking right he does. It is the reason he stole you from the Dungeon and tricked you into his collar. All his life he's been trying to reclaim what he believes is his birthright."

I groaned loudly, "Oh shit, then he is just like Byron. Both of them thought as boys they would be the ruler of all the Haus."

Claus shook his head as he replied, "Nein, Peter is nothing like Byron, boy. Byron is a brute full of hate and stupidity. Peter you may think the monster with only eyes for power but in truth there is heartbreak that drives him to do the horrible things he has done."

That caused me to pause as I said, "Heartbreak? Are you about to attempt to get me to feel pity for that son of a bitch that raped me as a little boy and continues to use me to fulfill his lust for power? Seriously, Claus? I would think you of all people wouldn't dare to insult my intelligence in this way."

"Nein. I don't make excuses for Peter's wrongdoings, Christian Axel. I merely say, Byron is without reason and Peter is within reason. Allow me to explain before you go accusing me of such foul attempts to protect the guilty." Claus glared at me hard as he said that.

I shrugged and crossed my arms as I replied, "Okay Claus. Go ahead and say whatever you want. Nothing will ever change my mind about Peter. So, waste your precious last breaths on his story and I will laugh as I dance on yours and his graves."

Claus sighed loudly and said, "Fair enough, I guess. Gott knows we both have earned your hate. However, that doesn't change the fact that just like you, my love, Peter was twisted into an evil man he is but was not born that way.

As I was saying after the death of Bernt, his unfortunate Frau found her own grave in a most suspicious manner. This left the tiny boys Peter and his younger brother Friedrick the orphans. Even though Bernt was gone as a potential rival for the Fur throne, Xavier wasn't satisfied that Peter and Friedrick had been neutralized as threats.

So, only one week after these little boys, babies really, were handed the worst news of their parents deaths, Xavier summoned them to attend him in the Fur Palace. Though no one knows for sure, most had a very good idea what terrible things happened to the brothers while trapped in their attendance to that perverted old King.

This was the way it was for Peter and Friedrick for many weeks, until one day the two broken little boys were traveling down to the kitchenette to collect the breakfast trays for the Fur Monarchs. It so happened that Friedrick, being far too small to carry a full breakfast tray dropped Xavier's meal onto the hallway floor.

While his overly protective brother Peter did all he could to collect the scattered food, a couple of Guards in Xavier's employ happened upon the helpless boys. After a bit of loud harassment, the grown fellows decided to up the sport a kick. Oh, and I do mean that literally.

Peter was held hostage and forced to watch as two of these brutes took up his little brother to use as there football. Friedrick was pummeled without mercy until his nearly lifeless body was tossed like used garbage at the tiny Peter.

Before that terrible tragedy, Friedrick was the handsome, intelligent boy just like his brother. After that moment, though he barely beat the call of the reaper, his mind was forever damaged. It was well known throughout the Haus that Xavier had ordered these brutes to do what they did, only they mistakenly grabbed the wrong boy. It was Peter that was the real target. Xavier of course, pretended he was horrified by the entire scene. Even so, he never punished the men responsible for the damage they done.

But that was far from the end of the trauma poor Friedrick would suffer. Thanks to his fragile mind and badly damaged looks, Xavier found him far less interesting than he had. This is where his true cruel nature shown through. By this time his illegitimate son Byron had become almost as fearsome as his father.

For Byron's birthday that year, Xavier gave him the gift of Friedrick. From that they until Byron finally tired of him,

Friedrick was his plaything. Friedrick was too mentally deficit to understand he was being badly misused. In fact, when Ingrid finally was able to prove Birgit wasn't born Dominant, which meant Byron was a half breed like Olaf and Noah, thus sending him and his mother to the dungeon, poor Friedrick went with him.

So, Peter was left with the guilt of being helpless to protect his little brother and the fear that Xavier would get him too. Sadly, becoming the retard would have been a mercy, I think. The things Xavier most likely was doing to him up there in that room with the red door, well, you of all people can imagine it I believe."

I stared at the Elder unable to even blink as I said, "You mean, Xavier did to Peter what he did to me? Nein. You are lying again, Claus. Peter is a monster and he learned to be that way because he was trained to be that way, not because he suffered it himself."

Claus snorted and replied, "Say what you want, Christian Axel. I tell you the truth of it, whether you choose to believe me is up to you. I tell you that Peter was one of Xavier's first victims during the years of the War, and he only survived it because Justus managed to help him escape to the children cottages. There Oliver, Rolf and your buddy Jacob kept the badly abused Peter hidden from Xavier's sights. For all of his youth, Peter was forced to stay in the shadows, praying that the cruel Fur King's hatred for him would one day calm."

This revelation was simply too much for me to hear as I squeaked out, "But he did survive, didn't he. That means eventually Xavier did forget about him, ja? None of this information gives Peter the right to do what he did to me, anyway. If any of what you say about him is the truth of it, then I hate him even more because he of all people should have known better." I finished my statement yelling till I was red in the face full of the fury.

Claus sat there with a strange little smile on his face as he replied, "Ah, did I hit a nerve there, Christian Axel? You realize that I do tell the truth of Peter, don't you. That would mean maybe I am not lying about anything I've said now, doesn't it? The reality of your conception and life since is uglier than even you dared to imagine. You see, Xavier didn't forget about Peter at all. He merely waited until he got the chance to strike the young man as deep as any wound could go without actually killing him."

I growled out, "Oh? And how exactly did he do that Claus. Go ahead, I'm dying to hear this story since you know damned well I think whatever Xavier did to Peter he more than deserved it."

The Elder scoffed, "Did he really? I beg to differ, my beloved, but then again, you and Peter parallel each other so much I've often wondered if this isn't proof there is such a thing as fate.

So, Peter grew into being a man, despite his being target number one of the children killer Xavier. Love found the lonely, young man easy enough the year he turned fifteen.

While you were misled to believe it was his dark bonded lover Felix that turned his head, that was not truth. It was a beautiful young FemDom named Rachel."

Chapter 12: The Prince that Never Was
Mad Maxx and submissive Meine Liebe

Ah, yes. I remember Ryker once told me Peter was married a long time ago. So, this is Rachel, the woman stupid enough to call that bastard husband? Finally, you are saying something I want to hear Claus. I've always wondered if the rumor was true, and if so what had happened to end their marriage. Oh, I know. She recovered from her stroke and realized her mistake, right? Hahaha," I snorted out rudely interrupting the Elder mid-sentence.

Claus glared at me angrily as he replied in a flat tone, "There is nothing comical about the things I am about to tell you, Christian Axel. I confess I adore you more than my worthless life, but if I ever hear you making mirthful noises again when I am about to discuss a senseless tragedy, I will make you sorry for it. You hear me boy?"

I shrugged, unable to stifle my giggling as I said, "I refuse to apologize that I appear non empathetic in this case. You can threaten to kill me if you want, but anytime you wish to discuss subjects that brought Peter misery, I will always find pleasure in it."

The old man snorted loudly then replied, "Oh is that so? Well, let me tell you something. Had Rachel lived you would not be sitting here on the side of my bed with chocolate on your face and the taste of my cum on your tongue."

That caused me to pause as I responded, "Huh? I don't understand your meaning, Claus. Stop trying to blame

132

everyone in this House for the awful things you've done and will do. I am trapped as your sex toy because that is the way you wanted it. Whatever the powerful leaders of this House want they always get. I'm warning you old man. If you are going to try to convivence me that Peter wouldn't have raped me into his collar if this imaginary wife of his hadn't died, forget it. I know better. Peter is just like all the rest of you, a disgusting pervert. He likes to hurt me because it brings him joy. Hell, he has told me at least a million times that he likes nothing better than making me cry and beg for mercy he never grants. That kind of freak doesn't stay satisfied with the love of a good woman."

It was Claus's turn to chuckle as he replied, "Well, you are half right but not completely. Be still and I will correct your misperception of how a plot was hatched to create an indestructible Prince, after a weak one was murdered.

"So, before we discuss the epic affair of Peter and Rachel, first I must return to the last few years of World War II. That is because around 1942 our country had begun to show signs that Hitler had bitten off more than Germany could chew. Reports were coming through rumors all around the countryside that his battle with the Russians was failing.

The idiot had taken an offensive on too many fronts thanks to his megalomania idea that he was going to create a new, pure race with Germany being the center of the universe. Oh, what a mess he had made indeed. I won't get into the history of that terrible war. You are an educated man and no doubt you've read one or two good history books dedicated to Hitler's foley. If you haven't I suggest you get

Leo or that hideous husband of yours to loan you one while you have years of nothing to do down below. I assure you, the devastation caused by that Antichrist will keep you from focusing on your own deplorable situation down in the Palace.

Anyway, it was spring that year that I received a letter from my only nephew, Leo. He was certain Germany was soon to lose the war and although he had done a passible job avoiding the Gestapo and SS scrutiny, he believed his homosexuality had been uncovered.

I was aware of the death of his beloved sister, my niece. A beautiful young lady we all called Maus. The years since she'd taken her life had been hard on the soft-hearted Leo. It wasn't a surprise to me that the silly boy had managed to get himself into hot water with the vicious German soldiers. I had been expecting to hear word of his joining Maus in the hereafter for a few years by that time. But to my surprise he wasn't writing me to report an execution date with the firing squad. Not yet anyway.

Instead, he wasted several pages of precious paper begging me to lobby Xavier to permit him asylum within the walls of Das Kaiser Haus. Leo was already twenty-five years old. I had to agree with his assessment of Xavier's unlikeliness to allow him admittance. He nor I believed the would be Fur King would be too willing to hear his pleas for mercy given he was an adult, and worse an Albrecht.

Despite my misgivings, I barely finished reading Leo's tear strew letter before I took off to find the evil Xavier.

Though I had no hope he would help, I assumed it didn't hurt to ask. At the time, it wasn't a secret that I adored both Leo and Maus. It was easy enough to think fondly of them since in reality, I had never met either one of them in person.

If Leo's request caught me off guard, then I have to say Xavier's response stunned the hell out of me. He had that nasty little grin tugging on his thin lips as he quickly agreed that the House could benefit from the addition of my dear nephew.

I didn't want to stick around and give Xavier a chance to change his mind, but before I could haul ass off to write Leo back he yelled after me, "Just as long as your kinsmen doesn't mind a little hard labor he will always have a place here in the House. Bladrick has great need of all the strong backs he can get."

I stopped dead in my tracks and responded, "So it is the Dungeon for Leo then?"

Xavier's laughter boomed as he replied, "Oh now Claus, did you really think I would allow an untrained and likely unruly relative of yours to run around wild in the halls? Nein. He will be provided safety here if he is willing to work. However, he will agree to be brought to heel by the Head Dungeon Master or he can take his chances out there among the doomed population in the countryside."

I grimaced as I said, "I'm not sure Leo is cut out to endure life below, Xavier. He is more blessed than you or I ever were when it comes to wealth. Maybe, you could charge him a more expensive entry fee or inflated rent for an

135

apartment instead of sending him to do grunt work in the cells."

Xavier shook his head then growled out, "What's the matter with you Claus? Your memory seems to be slipping. Have you forgotten what happens when our armies crumble? If this war is heading the way I believe it is, you know damned well money will soon be useless for anything but burning for the shitty heat it can offer. I'm going to need loyal men to help cull the unnecessary soon. So, either this nephew of yours will do his time burdening his soul with the ghosts of the helpless or he can join them. It really doesn't matter to me. You may go now." He then arrogantly waved me away as if I were nothing more than a tiny silver trainee.

I stood there with my jaw on the floor for a moment but then realized myself. By this time, no one was dumb enough to hang around Xavier unless they were wearing armor with wings. Without any idea if Leo would accept Xavier's offer or not, I went ahead and wrote him back with the details of it.

Well since Leo holds the fourth Fur throne, you already know his desperation overrode his good senses. I welcomed him through the front door of the House two days later. There was no time for proper introductions. Olaf and his butt buddy, Wilber, promptly grabbed a very shocked Leo by both his upper arms. I was helpless to stop the brutes as they dragged my young nephew down the main hall and kicked his ass right down the Dungeon steps. I wouldn't see Leo again for five years.

However, I did hear from him almost daily after he arrived. Okay, to be honest, I heard about him through the House grapevine. It turns out that Leo is made of far sturdier stuff than me or any one of us that served in that hell hole below the ground.

Xavier had reported accurately that Bladrick and Hemmel were in desperate need of help in keeping the Dungeon from becoming overpopulated. It teemed with those deemed unworthy of life by Hitler's rules. The fires lit to burn the pathetic remains of the unfortunate were raging day and night by this point in the war. I dare not consider the number of poor souls who can claim the last face they saw was that of Bladrick and his sidekick Hemmel. If this sickening fact ever bothered Bladrick, he never claimed it. I know it must have upset Hemmel because his wanton killing of the female silver trainees had thankfully ended, at least during the next five years. I suppose he was curbing his angry streak without having to add a crying baby girl to the mix. Yikes.

As for Leo, he wasn't going to be counted among the guilty when God comes to judge us all. Bladrick sent complaint after complaint to me over my nephew's refusal to slit a single throat. I admit at first, I found it rather humorous that Bladrick was fit to be tied over Leo thumbing his nose at his orders.

However, my pride and laughter stopped the second Bladrick began to threaten to take his case to Xavier if I couldn't get Leo to comply. Believe me when I tell you I ran so fast I nearly tripped and fell to my death in my haste to visit Leo. My wayward nephew was in real danger if I couldn't manage to keep Xavier out of this family situation.

As I searched around the Dungeon cells for my troublemaking nephew, I happened upon Hemmel, and oddly he was not in the company of Bladrick. I didn't wish to deal with him, so I attempted to push past without engaging the man in conversation. Much to my dismay, he refused to get out of the way. I had to assume Hemmel wasn't going to be denied his chance to lodge a complaint to me regarding his misuse at the hands of Bladrick.

The young man looked me up and down appearing near ready to burst into tears as he said, "Honorable Voter, could you spare a second to speak with a low worm such as myself? I swear to you with my entire being I can make it worth your time if you would grant me this small favor."

I grimaced over what I assumed he meant by making it worth my while, but I politely replied, "Alright Hemmel, what the hell do you want? Make it quick, I'm a busy man. Oh, and have you seen Leo? I am seeking an audience with him."

Hemmel nodded then said, "Yeah, he is in the isolation pit. Master Bladrick sent him there for refusing to cull the gypsy kids that arrived last night." I nearly took off in absolute terror both over his words and the fact that as he was talking he was dropping to his knees.

I gasped then screamed out, "What the fuck are you doing, Hemmel?" Just as I got that out of my mouth the idiot reached out and tried to undo my fly.

Hemmel stopped his attempts to make it worth my while as he sheepishly responded, "Oh I forget myself Honorable Voter. I suppose you'd prefer we do this somewhere more private. I apologize for my rudely assuming you enjoy public sex like Bladrick does."

I stammered back, "Hemmel, I don't wish to have sex with you in public or in private. For Christ sakes, are you and Bladrick still doing this shit where everyone can see? Has anyone told you the punishment for homosexual activity if anyone above were to find out about it?" I stepped away from the bowed man, looking in every direction praying no one else was witness to this taboo behavior.

Hemmel nodded and dropped his eyes to the floor, "I'm hoping someone does report us for it, Honored Voter. That's why I wanted to speak to you. I wonder could you lobby Xavier to see me put to the yard?"

His trying to blow me there in the Dungeon hallway was a shocker, but this latest revelation caused me to nearly faint dead away. I couldn't believe this handsome, sturdy young man was literally begging me to have him executed. Damn me for it, but I felt extreme pity for him, even though by this time his killing of the innocent girls was a well-documented and a known fact.

I shook my head as I replied, "I won't pretend I don't understand why you ask such a favor from me Hemmel, but I'm not the one to ask for this favor. I apologize for all the hell Bladrick has put you through. Even if I wished to fulfill your request Xavier doesn't heed my counsel. Besides, if you tell the truth of it, and Bladrick is dishonoring you regularly in public, then I must assume Xavier already knows about the indiscretions. Very little happens in the House that escapes his notice. That means, he either doesn't give a shit, or worse still he condones it. So, get off the floor and stop harassing me about troubles I've didn't start nor can I finish for you."

Hemmel wiped his wet eyes and took back to his feet as he mumbled, "I guess then I will have to stop this nightmare myself. My brother was the smart one to take his life you know. Can you imagine how many times I have thought I should have killed myself?"

I glared at him as I said flatly, "Nein I have no idea, but I do have to wonder why you haven't. If you had shown the honor your brother did then perhaps the first floor would be better populated with pretty young silver girls."

The Dungeon Master sniffed loudly and kept his eyes to the floor as he responded, "I thought Bladrick would lose interest or that eventually I would be released from this hellhole dungeon. As it is, my reputation is so tattered, suicide wouldn't repair my honor anymore."

I nodded then replied with a snort, "Well you are correct on the second part. As to the first, you do your job to perfection down here. Xavier isn't going to let a stone-cold killer lose in the House halls. you fool. So, if you are done assaulting my ears, I would like to politely ask you to stand aside. I need to speak with Leo."

Hemmel glanced up at me then said, "Forgive me for butting into your family business Honored Voter. but if you have come to try to get him to stop refusing to follow Baldrick's commands, you may as well forget it. Leo said he will happily go to the orchard to prevent his hands getting dirty with the blood of innocent people."

I growled out angrily, "I will not forgive you, Hemmel. First you nearly rape me, and now you think you can tell me my own business. Maybe after I visit with Leo, I'll go see Bladrick. I bet you'll think twice about fooling with your betters with the stripes of a whipping to remind you of your place." I started to storm off.

Hemmel yelled after me, "If you won't help me talk Xavier into seeing me relieved of my duty to Bladrick, then maybe you can do something else to offer me some comfort Honored Voter. I can save Leo in return for this thing I ask and I know this time you can provide the service return."

I halted immediately and turned around ready to stomp this child killing bastard right into the stone floor. "Hemmel, if you are trying to get me to do what you are too much a coward to do, you can forget it. Shut the fuck up and stop bothering me. I mean it."

He smiled wickedly as he replied, "I wouldn't dare to expect you to have more blood lust in you than that worthless nephew of yours. Oh, and I say that with respected Honored Voter. However, I can do what Leo won't for him. I'm his trainer. It isn't relevant who does the work, so long as the job gets done. If you'd pay my price, I'd be happy to do this and keep my silence in the matter."

After a startled pause I calmly replied, "Name the price before you say another God damned word Hemmel."

Hemmel's smile widened as he said, "I have five Krauss family members seeking asylum from Hitler's dogs. If you were to pay the door guards to look the other way so I could smuggle them into the House, I'd be most eager to repay the debt I'd owe you."

I sucked in my breath and rushed back as I replied in a whisper, "Lower your voice Hemmel. Xavier has ears and eyes everywhere. What you are asking is a serious crime. The death penalty is the sentence if I or your family were caught. Bad enough you want to bring in more Krausses but they are no doubt Jews on top of that. Are you out of your fucking mind? Oh wait, I get it. You want to be caught, right? Then Xavier would see that you get that honorable death. Well, you can forget that shit."

Hemmel chuckled and said, "You are wrong, Honored Voter. If I find a way to bring these people into the House, the last thing I'd want to do is die."

I shook my head in wonder. "Okay, so one of these five have a plan to kill Bladrick or Xavier then? I think if that is your hairbrained scheme you should have them murder Hitler before taking on the smaller monsters."

That caused Hemmel to laugh hardily as he replied, "Oh don't I wish for the death of all three, Honored Voter. I say that with respect, but that isn't the reason I wish to save them. You see, one is a woman that has agreed to be my wife. If I had her by my side, I just know I could suffer anything for as long as I must. Please do this for me Claus. You would be saving Leo, five innocent people, and even though you don't care, me too." He looked at me with desperation in his eyes.

I stood there feeling I had floated out of my body as I nodded my head in agreement, "And if I can find a way to do this, you would swear to never speak my name if you got caught and save Leo?"

Hemmel spit into his hand then held it out to me as he said, "On my mother's grave you have my word. The five of them are in hiding just outside the House border. The back door guard has a son named Almut. He had to sell him into this Dungeon to pay a debt he owes to some fourth floor Dominant. If you can pay Helga to paint that boy black, well the guard swears he will smuggle my family into the House."

I shook my head and whispered back. "Then what? Are they going to hide in the walls, Hemmel? Do you really think you can sneak five people around without someone noticing?"

He leaned in close and said, "Ingrid will help us once I have them inside. The two boys are Gregor's children from his first marriage. The three girls are his brother's daughters. They are all that Hitler left of our village and family. Please Claus, if I can't save them, the direct line of the Krauss founding family is lost forever."

143

I sighed. "I've spent most of my adulthood hating you and your family line, Hemmel. I won't lie and tell you I didn't wish a thousand times all of you Krausses were dead. However, I can't swallow the idea that some outsiders with an insane agenda are the culprits instead of each man or woman having a fair fight. I will go visit Helga and see Almut painted. I will even go talk with Ingrid about this for you. Hey, wait a minute. What makes you so sure the Queen will help your people just because Gregor is related to them?"

Hemmel winked with a smile and said something that chilled me right to my bones, "Because our beloved Queen has always put the needs of her family first, hasn't she?" He then took off in a rapid stride leaving me standing there stunned to near stupid over his probable knowledge of Ingrid's secret connection to the Krauss.

"Are you saying Almut was originally a silver? Bullshit. That bastard wears the black too naturally to have ever been a pleasure submissive, Claus. Stop the lying damn it," I blurted out.

Claus glared at me as he said, "You don't have to believe me, Christian Axel. Ask him yourself and see if I lie."

I chuckled evilly. "I will ask him after Valitin and Magnus are done having their thrills with him. If you do tell the truth, he is likely very pissed off that I sent him back to where he started."

The Elder let out a gasp, "Christian Axel, how could you of all people do that to Almut."

I shrugged as I said, "He shouldn't have fucked me over. Afterall, everyone knows I always provide a perfect service return."

Claus replied bitterly, "So many have indeed come to learn that the hard way. I would ask you what crime he committed against you that demanded such a harsh punishment, but I know better. He was a fool to ever claim allegiance to our Mad Mortar King. That is reason enough."

"So, are you finally going to get to this marriage business of Peter's, or do you wish to reminisce about a tea party you had one time with the Kaiser," I retorted angrily. I was pissed Claus had called me insane, but I wasn't stupid. I didn't dare call him out on it after that rough oral sex. Yikes!

Claus snorted then with a bit of irritation in his tone said, "You are one rude little bastard. I would have expected impatience out of golden hound Maximillian but not my beloved lamb Christian Axel. I'm almost positive you are the boy I once thought so gentle, I nicknamed him after my loving mother. What happened to you my darling Felicity?"

I startled. "Huh? You call to Felicity? Claus, are you okay? She sits over there on the table where you put her."

He shook his head. "Nein. You put yourself into a lamb toy Christian, and your dead brother inside your head because you couldn't deal with his loss. You blame yourself

145

because he saved you, but you couldn't save him back. You seek that grave Gerard buried you boys in, far out there in green fields of Bavaria, and try to find the mother that died the day Peter showed her the blood-stained sheets after he defiled her only remaining grandson. You could only say two intelligible words when they found you half dead by the burning hovel, Mor and Maximillian. The only two people that you believed truly loved you, and you've lost them both. I suppose if I were in your troubled shoes, I would rather not be me either."

I felt my throat go dry as I squeaked out, "Stop it Claus. I've said I don't believe you and still you persist on trying to twist my mind."

Claus sat up and looked into my eyes as he said, "I tried to straighten out your psyche, boy. The mangling was done by someone else and you fucking know it. Tell me something, what color are my eyes?"

"I woke up in the straw. I looked around the cell with trepidation. Falling asleep wasn't a good thing. I would lose track of the time when I got rest. Noah would be coming soon to bring my food. I hated his lessons and he always hit me when I messed everything up. No matter how hard I tried I couldn't understand why he insisted on making me do stupid things like tie my shoes, pee in the wooden privy, or eat with a spoon. It seemed to me all those things were a waste of time. I had fingers to pick up the food, holding my urine till I got to the potty was uncomfortable and why did I even need shoes?"

The door opened as I sat there contemplating chewing on the chain that held me to the wall for the millionth time. Noah stepped inside carrying my dinner on a tray and a smile on his face.

"Well, look who is bright eyed and ready to practice behaving like a human instead of a beast, ja," he chirped out to me.

I growled low in my throat. "Go away, Noah. I hate Noah, Ficken Dich bastard. Mor. Help Maximillian."

Noah chuckled. "You know better than to speak to me like that. Christian Axel is your name not Maximillian, so stop saying otherwise. Although, your German is improving. I suppose we should be grateful for that at least. Come on boy. Time for supper."

I glared at him. "Nein. Noah hurts. Help, I screamed out.

The Dungeon Master ignored my demands to leave me alone. As usual he hauled me out of my corner and forced me to my knees in front of him. Then after watching me eat my meal rapidly and throw my spoon across the cell in a desperate bid to distract him while I retreated, he threw me to my face.

I clawed at the dungeon floor while he took his mount fully clothed. "Hold still, you little bugger. Listen, we are just playing a game. There is no reason to get so upset about a little wrestling match."

I stopped trying to escape him and called out, "Play a game? Game? What is a game?" This series of words sounded interesting to me for some reason.

Noah abruptly let me free of his grip. He then rolled me to my back and stared into my eyes intently for a few moments.

Then he blew out his breath as he said, "This game is called wrestling. Do you like to play games, Christian Axel?"

I nodded. "Play a game, Maximillian. Ja, wrestling Maximillian."

He rolled his eyes. "Not Maximillian. You are Christian Axel, damn it. Okay, look we can correct your name issue shortly. For right now you turn over and I will play the wrestling game with you, ja?" I giggled and rolled so Noah could play this wrestling game with me.

He grabbed me by the shoulders as he said, "Wait, if you want to play this right you have to get up on your knees, here pretend you are a sheep. You know, baa. baa."

I nodded and responded, "Baa, baa. Felicity, Felicity. Baa." With that I took to all fours.

Noah laughed as he went to the mounting position behind me. "Oh, you are very good at this, Christian Axel. There you go, my little lamb. Now you be still and I will teach you how to play this game, ja?"

I wiggled in his grip with thrill over getting to play a game for the first time since, oh my Gott. Maximillian, please don't go to sleep. Christian, please don't die. Maximillian the worms are everywhere. Christian, it hurst so bad. No, please, we are dying. I am Christian. I am Maximillian. Gerard, please don't. Mother, he's hurting us. Where are you Mother? See the baby lambs? They are eating the grass. I am in the green fields. Christian, help me. I am in the ground. Maximillian save me. We are one. We are one. We are the lamb, baa. We are the hound, aroooh.

"Christian or Maximillian, wake up honey. Please wake up," I heard Claus screaming just as a rush of freezing water poured over me.

I opened my eyes and saw his wizened face staring into my own. "Claus? Did you finish the story?"

He took a deep breath then said in a frightened sounding tone, "I thought I lost you, honey. What happened there? I thought I knew which child I'm holding in my arms but now I'm not so sure."

With a snort I backhanded the old man as I shouted, "Enough of this game. I'm leaving if you don't cut the shit and I don't care if you do send me to the yard for it." I sat up from my prone position in the wet spot on his bed. I suppose the idiot threw his jug of water on me, sheesh.

Claus's eyes rolled back into his head for a moment and his hold on me loosened. I watched as he managed to hang on to consciousness.

Then he spoke in a raspy voice as he slowly recovered from my blow, "Alright, I suppose I had that coming. I shouldn't have forced you back into your traumatic memories without giving you more time to recover since the last session."

"Fuck me. Claus, is that all you have to say for yourself? Really? Thanks to your nasty tricks with that drugged candy, I can't get the vision of an imaginary brother that died and I can't even say it. What have you done to me? More than that, why did you do this to me? I thought you said you love me. Is this the way you show it? No wonder no one ever loved you either," I shouted out at the Elder.

Claus's expression turned mournful as he mumbled in return, "Hurting my feelings isn't going to make your terrible reality go away boy. Schizophrenia sure does help you hide from it though, doesn't it? Well, I will get back to the story before one or both of us says something that leads to us ending this visit far too soon.

So, as I was saying, I agreed to help Hemmel smuggle his five refugee family members through the back door of the House. Ingrid was most thrilled to aid me in this quest much to my dismay. Within two days, with her by my side, we had managed to save Almut from his life of terror as a pleasure submissive. It goes without saying, Helga, always the bitch, charged us a king's ransom for the boy.

That part of the plot completed, we headed for the back door to await Das Kaiser Hauss newest members. I will never forget that foggy morning the seventeen year old Karl, his twelve year old brother Malfred came barreling into the House. Both boys were nothing more than skeletons with a bit of flesh hanging on them. The sight of these poor kids was horrific, but the two females with them caused even the tough-skinned Ingrid to weep.

The oldest girl, named Awiwa, was only seventeen and covered in sores. She was skeletal like the boys and bald from a forced shaving. Her youngest sister who was like Malfred, was twelve was in the same pathetic condition. She introduced herself in a hollow tone as Rachel. Both girls were bleeding rivers from between their legs.

I assumed that the young ladies were enduring their monthly flow simultaneously. With the deplorable condition of their threadbare clothing, it was inevitable that nature's curse to females wouldn't be easy to hide.

However, my belief regarding this was quickly dashed when Ingrid inquired as to the whereabouts of the fifth Krauss expected.

Karl dropped his eyes to the ground as he said quietly, "We ran into a group of German soldiers last night. Malfred and I managed to escape but the girls were captured. Before we could find weapons to fight, they gang raped our poor cousins. We were able to free Awiwa and Rachel but Dina, she didn't survive the assault. She lost too much blood. Don't worry, no one will find her body. Malfred and I buried her along with the monsters that took her life and our cousins' innocence." Malfred wiped his eyes and kept his head low while his brother reported the terrible news.

I glanced at the two remaining girls and noticed both had a vacant look in their eyes. Until that moment, other than the constant smell of burning flesh from the non-stop fires, and my altered lifestyle, I hadn't truly seen the terrors brought about by Hitler's war.

Ingrid stifled her tears as she gently took Awiwa's fragile hand, "You are safe now my dearest cousins. Come with me and we will wash away the dirt, grime, and blood of the past. Today you are reborn and yesterday must be forgotten."

Rachel barely able to stand, she was so damaged, said weakly, "Our unborn sons and daughters will never forget your kindness dearest Queen." Then to Ingrids shock all four dropped to a kneel before her and kissed her hand while shedding tears of gratitude."

I rolled my eyes. "Boy you really are a fiend, Claus. Now you expect me to feel sorry for that dirtbag Malfred and that bastard Karl too? Okay, so why stop there? Go ahead and tell me that Lucus is really a saint in disguise and the Vampire is related to Jesus while you are at it."

Claus shook his head and sniffed loudly as he replied, "Nein, though you accuse me of it I refuse to lie. I didn't say anything about Karl or Malfred's nature now did I? I am merely telling you the story of Peter and Rachel as it happened. All of it."

I crossed my arms and chuckled bitterly, "Okay, wait a minute. So, this Rachel that Peter married was a Krauss? Oh that is rich. No fucking way."

The Elder nodded, "Indeed she was. In fact, she was Karl and Malfred's first cousin."

I really started howling at that, "And Jewish. Good thing that Wilhelm and Ryker are dead already, because if they weren't I'd fucking kill them myself for telling me Peter was a known Nazi."

Claus appeared startled as he replied, "They said that about Peter? Wow, that Gretta is truly a low bitch to put those boys up to spreading that lie to you. Peter is a lot of foul things, but a Nazi, never."

My mirth slowed as I said, "Yeah, seems Gretta has been up to no good a lot longer than I realized. No worries though because she can't stay pregnant forever. One say I will have my revenge, and so will both those idiot boys."

The Elder clicked his tongue then said, "So be it. However, you missed one of the most important points of this part of my story. Hemmel wanted me to help the Krauss family find asylum for a reason remember?"

I nodded. "I do. I have to assume since he was a single man till the day Olaf and Wilber laid him low on my command, Dina was the woman that agreed to marry him."

Claus looked at his lap as he replied, "Unfortunately you are correct. I suppose you are aware the Krauss always marries cousins. Not usually first cousins, but thanks to Hitler nearly wiping them off the face of the Earth, Awiwa betrothed her hand to Karl and Rachel to Malfred. The oldest daughter Dina had just married her third cousin when the war broke out. He was taken away to the camps, and she was left widowed at twenty-one. In a desperate need for a man to care for her and sire children in their line she readily agreed to make Hemmel, her very distant cousin, a happy man, sight unseen."

I did a double take then blurted out, "Wait, I thought you said Peter married Rachel. How did he do that if she was already promised to Malfred? You are not making any sense, Claus."

He let out his breath sounding frustrated as he replied, "Be still. I was trying to answer that question before you rudely interrupted, yet again."

Anyway, Ingrid managed to get all four Krauss's accepted into the House by unanimous vote. There still was no official Fur or Silk monarch but the voting counsel of Drexel, Barnim, myself, Xavier, and strangely Bladrick gave the ravaged refugees full rights.

Now I said strangely Bladrick because the moment the Krausses arrived at the back door, Xavier raised him from below at last. Hemmel didn't get the comfort of a wife that he desired, but he did receive a reprieve. With Baldrick's rise, he was named Head Dungeon Master. His misuse had come to an end and in his gratitude, he put Leo on corpse clean up duty.

For a moment, things seem to be looking up. At least for Ingrid and me. The rest of the world was drowning in piss and blood.

However, none of that mattered to us. We had Bladrick back, and with Leo doing his time in the Dungeon, plus four loyal Krausses slowly convalescing, I really believed we could somehow bring Xavier and his men down in a few short years.

Things remained pretty quiet for the next two years. Karl, Malfred, Awiwa, and Rachel turned out to be valuable members of our little inner circle of Xavier haters. As they healed, and learned the House rules, all four used their incredible intelligence to lobby those around them to stand against Xavier's bid for House take over. It didn't hurt that with enough to eat and regular bathing the Krausses possessed as much physical beauty as they did epic verbal skills.

Our old ally Bladrick redeemed himself to Ingrid by dutifully doing his part to try and sway other Dominants to work with us to overthrow her bastard husband. Below, a grateful Hemmel and peaceful Leo worked the Dungeon staff to stand with us above them.

By 1945, the halls of Das Kaiser Haus began to echo with the sounds of rebellion. Had the war dragged on just a little longer, Xavier's takeover would have been nipped in the bud. But, that spring, Russia broke through the lines, invading Germany's borders, and they burned a path through our country. Right to the front door of Das Kaiser Haus."

Claus paused here, closed his eyes, and took a deep breath before he continued with relaying his troubled memory of the sack of the House.

"I recall that morning the Russians arrived because I still have nightmares about it. It wasn't that we hadn't heard those Red bastards had gotten past all defenses. It was just that they moved too swiftly for any of us to have time to flee. The sounds of gunfire, explosions, screaming, the smell of blood filled the air as all the residents, big and small, furiously tried to get out. Some of us were trampled to death in the stampede headed for the exits. Others were picked off by Russian rifles as they came swarming in through the busted front entry.

I was with Ingrid and Bladrick fleeing down the back stairwell when to our horror the Russian horde reached the back door too. I saw the first of those hairy monsters let loose their weapons into the crowd of desperate residents. As each wave of shots rang out, dozens fell and didn't rise again.

It didn't take thirty minutes for every surviving resident from Xavier at the top to Hemmel at the bottom to be taken hostage by the Red army. They rounded us all up into the main entry, shooting anyone that couldn't easily fit into the packed mass of frightened prisoners.

To be honest I thought I would die of suffocation before the Russians got the chance to execute me. None of us could understand a fucking word our captures were shouting but one thing was clear, we were fucked.

Well, that is not exactly accurate. Only a little more than half of us were. I mean literally. The Russians didn't fool around. Once they were sure they had collected everyone, they separated out the females from the males. Then right there in front of all of us, they began to sexually assault the House women.

From the youngest baby girl to the eldest FemDom they raped with abandon. Wives screamed out for mercy to their husbands, little daughters cried in agony for their mothers. The males, we wailed in anguished misery for the mothers, sisters, daughters, and lovers that we couldn't help.

I fell to my knees with all the other men, weeping in despair wondering what would become of us, when I caught sight of Xavier. My chest nearly caved in as I noticed his eyes were on the group of Russian's gang raping our precious Ingrid on the House stair case. My heart wasn't breaking just because our sweet lady was being defiled, but because, I swear this to God, Xavier was smiling. That motherfucker was enjoying the sight of the mother of his children being treated like nothing but a sex toy by those Russian pigs.

For the next seven days, this was to be our fate. A conquered nation, and our people were the spoils of war for the victors. The Russians did provide sparse rations, but many were left wanting no matter how carefully we shared the measly portions.

They took their liberties with our women folk. The youngest girls were killed either outright by the rough treatment during the rapes or shot when they stopped responding. Many of the mature ladies also died from injuries caused by fighting their attackers.

The most beautiful of our girls suffered the most vicious attacks, and only Ingrid, Rachel, and a handful were still alive by the time the soldiers' commanding officers arrived to secure the scene, thus ending the worst of the carnage.

Sadly, almost as many men of the house died during that week as did the women. A few committed suicides after their beloved wife, lover or daughter found her death at the end of a Russian's cock. Others refused to obey commands to stand down and allow the monsters to abuse their girls. They were shot for their attempts at honor. Some of the eldest of us simply dropped dead. Likely from heart attacks or stroke brought on by the stress of this horrible situation.

As you already know, all the Voters survived including Ingrid despite her injuries. Karl, Malfred and even Rachel survived this terror as well, but sadly not Awiwa. She was killed on the second day when she hemorrhages during a particularly nasty sexual attack. I don't think Karl ever truly recovered from the loss of his beloved first wife. Awiwa was almost full term with their first child, but those brutes didn't care. They brutalized her anyway and poor Karl's baby died with its mother.

I gulped and whispered, "Then he lost Ryker too."

Claus nodded, then said in a serious tone, "Yes, he did. You need to understand something boy. Karl was wrong for what he did to you, so was Malfred for that matter. However, his belief that Ryker was killed because of you, after losing his first baby, and Jonas's announcement that you are

158

betrothed to his only living child. Well, I suppose it made him snap his last gasket."

With a shutter I replied, "He should have asked me if I was really going to do as Jonas says I was going to. I would have told him his daughter was safe because I wouldn't marry that baby for anything."

The Elder lowered his brow and looked at me hard as he said, "Oh? Not even for your freedom from the House?"

I stammered out, "Don't be stupid Claus. How can marrying a baby Krauss give me freedom."

Claus's replied in a deep voice, "Don't you play me for a fool boy. You know damned well it's not that baby girl that holds the key to the front door but the uncle you both share. If you marry Karl's daughter, Malfred becomes the God of the House because he is a Fur Prince that is related by first degree kinship to both the Mortar King and Queen. Once he is God, he can order you both released forever. Only the God of the House has the power to free the foundation Monarchs."

With a snort I replied flatly, "You assume too much Claus. First of all, the baby would have to survive that terrible mother of hers. Second, she would have to break her metal, which is nearly impossible to do. Third, she'd have to forgive Malfred publicly for raping his own nephew. Then if all that happened, I would have to trust Malfred to keep his word to give us our freedom. That last part is the most unlikely of all to happen."

Claus chuckled lightly then said, "Oh that last thing is the only part of that plan that I actually can be sure of boy. Malfred will release you and that niece of his. The rest of it is up to you."

I narrowed my eyes suspiciously at him as I replied, "How can you be so damned sure of Malfred's word? I seem to recall not so long ago you helped put him into a position of powerlessness. You killed his kinsmen involved in that plot to take over the Fur throne too. Then when that went wrong, he had his brother and all their friends gang rape me. So, why the hell would you suddenly trust a guy that has betrayed almost everyone he's ever met in every instance?"

He smiled at me as he said, "Because of Rachel, which is why I trust him this time."

That made me guffaw as I replied, "Rachel is too little for him to even know the girl. You really think that power hungry nut will become a trustworthy ally just because I marry her?"

Claus shook his head. "Wrong Rachel my boy. Now, if you are through asking stupid questions can I please get back to telling you about the Rachel to which you can thank Malfred's allegiance to in this plot to escape the House?"

I sighed loudly and said, "Do I have a choice? Go ahead Claus. I'm all ears."

He looked me over with his cloudy gaze as he said, "Choice, now that is an interesting word you use. So, as I was saying the Russians had arrived and as you already know, they were here to stay.

While the arrival of the high-ranking Russians signaled the end of the wanton raping, and pillaging of our residents, it wasn't even close to the end of our travails.

The Russians exited the House proper, but a large battalion was left behind to keep us held hostage within the wall. Xavier and Bladrick were selected to sit in with one of the Russians top officers to discuss our role within the occupied territory. While these two men did their best to talk the Red Army from blowing us all to kingdom come, the rest of us did our best to pick up the pieces and bury our dead.

Food was scarce and nerves were frayed. Sickness of all kinds began to break out among us, and soon enough even more corpses had to be dispatched. It truly seemed eventually all of us would be nothing more than a distant memory, best forgotten.

I wish I could tell you more about those two weeks during Xavier and Bladrick's desperate pleas for mercy from the Russians. However, it is still a bitter blur in my memory. Perhaps like you did about your childhood, I have erased it, or at least deeply repressed it. What I can't block out is the intense feelings of shame, pain, fear, regret, and remorse for, well everything.

I didn't see Ingrid for many months after the raping of Das Kaiser Haus. I must assume she needed to be alone in her attempts to heal both body and mind from those terrible indignities heaped upon her. I wondered if she wouldn't find it impossible to face the surviving House members knowing they would surely never forget what they saw.

Fourteen days after the Red Army officially took over the House, Xavier and Bladrick were returned to us by the Russian Guard. But those hairy fuckers weren't the only strange faces in tow. I was standing there with Drexel and Barnim ready to greet our returning brother Voters when I first laid my weary eyes upon Jonas.

We had all been eager for Xavier and Bladrick return, praying for good news but this creepy looking new guy set even the usually unemotional Drexel on edge. I decided to wait till our brother Voters gave us the run down on our chances of survival before I panicked, but I admit I didn't think this was looking good.

Xavier spoke while Bladrick and Jonas stood behind him in a weird silence, "Well brothers, we need to gather together the House. Claus, you and Drexel send out word for everyone to meet in the Great Hall in two hours. Barnim, you go collect Hemmel and Leo. I want the House Nursery collected and brought to the Dungeon. Every child under the age of eight is to be put into the cells to await my inspection set for tomorrow. In fact, if you find any child in this House collared or not that has survived, they are to be hauled down below. Okay boys, you have your orders. Get to them."

I watched Barnim and Drexel hurry off to mind Xavier, as I cleared my throat and held my ground.

Xavier's yellow eyes burned like the sun as he gruffly said, "Well? Are you going deaf Claus? I told you to go collect the residents."

I gathered all my courage and replied sounding as tough as I could, "Who the fuck died and made you the boss, Xavier? Any man here is as fit to bark orders. I am not your bitch that fetches your slippers on command. And who the fuck is that scary looking motherfucker?" I pointed at Jonas as I said that.

Xavier nearly blew his top as he yelled back, "Claus, I could see you shot for daring to speak to me like that."

I nodded as I said, "Do it then because I am not moving until you answer my fucking questions."

The old rat then seemed to calm down as he replied in a mocking tone, "Well, Claus, the fucking Russian army gave me control of this property and everyone inside, including you. As for this fine fellow over here, this is Jonas Weise, our new Silk King. Now, I suggest you be a good little bitch and fetch your Master his playthings. Say another word to me and so help me I'm going to send you to my personal vet to have you fixed."

I swear to all that is holy I nearly died from the shock of his words, my boy. It seemed like the whole world crashed and burned at that very moment. We had all become Russians. Xavier was undisputed Master of the House and some stranger was second in command. And all this trauma within only three weeks.

I gasped loudly, "Jonas showed up and just like that he was Silk King? How the hell did he do that, Claus? I just assumed he was somehow related to one of the founding families, but am I hearing you right? He wasn't even a House member before the Russians took over?"

Claus glared for a moment then nodded as he replied, "He isn't related to anyone in the House that I'm aware of, and before that day I'd never even heard of him. I suspected immediately he was with the Russians somehow. At first, I thought maybe a Russian officer that was given the title as a reward for some heroic deed during the war. But over the years, I've come to believe he was or is involved with the KGB somehow."

I blew out my breath making a faint whistling noise then said, "That would sure explain the reasons Ivan and those Russian snakes mind that bat. The one thing I don't get though is if he is KGB then why didn't the big guys in the Russian army make him the boss instead of Xavier? For that matter, why would he still be here now that the Stasi are running our puppet government? I would think that if he had that kind of power, he would have just had some big wig order their Stasi dogs to make it so."

Claus shook his head as he replied, "Those are very good questions but one I have never been able to answer. Only three men know the truth of what the top brass had to say about the House. Two of them are long dead and the other one has good reason to keep his silence. It has occurred to me, there is one other very likely explanation for Jonas."

I groaned then interrupted the Elder, "He could be one of the Russian officers they wanted to be gone, but his connections made it impossible to kill him outright."

The Elder nodded, "Or worse, he did something that is a crime in his country and the House is his prison sentence, just like Ivan and all the others."

With a frown I replied, "That certainly would explain a lot about Jonas, wouldn't it. It only makes sense from the Russian point of view. You know that would mean that Jonas likely hopes that one day they will forgive him, so he goes home, just like all the rest of his brute crew around here. It sure would be great if you are telling me the truth at least on this one thing."

Claus chuckled hard then responded, "I know you think this means it possible that one day, just like old Hemmel so long ago, you will be granted a reprieve from your biggest offender. But let me tell you something, boy. Jonas may be a spy, criminal, Russian officer or even from a real Transylvania vampire. However, be assured if he gets the message, it is safe to return from whatever rock he crawled out from under. He's not going to leave here without his Priceless husband."

I shook my head, "Over my dead body. Besides, if he were called to go back, then he would become just another outsider, right? I could legally kill that dirty bat, and no one could punish me for it. Hahaha."

The Elder looked at the roof and took a deep breath as he said, "Oh my dear. I didn't realize Peter nor Leo nor even that idiot Jonas has prepared you for living outside of the walls of the Haus. You need to be aware that out there on the streets you can't just murder anyone that gets on your nerve. This is a problem that needs to be corrected immediately. Those fools are running out of time."

That caught my attention as I leaned in closer and said, "Claus, you are talking nonsense again. I'm dying to hear the answer why any of them would bother to teach me anything. Oh, maybe they might bother to give me lessons on how to suck their cocks the way they like it. Everyone in this House is a pack of liars, even Leo. I seem to recall all of you told me that if I broke my collar and became the Dominant, I could finally leave this place. Funny thing though, is when I tried to walk out the door, you all made sure I didn't get far. Heslach wasn't exactly that freedom of choice I was promised. No one, not even you on your death bed, is ever going to let me go free. Lucus is going to force me to name him the regent, then it's off to the Palace hell for me. Like it or not, I'm a grown man now, Claus. I no longer believe the fairy tales that old men who fuck and then kill their children told me."

Claus winced then replied, "I know you have no reason to trust me, but I swear on my beloved Felicity's grave one day I will pay you back for all the harm I've caused. As for all the others, I refuse to answer for them. More than that, I won't protect them from your righteous wrath any longer either."

With a sigh I responded, "Well then get back to the story Claus. You're wasting my time."

166

The Elder chuckled as he said, "We can't have that now can we my boy? Okay, so Xavier had called a meeting of all the survivors of the Russian sacking of the house and every child eight years or younger had been seized. The Dungeon was packed wall to wall with "Hitler's war babies." I didn't know for sure why Xavier had ordered the children rounded up, but deep inside I think I suspected he had the most sinister of motives for it.

Two hours was more than enough time to gather the rag tag, worn, and frightened remains of the House residents. Xavier arrived in the Great Hall, flanked on each side by Bladrick and the new Silk King Jonas. He marched through the subdued crowd in a goose step almost as dramatic as any seen by the SS guards.

I stood in the very corner of the room feeling queasy at this most irregular get together. The atmosphere seemed as heavy as our hearts as Xavier took to the podium and began his speech. I couldn't forget his bone chilling words if I were to be dying of dementia instead of cancer.

His voice boomed through the air as he addressed the crowd, "I have managed to convince the Russian forces to spare our beloved Das Kaiser Haus." The mass of residents let out a collect rushing sound as each man and woman finally took a breath upon hearing his first sentence.

Xavier was forced to wait until the raging applause and shouts of relief calmed before he continued. There is no doubt no one there believed the Russians were going to just walk away. However, I was likely the only among them that realized he had chosen his first words very carefully. He said the House was saved, but not necessarily her people. Claus sighed mournfully.

It was a good five minutes before at last he could speak and be heard when he said, "You may all thank me for the mercy of this blessing later. Well, those of you that survive the examination that is." The joyous crowd fell silent as each looked to each other in understandable confusion.

The Fur King chuckled diabolically as he motioned for the black collar guards at the Great Hall doors to close and lock them. "It is an unfortunate reality that Germany has been defeated. When a country becomes the property of another nation, the cost must be absorbed by them. Our Mother Russia has been most generous in granting this House protection, and a regular stipend of rations to provide for us until we can once again produce for ourselves. While we are most grateful for this mercy, I fear that there is only so much aid they are capable of parting with, giving they have many mouths to feed already. So, to prevent the illness, crimes and mass starvation that will come from shrunken larders, I intend to weed out the weak, the sick, and those too young or elderly to be of use in the massive job of rebuilding our community."

Gasps, yelps, shouts of anger and screams of terror filled the room as his words began to sink into everyone's disbelieving ears. Xavier had just officially announced many of them were to be executed with little to no recourse. Worse, no parent in the Great Hall that day misunderstood that their leader intended to exterminate all of the House children.

168

The mob began to rip apart the tables and chairs, apparently to create makeshift weapons. I could see from my distant vantage Bladrick and Jonas expressions were those of men afraid. But Xavier remained stoic with that irritating arrogant grin on his ugly face.

A gunshot rung out just before the first of the blood frenzied residents managed to reach Xavier and his men. Silence hushed the crowd as, yet another shot cut through the air. We all looked in every direction trying frantically to discover the source of those noises of death.

Then a woman shrieked out, "Oh my Gott. The babies. The Russians are killing our babies." The mass rushed for the huge windows of the Great Hall to witness for themselves if the female voice spoke the truth.

And she was.

The crude clubs made of the fine dining table legs were used to crash in the glass, rather than brain Xavier and his crew. Men and women, old and young poured from the ravaged windows running as fast as their legs could carry them in a vain attempt to save their newborns, yearlings, and toddlers.

But it was too late.

By the time the first set of parents reached the Russian killers, every youngster under the age of three lay dead. The carnage was almost surreal. The south lawn was speckled pink with little bodies of hundreds, shot or bludgeoned to stillness forevermore.

Woman fell over the tiny corpses howling in heartbroken agony, and many men attacked the hairy murders, some with their bare hands. Soon enough, the babes were joined in eternal peace by many of their grieving mothers and fathers.

I was already an old, tired man in 1945. I had celebrated my fifty-fifth birthday only a few weeks before that nightmarish day. A life of hard living, and harsh memories had taken their toll. While my horrified eyes took in the sights of this unimaginable massacre, my legs gave way from under me.

I fell to the floor just inside the shattered exit, trembling from the weight of the burdens I could no longer bear. I would have happily died right there that very minute, but the fates still had not finished with me yet. A strong pair of arms reached out of seemingly nowhere and pulled me back to my boots. I turned to look upon the face of the one that aided me to stand when all I wanted to do was fall. Through my tears I could barely make out the pretty features of Malfred's betrothed.

Rachel's eyes were wet, but her expression was fierce as she said to me, "Claus, don't let them see they have hurt you. If they find your weakness, then you are as good as dead. The dead can't seek revenge, nor work to end the madness that evil men do. You have already come so far. It would be a pity to lose it all, just moments from the finish line, ja?"

Such wise and brave words coming from a young girl that already suffered more loss than I could imagine immediately awoke me from my nervous breakdown.

I did all I could to calm myself as I replied, "Aren't you afraid, Rachel?"

She flashed me a bitter smile as she said, "More than you can imagine, Claus. That won't stop death from coming to claim me eventually. No one lives forever. Until then I must live with memories I can't change. It would be a mercy if these brutes did send me to my grave. Because if they don't, then I know no matter what I do I will never know peace again. It is life that hurts, but death is painless. Do not waste your precious time in mourning for those who suffer no more. Instead, join those of us that continue to struggle to prevent the future from sharing in our ill fate."

The girl was only fourteen in the flesh but the brutal world around her had aged her soul by decades. I was in awe of the tiny frame that concealed the heart of a Lioness. I swear to you, had I been a straight man, I would have done everything in my power to make her my bride. Be that as it may, her unbroken resolve was enough to reawaken my own sleeping warrior within.

It was at that moment, one of the most tragic the House has ever known, that an idea so amazingly clever began to hatch in my mind. I knew the plan wasn't going to help if the Russians decided to burn the House down around our ears, but if I could survive and if Rachel could too, well, I was sure I'd discovered the way to finally put an end to Xavier's despotic rule and return the House to the serene place of equality it once had been under Mother Felicity.

I saw the answer had always been right there. If a King has become a threat to his country you depose him with a legitimate heir. A Prince to overthrow a King.

Chapter 13: The Sacred and the Sacrificed
Master Mad Maxx and submissive Meine Liebe

The next several months after the mass killing of all the House babies and toddlers were the hardest in my entire life. Knowing all that I have told you about the terrible pandemic and starvation after the First World War, it almost goes without saying how bad things were.

Every survivor of the Russian sacking from the youngest to the eldest was forced to work. Most toiled in the fields but if they possessed some building skills, they were tasked with repairing the damaged House. From the powerful Xavier to the four-year-old Jacob, no one was exempt.

At the end of the Russian's rifles, we slaved around the clock. The Russians granted us almost no rest, food, or mercy. Those who fell ill, or for whatever reason couldn't pull their weight, were shot without warning nor care.

Worse than any of the personal miseries we endured during these hard times were the terrible tragedies we were forced to witness. Within six weeks after the Russians took possession of Das Kaiser Haus, many of the surviving women, began to drop dead. Only this time, it wasn't because they were defending their children or fending off our oppressors' sexual assaults.

Well, that's not exactly true. Many of the girls had found their Russian rapists seed had taken root within them.

If the lady was lucky, a carefully executed leap from the third story balcony resulted in an end to her all her troubles.

For those women in the unwanted motherly way but stuck outside working in the fields, things were a bit trickier. Our Russian overlords had become wise to the girls intended mass abortions pretty quickly. Because of that, they suddenly weren't in a hurry to shoot females that rushed at them. Even when the desperate lady did it with her fist flying while hurling terrible curses at them.

The unlucky ladies in the fields witnessed a few of their sisters subdued then tied up to prevent the suicide attempt. After that, the unwilling mothers to be began using surer means of termination. Hangings, slit wrists, and even climbing the trees to jump to their death became almost the daily event.

It should also be said that the youngsters didn't die in the numbers the pregnant females did, but they too claimed heavy casualties. Some expired from malnutrition and disease. Others found their graves through work-related accidents, or from a bullet when they didn't perform up to expectations.

I suppose it is almost unnecessary to tell you that all the residents over sixty-five, the chronically ill, and those who fell ill were exterminated within the first thirty days. The Russians wiped them out without firing a shot. They simply worked them without rest or food until they dropped dead.

Within three months the population of the House went from hundreds to less than fifty left alive. The males outnumbered the females six to one. Of my generation, only myself, Ingrid, Xavier, Drexel, Barnim, Bladrick, Heidi and Helga survived. There was no one left in the House older than Bladrick and Xavier. Both men, at that time, were both only fifty-six years old.

Several of the founding House families had either been wiped out or had escaped into the countryside. Those lucky enough to get away, left with only the rags on their backs. I heard over the next few years, none that left had faired any better outside the House. The entire country had been war ravaged. The fields had been burned, all the food taken by the Russian hordes and the animals slaughtered from Germany's borders to Berlin. Most that had fled never were heard from again, presumed, likely correctly, to have died of starvation or murdered by roaming Russian soldiers.

Despite this hell on Earth, though I'm still unsure how, the House survived. Of course, that wasn't a good thing for you, my boy, but for those of us who rebuilt her it was a miracle.

Six months into our defeat, things started to show slow signs of improving. The resident deaths stabilized, and food became less scarce. Although, our menus were still pretty shitty, there was enough of it to sustain the tiny population of survivors."

"Wait a minute," I interrupted, "You said everyone had to work. Does that mean Jonas was forced to help rebuild the House too?"

Claus glared at me as he spat out in a frustrated sounding tone, "Yes. That idiot was right there with Xavier and Bladrick working like a slave among the rest of us."

I chuckled as I replied, "No shit? What was his job duty, Claus? Oh, I know, they had him stand in the fields to scare away the crows, right? Hahaha."

The Elder groaned as he said, "I'm glad you find some humor in the nightmare story I'm telling you, boy. Have you completely lost your soul? Whatever happened to that sweet little child I used to take to feed the ducks? I seem to recall you used to hate the idea of people suffering."

I stopped laughing and growled back through my dentures, "When you start telling me of the travails of humans suffering, I will shed tears. So far, you only spew descriptions of a bunch of assholes that had not given a shit over these very same terrors they did or allowed to happen to others."

Claus stared at me for a moment, then sighed as he replied, "You do have a point, my boy. But you forget, not everyone that was being punished was guilty of the crimes you say our people ae guilty of. What about Malfred, Karl, Rachel, and Leo? Or the babies like Jacob, Rolf, Oliver, or Peter?"

I rolled my eyes, "Oh go fuck yourself, Claus. Malfred, his brother and cousin, even Leo should have joined the Russians and helped them killed the Germans. Instead, they switched teams and became one of the monsters. Except for Leo, Jacob, and maybe Rolf, and I never met this Oliver guy.

All those babies you felt sorry for grew into monsters. It would have done the world a favor had they been put to the yard before they got the chance to hurt others."

He snorted then said, "I must say those are bold words for the King of Killers to utter. Tell me something, my boy, how many notches do you have on your belt? Or have you lost count of the number of skulls rotting away in your Palace?"

I leaned in close and gazed into his watery eyes as I said low, "I don't have so many I couldn't use one more, old man. You'd better choose your next words very carefully or I can undo all the fine work you did so long ago. This House is an eye sore, a blight on the perfect landscape you know. Perhaps you are eager for a proper demonstration of why I am leveled Priceless."

Claus's eyes went wide as he gasped then croaked out, "Who is it that I'm speaking to right now? I don't recognize this thing sitting in front of me wearing the skin of our beloved Mortar King."

I chuckled as I growled out, "I am the cracked foundation of this debauched House. The true son of Joseph, and Master of all the filth that you see. My throne was carved out of mortar and my heart created from stone. I wear the metal crown upon my boney brow."

The Elder trembled visibly as he said, "Are you saying this is Florian I am speaking with?"

I nodded as I responded, "I say nothing at all because the dead can't speak. But they can still haunt the nightmares of corrupted men and women."

Claus whispered through his shaky lips, "Answer me this my dearest Lord and Master Florian, what color are my eyes?"

With a deep snort I replied, "Sunken sockets, deep and dark. Speak no evil or from your body your head I part."

The Elder didn't break from our stare down as he yelled out with suddenness, "Be still. The lambs are near. They call for you. You must follow them or you'll never find the green fields."

I sucked in my breath as Noah released me from his grip. I shivered in the cold air as the fresh water dripped down my naked skin.

"Damn it Christian, I thought I'd made it clear. You must use the privy every time." Noah threw the soiled sponge into the bathing bowl at my feet.

I dropped my eyes to the floor as I replied, "I'm sorry, God damn it. I hate you, Noah. This piss won't happen for crying."

Noah stopped fuming for a moment and locked his eyes on me as he said, "What did you just say?"

I shuddered then responded, "You little brat. I kill you. Peed the breeches more."

The Dungeon Master startled me badly when he started laughing wildly and said, "Oh my God. Your German sucks, but I must admit it is certainly funny to listen to you butcher our language."

Tears well up in my eyes as I replied, "Why angry bastard? I beat you, asshole. Eat fucking spoon. I hate you, Noah." I didn't understand his humor over my attempted apology.

Noah recomposed himself then he grabbed me by the hair roughly and said, "Stop talking idiot. I think I preferred your constant screaming. It bothers my ears less." He pulled my head back till I yelped.

"Nein, help. I spoon momma. Maximillian, don't eat momma." I wailed out in agony as the Dungeon Master dragged me to my favored corner of the cell.

Once there Noah let go of my mane and yelled out, "There in the straw," he pointed at clothing lying next to me. "Put those on by yourself this time. If I have to aid you in dressing, I will beat you for it."

I cowered as I crawled rapidly to retrieve the fresh rags. "Don't beat. I hurt the God damned spoon, Noah," I sobbed out while I attempted to do the thing I thought he wanted me to do.

He watched me as I flailed and made several mistakes before I finally got the task completed. Once I was clothed, I rolled into the fetal position and wept hard full of terror Noah was going to hit me like he always did.

Instead, the Dungeon Master walked over and stood above me as he said in a gentle tone, "Good boy. You still have a long way to go, but I see you are trying. That is a huge improvement from only a few months ago when you first arrived. Come on Christian, stop crying. I'm not angry at you. Hell no. I'm proud for a change."

I heard his words, but I didn't understand what most of them meant. This man, this cell, the chain and all the weird rituals were so confusing. The tears kept falling as I lay there wishing that my brother was with me. He always knew what to do. Wait, where is my brother?

With a sudden gasp I awoke from the trance, "Claus. The manacle I wore in the dungeon, what did Peter do with it?" I felt a tremor in my stomach as I asked the Elder.

Claus raised an eyebrow and replied, "It is in the Palace where all the removed silver goes. You know the law. Why does that matter?"

I shook my head wildly. "My name is the reason I ask. That was the manacle Gerard put on me the day he chained me to the barn wall. I remember he scratched my name on the inside of it."

Claus let out a sudden agonized rush of air, "Hell no. Oh fuck me. Please tell me you are kidding."

"No. I am not Claus. I saw him do it just after, after, he ripped up the stuffed puppy." I sniffed back a rush of intense sadness as I said that.

The Elder leaned back his head and covered his eyes with his hand as he said, "The answer was there all that time. Neither I nor Ingrid thought to exam Gerard's blasted manacle. Okay, too late for all that now, but tell me boy, can you recall what name he scratched into the metal?"

I took to my feet and started pacing as I did my best to remember the word Gerard forced me to see before he put it around my neck. "It was so long ago, Claus. I'm drawing a blank. Oh. I know, make me do that trancing thing again. I can remember it that way, right?" I rushed back to his side in desperation, sure that if I could recall that name, I could finally prove I didn't have a dead brother named Maximillian.

He removed his hand then sat up as he replied, "I don't think it is safe to take you back to that moment. You nearly fractured last time. I think it best to get back to my story, and if you still want to try in a bit, we can do it then."

I shrugged and responded. "Alright if you say so Claus, but please hurry this up. You might have all day to talk, but I don't have forever to listen."

Claus chuckled bitterly as he said, "I never thought I'd live to see the day the Priceless would be in a hurry to return to his abusive life. Okay, have it your way. I will do my best to get right to the business of finishing the story you need to hear.

So, Ingrid eventually healed from those vicious sexual assaults. I realize, she likely was returned to the meager population long before I saw her. As I said, no one was given excuse to evade rebuilding detail, not even the new Fur Queen.

It was clear by the time I ran into her again, the Russians were going to let us live. At least for a while anyway. The first time I saw her, I couldn't approach her with my idea for retaking the House out of Xavier's power. Assuming of course, after all that had happened any of that even mattered. Xavier and his cronies were surrounding the fragile lady. I didn't dare increase my odds of being murdered if the Fur King overheard the things I wished to discuss with Ingrid.

When next I spotted her, I was painting the walls on the third floor and so was she. I noticed right away that this time she wasn't surrounded by her husband or his sympathizers. With a wary eye on the Russians assigned to assure we didn't skimp on duties I calmly moved my position to get within ear shot of my oldest friend.

Ingrid saw me and without requiring a signal or sound, she nonchalantly began to paint with fury. The Fur Queen moved toward me slowly while trying to appear deeply involved with her task.

"I think I have come up with that plan we discussed before everything went to hell. If we are still interested in reaching that goal," I whispered.

Ingrid nodded slightly as she responded in a hushed tone, "I'm listening Claus. I've must tell you I overheard Xavier saying after the Russian's tire of their sport, they are turning the country back over to a puppet government. Then he is positive no one will be capable of stopping him."

182

I winced upon hearing verification of the rumors I'd already heard circulating around among the House survivors. "First I need to know, have you seen Rachel anywhere? Or do you know if she has been killed."

Ingrid glanced at the attending Russian as she mumbled, "Rachel was alive yesterday. Today is anyone's guess."

I nodded as I replied, "Good enough. Listen, do you remember that law about any sons that a Fur Monarch bares while sitting on the throne?"

She snorted as she replied, "Of course I do, Claus. What does that have to do with anything? I can't have any more children, and Justus was born before Xavier became King. He can try to wrangle in that little brat Birgit bore him, if the cuss lives, but the law says the son must be accepted as the child of both the Monarchs. I will never claim that half-breed bastard Byron as my own blood. So, I ask again, what the hell does that law matter to us?"

I leaned in close and whispered, "Tell Xavier if he truly wants to become the legend by fathering the Prince of Princes, you will agree to adopt Peter. He will go for this compromise. Just think, you end any chance of his champion Byron rising, plus the horrible treatment Peter has endured will make him easier to turn against Xavier, ja?"

Her eyes went wide, and she nearly dropped her paint brush as she breathed out, "Oh my God Claus. That is a brilliant solution. But wait, Xavier is very clever. He could find a way to obtain Peter's loyalty despite all the damage he's done to him and his family. Oh, and what about that

183

horrible man Jonas? He holds the Silk throne, and no one knows how he got that appointment. He might be difficult to remove. Also, Peter is barely six years old. We'd have to wait years before he'd be ready to assume the power of the House. Not to mention it will take luck and at least a year more before he could come to full power by producing a legitimate heir to the Silk Throne. Then I must wonder who among our surviving FemDoms could we trust to become the mother and regent of Peter's Prince?"

I smiled as I replied, "Just get Xavier to agree with you to adopt him. No doubt our country's lot will not improve for the next several years. I suspect we have plenty to keep us busy while we wait for Prince Peter to come of age. Of course, we will have to marry him off the second he becomes a man. Then we let his bride convince him he must get to work creating his dynasty with urgency. I'm sure with you as his mother to guide him, Peter will be eager to depose his father the King and take over his throne. As for a wife for the Prince, I already have the perfect girl in mind. I believe she would behave the gentle mother and wise regent till their first born son is old enough to take full possession of the voters."

A huge grin broke out on Ingrid's face as my plan began to sink in. "That is why you asked me about the health of Rachel Krauss, ja? Oh Claus, she is the perfect choice, but do you think she would do this for us? Peter is so much younger than her, and there is her betrothal to Malfred to consider. You do realize the Jewish people put their family and traditions above everything else, right?"

I nodded as I whispered back, "Ja, I am aware of the possible complications. I will see what it will take to get Malfred to withdraw his promise to the girl. As for Rachel, I wouldn't have considered her if I didn't already have reason to believe the young lady eager to act as savior of this House. Do you want to speak to her, or do you think it best I speak to the pair of Krausses on my own. Might be safer to keep you out of this just in case Xavier gets wind of it before we can spring the trap."

Ingrid shook her head and replied, "Nein, I've never been afraid of that brute. I will get Xavier to agree to adopt Peter and speak to Rachel about becoming my future daughter-in-law. As for Malfred, I leave him to you. Claus, I swear to the Gods, you are a fucking genius."

I frowned and said, "I will accept that kind ego stroke if and when Xavier's power is neutered."

With a yelp I interrupted Claus. "What the fuck. Are you serious Claus? Please tell me Xavier didn't agree to adopt Peter as his son."

The Elder snorted then replied, "I can't do as you ask boy. Like it or not, Ingrid was successful in her bid to adopt Bernt's orphaned son. However, it wasn't easy. It took her a full year of threats and begging, but finally in 1946, Peter officially became the legitimate Prince of Das Kaiser Haus. The very day Peter became their son, Xavior's previous favored child, Byron, was exiled to the dungeon along with his mother and Peter's mentally deficit brother, Friedrick."

I took a deep breath then said, "You are making my brain hurt, Claus. So, Peter isn't my father. He is my brother and uncle. And Justus isn't my blood brother, but he is Peter's real brother, and Byron, oh, fucking bloody hell, he is also Peter's brother but also Peter is his uncle. Is there any motherfucking Schmidt that isn't in the habit of fucking his brothers, cousins or uncles?"

Claus snorted as he replied, "Ja, Oliver and Rolf, Derbeck's boys. However, I think you are missing the point. boy. Think a minute. Peter went to a lot of trouble to trick you into his collar. By now you must be aware your collar was promised to Gretta, not Peter. He betrayed Ingrid and me for reasons I've never understood and took you for himself. I must assume he couldn't bear to see another male take the power of the House after he lost his own bid to be the Monarch of Monarchs."

I glared at the old man as I spit back, "Peter told me he betrayed you because he overheard you telling Bladrick you were giving the Silk throne to Gretta instead of to him like you promised.

He startled and said in the near whisper, "What? How the hell did he find out we had cut him from the plot? Only Ingrid, Bladrick and me knew we were going to bypass him in favor of Gretta. No way they would have betrayed their own blood kin to Xavier's Prince."

I rolled my eyes and replied, "Peter told me that he forgot his hat during one of the secret meetings you bastards had regarding some other stupid plot. He returned to get it but none of you saw him sneak into your apartment. While getting it, he eavesdropped on your conversation. That's when he overheard you discussing cutting him out of the deal. Oh, by the way, Thanks a lot for that huge mistake. My ass wishes you to know it truly appreciates that neither of you old fuckers thought to lock the God damned door when conspiring to betray a monster."

Claus rolled his eyes and said, "Ah, well I'm glad to finally know the answer to that riddle after all these years. Damn that sneaky Peter to hell. I suppose what is done is done. I do regret that mistake more than you can imagine, but to be honest despite the pain it causes you, it is far from the worst misstep I have ever made."

I groaned out, "So you have been insisting over the last few hours. God Claus, give this fake attempt to offer excuses for the evil you have done to me and others a rest, will you? I'm warning you my patience and temper are wearing thin."

He glared at me angrily. "I am not attempting to gain your forgiveness boy. I assume no matter what I say, you'd never grant me the mercy of forgiveness anyway. Why would I bother to waste my precious breath on it? Besides, I truly don't give a fig if you blame me for all your troubles. Better you hate me than turn that loathing toward the boy I love, ja?"

"Enough Claus. Tell the fucking story or release me, dammit," I shouted out.

The Elder took a deep breath then without bothering to address my rudeness continued his story.

"Well, the months marched on with mild improvements in our situation occurring very slowly. As I said, Ingrid did manage to get Xavier to formally adopt Peter. It was a win for me and the Fur Queen, but the boy in question was not thrilled to learn of his 'lucky' rise."

You probably recall that I told you Justus had helped Peter escape Xavier's cruel tortures just before Das Kaiser Haus was sacked. He had been snuck out of the Fur King's apartment and spirited away to live among the House children in the nursery cottage. There the kids hid Peter away from Xavier's gaze. For a short time, he found peace lurking in the shadows, sharing the meals with his beloved cousin Oliver. That sweet boy was Peter's best friend and greatest champion.

After the Russian take-over, Xavier had his hands too full with problems to bother a retaliation against his son Justus. He also didn't have time to send his goons to retrieve his escaped plaything. So, the announcement that the Fur Monarchs had formally adopted him, likely was the nightmare Peter feared more than death itself.

I witnessed Olaf dragging Peter back to the Fur King's floor with my own eyes. It may sooth your tormented soul a tad to know he wailed, wept, and begged for mercy the entire trip up to the seventh floor. It was to be expected given Peter was only a nine-year-old child.

However, even if it had been my elderly ass being hauled up to suffer only God knows what, I doubt the scene would have been different. Xavier was by then a well experienced torturer. He had honestly earned his bloody reputation by amassing almost as large a body count as any Russian guard could boast.

I tell you without any regret I did feel a twinge of guilt over sacrificing the boy to the cruel Xavier. The feeling of remorse wasn't strong enough for me to rethink my plan, but it was enough to incite me to question Ingrid often about his welfare.

The next few years, reports from your grandmother were grim regarding Peter's treatment. She told me horror stories of Xavier spending many hours with him in the room with the red door. She said it was common for the sounds of Peter's screaming and pleas for mercy to be so intense she couldn't sleep without ear plugs and heavy sleep medications.

That was the way it was to be for that boy from 1946 until 1950. In fact, no one in the House saw Peter for those four years except Ingrid and Xavier. Olaf told Bladrick on several occasions not even he and Wilber laid eyes on him despite serving Xavier daily. There was speculation that your evil father of yours kept Peter either chained to the wall in that room or perhaps caged him.

Whatever happened, only Xavier, Peter and Ingrid know, and none of them have spoken a word of it that I'm aware of. Claus stopped and cast me a glance with a curious expression.

I shrugged and replied, "Do you really think Peter told me any of this? This is the first time I've heard he was adopted for Christ's sake."

He nodded then said, "It would seem Peter did go to great lengths to prevent you from finding out anything about his violent childhood or ties to Xavier."

I stared at him hatefully as I responded, "Gee, I wonder where he learned that bad behavior? Claus, I just can't sit here and say nothing while you try to fill my ears with obvious lies. Do you think I'm stupid? You must if you expect me to believe Peter lived chained to Xavier's torture room walls for four years. I think you've forgotten he's been using me as his cock warmer since I was eleven. That kind of sustained abuse would've left lots of scars behind. This is something Xavier taught me personally. I've seen Peter naked millions of times and believe me. His flesh is without significant blemishes. You can tell a fish tale to strangers but the guy that cleans your catch knows when you lie about the size of your prize, Claus."

The Elder chuckled over my clever analogy for a moment then replied, "I've always thrilled over your wit, my boy, but I swear I'm not fibbing to you. Peter did suffer Xavier's heavy hand and cruel perversions for many years as a child. Please recall, I didn't claim I witnessed the actual implementing of any kind of tortures on Peter. I merely report what others told me about it. I would also remind you that scars on the skin are not nearly as devastating nor as deep as those hidden from the naked eye."

That truth caused me to sigh as I said, "Okay, I'm willing to concede an abusive childhood certainly would explain Peter's nasty nature. That still doesn't excuse the terrible things he did and does to me though. So, you can save time by skipping the details of Peter's troubles and get to the point like I asked you to do hours ago."

He nodded and said, "I can't argue that. Anyway, as you know, in October 1949, the Russian menace allowed the German Democratic Republic to form. Our nation became a satellite nation of the USSR, and to this day the government is supposed to be a socialist state.

However, we in the House discovered quickly the GDR is a totalitarian state. I say that because the February following the formation of the GDR, the Stasi paid a visit to the House to discuss the punishment its residents would receive for our part in the war crimes committed in World War II. No one other than the Fur and Silk King were permitted to sit in while the head officers discussed our future or lack of it.

I think every House survivor held their breath while that historic meeting took place behind closed doors in the Great Hall. From the second they had arrived, the snotty Stasi had been made clear to everyone they viewed every man, woman, and child of the House as war criminals that should be executed immediately. I suppose we all feared the outcome of their visit because it was the truth. All were guilty either directly or by complacency.

Since we are here today, burning us all at the stake wasn't to be our penalty for our part in the madness of Hitler's rein. Much to our horror we were to find out the Stasi had decided the House residents would be made to suffer a much harsher sentence.

Xavier and Jonas gathered the sparse survivors together almost before the Stasi top brass had exited to share the bad news.

Xavier stood before us with a huge grin as he said, "Brothers, and sisters, I bring good tidings. Our dark days of uncertainty have come to an end at long last. Your Silk King and I have been able to lobby our new government to show our population mercy and forgiveness for our stupidly believing the lies spread by the criminal Hitler."

He shot a look of triumph towards Jonas and that Vampire bastard shouted out, "You should all be grateful to the wisdom your Monarchs have demonstrated. If it were not for us, this House, your home, would be keeping the night at bay with the light of her inferno. Kneel while your King speaks to you worms."

My jaw hit the floor before my knees did upon hearing that stranger demand honorable Dominants engage in such humiliation. Despite my anger over the indignity of it though, I was too frightened over what may or may not have occurred during that secret meeting to refuse the Silk King's orders.

Everyone else, apparently, felt the same as I did. All the residents followed the command in silence. Within only moments, Xavier and Jonas stood tall as giants over their subjugated and terrorized people.

The Fur King's evil laugher rang through the halls as he barked out, "I see that the dogs of this House have learned their place with only minimal training. This is good to know. Now I demand each hear my warning loud and clear because I've no tolerance for repeating myself. The honored Stasi have informed your worthy Kings there will be no attempts by the new government to seek the death penalty for war crimes attributed to this population. However, they are unable to overlook the past without demanding retribution. Therefore, they have decided if we are not to pay with our flesh, we shall pay with our coin. A collection of an annual fine of ten thousand dollars is to begin immediately." Several wails of disbelief rippled through the crowd upon hearing this terrible and impossible decree.

Jonas roared out, "Be still, worms. How dare you insult your King that has managed to grant you mercy." He rushed forward and kicked the closest kneeling resident in his face.

The man fell unconscious at the fuming Vampire's feet with a thud. Terrified gasps, yelps, and screams erupted immediately. Thanks to this impulsive move, panic was spreading faster than the plague all around me. Xavier realized he needed to calm this situation before it got further out of hand.

That old bastard raised his hand high and yelled out, "Silence, dammit. Honorable Jonas, please withhold your temper. You are not totally familiar with the customs of our people yet, so I beg you to use the patience reserved for children. The rude behaviors of these nothings shall be dealt with in time I assure you. Until then, I command all of you to keep your complaints quiet. The Stasi are aware that most of the House's fortune and income have been compromised. They are not unreasonable men. I've reached a compromise regarding this situation that will relieve most of you. For those unable to fulfill the new obligations, well, they shall be eliminated." When he said that, I finally regained the strength of my heart.

I took back to my feet and glared at the despotic Kings without fear and said, "And who is to play the judge regarding if the price has been paid Xavier? You? This stranger?" I pointed at Jonas with hate in my expression.

Jonas started to march toward me with an expression of murder on his ugly face, but Xavier halted him by laying a hand on his shoulder as he replied:

"Ah, my dear old friend Claus, I must ask you to put aside your anger for a moment. I tell you, all of you, I understand. Have I not also been the victim of indignity and grief right next to each of you over these many years since the end of the war? No one in this House can claim they are unscathed by the terrors, nor free of the anxiety over our future in this unproven political environment. But honorable Claus, you and I, we have suffered many travails in our troubled past, ja? Yet here we stand. I swear to you comrade, this latest wrinkle isn't one that in time will be ironed out."

I snorted loudly as I crossed my arms in defiance and responded, "Can the formality and stop filling our ears with impossible demands. If the Stasi are aware we are an impoverished people, then why do they impose annual fines no one in this House can hope to pay? The Russians have stolen our treasures, plundered our food stuffs, and killed our sons and daughters. Am I to suppose the new governments expect us to find employment in the village? Unemployment is at horrific levels everywhere, and the entire country starves in equal numbers. Most among us don't possess useful skills even if jobs can be found. And what about the few children among us that still cling to life? They are too small to earn a wage large enough to fill their bellies much less extra to line the coffers as the Stasi order."

Xavier shook his head as that stupid smile of his bent his lips, "Claus, I see age hasn't brought the gift of patience it usually blesses to elders. Please hear me out, all of you. The Stasi believe that the path toward meeting our obligations to them can be accomplished by resuming the industry that has proven successful to us historically." Everyone gasped collectively upon hearing that.

I replied through trembling lips, "Xavier, even you surely realize the House's fortune was built on a trade that both Hitler and the GDR have outlawed. If we are to believe the Stasi wish us to resume the profession of 'entertainment' that they have deemed morally and socially deplorable. Then I must wonder how such could be accomplished given our critically low population, lack of skilled staff, not to mention loss of important and worthy clientele."

The Fur King chuckled evilly as he said, "Ah, well you see old friend, if I stand here saying this House is to return to her roots, then I already reported our original business expertise has been approved by our country's leadership. As to your other questions, you already pointed out a few of the answers in our discussions. The children and young adults left among us are to report immediately to the dungeon. There, our Dungeon Masters, and Mistresses will solve the lack of trained entertainers by teaching them the finer points of, as you call it, 'entertainment.' The ones among us deemed too old, unattractive, or incapable of rebuilding the House's stellar reputation are permitted to contact all family, friends, or connections they still possess around the world. They will either provide this House with useful fresh clientele or obtain the money to pay their personal debt before it is collected annually. Those who are unable to provide the services, offer fresh clientele of worth or shell out the fines will still be useful. As fertilizer."

I began to shake wildly with the understanding that a man such as myself could do none of the things Xavier reported assured continued life, "This solution you offer Xavier, I cannot find reasonable fault to argue against. However, you failed to inform us of the length of our sentences."

The Fur King sucked in his breath but didn't stop grinning as he replied, "I also neglected to report the entirety of our sentences." The crowd moaned, and a few wails rippled through it. "Look around at each other, my children. These faces you see are the last you shall ever be familiar with in this life. The House is no longer just a home. It's our prison. No one is permitted to leave the boundaries as determined by the Stasi from this day forward." All the residents glanced around at each other with the expression of fear and disbelief in their expressions. "To assure no one attempts to flee from their punishment, the Stasi have ordered a colony of Russian Guardsmen to take residence among us. We must build them reasonable lodgings on the House grounds and provide them an honest wage."

I fell back to my knees nearly fainting as all around me the residents began to weep. The weight of our burdensome and impossible task overwhelmed everyone present. Only Jonas and Xavier appeared unaffected by the gravity of our fate.

This outpouring of grief continued for a few moments before Xavier shouted out demanding silence once more, then he said, "So, I command everyone under the age of forty to report below. There you shall be examined by Hemmel, Heidi and Helga. If you are lucky enough to be selected for collaring, you're to be trained as either a House submissive or as a Pleasure submissive. Those able to contact relatives or obtain the funds will be forgiven from enforced services. Those turned away or capable of paying their way out of service will report to Jonas for assignment to apartments. He will determine your status based upon your ability to provide either financially or by the quality of your connections for the future clientele. You will be given two weeks to meet the quota as set down by our Stasi rulers. I told you I don't repeat myself, so I'm not going to say again what happens to those in two weeks that are found to be 'worthless.' Claus, you, Bladrick, Barnum, Drexel, and Ludwig are to report to the sixth floor. Each of you have been granted reprieve if you can provide enough money to pay the wages of the Russian Guards monthly salary. I don't care how you do this, only that you will. Jonas has selected Johannes, Hans, Christoph, Alice, and Rachel to serve on the fifth floor in the Silk thrones. The Voters are to resume the job of collections of rents, fines, and to enforce House Laws. Each of you will be provided free apartments and food, but in return you're tasked with contacting wealthy clientele. My wife Ingrid and son Peter are forgiven from the examinations, but you Justus, and you Byron shall follow your brothers and sisters below. Olaf, you and Wilber are also forgiven the examinations but are hereby tasked with enforcement of all I have commanded. You are ordered to kill without argument any resident that refuses or gets out of line. Ow why are you worms still here? Get your asses in gear or the next thing you hear will be the sound of the bullet ripping through you empty heads."

I watched helplessly as the mass of frightened residents scurried with haste nearly crushing each other in their haste to get to the dungeon. It goes without saying, all the names forgiven the examinations were mentioned as either Voters or Elders were the only residents left over age forty. Well, other than Rachel who I assumed Ingrid had a hand in assuring was spared."

I let out a yelp interrupting Claus's story, "Bullshit, Claus. No fucking way all the assholes that have raped me since I was a boy were ever used as submissives."

198

Claus rolled his eyes as he replied, "Boy, I've told you the truth. This madness did happen in 1950 just as I've said. Believe it or not, Killian, Anna, Oliver, Friedrick, Karl, Rolf, hell even that bitch Byron were forced into a collar for a few years when still children. Xavier, with the Stasi's help made that entire generation into professional whores. Do recall I told you the kids born during the war would have a great deal of difficulty finding someone they hadn't fucked. Now you realize why I said that."

I sat there staring at him suspiciously as I said, "Karl you say, but not Malfred or Leo? How about them? Or Noah?"

The Fur King yawned as he said, "Yes, Karl and your old buddy Wolf were collared black for a bit. Leo was able to buy his way out, and as a favor to me, he managed to fund Jacob and Malfred out of being collared silver."

With a snort of disbelief I responded, "Okay so you saved Malfred through Leo to get him to owe you a favor, right? That's how you got him to break that engagement off with Rachel. Clever and lucky I suppose, but why did you save Jacob?"

Claus shot me a hateful glance as he said, "Because he was still just a baby for Christs sake. You must think me a monster to just sit back and watch a man I know you adore be ripped apart by lusty businessmen."

I nodded then flashed him a sheepish look as I replied, "Well I'm glad you did have compassion for Jacob, Claus. He has a good heart. The metal hardens a person and that would have been such a tragedy had it happened to that angel. Look, not that I'm saying I believe a damned word of your story, mind you. But if Rolf and all the other kids were collared, why are they Dominants now? Come on. Don't you know if you are going to lie it should make fucking sense."

Claus dropped his eyes to his lap then after a deep sigh he said, "That answer has been the one that has haunted my worst nightmares for the last many months, my love. You see, the next two years were horrific. Most of the House was judged useful as submissive material and very few were able to find a way to pay their way out of service. Xavier, with his trusty Silk King, Jonas, began to invite outsiders from all over the world to demonstrations of the 'taboo and unrestricted' pleasures the House could provide them. At first, the unwilling 'entertainment' was selected from the working pleasure submissive classes and always an old enemy of Xavier's. As you recall personally, Xavier's public displays of House specialties eventually proved fatal for the silvers in his chains.

When that old bastard ran out of long-term enemies, he started working on eliminating foundation family lines. In less than twenty-four months, the House had managed to refill her coffers, but at the cost of a huge number of its 'employees.'

Oliver, Rolf, Friedrick and Byron managed to avoid death in Xavier's red door room only because they share his last name. However, Killian, Anna and Reece were without a doubt targets. Reece finally managed to locate his father in the unoccupied part of Germany. A tear-filled phone call, with a promise he would emigrate to West Germany to take up his father's legacy saved the Altergott children at the last moment.

Malfred managed to convince Leo to pay his brother Karl's debt after watching his big brother suffer for a year in black. I have no idea the exchange of service promised by Malfred to Leo, but I must assume either the boys paid him or perhaps Karl's son Ryker did.

My eyes nearly exploded from my sockets as I yelled out, "What? Are you saying one of the Krauss let Leo fuck him to save Karl?"

Claus nodded slowly but didn't look up as he replied, "Leo is a gay man, that you already are aware. I told you I have no idea which boy completed the service return, but one surely did. Leo is a true gentleman, and to this day has never discussed the terms of this salvage favor."

I closed my eyes tightly trying to ignore the pain at hearing Leo would be so cold as to demand dignity, even if it was from my enemies the Krausses, in return for doing the right thing. "Okay, so again, I say I don't believe any of this bullshit, but you still haven't told me why I see no silver collar on the Schmits. Did you get Ingrid to let them break the collars, or did Xavier free them so he could take over the Voters' floor?"

Claus took a pause then said, "I really wish you didn't want to know this answer so much. Okay, I will tell you, but you must swear not to become angry. I had no idea I was saving children only to completely torment another one."

I opened my eyes and set them on him full of fury as I replied, "That is how Gretta and Lucus got in this fucking House isn't it. You invited them and charged those two freaks enough to buy the Schmits and maybe all these other assholes around here out of their collars. If that is what you are about to tell me Claus, then forget it. I'm going to be pissed off at you and I refuse to swear to a lie like you do."

Claus winced as he said, "I suppose that asking you to calm the demons you righteously have cultivated over those two isn't a fair request. It is my fault Lucus and Gretta are here, that is the truth. I contacted my family because I knew Leo's father had embarrassed the family by screwing around with a maid. Gretta was the result, and Leo's mother, my aunt wanted the girl gone. I promised to make her disappear for a hefty price. The Albrecht name was saved from being tarnished and the House reaped a huge reward. I used the money to free Oliver and Rolf from their service. But I fell short saving Friedrick and Birgit."

I growled out angrily, "So, you contacted that snotty asshole Lucus."

He nodded, "Yeah, I confess it. I heard through various sources the royal family was looking to unload him somewhere far away from the thrones of Europe. It seems, and I believe you are personally aware, Lucus's proclivities were too shameful to allow to exist outside where nosy media sources could catch wind of them. For a king's ransom in the summer of 1952, the House population welcomed its royal prisoner. The money I extorted for this find, paid the collar fees for Justus, Birgit, Karsten, Kay,

Eric, Friedrick, Viviana, Byron, Bren, and Bartram just to name a few you know."

I yelled out in disbelief, "Are you fucking serious. Oh my God, Claus. Why the hell did you save those last three monsters."

He groaned then replied, "I am ashamed to tell you I didn't intend to save any but Friedrick, Justus, and Birgit. Bladrick was behind the money collected from Lucus's membership to buy out of the silver several of the others mentioned. In fact, Ingrid and Bladrick had been busy those two years after the mass collaring offering asylum to the unwanted or embarrassing members of wealthy families all over the world.

By 1953, every surviving Dominant from the original sentencing had been freed of their metal by one of the Elders or Voters. None of us bothered to attempt to buy the freedom for the few left alive that had been submissive before the Stasi sentencing, except for Birgit and her sister Viviana. It shameful to admit that my years as a Dominant had given me the diseased belief that those not part of the founding families were less than us. I realized too late, that's both inhuman and unnatural but I can't go back to undo the harm I helped cause."

I set my blazing gaze upon the Elder as I asked, "May as well keep your feigned remorse to yourself Claus. Maybe when you meet the Devil shortly, he will forgive you, but this Demon doesn't want to hear it. I do wish to know why you bothered to save Birgit and Viviana from the metal though. I had wrongly assumed Xavier freed them in return for Birgit providing him my brother Byron."

Claus blew out his breath as he said, "I felt sorry for Birgit and her sister. I'd been painfully aware of the cruelty Xavier used in his attempts to seed a Prince of Princes. Both sisters had been badly misused by that bastard, and being black collars, they were helpless to deny his interests in them. Birgit and Vivianna are pure souls that deserved better than they got. There is no other excuse for my stepping in and raising them when providence provided me the chance to do it."

My anger softened as I responded, "I suppose I should thank you for that mercy at least. I wouldn't have survived the Palace had it not been for them. Birgit has made a fine and fair Head Dungeon Mistress, and I dare say has saved enough silvers to have paid back her good fortune a hundred times over."

The Elder nodded with a bitter smile breaking across his face, "A better choice to mother the next generation of the unlucky couldn't have been made. I've never discovered her origins, but I suspect that lady and her sister fell to Earth from Heaven." He chuckled lightly.

I nodded. "Maybe. So, you have explained how King Lucus and that shady bitch Gretta got here. Still, I think you attempt to avoid telling me the rest of the lie you've concocted regarding that motherfucker Peter. Get to it Claus."

He stopped laughing and glared at me barely veiling his fury as he spat back, "I don't avoid shit. All that I've said had a lot to do with the circumstances of Peter's failure to take his place as Monarch of Monarchs. Now, be still and I will continue.

Peter had been thirteen the year the Stasi came. His place among us remained a bit of a mystery for the remaining three years during the restructuring of the House. He was rarely seen in the halls, and when spotted at all, Xavier was not far behind.

I was so busy trying to liberate my enslaved brothers and sisters, I didn't have much time to visit Ingrid to inquire about his health. She would tell me a few years later, Xavier had seemed to have broken Peter to his will.

However, she had faith Peter's legitimate anger over his harsh treatment would save the day. Just to be sure though, she spent many hours preparing Rachel to successfully seduce her would be husband. If anyone in the House knew how to wrap a man's heart around a finger, it would be your grandmother.

Within those first three turbulent years, the Russian Guards you know so well, dug in and Ivan was introduced to us as the captain of them all.

The first floor slowly filled up with the newly freed Dominants and those members reclaimed from the ravaged countryside. The second and fourth floor apartments welcomed the wealthy among us. The third floor remained open for the hundreds of rich visitors coming to enjoy all the thrills the House could offer them.

The fields recovered, the flocks grew in number, and the coin flooded in. By Peter's fifteenth birthday in 1953, the House could once again afford to outsource a skilled labor force.

Unfortunately for untold numbers of helpless children, the villages no longer sent their orphans to the dungeon back doors. This lack of willing submissive material resulted in Xavier and Jonas contacting the underground markets that specialize in human trafficking.

Soon, the only outsiders more commonly witnessed heading to the seventh floor than some fat-cat dignitary looking for kicks was the shady figures of coyotes. Xavier brokered deals of unimaginable numbers until in only a few months the House dungeon barracks were once again teeming with crying, lost, unlucky youngsters. Hemmel, Noah, Heidi, and Helga worked day and night preparing these unwilling recruits for their short lives of cruel subjugation.

The days of treating the lowest levels of House residents were long forgotten under Xavier's icy rule. He and Jonas bullied us Elder Princes and Voters into passing laws designed to prevent any collar from escaping their metal. They were not stupid enough to take away the hope of these poor hostages though.

Xavier and Jonas used the rumor mills to mislead the silvers into believing in a Dominance training program to persuade them to serve without argument. The Black collars were kept loyal by being paid a measly wage and given meager lodgings. They also managed to put a rift between the two colors by filling their ears with lies about the favor shown to each class by their betters.

As you are now aware, over time, silver and blacks came to believe the lot of the other was much more rewarding than their own. This universal resentment prevented the two groups from unifying in rebellion against their torturous oppressors.

I felt like a coward, and I was one too. Xavier had grown so powerful, no one dared to refute anything he did or demanded, no matter how awful it was. He'd successfully murdered most of his open opponents, and those of us that hated him had to remain silent or join them.

Other than Ingrid, Rachel, Malfred, and Bladrick, and I was still nervous that he wasn't to be trusted, I had to assume anyone else would betray any plot against our Fur and Silk Kings. And so, it was in this environment of fear and terror that Ingrid sent Rachel into action to capture the stoney heart of the Prince of Kaiser House.

Ah, Rachel was perhaps the most beautiful weapon I have ever laid my eyes upon, my boy. Mother nature had blessed that young lady with an arsenal more impressive than that of Aphrodite.

Despite her many hard years since the War had stolen her family and changed her fortunes the twenty-five-year-old lady had retained her loving soul. Peter, as a fifteen-year-old spaz, was no match for her well-honed wiles. Claus chuckled briefly before continuing.

Because the number of FemDoms to Dominants was still horrifically unequal at that time, Ladies of the House were treated like treasure most rare no matter her status. Even the violent Xavier was unwilling to impose severe penalties on any of them, even if one was accused of a crime. Women like your mother and Gretta have often abused the attitude regarding the fairer sex that is left over from the war.

Peter, his reluctant protégé, also had been brainwashed into believing House females were to be treated with nothing but the highest of respect. Therefore, it was easy enough for Rachel to manage to meet the Prince of Kaiser Haus without fear Xavier would block her attempt to gain Peter's attention.

I wasn't witness to the first time the infamous lovers set eyes upon each other, but Ingrid was. She said the second Peter's gold gaze focused on the blond beauty, he was blinded by her. Rachel stole the prince away from the Fur King's grasp without a bit of struggle. From that day forward, nothing Xavier did or threatened to do would stop Peter from following his Princess anywhere she told him to go.

With a loud snort I said, "Come on Claus. This is the biggest lie you are attempting to feed me yet. No way a woman was able to enslave Peter to her will. I don't care how gorgeous you claim this Rachel woman to be, Peter always fucks his lovers and leaves them heartbroken. It's no secret around that House that he lets his cock lead him around, but

I've never heard any rumors that anyone has ever been capable of taken him hostage by it. And I heard tale there have been many who tried."

Claus shot me a glance that appeared cautious as he replied, "I don't deny the stories about Peter's unhinged sexual conquests are truth. That man has surely been intimate with almost everyone in, and around, the House by now. His indiscretion in partners wasn't always the case. I suspect there is a damaged psychology that drives him from bed to bed, but that's not relevant to the story of his failure to take his rightful place as Prince of the House."

I shrugged, "Okay, fair enough. So, he fell in love with Rachel, a woman ten years older than him. I suppose you are going to tell me her death is what caused him to become the bastard he is today? If so, go ahead. Try to get me to feel sorry for him that life wasn't kind to him. I dare you."

Claus rolled his eyes and said, "I will do no such a thing, boy. You listen closely to the story of the fall of Peter because I believe with all my dark heart there is a lesson in it for yours.

Anyway, Xavier was at first very angry that Peter defied him by publicly courting Rachel the fifth chair Voter. It was during this time that the prince began to demonstrate admirable strength against his evil adoptive father.

It's the truth, Xavier wasn't the brutishly built fellow anymore. The boy however, had grown into the robust young man that could tolerate a lot more pain than the tiny child he once had been. That fact afforded Peter the power he needed to deny the Fur King's attempts to beat him back into submission to him.

Ingrid was also helpful in Peter's bid to gain his freedom from Xavier's grip. Your grandmother provided the young lovers ample opportunities to find alone time together. It didn't take the overly ripe Rachel long to announce the long-awaited child of our dreams had taken root within her womb.

Once Doctor Britton verified Rachel wasn't imagining her delicate condition. Ingrid thwarted Xavier's finding out about this potentially damaging situation before she could clinch the deal. I was there in the Great Hall dining along with the other Elders the night Ingrid announced the good news.

Xavier and Bladrick were deep in conversation about a potential new House member, when the Fur Queen shot me a smile with a wink across the table.

She took to her feet and tapped her wine glass with a silver spoon to command the attention of all the Great Hall diners as she said, "Honorable Brothers and Sisters. Please lend your attention to your unworthy Queen. I wish to share amazing information with all the treasures of Das Kaiser House. Our beloved Prince, Peter Schmit has chosen to honor a lucky lady among our number with a bond of blood. In response to her Prince's favor, his bride has blessed all of us with the gift of a Prince or Princess of the third generation. Please stand up honored Voter Rachel. Allow this House to see their new Queen of Queen, and future mother of the Thrones. I wish to welcome you my beloved daughter by embracing you and my grandchild with my most humbled arms."

Rachel didn't hesitate to take to her feet. She then rushed across the room from her place at the Voter's dining table eager to receive the Fur Queens blessing while thunderous clapping from every onlooker rocked the Great Hall.

I stole a glance at Xavier and had to cover my mouth with a napkin to hide my smile. He was glaring at Peter who sat across from him. I noticed the Prince was defiantly refusing to look to his lap in shame over the announcement of his secretly marrying and fathering a child behind the Fur King's back. Xavier's face was red with underlaying fury that somehow his little plaything had managed to outfox him.

I admit while I watched this exchange between Peter and Xavier, I silently prayed for the first time in many years. Only it wasn't to request God grant Peter a son. It was that our Creator would send a lightning bolt from the heavens and strike Xavier dead that very moment.

Looking back on that night, I suppose deep inside I knew if someone very powerful didn't end Xavier's life, my plan for the House take over was doomed. Ingrid was smart to make it widely and legitimately known that the Prince of Princes had formally deposed him. Had he found this out before everyone else, he no doubt would have destroyed Peter to prevent him from rising before Xavier was ready to step down, if he ever would be.

You see, because this had been made public, it wouldn't be so easy for Xavier to undo the very plan he set into motion. In his hurry to keep his family in control for all time, he'd accidentally knocked himself right off of the throne. Worse than not being in control of when Peter would take the Fur throne, was his impudence at selecting the name of the woman that would behave as the Regent and mother of the Silk King. If he killed Peter now, it would be no different if any regular Dominant murdered the Fur King."

I gasped then leaned closer as I whispered, "Wait a second, Claus. Are you saying because Ingrid announced Peter married and got Rachel pregnant the Peter was the Fur King?"

Claus shot me a mischievous grin as he nodded and replied, "I believe that is what I just said."

I shook my head and said, "But he was only fifteen years old you said. And he certainly wasn't the Fur King when I met him. Plus, no one and I mean no one, told me any of this shit. If Peter had even been the Fur King someone would have said something. You are lying. You go to be."

I confess this is what I said to Claus. But inside my head I thought if this was truth, Ryker, Felix, Rolf, Leo, Justus, Jonas, Jacob, Cary, everyone had kept me from finding this out and that meant no one could be trusted.

Claus clicked his tongue then replied, "There is a good reason you never heard of the year that Peter reined as the King of Kings."

I gasped and nearly choked on my spit as I said, "Year? What the fuck. What happened?"

He nodded then his expression went dark as he replied, "Dammit boy. I've been trying to tell you. So, my plan worked. Xavier and Ingrid were relieved of their duties as King and Queen, and of the seventh-floor apartment. There wasn't a person among the masses not happy to see the pair of Elders sent to live in an empty apartment on the third floor. Even Xavier's hard-core ground level supporters turned their backs on him. Instead, the House celebrated the rise of the legendary King of Kings and his beautiful wife, the kindhearted Rachel. Everyone believed the dynasty of Peter and Rachel would lead us out of the ashes of destruction into a new era of peace.

Peter was too young and unpolished to be of much use in healing the House ills at first. Rachel, ever the loving partner, stepped up and despite her fragile condition did her best to help him grow into his role. Together they managed to gain control of the Voters and end the worst of the wasting of our most precious resources, the silver collars.

Most in the House were patient with the young King and Queen. We all understood, like it or not, if we couldn't meet the annual fines set down by the Stasi, the outcome would be devastating for everyone in the House, even the enslaved classes.

That said, a solution that was both workable and humane wasn't an easy thing to conceive. Peter's faith and love for Rachel's good counsel was admirable but unfortunately his weakness. The poor girl, while a strong leader at first, suffered a difficult pregnancy. Within three months of their takeover, the doctor ordered our Fur Queen to bed rest. She was not to be stressed for any reason as it could compromise the unborn prince or princess.

Peter was forced to continue the nearly impossible task of bringing the House to heels on his own. Much as we expected, he began to lean heavily upon your grandmother for advice after Rachel was leashed to her room.

Things had started slowly improving over the next several months. The coyotes were not such a common sight anymore. The young recruits in the dungeons were being treated as kindly as possible given their stations. The black collar workers got raises, and their rents prices lowered. The public displays of torture for outsiders' entertainment were abolished. Anyone caught abusing a silver or taking bribes from wealthy patrons to look the other way while they did it were severely punished. A few House members that were caught committing the worst crimes were executed.

Things were truly looking bright the day Peter welcomed his son Emmerick into the world, exactly eight months and four days after he rose to the throne."

With a growl I interrupted, "Wait a second, Claus. I believe you said Rachel died while expecting."

Claus glared at me as he said, "She did boy. Shut the hell up and let me finish please. Emmerick was born in 1954 and the legend of the Monarchs of Monarchs was completed. This meant that Jonas's days as the Silk King were over. The second Emmerick took his first breath, Rachel assumed the role as Regent Queen of the Silk, and the Vampire was sent to live next door to Xavier."

I sighed loudly and responded, "Oh, okay. I don't think you need to finish this story. I found it hard to believe Xavier would sit on his thumbs and allow Peter to steal his throne. But that shady fucker Jonas wouldn't be so tolerant. He killed Rachel to keep his Vampire ass in that seat, didn't he?"

The Elder groaned and replied, "I wish I knew boy. Truth is that the mystery of who is or was responsible for the death of our beloved Silk Prince and his Regent mother is one I have never solved. Perhaps, one day you will uncover an answer that has escaped me for nearly twenty-two years.

As it was, Jonas did as commanded and moved off the fifth floor without quarrel. He knew Peter was aching to send him to suck on a Russian rifle. That bastard might be arrogant, but he isn't stupid. Rachel took the throne of the Voters, with the tiny Prince Emmerick in her gentle lap.

But not even three months passed when to our thrill and astonishment the Silk Queen reported Peter had blessed her womb yet again. Their love for each other was evident in both the emotional and the physical, so most of us assumed in no time the House would burst with Bernt's grandchildren.

It was around this time, Malfred showed up at my apartment interested in collecting the remaining favor he held with me. You see, it wasn't just his freedom from the silver he bargained with me to give up his precious Rachel to Peter.

A silver of uncommon grace, charm, beauty, and value had risen from the dungeons. Her name was Tamina. Malfred had become smitten with her but didn't have a penny to his name. Her collar belonged to a no account fourth floor Dominant, and this fellow was quite cruel to the helpless girl.

He wanted me to find a way to purchase Tamina for him. Even back then, Elders were forbidden the ownership of silvers. He knew I could easily turn her over to him without having to explain myself.

I tried to talk him out of this silly idea. The laws about a silver being unable to break a collar unless they were high born were not abolished. It didn't appear that it was going to change any time soon either. But Malfred wouldn't listen. He loved this girl, and believed with all his heart she was the fair trade for the one he had to let go.

Well, I went to this low life Dominant and tried to bargain for Tamina. He wasn't open to negotiations. After several attempts to get him to relent his claims, I decided to remove his voice of refusal, permanently. The fellow tripped down the stairs right into his grave, and Tamina went up for auction.

During the war, Xavier had warned me that my homosexual nature and interest in cross dressing was dangerous. I was told to get rid of all the beautiful dresses and fine jewelry my beloved Keifer had gifted me during our marriage. Well, fuck that. I disobeyed the order by hiding all my pre-war possessions.

You see at that time I was living in the apartment that Voter Rolf now lives in. After Keifer died, one day I was grieving and went to my closet to find the dress he loved on me the best. I knew being caught in it was a crime, so I hid myself inside while I put it on. It was cramped, and I tripped over a pair of my best pumps. I fell into the wall and to my astonishment instead of holding my weight it gave way to revealing a secret room.

Apparently, an unknown Voter in the House's long history had created this amazing little hideaway for reasons lost to time. I have always believed Keifer was with me in spirit that day and he guided my lucky discovery. He must have known that one day it would be the only thing that could save the things from our life together from being found when the Russians sacked the House.

Thanks to that bit of providence, I was able to sneak into that apartment while the Voter Alice was at breakfast. In only a few moments I had retrieved a piece of jewelry that I sold for more than it cost me to win Tamina's collar auction."

I groaned loudly and put my hands over my face as I said, "Oh shit. So that is why Malfred went to you after Olaf told everyone he got Tamina pregnant. And the reason Malfred loaned her collar to you for that asshole to misuse in the first place. Fuck me. It's also why he targeted me in that gang raping shit and explains his interest in getting to

217

the Sixth floor. He wasn't really coming after the Fur Throne. He was trying to become Elder so he could get revenge on you without being executed for killing one below him in status."

Claus sighed and replied, "Ja. I can never apologize to you enough for not warning you about Malfred's righteous anger."

I removed my hand and stared at my lap as I said, "Your apology isn't a fair service return, Claus. I will murder you to make us even, but before I extract my refund I demand you tell me what happened to Rachel, and how did her death result in Xavier getting back the throne he apparently never earned in the first place."

The Elder nodded then said, "So, Rachel's second pregnancy wasn't the hardship Emmerick's had been. She was nearly six months along and all signs indicated Peter was about to become the proud pappa of a treasured daughter when…"

Chapter 14: Bloody Fallen Monarchs
and Frozen Winter Tyrant
Master Mad Maxx and submissive Meine Liebe

I was walking next to Peter up the main staircase. We were deep in a discussion of a proposed law change when a woman's scream ripped through the air. To our absolute horror, only seconds after that call of distress, a form flew past us headed to the first floor with speed. We were on the fourth level steps. The hapless victim no doubt had jumped, been pushed, or slipped from at least the fifth-floor banister.

The sight of watching a fellow resident fall to their death was disturbing. However, my terror was intensified as I realized I recognized the identity of the victim. It was without doubt poor Rachel I'd heard announce death had come to lay claim to her soul.

I shot a frightened glance toward the Fur King. It was obvious he too had realized it was his wife and his unborn daughter that we'd unwittingly witnessed die. Peter's color had turned pale and he stood there frozen to the spot too shocked to stir. Instinctually, I took off running, but not down to offer aid to the unsavable Mother Regent of the Silk King.

Nein, I hauled ass up the stairs hoping against hope to lay my eyes on the sonofabitch that had committed the foulest of crimes. I swear to you my boy, if I had been able to capture that fiend, I'd have ripped him to pieces with my bare hands right there and then.

Sadly, despite my quick actions I found the fifth, sixth and even the seventh floors devoid of life. Everyone suspected Xavier, Jonas or one of their dogs were behind the expectant mother's death. There was not a shred of evidence ever uncovered to prove it. Each person that stood to gain power by her demise managed to provide a solid alibi.

Only an idiot would have expected that these beasts did the dirty deed personally. I assumed – as did Peter, Ingrid and most in the House – they'd offered a favor or coin to someone that could slip past all eyes unnoticed. As you are aware, the fifth and sixth floors are forbidden to everyone in the House but to a select few. It seemed the most plausible explanation that they bribed one of the Voters or perhaps a black collar.

However I discovered that the whereabouts of every Voter and Elder were accounted for during the murder. None were in close enough proximity to have tossed her over and then manage to escape the scene without being seen. I then turned my attention to the fifth and sixth floor black collar staff.

Again, I encountered a brick wall. All the men and women assigned to the leaders had verifiable stories. One by one, I painstakingly traced their movements during the hours leading up to, during and after her death. I rapidly found myself running out of leads. It was as if Rachel and the baby had been pushed off the banister by a ghost.

That bastard Doctor Britton's autopsy report wasn't of any use in my investigation either. He stated his belief was that Rachel had tripped over the railing. Likely due to a fainting spell brought on by her difficult pregnancy.

As I told you already, there hadn't been any signs that Rachel was encountering trouble with this baby. Peter knew better than to listen to Doctor Britton's opinion on the matter. He, like most in the House, assumed the doctor's report was tainted with a well-placed bribe.

But there was nothing the Fur King could do but grieve. There simply wasn't any proof his adoptive father or the ex-Silk King were behind Rachel's death. So, with a broken heart and his toddler son held tightly to his chest, he buried the Regent Mother and his lost Princess.

I confess, I cried as hard that cold fall morning as I did the day I'd been the man in Peter's shoes. There wasn't a single resident in the House that didn't deeply mourn the loss of that great lady.

Well except Xavier, Jonas, and no doubt the murderer. I kept my drenched eyes on those two monsters throughout the entire funeral. You won't be surprised to hear neither man shed a tear. Though I can't be sure my sorrow wasn't playing tricks on me. I do believe Xavier cracked several smiles while he watched the House lay Rachel to rest.

The usually stoic Peter, believe it or not, demonstrated an epic display of intense agony. It took Bladrick, Barnum and Drexel working together to pull him off his wife's casket as the gravediggers started to lower her in the ground.

Believe me, you could hear him wailing for miles. In his pain, he threatened to execute anyone that dared to stop him from keeping his lover from being taken away from him. His Fur Princes ignored his empty curses.

Despite Peter's unmanly behavior of kicking and screaming the three Elders hauled him back to the gold Palace. The rest of Rachel's internment went without interruption.

For the next several weeks, the House residents weren't greeted by the sight of their young Fur Monarch or their even younger Silk King. The halls were traditionally silent of laughter or loud noises. That is of course customary for thirty days after the death of a monarch. While this tradition is one I honestly respect, I took it upon myself to pay Peter a visit.

There was this feeling that I couldn't shake. I feared Peter's love for Rachel was so powerful he might not recover without attempting to join his Queen.

When I knocked on the door, as usual his black collar lover greeted me. I informed Felix I had come by to offer my sympathetic ear to our grieving King. To my surprise, Felix stated Peter's need for affection was being amply attended to by him personally.

As you know, due to your own Shadow King's lessons, a Dominant doesn't enter the Dark Bond lightly. Felix and Peter's private relationship had long since been the topic of rumors. Only Peter can say when the two took the 'Oath of Condemnation" and officially bonded. That said, the news of Felix's special place in Peter's heart began to circulate only a few months before Rachel began her attempts to seduce the young Prince.

Despite my protests, Felix refused to allow me to speak to Peter. At that time, I was nearly powerless because I sat in the fifth Fur throne. The only person I could lobby to force the Fur King grant me audience was the Silk King. The problem with that was Emmerick was only nine months old and without a mother regent. It was this worrisome fact, among other pressing topics, I had wished to discuss with the Peter.

I knew Peter was aware of his duties to the House. Like it or not, the Foundation Laws bound him to select a fresh bride to act as the Regent for the immature Silk King. He was permitted the mercy of twelve months to properly mourn but not a day longer.

I wanted to convince him that it wasn't wise for the Fur King to waste precious time. He needed to dry his tears and start wooing an honorable candidate quickly. Otherwise, in his haste to beat the deadline, he might be forced into a disastrous match. I was worried Xavier, Jonas or any of their cronies might use Peter's weakened state to their advantage.

The air around me as I walked down the seventh-floor staircase that day seemed heavy with bad omens. It took all the strength I had not to turn back and knock Felix's stupid ass out of my way. Deep inside I knew if I couldn't get my message of warning to Peter first, someone else would.

It took a bit of patience, but I managed to catch Ingrid out without Xavier. She didn't even allow me to finish voicing my fears before the clever gal told me she'd already been examining prospective Regent Queens.

I felt a pang of relief as I asked her, "Do I know any of the lucky ladies you are considering?"

Ingrid cast a nervous eye down the hallway to assure we wouldn't be heard as she replied, "Yes and no. I've determined none of the typical FemDoms available in the House are worthy to act as Regent for our beloved Emmerick. Thankfully, I still managed to find the perfect girl for this job. Best of all she has been training for this position of power all her life. She also swears she will be loyal to our cause."

I was startled upon hearing this news as it too good to be true as I asked, "Oh thank God. Who is this amazing FemDom? I assume she is one of the fourth-floor ladies. I need not remind you the House residents won't be pleased if you are thinking of pairing their Fur King with less than the highest quality. Wait. How can we be sure Peter will accept your proposed match? The girl must be very special to capture his interest after he's lost so deep a love. When can I meet her?"

Ingrid chuckled sounding mildly anxious as she replied, "Calm down brother Claus. I know you are eager to plug the hole Rachel's loss has created in the power structure. But when it comes to dealings with the heart one must tread carefully. All will be revealed in good time, I swear it."

I frowned then leaned in close to Ingrid as I growled into her ear. "Do not think of us as such old friends that I won't call you out when I catch you attempting to lie. I noticed you still haven't given me the identity of our would-be savior. Dearest sister, if I have done something to cause you to question my trustworthiness, I beg you to tell me the conditions of my infraction against you. After all we have been through, I've earned at least the mercy of attempting to defend myself. I swear the allegations, whatever they may be, are false."

Your grandmother sighed then with a glance of fury whispered back, "You misunderstand me Claus. I didn't wish to divulge the plan in its entirety because I'm not sure

I can trust the one I've paid to see she is smuggled inside the House. I was trying to protect you as much as possible if her truthful name is ever realized."

I let out a wail that interrupted the Elder with suddenness as I yelled angrily, "Claus, shut up. Shut up. I don't want to hear anymore." I covered my ears tightly with my hands.

Claus yelled back, "You can try to ignore me, boy, but I refuse to deny you the answers you came here today to find out. Stop acting the ass. Did you really think the story of a legendary King Priceless was going to be fun to hear.?"

I dropped my hands and stifled the tears that began to form behind my eyes as I responded sounding defeated, "Agnette is the girl Ingrid selected to take Rachel's place as Regent to Peter's son. There it is said, so you don't have to. Now your wicked story is done. Please release me Claus. I'm sorry for so many things in my life but seeking you out to ask about that stupid dream I had is fast making it to the top of my list."

Claus blew out his breath and looked to the ceiling as he said, "If you've figured out the plot that led to your existence then I say you can go with my blessings. However, I know that you don't know. Tell me boy, why doesn't Agnette sit on the Fur Throne next to Peter? Why doesn't the Royal Emmerick sit on the Silk as he was born to do?

A tear ran down my bruised cheek as I replied, "Agnette did what she always does. She betrayed Ingrid. She took one look at Peter and tossed him aside for that old creep Xavier, thinking he was a better deal. Then the two of them threw Peter out of the Gold Palace and laughed while they did it. Peter was forced to hide out with his baby. No doubt Peter fucked the poor kid to death because he couldn't slip into the House to fuck anyone else. Agnette accidently got pregnant with me and decided to use me to blackmail Ingrid into giving her the Silk throne. When that didn't work, she ran away. I know she married Gerard and ran away from him too. Then she needed cash so she made him give me back to her. Then my mother sold me to Ingrid. As if that wasn't bad enough, then all you rat bastards used me to warm your cocks. Which all of you still do. There, see, I do know this story. Now can I fucking go?"

The Elder took on a look of disbelief appearing ready to cry himself as he said, "Oh my dearest boy. You are wrong on every detail. I can understand why you believe the worst of Ingrid, your mother and me, but I swear to you it didn't start out that way. I know I've caused you unfathomable pain and I apologize for it. However, I must now cause you far more. It is the only way to set you free. Not of the House, not yet anyway, but of demons that are born of misunderstanding. So, I can't make you hear my words, but I can and do order you to listen to them."

I began to openly weep as I replied, "Damn you Claus. I don't believe in God or the Devil, but I'm thinking it wouldn't hurt to summon Satan. Perhaps I could sell him my soul in return for the ticket I'd need to watch you burn in hell."

The Elder broke out in a sudden chuckle as he said, "Ah, but dear boy, no matter how hard you call out for Beelzebub he won't respond. He doesn't owe a service return to gain property he already possesses, ja?"

I spit out angrily, "Why don't you die already, old man? Go ahead. Pollute the air with your disgusting words and lies. After I kill you, I will cut off your head. Florian will happily accept your attempts at empty apologies for all eternity. The second I deliver you to his boney hold. I will dig up your precious Keifer and add his empty skull to the Priceless collection too. Then, in six months, I will be trapped with all three of you. Till the day I join Florian in his death, I will force my cock into both of your useless mouths and defile your worthless remains."

Claus began to laugh so hard he nearly fell out of his bed as he replied, "Oh my, you are dark, my boy. I must confess I've never found you sexier than at this moment. What a sad story for Claus. I'm too old and you're too damaged to further explore this most thrilling secret side of you I have never seen before. I do thank you for the mercy of that promise to honor me and my beloved Keifer with your amazing artistry long after I'm gone. I don't think it fair to speak for your uncle, but I can tell you till I breath my last I will fantasize about my most blessed fate to act as relief for the boy I loved the most."

I sniffled loudly, then squeaked out, "Shut up Claus. I hate you so much right now. I can't even think of anything bad enough to punish you for the harm you have caused me." I rubbed my tear-filled eyes roughly while whimpering like a little child.

Claus's humor ended abruptly as he replied with a pity filled expression, "Ah, poor little one. It's not like you to give up so easily. The Mortar King I know and love never admits defeat. Tell me something child, what color are my eyes?"

I glanced up startled by his question. The walls of his room melted rapidly into the stone barriers of my dungeon cell. I gasped in shock as the smell of damp straw and musty air filled my nostrils.

The sound of Noah's commands boomed out breaking me from my stupor, "God dammit Christian. Stop acting a fool. I said I want to wrestle." He grabbed my tiny shoulder and forced me to my face.

With a loud wail I screamed out, "Nein, I win Noah. I win. Nein, baah, baah. I break the spoon. You brat, God dammit."

Noah leaned into my ear and growled, "You didn't win the game, Christian. I said you had to be nice for Heidi. You bit her as usual. So, I get to wrestle. That was the agreement, remember?"

I shook my head wildly. "I don't bite Heidi. Nein, I eat the spoon. I win Noah. Nein baah baah. Nein wrestle."

He got off me and rolled me to my back then said while staring into my eyes. "Maybe you didn't bite her. I know she lies. I've seen the stripes she leaves on you. That bitch is relentless but not the worst thing that this House has to offer a pretty boy like you. I suppose you don't understand everything I say even after all these years together, but you are the closest thing I have to a friend. Please don't give me trouble about this little secret thing we do together Christian. I'm just so damned lonely. My father made sure I would never have a wife or lover by condemning me to this accursed dungeon for life. I know Hemmel and those twin bitches have no problem destroying little kids to fill their lusts. I am not them. It isn't right to ruin those poor kids like they do, nor to kill them. Isn't life terrible enough without adding to it? Oh, I don't know. Sometimes, I think maybe I would find peace by giving into the devils this House puts into everyone. But not today, not with you my little buddy. Now, you be the lamb and I will wrestle with you. After you do the great job you always do, I will give you candy. How does that sound?" He reached into his leather pants and produced a colorful wrapped candy bar holding it where I could see it.

I smiled with joy and nodded as I said, "Ja, ja. I eat candy. I do baah baah, Noah. Do the wrestling. Baah, baah," I yelled out in joy while I took to my hands and knees.

Noah chuckled and wrapped himself in the mounting position over me. "I swear to God I love you my little lamb. What would I do without you? If only the world were a different place, I could have you for a brother instead of that bastard I've been cursed with." He began his dry humping as I continued to bleat happily and ignorantly.

Noah's moans of pleasure suddenly went silent. I watched in horror as the straw rose from the stone floor until it had completely covered me. Choking dust filled my lungs. I attempted to scream. A hand reached into the pile and pulled me out. For a moment grime from the prickly stuff coated my vision with haze.

A voice I recognized as Gerard's boomed, "Goddammit, stop being stupid. When are you going to understand there is nowhere to hide? Get over there and eat that slop your stepmother worked so hard to make for you. Christ, you stink. Oh wait, that is that brother of yours creating that putrid smell. Guess that will teach him to piss me off, ja? Hahaha." He pushed my face into the dog bowl demanding I eat the nasty stuff in it.

I gurgled out, "Help, mor, mor. Ah!"

Gerard pulled me out of the mess and glared into my frightened eyes. "Why do you call for that bitch mother of yours? Where is she, huh? Do you see her here? Nein. She ran away and left you with me. I'm your daddy boy. Look here, see it is written on this paper." He reached into his suit jacket and produced an official document holding it where I could see it.

I shook my head wildly. "No, liar. Momma loves us. You are not my father. Momma, momma, help Maximillian. Help Christian. We are lost."

Gerard knew I couldn't read. He smiled evilly as he held it to his face and said, "Gerard Albrecht is the father and Agnette Kraus is the mother of Christian Axel and Maximillian Keifer. This is a birth certificate fool. You are my son, and so was that thing attached to you. I decided I didn't want two kids. Maybe if you keep pissing me off, I'll decide I don't want any. Now eat, you motherfucker." He forced my head back into the dog bowl.

I refused the food by locking my lips tightly. This angered Gerard beyond reason. He flung me into the wall. I whacked my head on the bolt that was holding the chain preventing my escape. The force of it sent me to the ground in a swoon. Gerard grabbed my hair and began to slap me anywhere his hand could make contact.

All I could do was cry and beg for mother to save us. I was too weak to fight back. The weather had been viciously cold and I was without proper clothing. I'd gone many weeks without much food. Gerard's cruel bondage had caused my limbs to become nearly paralyzed from lack of use.

Gerard finally tired of his brutality. He grabbed me by my threadbare shirt and tossed me into the wall once again. I landed but this time I remained still hoping he would believe I fainted. The ploy appeared to work. After a few moments of watching me closely, he picked up the dog bowl and left the way he'd come. I was once more alone with only my brother and the make-believe animals in our fantasy to keep me company.

I let out a grateful sigh and rose slowly from the prone position. I turned to check on my brother to see if he was alright after that terrible attack. Fear gripped me when I saw him laying with his back to me. I noticed right away he didn't seem to be breathing.

I gingerly rolled him over and let out a mournful wail. I was staring directly into the empty sockets of the mummified corpse that used to be, ah, no. A loud snap and intense stinging in my face woke me from the trance immediately.

I shook my head trying to clear away that gruesome sight from my memory while Claus let out a loud sigh then said, "So that's why you thought Gerard was your stepfather, but instead he was your abductor. I guess I'm not too surprised to learn of this latest cruelty he pulled on your troubled mind. Obviously, he was capable of almost any horrid thing given the crimes he committed against you and your brother. But I must say brainwashing you into thinking him your dad makes me wonder if he and Agnette planned to use you for more than just gaining entry into the House."

I stared at Claus angrily as I replied, "What the hell are you talking about? I thought you said Ingrid smuggled my mother into the House to marry Peter. If she wasn't successful, then I'd have to wonder if I've been misled into believing Xavier is my father. Otherwise, according to your story about everyone in the House being held as a prisoner, which couldn't be possible since not even the Fur King could leave if that were true. So, why would Agnette get involved with Gerard in a plot to get inside the House? You aren't making a bit of sense."

The Elder glared at me a moment then responded, "As it were, Agnette had been exiled by Ingrid after she became pregnant with you and your brother. Your grandmother didn't send your mother away to be cruel, she did it to protect Agnette's unborn children from becoming Xavier's victims."

I rolled my eyes as I said, "Again, I say you are becoming deranged Claus. If Xavier wanted to depose Peter as the Monarch of Monarchs, then why the hell would the old bastard injure any babies he managed to sire with my mother?"

Claus growled low in his throat as he replied, "Dammit you are an impatient bastard. I think you are attempting to deflect our conversation from your painful recovered past but have it your way. I will get back to the story and we will return to dig deeper into the things you've told me about Gerard's torture later.

Anyway, not even a few months after Rachel was lain to rest with Peter's daughter, Ingrid appeared at my apartment door. Only during this visit she wasn't alone. This was the first time I was to ever lay my eyes upon the woman that would lead to both my greatest pleasure and worst pains in this life.

It seems like only yesterday Ingrid stood there next to one of the most beautiful women I had ever seen. Agnette was the spitting image of her mother, before time and loss had taken its toll on her. Even as the gay man, I dare not deny your mother had more than her fair share of physical appeal.

Mind you this was before I knew her well, appeared demure, intelligent, and shy. There wasn't any doubt in my mind that this lovely girl was more than capable of capturing any man's heart she wanted. If only Agnette's heart had been as lovely as her face, well then every terrible thing that has happened in the last eighteen years wouldn't have happened.

There is no point in mourning for the glorious future that never was. The brutal truth is, the moment Agnette stepped foot into the halls of Kaiser House marked the beginning of the end for all of us. We just didn't know it.

The original plan was pretty simple as I told you. Ingrid brought your mother into our lives, expecting her daughter would easily seduce her way into the role of Regent for the Silk King. I hate to admit to it but Ingrid and I rejoiced upon watching our grieving Monarch fall under Agnette's spell. The girl didn't even have to try too hard. The minute Peter laid his eyes on her he was her slave.

Unfortunately, our Fur King wasn't alone in his desire to possess the gorgeous lady with a mysterious past. I doubt there was any man from the first to the sixth floor that didn't do his damnest to capture the attentions of Agnette.

This alarming fact did two things that neither Ingrid nor I had anticipated. First, it caused the initially insecure Agnette to begin growing into the arrogant bitch you had the misfortune to know. The second more serious result was Peter became dangerously paranoid of the House residents and possession of Agnette.

He started to shirk his duties both to his throne and to his son. His behavior was pure madness. Believe me when I tell you, Peter stopped at nothing in his bid to maintain constant surveillance on the movements of his bride to be.

To be fair, Peter had just suffered the pain of losing Rachel after enduring terrible torture all his young life. Being a little worried that something bad would happen to his latest effort to find joy should have occurred to us. It didn't help this dangerous situation that Agnette was openly thrilling in her new status as the most coveted woman in the House.

You are aware of your mother's habit of openly flirting with anyone that granted her an ounce of attention. So, I won't bother boring you with discussing too many details about her disgraceful actions with Peter. It suffices to say, Agnette wasn't coy about letting him know he'd better give in to her every whim or else she'd seek out someone who would.

Ingrid did her best to keep Agnette's willful nature in check, but the girl refused to listen to her mother's good counsel. Instead, that idiot woman upped the pressure on Peter by increasing her demands for money, jewels, and undivided devotion. This last imperative led to Peter's utter neglect of his baby son's safety and good welfare.

Ingrid did her best to take up the slack by pleading with him to allow her to manage the baby Silk King's needs. Peter, however, still viewed Ingrid with extreme distrust. He honestly believed she was at the very least complacent with the harsh treatment he'd been victim to at Xavier's command, if not an instigator of it.

For the next few months, the House residents prepared for the epic wedding that would unit their Fur King with his latest obsession, Agnette. Emmerick took his first steps and had his first birthday. Both milestones were ignored and uncelebrated by his distracted father.

As for Agnette, she took this time to become overly familiar with the one person in the House whose appearance was more shrouded in mystery than her own, Jonas the Vampire.

I gasped then whispered to Claus, "I must confess, Justus shared his diary from this time with me a bit ago. His entries had suggested that my mother had been the Bat's lover."

The Elder sighed while he nodded then said, "Of course Justus was correct my boy. He of all the people in the House would know the details of the shady relationship between Agnette and Jonas since he was involved in it."

I nearly choked on my spit as I blurted out, "Justus helped Jonas seduce my mother is what you are saying?"

Claus nodded again then replied, "You bet he did. You see Justus was angry with Ingrid because he felt she hadn't tried hard enough to get his father Xavier to recognize him as the rightful heir to the Fur Throne he believed himself to be. It wasn't true, but Justus is just as hardheaded as his real father Bernt ever was. When Xavier abandoned Justus in favor of Byron as his pick, instead of sending Byron to hell like he should have, he turned his hatred toward his mother Ingrid. Then when I managed to talk Ingrid into adopting Peter, well need I say more. Justus's fury at his mother was all consuming. I believe with all my heart that Justus was and still is intent on seeing that any plot Ingrid was involved in results in total failure. You'd be wise to keep eyes in the back of your head with regard to that man. Like most things in this House, Justus isn't the meek puppet he attempts to appear to be."

I glared at Claus for a moment then responded, "Why do you tell me this shit after I already raised that bastard to the status of Elder? I fucking bonded him to my worst enemy the Silk Queen too. Dammit Claus, if I am to believe Justus is the monster in disguise you say he is, then I must believe he, rather than Gretta, made sure I was the entertainment for that nasty Stasi Christmas party."

Claus groaned slightly as he sat forward and said, "How can you think to blame me for that error in your judgement boy? You didn't seek me out to ask any questions about that man's nature before you ordered him raised and married now did you?"

With a snort I replied flatly, "Why would I Claus? You have always been a liar to yourself and everyone else, including me. If I ever doubted that, and I didn't, you have been God damned sure to spend the last several hours reminding me of it."

The Elder smiled bitterly as he responded, "Touche! I suppose there is no reasonable defense to your correct assessment of me as the king of lies. Despite that, I need you to believe that no matter the evil I've done in my life, everything I've said to you today is the truth. Justus is dangerous. Not just because he is fraught with unjustified resentment that his greatness has been underused, but also because he is aware you are the real heir to the thing he covets the most in this world. Not to mention he has spent all his life cultivating a reputation as being a mealy mouthed, weakling without friend or connection."

I leaned back into his bedpost and crossed my arms as I said, "Alright, I will be wary of Justus, but that isn't an admission that I believe a thing you say."

Claus nodded then said, "Fair and good enough. As I was saying, as the big wedding approached, Ingrid's attempt to prevent the fall of Peter from the throne unraveled. It's unclear how deep Xavier's fingers were in the plot to see himself reinstated. I don't doubt he had a major part to play in it or at the very least pulled the strings from behind the scenes.

However, Agnette, Justus, and Jonas's role in the mess is not disputed. About a week before the blessed wedding day, the Vampire made his move. Justus helped that dirty bastard by coaxing the Fur King to join him for a few celebratory drinks in his apartment.

Peter and Justus arrived at his third-floor apartment door, just in time to catch a glimpse of Agnette sneaking into Jonas's. It goes without saying Peter was beyond livid over seeing his bride to be carrying on a secret affair with his sworn enemy only moments before they were to take vows of monogamy.

I had been visiting Ingrid and Xavier only two apartments away when that hell between the promised lovers broke loose. The three of us had barely come out into the hallway to investigate the cause of Peter's shouts of anger before shrieks of horror rang out from the floors above us.

If I close my eyes, I can still hear Emmerick's nursemaid as she desperately screamed, "Oh my God. Blood is everywhere. The little King is broken. Call the House doctor. Please help." All of us, even Justus rushed toward the sounds of the pleading woman.

The sight awaiting us in Emmerick's sixth floor apartment was one right from the depths of hell. In the center of his bedroom sat a tiny bed with white bed sheets stained red with clotting blood. Each of the four bedposts had been tied up with rope that had obviously been used to restrain the tiny boy while his attacker assaulted him. Then on the floor next to this gruesome scene lay a discarded blade. It was soaked in crimson, no doubt the weapon used upon the child to end his torment.

Everything an investigator would require when piecing together this horrific crime was there for all to see. Except for the most important item, the king himself. The knots no longer held their tiny victim, and the rest of the room appeared devoid of any sign of him. While there was no body, the sheer amount of life giving bodily fluid assured that wherever his killer had stashed him, Emmerick was a corpse."

I sucked in my breath then said in a near whisper, "Wait, someone stabbed Peter's little baby to death. But who could have done something so terrible Claus? If Xavier, Jonas, Agnette, Justus, and Ingrid were all on the third floor together, then who could have done it?" I winced at the concept that anyone could be cruel to an innocent year-old child even in the House.

Claus's eyes glistened with hatred as he replied, "Oh my dear boy if only I knew the identity of the culprit. I swear to all that is unholy I would have ripped the sonofabitch eyes and cock out by the roots if I could find him.

In fact, I can almost assure you, I wasn't the only person in this House that would have enacted the most brutal of torturing had the one responsible for the death of Emmerick. You see, at first glance it seemed the killer had escaped taking the Silk King with him.

It took mere moments after our arrival for Ingrid's overly vigilant eyes to spot a pair of tiny feet sticking out from under the savaged bed. An unearthly wail escaped her throat while she rushed to pull her deceased baby grandson from his place below the mattress.

Oh my God the sight of Emmerick's terrorized flesh was soul wrenching. His little eyes were open wide, and on his tiny face was fixed an expression of pure horror. When the inconsolable Ingrid lifted him to cradle in her lap, a flood of crimson poured from his backside onto her dress.

Doctor Britton would later verify during his autopsy what no man or woman in the room that day could deny. Emmerick's cause of death wasn't from that knife. Someone had violated the baby boy so violently; he'd succumbed to shock and blood loss before the killer got around to slitting his throat. The monster that took his life hadn't even bothered to attempt to hide the evidence of his soiling that precious treasure."

I let out a cry and then through budding tears interrupted the Elder, "Nein. Claus, I can't listen to this sickening story you are telling anymore. A twin brother's mummified corpse attached to my collar in Gerard's barn, then I got buried alive, after cutting myself up with a razor, while you spent your youth murdering children in the dungeon, and now you tell me that some pervert in this House raped Peter's newborn baby to death. And you tell me all this on top of what I personally can prove I've suffered within these walls. Christ, what the fuck is wrong with you, pervert? Don't you think I've enough nightmares to keep me awake for the rest of my life without this cruel attempt to add more?"

Claus's eyes began to leak tears as he replied, "I can't do anything to change the past boy. Please understand, these things I share with you are all I can do to alter your future. It's not my goal to cause you more pain by telling you the events of Emmerick's death. I want you to do your best to view my sharing these appalling details and notice the familiarity of them."

I shook my head while my own eyes became wet with water and said, "Claus, nein. I can't. I won't."

He reached out and grabbed my arm, pulling me toward him as he said sternly, "You can and you will boy. You asked for the answers. Surely you didn't expect them to be pleasant ones. I've served you perfectly in your request, but now it is time for you to return the favor. Tell me about that morning that Peter tricked a little boy into wearing his collar."

My breathing began to become shallow as the walls melted around me into the dank stone of the dungeon cell.

I huddled in the corner behind the fort I'd built from straw. I was keeping myself busy thinking over the events happening in my deary world over the last few days.

A man with gold eyes, named Peter, had been showing up to watch while Heidi forced me to sit still on her classroom desk. The way that strange man looked at me made me nervous. I'd asked Noah about him. He laughed and told me that this man was interested in buying me. Then Peter would be my Master, whatever that was. Noah had told me one day he was going to take me up the steps to serve as a slave to someone's every command.

I didn't like the idea of being forced to mind some mean person's rules. I wanted to stay in the dungeon with my friend Noah. Besides, this guy named Peter reminded me of that horrible Gerard and another man with lots of wrinkles I saw once a long time ago. I had decided to get rid of Peter by misbehaving and ignoring Heidi's orders. I'd gotten thudded for acting the ass, but I'd decided a few beatings were worth it if it made Peter go away.

My deep thoughts were interrupted by the sound of the stone door coming open. I watched Noah come into the cell. His face wore an expression that made fear race up my spine. I'd not seen him looking this worried since I'd been very small.

He approached me slowly, cleared his throat then said, "Christian, my little friend, the day I've dreaded has finally arrived. Orders have come that you are to be taken above. I knew this would eventually happen, but I didn't realize how much it would break my heart to say goodbye to you."

I startled over his words, some of which I still couldn't understand. "Nein, Noah. I don't go to stairs. I stay with spoon. I don't bite. Goddammit brat," I yelled back at him.

Noah chuckled gently then with a sad expression in his eyes replied, "Please stop speaking, Christian. I swear I can't keep my stoic demeanor if you do. The laughter you've given me over the years with your brutalization of our language is only a tiny part of the thing I love about you the most. Oh God, what will I do without you here to make my ghastly existence worth enduring? Who will I wrestle with now that you're leaving me?"

I rushed forward and took to all fours as I yelled out wildly, "Nein, Noah. I don't go to stairs. I play wrestle, ja? Nein to Peter. Baah, baah. I don't bite spoon. Stupid brat. I beat you to death, ja. Please help momma. Baah, baah."

Noah walked over and pulled me to a kneel and knelt in front of me while staring into my eyes as he said in a calm tone, "Nein wrestle, Christian. Not today. Not anymore. Listen my little lamb, you must mind Peter like I taught you to do or he will beat you. You don't like the beatings, ja?"

I shook my head and replied, "I don't like beating. Please help Noah. Nein Peter. I stay lamb, Noah. Please? I wrestle, baah baah, ja?" I attempted to pull his hands to take me by the waist while I again fell forward to take the lamb wrestle position for him.

Noah forced me back to my knees and to my horror I saw tears running down his cheeks as he said, "Christian, I know you don't understand but please don't make Peter angry. Do what he says to do and one day we will meet again. If you deny him his revenge, he will kill you for it. He believes this house owes him for what it took away from him. It's unfair that you must pay the bill Xavier and Ingrid have made but it is your fate. Always has been. I love you little lamb, far more than I thought I could love anyone. I want you to promise never to forget that. No matter what they do to you above us in this hell hole, Noah will always and forever be your friend. They will try to lay claim to your dignity, your mind, and your soul, but try as they might, they can't take our special bond away from us if you don't let them. One day, if you survive, you will be a powerful King. When that happens come find Noah. I will give up everything, even my life, if need be, to bring you the happiness you brought to this worthless man."

I stared into his tearful eyes and replied, "I love you Noah. I am your lamb, ja? I do happy for Noah." I reached up and stroked his wet face with a peaceful smile.

He shivered at my touch but smiled back and said, "Ja, you are, and I thank you for the mercy of it. Now, I am going to release your chain. Follow me and don't fight or I will have to beat you for it." I watched as he used his key to unhitch the chain from my silver manacle.

I quietly stood up and then took a place behind him as he led me to the door of the cell. The second he opened it; I immediately disobeyed his order by taking off in a run down the dungeon hall. I had no idea where I was going, but I did understand the stairs that led above is a trip I wasn't willing to take.

Within only moments Noah, and the huge Dungeon Master called Hemmel were in hot pursuit. My youth and nibble legs prevented them from easily capturing me. I dodged and zig zagged hauling ass as fast as I could down the dark, dank corridors of that underground world, headed for nowhere.

I rounded a crumbling corner of the eastern block of the holding cells and ran smack into a hooded figure. The force of that unexpected collision sent the mysterious person to their knees and me to my back. A yelp barely escaped my mouth before Hemmel and Noah lit upon my momentarily helpless frame.

It goes without saying the two big men had me bonded in ropes before I could struggle or offer protest of worth.

Once I was subdued, the strange fellow in the black robe motioned the Dungeon Masters to back off me. I laid there trembling as the man knelt on the floor so he could force a piece of chocolate into my mouth. I tried to spit it out, but he held my jaws closed while pinching my nose off. I had no choice but to swallow the candy or smother for refusal.

A drowsy feeling overcame me quickly after I dispatched the delicious treat. The hooded man backed away and motioned Noah to him.

The man's voice sounded as if it was under water as he said to Noah, "Hurry up and get him to Peter's apartment. Don't let anyone see you and don't ever repeat anything you see or hear from this moment until you return or you know what will happen to you."

Noah cast an anxious glance at me as he replied, "Please don't do this honorable Elder. He is a sweet kid. If for no other reason I wish you'd reconsider because he isn't ready for this. He still can't speak German worth a shit and he barely can dress himself. His mind has not fully recovered as it is."

The hooded man raised his hand to command silence then said, "Shut up and do your job, Noah, or far worse than is going to happen to this boy is in store for you."

Noah scoffed then growled out, "Worse than a life of nothing? Go ahead and threaten me all you like. Won't do you a bit of good. Just know the only reason I'm going along with this bullshit is because I believe with all my heart one day he will make you sorry for it. All of you." He shot a glance at Hemmel as he said that.

His hood quaked as he chuckled and replied, "Oh do you think so, Noah? Well, now wouldn't that be something if he could. In fact, the idea that this little bastard will give me a run for my money has created much thrill in my old soul for many a sleepless night. Do you hear that, little nothing? Noah says you are going to get me. Try if you dare boy. I look forward to it."

My eyelids were heavy, but I listened to his voice intently. The sound of it seemed vaguely familiar. I just knew I'd heard it before but I couldn't recall where.

Noah lifted my bonded frame into the air. He gently placed me over his shoulder. It seemed like a dream as the two of us glided down the dark halls, finally reaching the dreaded stone steps that led to the top floors of the House. The Dungeon Master traveled with silence between us as he took the trip up the stairs onto the first floor.

I could barely hold off the urge to slumber as the amazing sights of the huge mansion came into my view. I couldn't believe the size, wealth, and opulence that surrounded us on every side. Nothing seemed real as Noah rapidly tore up the main staircase of the Kaiser House.

Quietly I counted the steps as we ascended to the third-floor platform. Then, Noah took off down the hallway, headed for what I would soon learn was Peter's apartment. All that time, the Dungeon Master had kept silent. The bewilderment of the meaning of all this strangeness had stolen my own tongue. I could do nothing but glance around unsure if I should be frightened or in awe of what was going on.

Noah halted in front of a door at the end of a long line of many and before he knocked, he said in a low but stern tone, "Christian Axel, though I want nothing more than for you to never forget me or everything you have suffered in your short life. If you are to have any chance at survival in this hellish place, you must. At least for now. I paid close attention to the things your benefactors have tried in their feeble attempts to bring you back from the abyss of your madness. So, listen to me closely, you must complete the mission. If you want to find your brother, you must find the green fields. He is there waiting for you to save him. Christian, you must follow the lambs. See there? Felicity knows the way."

A dizziness followed by intense confusion overcame my senses. I saw the lambs standing in the green fields under the mountains. A black hole blighted the beautiful scenery. I knew, that was the place I would find him, my long lost brother.

I let out a gasp as Peter threw me onto his bleach white sheets. I struggled in the ropes wildly as the naked man crawled onto the bed behind me. With a wail of terror, I attempted to wriggle off to escape whatever insanity my Master was pulling this time. I didn't yet understand the gravity of his strange request for the mysterious special services. But something about the entire thing indicated I should be frightened.

Peter halted my flight to safety by snatching me by the ankle. He dragged me back to the center of his bed and forced me to my face. I whimpered and called out for my mother as the big man drove my legs apart and took a place between them.

He leaned down and put his lips to my ear and whispered, "You will endure what you must. Maximillian. I would apologize for the pain, but there is no avoiding it. No matter how brutal you may find this act, it's nothing compared to what Emmerick was made to suffer. In a few moments no one will be able to steal what belongs to me ever again." Peter chuckled briefly then returned to his upright position.

My heart raced in total terror as the big man held me in place with one hand and began to ready himself and me for his consumption. AHHHHHHHHH!"

I awoke with a start to find Claus staring at me with his eyes wide in apparent shock. "Wake up, boy." He backhanded me again.

"Claus, stop hitting me, dammit. Why did you give me over to Peter? You knew what he was going to do. And Noah, that fucking rat. How the fuck did you make me forget everything that happened in the Dungeon that horrible night?" I wailed out feeling that I was going to explode as the truths of my miserable existence continued to replay in the repeat across the wheelroom screen.

Claus released his hold on me and then, still appearing deep in surprise said, "If your memory is correct, then surely, you've realized I'm just as confused as you are right now. This is the first I've heard that Noah, Hemmel and some unknown conspirator was also involved in Peter's betrayal of the plan Ingrid and I set into motion. I always assumed Peter took advantage of our being distracted by your grandmother's illness but this is far deeper than any of us ever knew."

I glared at Claus angrily as I replied, "So, you deny that was you in the hooded cloak that night in the dungeon? You better not try to point a finger at Ingrid or Agnette either. That voice I heard was male, not a female. If it wasn't you then who the fuck was it?"

He shrugged then said, "Only you can answer that question. Was it Bladrick? Or perhaps Drexel, Barnum, Olaf, or Byron maybe? You said you recognized it, ja? Think hard."

With a snort I closed my eyes and returned to that moment in my memory, listening to the sound of the hooded figure's voice hard. Suddenly, I realized where I'd heard it before.

My lids flew open as I wailed out full of despair, "The man in the cloak was my father. Xavier sacrificed me to Peter because, because, oh my God. He helped Peter betray all of you but never told him he did. Xavier knew by doing this if push came to shove Peter would be guilty of the same crime he'd surely claim against his adoptive father. Xavier did this in a perfect service by letting him rape his son in return for raping Peter. But that can't be right, Peter doesn't know I am Xavier's son. Does he?"

Claus shook his head slowly then sighed as he replied, "Nein, he doesn't. Far as I know or knew until now only Ingrid, Agnette, myself, Bladrick, and Noah knew your true identity."

That made me grimace as I responded, "Well you were wrong. Justus, Byron, and apparently Xavier knew it too. I'm afraid Rolf has also since figured it out. I suppose, not that it really matters anymore, you can finally put to rest the name of Emmerick's killer. I avenged that poor baby even though at the time I honestly didn't realize the scope of my father's brutality and perversions."

The Elder frowned and said, "Obviously you are partly correct. Xavier's role in the destruction of the baby Emmerick was never in question. At least not in mine or Ingrid's mind. He was the man that stood the most to gain if the Silk King died without a regent. However, I already told you that bastard was with me at the time Emmerick was misused to death. He'd hired someone else to do the unspeakable deed. That is the man I've waited a lifetime to throttle, at least as much as I ever desired to murder Xavier."

I narrowed my eyes at him as I replied, "You mean after all this time the criminal responsible for the death of Rachel, her daughter and Emmerick isn't immediately obvious to you? Seriously Claus, I thought you cleverer than you actually are."

The Elder snorted then spat out, "You dare to insult me? Okay smartass, if you think yourself a better sleuth than me, say the name of the man I intend to send to hell before I get there."

I chuckled evilly under my breath as I responded in a vicious tone, "You're too late, old man. I sent that demon to his justified end years ago. It was quite obviously Felix that sought Xavier's favor by enacting the cowardly acts of killing a pregnant woman and raping a baby to death."

Claus gasped then he said, "Shit, Felix, of course. As Peter's dark bonded, he would be capable of approaching Rachel without her becoming fearful of foul intentions. He also would have complete access to baby Emmerick's nursery, and more importantly be aware of the little King's nursing schedules. That sonofabitch. He knew due to his almost illegally infamous love for his Master Peter no one would ever suspect he'd do anything to hurt his beloved Fur King. But that is the point in question now isn't it? If he truly cared for Peter, why would he help Xavier destroy him?"

I chuckled with a hollow sound as I replied, "Claus, don't play coy with me. I do believe you are just about to answer your own question. That is if you ever get back to finishing this damned long winded story of yours."

The Elder grimaced as he said, "Ah, you are indeed one of the most intelligent people I've ever met, boy. Even if you are also the most insane. Yeah, the obvious culprit is Felix in the murders of his Fur King's family. With his legitimate Queen dead, his heir destroyed and his soon to be bride soiled by being publicly caught in an affair with the ex-Silk King Jonas, Peter was by House law unable to maintain his throne."

Felix knew he would have more access to an untitled Dominant than he ever could to a popular King. Xavier wasted no time demanding Peter be demoted the second Doctor Britton officially pronounced Emmerick dead. He also quickly pointed a finger at Agnette, implying that she was likely behind the deaths of both the Regent Queen and the infant King. She was immediately taken prisoner and ordered to be held in the dungeon until Xavier determined her innocent or she was found to be guilty of the crimes.

Peter was stripped of all his power, his son, and his bride to be. In fear that Xavier would find a reason to end his life, his old buddies Oliver, Rolf and Jacob came to his aid. The three men took turns keeping Peter hidden from the old Fur King's sight until either his anger calmed or one of them was dead.

Despite Ingrid's best attempts she couldn't protect her daughter Agnette from Xavier's brutal interest in her. That idiot mother of yours no doubt didn't require too much prompting to give in to his offer to spare her life in return for attending his lusts. Interestingly, after Peter was sent running and Xavier returned to power, this time Justus rose with his father."

I grimaced then interrupted Claus by saying, "Yeah, I read about that bullshit in Justus's diary too. So, that is why Justus followed my mother everywhere she went. Xavier let Agnette out of the dungeon, but he knew better than to trust that whore, ja? He set his minion to guard his pretty piece of ass."

Claus scoffed then replied, "Well that is a crude way of saying it but ja, that's correct. I suppose old Justus also wrote somewhere in his notes he had a severe crush on your mom."

I nodded then said bitterly, "He did. I thought it odd that Agnette seemed to be sleeping with everyone but that idiot. If your story is to be believed, I guess she's not as perverted as my father because she knew Justus was her brother. Trouble is, Justus didn't know that. It also explains why my mother appeared upset when she did find herself pregnant with me. She wasn't ever interested in Xavier but merely played him till she could do better. I suppose it should piss me off to realize that eventually she did manage to get what she wanted. The Vampire married the dumb bitch and once again I pay the price for her greed."

The Elder rolled his eyes then replied, "Stop pretending that Agnette didn't end up the loser in the end. I already told you I believe Birgit. If I were well enough I'd go down to the Palace if for no other reason to relieve myself in the Mortar King's toilet. Afterall, it would be wrong of me not to honor our foundation monarch's mother in the fashion she deserves, ja?"

I snorted loudly then said, "Ah, who is the crass one now, Claus? So, there it is. I am the sole survivor of a pair that was born from rape and raped as retaliation over a raped baby and stolen throne. Has anyone ever told you that you should've been a writer? That story you tried to tell me is a real page turner. Now, if you are quite satisfied that I will never ask you another question, can I respectfully request you release me from playing your unwilling audience?"

Claus glared at me appearing glum as he said, "Really? That is all you have taken from everything I told you?"

I shrugged then responded, "Oh I think it's unnecessary to repeat the terrible things you've said. I know you expect me to thank you for this feeble attempt to clear up all the terrible shit I've suffered for as long as I can remember. But that isn't going to happen, Claus. I am not grateful to you for your mercy as if you ever gave me any. I also don't say that with respect."

The Elder reached over and took up my lambs but kept his eyes on them as he replied, "You are a rude bastard, my boy. I guess that is expected. However, I must ask where do we go from here? If I say you may go, do you plan to end my life?"

A chuckle erupted from me as I held out my hands to receive my lambs and I said, "Now where is the fun in that, Auntie Claus? Didn't Bladrick tell you how much I enjoyed watching him die, slowly and painfully? Well, while I suspect he was behind the death of your lover Keifer and likely involved deeply with that shit that happened between me and his son Olaf. His part in this plot that landed me in the place as your cock warmer only slightly annoys me. You, however, have claimed to love me above all others. Yet, you are the one with more of my blood on your hands than most I've already murdered. I guess that means I will not be killing you anytime soon, but I sure as hell am going to be visiting often. You know me, I love to watch, ja?" Claus laughed till he coughed over my response.

Once he recomposed himself, he stared at me appearing somewhat sad as he said, "You know, the day Peter announced to me, Bladrick and Ingrid his betrayal, he brought those sheets soiled with your blood up with him. Your grandmother had already suffered a mild stroke the week before, hence Peter being able to sneak you out of the dungeon. Bladrick and I had been far too busy attending to her while she recovered her health to make our weekly visit to see you. Anyway, the moment Ingrid heard Peter boast of his conquest and laid her eyes on the evidence of her baby boy's defiling. Well, she wailed out, clutched her breast, and died instantly. I hope it brings you some peace to know Ingrid loved you so much that it literally broke her heart into two to realize she had failed to save you from the House's greed."

I stood up and placed my lambs into my jacket pockets as I replied, "That's sweet Claus. Tell you what. When you see her, let her know I appreciate that she managed to keep it together when it didn't matter, but turned into a coward when it did. I guess it isn't fair to pick on Ingrid without pointing out that you somehow maintained your health for many years after Peter showed up with those sheets. Ah and Aunty, the words I would like to say to you over your lack of remorse at my sad condition is, oh give me a second, damn, it's right there on the tip of my tongue." I shot him an angry look as I said that.

Claus nodded and used his hand gesture of release as he replied, "You are so much like Keifer. You never allow me to forget how much I owe you for bringing me joy. I suppose you are not interested in knowing why I told you Malfred is the one man you can trust to see you and your little wife free forever from the House. You are free to go my beloved boy, whoever you really are."

I scoffed loudly and said, "Dammit Claus. You have already nearly wasted my entire day telling me an endless story that did everything but answer the one fucking question I asked in the first place. So, why should I bother to stick around to hear another lie you will spin in your effort to deny me the only thing besides chocolate I've ever asked you for."

The Elder laughed hard as he said, "But I did tell you boy. Ingrid and I were using every technique from hypnosis to prescription drugs to attempt to heal your shattered mind. She did all she could to keep your madness hidden from the residents while we worked in secret to quell your trauma driven behaviors.

Noah was tasked with retraining you to attend to your most basic needs, though apparently that bastard was doing far more than we'd asked him to do. Everything we tried failed. Eventually, with deep grief, Ingrid was forced to see you labeled Priceless. If she hadn't, then sooner or later your mental illness would have been reported to the Guard.

You are already aware that only a single Priceless is permitted to exist in the House. Anyone else that is viewed as mentally ill is immediately sentenced to death. Ingrid consoled herself that even if she couldn't see her plot to raise you as the King of Kings, she could provide you with as comfortable a life as possible given the severity of your disease.

As you are most painfully aware, even her attempt to see your life as a treasured Priceless pleasure submissive was thwarted. She'd already suffered the pain of her beloved grandsons being abducted and held hostage for two long years. Then came the nightmare of discovering one of her beautiful boys had been murdered and the other so brutalized he was catatonic. Oh, I don't even want to think about the anguish she felt over failing to save you both.

Peter's betrayal though, well as I told you, was the final straw for her. A lifetime of woe caught up to her, Ingrid finally gave up all hope of successfully 'fixing what she believed she helped break.'

But there was plenty of misery to go around both before and after Peter's actions ended that great lady's life. The Krauss family had their own laundry lists of personal losses that by that time was decades in the making.

Karl in particular suffered heavy casualties in his short life. First his father abandoned their mother, leaving him as a young teen the man of the house. He was helpless as he watched his mother, sister and entire village hauled away to be exterminated by the Nazis.

Then came the terror of watching his cousins, wife, and child raped and murdered by the Russians. Till at last he found a bit of happiness with his baby boy named Ryker. That joy too was brief. I need not tell you the outcome of that doomed child, nor of Karl's second marriage after they were forced to uncollar their own son.

Malfred, as you know, is unable to father children. So, once again the burden of keeping his family line safe fell to Karl alone. This, paired with a paranoid fear that one day the Schmidts would destroy them, caused both men to grasp desperately for a powerful place within this prison.

As you are aware as it came to pass, Karl managed to father the baby girl required to salvage the Krauss's place among the House monarchy. Trouble was, after so many traumas, Karl couldn't stomach the idea of placing the fate of his family line within the grasp of one that he already blamed for the death of his son. And so it seems he was right to fear you, since it is you, he can thank for his ultimate outcome.

You weren't permitted to sit in on the emergency meeting Gretta called just after Malfred confessed to killing his own brother. No one doubted the Elder did the right thing, since he claimed to have ended Karl in a last-ditch effort to save our Priceless collar. But the House law is clear regarding being found guilty of killing a kinsman. Malfred should have been sent into exile or sentence to death over his admission.

Every one of us but the peace-loving Leo wanted to see that punishment carried out too. The reason it didn't happen was because during a brief recess, Malfred politely asked to speak to me privately. I decided it would be entertaining to listen to that asshole grovel and beg for his life, so I agreed to listen.

What he had to say changed everything. Malfred informed me that sparing him despite his heinous crime was in your best interest. He told me that Karl's used his last breaths to force Malfred to swear to him he would stop at nothing to see his daughter and her husband freed of Kaiser House. Malfred reported he wouldn't dare to deny his brother this last wish nor did he want to.

I could see in that old bastard's eyes, losing his big brother (the last of the small crew to survive Hitler's dogs) had broken his usually arrogant spirit. I decided, against my better judgement, to believe he was willing to keep his word to Karl.

Besides, I knew something that at the time he didn't know. Malfred is your mother's half-brother. If it was possible that Malfred was honorable enough to follow through with his brother's dying wish, then if you married the baby Rachel, he would have the power to see it happen.

I had intended to leave you a letter to be given to you upon my death that explained the connection between Malfred and Agnette, but as usual, you were clever enough to find that out on your own. So, now I must ask you to do as I have done. Do whatever you must do to fool Jonas, Peter, and even that idiot Lucus. Make them believe that you are complacent with their designs on you. But place all your trust in Malfred. Mind his counsel and regard him as your champion. If you can then I know, no matter what terrible things you have suffered, you will one day soon find the true happiness of freedom."

I stood there gapping at Claus unsure how to respond to the things he had said. He glared back silently refusing to break from our stare down.

Then unable to take another moment of this awkwardness between us I said, "I will consider it."

He nodded then replied, "That's more than I have the right to ask of you. I suppose if the Gods are kind, I will see you next Thursday at one, as usual, ja?"

I rolled my eyes and said, "I've always been a man of my word Claus. Unlike you and everyone else around here, I don't try to make excuses for the terrible things I've agreed to do. If you are still alive, I'll be here."

Claus sniffed loudly as he responded, "Thank you beloved. I suppose you are in a big hurry to check on the details of my story. You'd better get going your Majesty. Your time to tie up all the loose ends is running out." He rolled over till his back faced me, quietly sobbing just as he always did whenever his clock ran out.

I turned to head for the door, but yelled back before I exited, "I'm not the only one that has very few moments left Claus. If for any reason you manage to get an early release from this prison hell before I return next week. Tell my imaginary brother to come visit me in the Palace in about six months. I'm sure he will be delighted at all the skeletons I've collected to keep him company, ja? Hahaha!" With that I rushed from the Fur King's apartment headed as fast as my feet could carry me.

I had been interested in holding an audience with my brute brother Byron before I'd been rudely hijacked by Claus's demands. My plans had changed both because of the lateness of the hour, and because the Elder was right about one thing. I needed to verify some of the stuff he'd told me. The house residents, collared and Dominant, cleared from my path appearing frightened as I passed them by.

Nobody within eyesight that day could deny I was a man that meant business. I'd decided to start my serious investigation bottom up. Without hesitation, I rushed down the stoney steps, heading for the place where it all began: The Dungeon

Chapter 15: The Questionable Motives
of Unresolved Issues
Master Mad Maxx and submissive Meine Liebe

I moved with speed, ready to visit Noah and ask him a few things about that information Claus had given to me. And ask him a few questions about my own memories of his dishonorable behaviors with me.

It was a mostly uneventful journey through the hallways, except I noticed, no one was willing to slow my pace. All around me the silvers, blacks and the Dominants alike took to their knees. Obviously, the news of my loss of temper with the criminals of the Haus had made the rounds through the gossiping channels.

I confess to you, Meine Liebe, which was a good thing for them. I was no longer the patient man willing to allow even the minor disrespects shown to me to slide by unpunished. Despite my still fragile physical condition, I likely would have killed any man, woman, or child that bothered me that day. With the broken hands and other more sensitive places, I was a bit of the grouchy King, ja?). I am their fucking Mortar King and it was far past the time that every asshole in that hell hole understood that truth.

Anyway, the trip from Claus's first floor apartment to the dungeon was the quick one. I rushed through the dank, musty corridors feeling the rage over the things I'd recalled heating up inside my chest. I thought if I didn't discover

Noah's whereabouts fast, I may add the Head of the Dungeon Masters to Florian's ever increasing court.

Well, lucky for Noah, he wasn't the difficult fellow to find. I came upon him walking down a lightly traveled stone hallway, unaccompanied and apparently not in the hurry to get wherever he had been going. He saw me coming his way and his solemn expression immediately brightened. A huge smile broken out across his face as he halted his traveling and waited for my approach to be close enough for him to speak to me without having to shout.

Something about his seeming thrilled at seeing me pissed me the fuck off in ways I cannot explain. In my mind, I saw an image of me bashing his brains out all over that mortar floor with the flimsy cane I was using to aid in my mobility. Truth is Meine Liebe, had I not had the painful healing going on in my hands, further irritated by using that cane to walk with, I likely would have made my dark thoughts the reality.

However, I was in not in any condition to go picking violent fights with this burly fellow for that moment. Instead of attempting to rip his head from his wide shoulders, I decided to keep my fury in check. At least until I could get this dirty motherfucker alone, without witness nor ability to call out for help. Hahaha.

I stopped in front of Noah and said without any sign of aggression in my tone, "Good afternoon, Noah. Are you the busy man at this moment? If not, might I ask to speak with you somewhere private? I have some ideas about the treatment of the recruit collars I wished to run by you."

His smile smoothed into the expression of concern as he replied, "Uhm, sure thing your Majesty, but I must remind you that my opinion about anything you desire happen here below isn't relevant. You are the Dungeon Master Supreme, along with wearing the double crown of the Collars and the Mortar. I dare not tell my Lord and Master his business. You already know your words are the law. That said, of course, I'm your loyal servant and will be honored to serve you in any capacity you place upon my unworthy head. I do so with complete humility and understanding that I am far worse than undeserving of it. I am aware that I'm lucky to breathe the same air as the one that was born to rule over the hearts of men." Noah knelt before me with the grace usually only seen among the most talented of the silver submissives.

I held back my urge to kick him in the face as I growled in response, "If you'd remembered your place of subjugation before me sooner Noah, I dare say I'd be the less burdened Monarch today. Where the fuck were these wonderful manners you obviously possess that day you spoke to me in common at the Great Hall door? Get off your knees and stop acting like you mean the lofty things you say to me. It's not only obnoxious, but also sure to set me off into the blind fury. I think you mock me Noah. That's not a healthy thing for you to have me believing of you, now is it?"

Noah gasped and returned to his boots with speed as he said, "Nein. I swear to you, your Majesty I do no such a thing. I beg you to punish me as you see fit for showing that lack of respect that day, but please understand I am the honest man that swears what I've just claimed is the truth."

I nodded and replied by gesturing my head in the direction of the Dungeon Master's barracks, "Well that is good to know because truth is exactly what I desire. Let's go to your room and discuss further this change of heart you seem to have had, ja?"

He took off without hesitation headed for the destination I'd requested him to take me. I followed behind him close enough to smell his aftershave cologne wafting thru the air in his wake. I found that a strange scent for him to emit though I'd never thought much about the cleansing rituals of the men and women that lived in the rat hole below the Haus before. I guess I just assumed they would all stink of sweat and blood of the innocent children they tortured daily.

We had reached his room door before I realized it. I stood there mildly confused while he took out his keys and began to undo his locks. I was bothered that Noah's smell was overwhelming my senses. Not because he had overdone a brand of foul perfume mind you. It was of a pleasant odor and barely noticeable, but yet I had. This unexpected trigger had somehow distracted me to the point of losing my focus on kicking his ass for the rotten things he'd done to me when I was the little boy. I couldn't figure out why this insignificant detail managed to wield such a powerful reaction in me.

I shook off my weirded out feelings as Noah bowed and allowed me to enter the room before he did, which is the proper protocol given my higher status above his own. When he joined me inside the tiny space I motioned him to lock the door behind us.

I saw the expression of fear in his eyes when I indicated that. No doubt it was at that moment he understood, too late I may add, that my interest in an audience with him wasn't going to be the friendly chat he'd thought I come to have with him. Hahaha. This time, he hesitated to obey my command.

Without any emotion I barked out, "Are you blind Noah? I do believe I've ordered you to grant me your attention with the luxury of full privacy. You better lock that fucking door this minute or I'll use your lifeless body to block that entry." Noah observably shuddered but quickly did as I'd commanded.

I watched him with a cold glare and held out my hand as I said, "Good boy. Now give me the key. I warn you only this one time, Noah. Do not test my resolve to see your position open to be filled by a fresh Head Master. If you refuse to quickly obey me ever again, you will re-discover why Queen Ingrid leveled me the Priceless."

He gasped loudly, then trembled while he dropped the key into my bandaged hand and whispered in tone that sounded frightened, "Forgive me, your Majesty, but did you just say re-discover?"

I nodded slowly and glared even harder at the man as I replied, "Ah, you may be blind but you are not deaf, ja? Now tell me Noah, are you also forgetful? That would be such a tragedy if so. I cannot have the demented trainer running the show down here with the most precious treasures of the Haus in his possession."

Noah swallowed hard appearing to have the dry mouth as he responded, "Nein, your Majesty. My memory is sound. I must beg your pardon, but I wonder if you have perhaps heard that I've failed in the completion of my duties to the Haus somehow?" He backed toward his door one step as he said that.

I chuckled in the evil tone as I replied, "You seem worried. Noah. Now that's interesting to see from a strapping, strong brute such as yourself. What are you afraid of? Surely, not your Lord and Master." I took a step in his direction.

Noah retreated another step toward the locked entry as he stammered out, "Forgive me for saying this your Majesty, but I confess I'm scared of you. In all my years as the Dungeon Master I've never known anything even close to the brutality you dished out at the Funeral party for our lost Mortar Queen and Mortar Prince. May their rest in peace." He crossed himself but continued to keep his anxious eyes on me.

I approached the terrified Noah another two steps as I replied in the humored tone, "Ah, the things you saw that night have made you the fraidy cat, ja? Oh, well now Noah, there is no reason for you to be nervous. You of all the people in this fucking Haus know better than to believe what you think you saw. You are very aware that I'm not the dangerous man. Nein. I'm only the sweet little lamb, ja?"

Noah backed into his door with a thud and his eyes went wide as he whispered appearing about ready to faint from fear, "What did you just say?"

I took a place in front of him so close he could smell my breathe as I said with murder in my gaze, "I said, Baa, baa, baa."

Water fogged over his eyes as he replied thru trembling lips, "Nein. Please Master, I beg of you to show mercy that I know I surely don't deserve. I can't give you a valid excuse for the misuse I did to you. I swear I meant no harm by it. It is your will I obey, but if you could find a shred of kindness in your heart I would be most grateful. I beg that you kill me quickly. I don't care how, just please not burning at the stake, which I'm aware I earned." He fell to his knees and grabbed my ankles attempting to prostrate himself at my feet.

I chuckled loudly at this huge man trying to lobby favor from the Demon standing before him. I kicked him into the door with great force. He led out a yelp and covered his face with his massive arms. That silly move only managed to incite my need to hurt him more.

With viciousness I used my good leg to lay a strong kick into his exposed stomach. Noah retched and lowered his hands to grip at his injury. The second I saw his jaw exposed I let loose another blow from my boot right into his face. Blood and saliva erupted from his mouth onto the floor. He curled forward into the crimson puddle cuddling his belly, unable to get off his knees.

I bent down and took up as much of his hair into my mangled hand as I possible could, then I growled into his ear, "Now this is the proper way to wrestle, Noah. Don't you think?" With that I slammed his forehead into his stoney floor with extreme fury.

Noah wailed out in pain, but didn't attempt to rise from his place face first on the ground.

I limped to take the spot behind him and said with an evil chuckle, "You failed me as my trainer, Noah. It turned out that some of your lessons were lacking. Like the wrestling for example. I recall that when you taught me to do this, there wasn't any penetration. Only humiliation. Well, the fact that you left out that important part of the game was too damned bad for this little lamb of yours, ja? That's okay because Peter was happy to pick up the slack for you. I came here to kill you for introducing me to the game while lying about the rules of it but then something occurred to me. You can't pass on knowledge until you've learned it yourself, ja?"

Noah moaned from the agony of his unexpected assault and realization I recalled everything he hoped I'd never remember as he said in the breathless sounding tone, "I think the student intends to teach the instructor. I accept this punishment without quarrel, your Majesty. I thank you for the mercy of it because I am most unworthy of such coveted affection."

I laughed loudly then I growled out, "You misunderstand, Noah. There will be no pleasure in the punishment I give to you."

Noah shook his head without lifting it and responded in a grateful sounding tone, "If you intend to rape me, then I must dishonorably disagree, your Majesty. I expected to die here in this hell of rock and mortar the virgin, untouched and unloved by anyone. To have my last sensation in this brutal life be the act that's been forbidden to me all my life, granted to me by the Boy King himself, oh, my God. It is not only an honor, but also the dream. My world full of nightmares is about to thankfully end, and though I didn't earn it, and no matter how painful you make it, I swear to you I am forever in your debt for this. So again, I say I thank you for the mercy of it. I am ready to suffer your chosen punishment and then die as you see fit, my Lord."

I dropped down behind him and put my bandaged hands around his waist, pulling him hard into my groin as I bellowed angrily, "You die a liar, Noah. You are many things but the virgin is not one of them. I ordered you to take the Bartram stump first before any of your brothers got to taste his favors during the funeral party. I saw you go do as I commanded. So, you may possess the maiden head as the penetrated but you have no ignorance of being the monster that fucks the helpless. I should rape you with more than my royal cock for daring to spew falsehoods after I warned you to heed your words to me." Noah gasped as I thrust harshly into his hindside then held him against me refusing to allow him to escaping my dry mount.

The Dungeon Master trembled in my grip as he replied in a solemn sounding tone, "You did see me go to the stage ready to obey your commands, your Majesty. I must dishonorably admit to further crimes against you. I wasn't able to do it. I swear to God I tried, but this man Bartram is nothing but the pathetic stump of flesh. I couldn't find interest in completing the act of sex with it. I know you no longer trust my word, and I've earned this distrust I realize that. However, you can go ask my Dungeon Master brothers. They will tell you of the constant jokes they make about my lack of ability to perform the very act all of them know I craved the most. I thought if I were ever given the rights to engage in intercourse I wouldn't be too picky about the partner in it. That turned out to be the wrong assumption for this unlucky man. I swear it on my soul. I've never been guilty of not adhering to my sentence set upon me by Queen Ingrid so long ago. I've tasted no flesh, nor had a lover to call my own. Save that idiotic wrestling you and I did when I was assigned to train you." I thrust onto him with strength and chuckled when he let out a yelp from the force of it.

I then leaned down and draped myself over his back and whispered into his ear, "You insist on telling more lies on top of lies. What is this bullshit you're saying about Queen Ingrid giving you a sentence that orders you to remain the virgin till you die? I warn you, I've been to speaking with King Claus. He didn't say anything about that to me when we share stories about your dishonorable behaviors and poor training skills. That old sonofabitch didn't stop talking for hours about everything in the history of the world itself. If

Ingrid had condemned you to such a horrific fate, he surely would have told me of it."

Noah shuttered and then he blubbered in response, "I know you spoke to him recently, your Majesty. When you found me a bit ago, I had just left the phone call from him. He told me he learned from someone of many things I knew of the conspiracies surrounding you before you were taken to the third floor to become the property of Peter. I didn't realize until just this moment, it was your memory that he found out this information from. I already told you I have no reasonable defense for my crimes against you and against the Haus Leaders. You must do what will bring you peace, your Majesty. I am grateful that I lived long enough to repay the debt I don't deny I owe to you. After I am dead at your pleasure, I beg of you to ask the Honorable Claus if I tell you lies about my condemnation to chastity by the orders of Queen Ingrid. He will confirm I was at least the honest man about this. Olaf insulted the Queen and she wrapped him in the black collar for it, but this didn't calm her anger. Ingrid sentenced me to this place of dust and removed my right to know the touching of another. Everyone in the Haus knows of this, and therefore I've been without. No one has been willing to break the law. They all know if I were caught disobeying then I am to be sent to the circuit to be sold off as the catamite and my lover sent to the stake to be burned alive."

I chuckled softly into his ear as I said, "Ah, if you try to fuck anyone you will be sold off to be the whore, ja? Well, there you go, Noah. If you wanted to know touching of another so badly, there is the way out of your misery. The

Russian's would love to make you into their plaything. However, I think this is the farfetched tale you give me. I still don't believe you are the pure virgin without knowledge of sex other than those years of dry humping me. I demand you come clean and tell me how many silver collars have you soiled. Hemmel was your trainer, ja? Keep talking Noah. I am enjoying these fantasy stories you spew. It shall make killing you slowly so much more fun." I licked his ear and moaned out as if in ecstasy.

Noah quivered and sucked in his breath then replied sounding dreamy, "I never touched any collar. You can ask anyone down here. I respect the poor children that didn't wish to become the property for the rich above us to misuse. I confess that I was the young desperate man when I was ordered to train you. You were my first experience alone without Hemmel watching my every move. Back then I wasn't able to control my base urges as well as I've learned to since then. Plus, you are just so damned pretty, and those blue eyes of yours made me into the fool. I beg forgiveness for saying that, but it is the truth of it."

I nuzzled his neck with my nose and growled in response, "So, if you hadn't been condemned by Queen Ingrid you'd be the homosexual that preys on the little boys with light colored eyes, is that what you're saying?"

He moaned loudly and replied, "Nein. I'm not gay. I swear to you that I like to look at the females in the magazines when I can get them. I pleasure myself to their pictures exclusive. I also don't find thrill or fantasy when gazing at the males around here or in the books I read. I don't think children are sexy either. They look like babies to me. The breasts and legs of the mature woman are the things that drives me wild. I've dreamed a million times of what an amazing blessing it would be to hold one of them in my arms. I honestly don't know why I was compelled to do to you what I did when I was your trainer. I suppose I was just so frustrated and desperate. I swear once again on my soul I never did such dishonor to anyone else."

I unhooked one of my hands from his waist and grabbed his groin as I whispered breathlessly into his ear, "Seriously? Are you really going to dare insult me by claiming that you are straight despite using me for your masturbation? Well, I don't believe you and neither does your cock. The evidence that you are turned on by my threats to rape you is in my hand as we speak. Then you try to be cruel by claiming you only found your orgasms during our wrestling because you were the desperate man without the true outlet of the female you wanted. How about you attempt to tell the truth for a change, Noah? Tell you what. I will say what you won't. You're turned on by me because I'm sexy to you. In fact, you want me more than anything right this moment. Even if it results in your being sent to the circuit or gets you burnt at the stake." I gently rubbed on his erection through his leather pants which sent the man into spasms immediately.

Noah barely could catch his breath as he moaned out, "Please don't torture me like this, your Majesty. You are putting words into my mouth. I tell you that I am only a man, not a God. If you touch me after I've been denied such a pleasure for all my life, than you can't expect me not to respond favorably."

279

With a sudden move I rolled him to his back and took a straddle across his stomach. Noah laid there staring at me with his eyes wide in both shock and absolute terror. I sat on him for a moment chuckling and looking over his chest that was bare except for his Dungeon Master harness.

The silence was broken for those moments only by the sounds of his ragged breathing and my low humored sounds of evil delight. This man was confused, frightened, and perhaps somewhat relieved to finally be assured his tortured life was about to come to a conclusion.

The air was heavy with the scent of his aftershave. It was being steadily released by the copious sweat droplets erupting all over his flesh. The glistening of his fearful response made his well grown muscles appear to glow. As my eyes wandered over him, his chestnut mane and huge brown eyes caught my attention.

It was at this moment that it occurred to me that Noah was in possession of uncommon masculine beauty and rare grace, even at his mature age. I suddenly realized why my grandmother would have handed him such a seemingly cruel sentence of lifelong chastity.

Noah must have been as pretty as the twelve year old boy when Ingrid had to choose his fate as Dominant or submissive. She decided not to collar him but in order for him to remain free she was forced to send him to live in the Dungeon. Thanks to his status as the half-breed black collar he wasn't permitted the right to Dominance by Haus law. At least not above the first floor. That is unless his father

Bladrick had been willing to admit to breaking the law by making children with the forbidden black collar cook Evelyn.

Yet, I'd known Bladrick far too well as you recall, Meine Liebe. I can say with certainty that old beast would never have been willing to accept the punishment for such a serious crime. Not even to save his two bastard sons from becoming Haus property.

As the Queen of the Fur, my grandmother would be the one that had to decide what to do with two suspected half-breeds. It made sense that given her soft heart she'd never choose to condemn Olaf and Noah to the collar. So, without better options permitted her given the law, she granted them mercy by sending both boys to serve in the Dungeon. I had to assume she was hoping that one day the law forbidding half-breeds remaining free above ground, or outside the Haus walls, would be changed.

Well, according to Noah, apparently Olaf had pissed Ingrid off thru a terrible insult of some kind. In retaliation she'd had him collared and forced him to serve her brutal husband's interests instead of sending him below.

Noah on the other hand, was innocent of this crime against her. She'd spared him that terrible fate of his brother Olaf. W ell, she kind of did. Sending a handsome child that was far too small to defend himself in a place full of horny males that lacked female company, oh I think I need not explain the likely horrible results for Noah.

So, the clever Ingrid had given him the rare sentence of untouchable to prevent the older, stronger Dungeon Masters from raping the poor kid to death. The only thing I couldn't figure out was why she hadn't recanted this unfair, but protective, sentence once Noah was old enough to defend himself from unwanted advances.

I made the mental note to ask Claus about it the next Thursday. That is if he lived that long. Until then though, I had to decide how best to punish Noah for the foul things he had done to me personally and for the part he played in my ultimate downfall at the hands of Peter and Xavier.

While all this deduced information was flashing across the wheel room screen. I continued to allow my eyes travel across his massive frame. He didn't appear even close to his true age of thirty-seven. Believe me when I tell you that Noah was an amazing specimen of male beauty to behold.

I leaned forward toward him and drew in my breath deeply. His scent filled my lungs and to my surprise the emotions of peace and happiness came over me. Those strange feelings along with the heady mix of leather and blood from his busted lips caused my loins to tingle slightly.

I gasped as the realization that my cock was starting to rise with heated interest in the man I was holding hostage. Noah's own desire was making no attempt to hide from notice. I had to shift further up his stomach to avoid sitting on, uhm, him intimately.

With incredible fury I yelled out, "Goddam you, pervert. You had no right to play me for the little fool, Noah. I hate you. It's all your fault Peter made me into the sexual plaything of the Haus leaders. Why didn't you kill me when you had the chance? Or at the very least rape away my coveted virginity so that Peter would have to unlock his collar and send me to the yard as used goods? You are nothing but the coward that is too weak to take what he desires because he fears death, but not unhappiness nor dishonor." I backhanded him so hard it caused both of us to let out a wail of agony. Him from my blow and me from the sting caused to my mending finger bones.

While I held my aching hand to my chest Noah cast his tear filled eyes to the ceiling and mumbled, "You speak the truth of it, your Majesty. Send me on my way. I agree I have it coming a thousand times worse than you intend to do it."

I hopped up and then dropped onto his stomach causing him to lose his breathe momentarily as I replied, "Shut up. You don't even have the right to speak like the man because you are not one. You will address me in your mother tongue. Do it. Let me hear you bleat, you horny old ram."

Noah tore his gaze from the sky and looked directly at me as he opened his mouth and shouted out, "Baa, baa, baa."

Despite myself I started to laugh, and damn me, I couldn't stop that horrid mirth from taking root deep within. Noah lay still staring at me appearing surprised by my response for a moment. Then with suddenness my sounds of humor became contagious. We spent several minutes howling like hyenas over that pathetic attempt he'd made to sound like the baby sheep.

When at last I could get enough breath to speaking I said, "You know what I will miss the most about you, Noah? The way you butcher my language. Where the fuck did you learn to make the sheep calls? Not from this idiot, that I can be sure."

Noah chuckled a bit as he replied, "The closest thing to any animal I've ever been permitted to be around was you, your Majesty. I say that with respect."

I frowned as I responded, "What is this you say? You mean you never got to pet the baby sheep or play with the hounds? Not ever? Not even when you were the little boy before all this?" I pointed at the stoney barriers of his room.

Noah shook his head and his expression went from humor to sadness as he replied, "Nein, I've known only the walls of this Haus. I never seen the yard except through the windows. I heard you've been outside the Haus. Can I be so bold as to ask if you would tell me what that was like before you kill me, your Majesty? Was the air stale or pure? Does the grass feel soft as it appears?"

That admission from him caused my chest to ache with pity for him. I sat there staring into his eyes. They seemed to be pleading for me take him to a world denied him, that like me, was only the fantasy. Before I could stop myself, I leaned down and put my lips to his.

His body seemed to melt under me as our mouths met. I kissed him with eagerness and wrapped my hands into his flowing hair. Noah seemed unsure what to do. He held still, and didn't attempt to return my adoration nor did he move to avoid it. I ignored his lack of response and pushed my tongue into his head. Noah led out a whimper but continued his stance of stoic stillness.

I explored his dentition as if I were the expert dentist for a moment before finally withdrawing my fleshy appendage from his mouth. I put my nose to his and looked deep into his soft brown soul portals. The terror in his gaze overcame my good judgement. I started tearing at his harness. I was fueled with desperation that my damaged fingers were not releasing him from that cage of leather, as I wished them to.

Noah let out a gasp and his back arched as he wailed, "What are you doing, your Majesty. Please stop this. I don't understand what you want of me? If you desire to rape me then allow me to take the position but you keep this up you will injure yourself and that I cannot allow." Then he pushed me off him with the strength I recalled from my youth.

I rolled across the floor helpless to stop the journey till I collided with one of his threadbare bed leg. Noah sat up and with tears rolling down his checks he began to undo the buttons of his leather breeches. My attention was on his actions, as if hypnotized by them. I didn't move as I watched him remove his boots then pull off his only real article of clothing other than that harness.

He never took back to his feet but sat there on the bedroom floor doing this task, weeping all the while. Once unencumbered he dropped his water drenched eyes to gaze at his lap. He covered his face with his hands and sobbed quietly into them.

His unmanly display over the idea that I was about to roughly violate him didn't register within me. I ignored his grief and crawled back to his position barely able to contain my thrill over having the barrier to my desire removed.

The moment I was between his knees I pounced on the weeping Head Master. His shock at this move was audibly heard when he yelped. Because he wasn't expecting to bear my weight he was sent sprawling to his back dragging my eager frame with him. I didn't pay any mind to his apparent confusion. Without explanation I began to ply him with kisses, nips and licks anywhere I could make connection with his delicious flesh.

After his initial surprise seemed to wane, he tried to protest my interest in him by repeating his move to toss me off. This time I was ready for it. I blocked his arms with speed. Then without care for the pain it caused me used my damaged hands to pin his arms to the floor above his head.

I stared into his face and growled out full of lust and anger, "You have so many times called me your King. They say to the King goes the spoils. I intend to find out if that is the truth. Understand something, fool. I care not for what you think you deserve or don't. You say you wish to serve me but then lay there and suffer my affections like the corpse. However, let me make it clear to you since you appear to still be the idiot I remember you to be. I'm commanding you to be my lover Noah, but maybe you may prefer to die a coward. Hurry up and speak with that useless tongue of yours. You demand I stop, or you better start putting it to the proper service to your Lord and Master."

Noah's eyes went wider than I ever saw them go before as he stammered in response, "What? You want me to, but I don't, I mean, why, my Lord? I'm a nothing and worse still, even you as the Mortar King cannot claim me as lover without inciting the full punishment as the Haus law demands."

I leaned in and bit his neck till he yelped then said in the furious tone into his ear, "Everything in this Haus bows to me. I am the law. I am the Master and you are my servant, Noah. If I wished to I could even remove that silly sentence that holds you the prisoner to loneliness. But you already knew that and now you know I do too. That's the real reason you placed the burden of the Gold Buckles on my chest. And it is why you made the trade with me that demands that I lift you to become the King of the Fur when you turn fifty-five. Well Noah, you have many years left to serve in this lonely wasteland before you can force me to keep my promise to you, don't you? Perhaps you desire to spend the rest of your pathetic life forbidden the pleasures the flesh can give to you. Funny, you don't look like the priest type to me. I also think your cock isn't willing to deny me what is mine either." I rubbed my erect groin against his hard on.

Noah moaned out sounding enthralled, then he replied, "Are you saying you will release me from my sentence if I agree to sleep with you, your Majesty?"

I shook my head and put my mouth right up to his ear and said, "Nein. I will never release you, not ever. You will agree to belong to me only or you will die the virgin. I don't share my things, Noah."

He gasped then turned his head to stare at me as he responded, "Then you aren't doing this as punishment but because…" his words trailed off.

I glared at him wantonly as I finished his sentence for him, "I want you to be my lover, Noah. Beware before you answer because I won't ask you again. Say nein and discover I can be as cruel as I can be generous with my affections. Say ja, and I will take you to that place only true passion can. I swear on my honor I'll never leave you unsatisfied nor will you ever be far from my thoughts or heart. I love you completely and honestly. I never realized it till now, but I always have. If I cannot have you, then I'll make sure no one else ever will either."

Noah closed his lids tightly sending fresh tears rolling down his cheeks as he replied, "I think this must be a dream that I wish to never awaken from. You will never know how many times I thought of your beautiful face and found myself miserable that I would never hold you in my arms like I used to."

I blew out my breathe then said in the frustrated tone, "That isn't an answer to my question is it. Will you become my lover or do you wish to remain the untouchable with a lifetime of the same."

His beautiful eyes fluttered open and he said, "I say a thousand times it is my honor to accept your offer to become your lover, your Majesty. Do with me as you wish, and I will love you till forever comes to claim me for her own."

I chuckled with evil sounding humor as I replied, "Then I hereby condemn you for the second time in your worthless life, Noah. You shall serve me in all my pleasures, exclusively. I forbid you to touch another's flesh even if you are merely attempting to prevent them from falling to their death. Do not ask me to remove my grandmother's sentence because I will die without uttering the words that could set you free. I also won't tolerate you ever turning away my brutal affections when I come to take you for my thrill."

Noah smiled thru his tears and said, "I will never ask you to set me free because I never want you to let me go, your Majesty."

I moaned in delight as he leaned forward and began to kissing my neck, then I responded, "You are to call me Mad Maxx when we are alone, Noah. For a bit, we will need to proceed slowly in our intercourse. I'm not healed from that tragedy those bastard Stasi did to my flesh. You will follow my lead until you are trained to wrestle with me properly. This you understand, ja?"

He chuckled for a moment at my statement then said, "Fair enough, Mad Maxx. I am your student and you have always been my Master. I say only that I have adored you since I first laid eyes upon you. I waited all my life for this moment. I am content to wait a thousand years more as long as during that time I could gaze upon my only true love."

I snatched his lips into my own before he could say another ting. This time his arms wrapped around my waist in response and his tongue greedily met my own. We rubbed and petted each other's flesh for several moments before he realized I couldn't remove my clothing without his aid. *Noah was only too happy to assist in the undressing services for your Master, Meine Liebe.*

I gasped then turned around in his lap to stare at him as I said, "Wait a minute, Master. This was some kind of trick you were playing on Noah to pay him back for that naughty stuff he did to you, right? I mean, you only are with Leo because he loves you. And with Cary because Der Hund said that you needed his help. I think you did learn to like him a little, but you said you aren't interested in men." I let out a yelp as the cane cut through the air and connected with my naked thigh.

Master Mad Maxx glared at me for a moment then replied flatly, "Noah is different than Leo or Cary. I think of him as in the same category as Jakob but our relationship is more like the one I have with you."

Despite my burning welt I narrowed my eyes and said, "But you described Noah as very manly, not female looking like Jakob. Oh, I get it. You are teasing me, and I say this with respect, but I'm not falling for this story. You must have had a good reason to mislead Noah into believing you two were going to be secretly having sex because I know you didn't go through with it. Or at least, didn't enjoy it."

I squinted, my lids closed and waited for the cane to hit the mark again, but after several moments when it didn't, I opened my eyes to see him sitting there staring at me strangely.

Once he saw that I was paying attention he said, "This wasn't the trick. I love Leo, and care for Cary. I adore Jakob, but Noah is him that I truly love. The sex with him isn't a burden. It is my pleasure."

I shook my head then replied, "But if you really loved Noah, you would have released him from that awful sentence Ingrid condemned him to suffer. Besides, I know you said that you are not completely straight, but Noah is still a man. You've told me a million times you can love a man but never voluntarily have sex with them unless they are paying you something. And you never enjoy it. I admit it, you have me confused this time. I mean, Noah was already your servant and had nothing to give you that you didn't already own. So, this agreement to have sex with him was just to get what from him?"

Master Mad Maxx chuckled then said, "I'll never release Noah from his sentence, not ever. He is mine and will remain mine till the day he dies. I've already told you, Meine Liebe, that Mad Max is the pansexual. He is your husband and he found love for Leo and Annette too. Der Hund is bisexual. He chose Cary to play our Dark Bonded lover because he is a loyal friend that desires to fuck us in return for his aid. Christian and Maxximillian are the straight men that thrill only for you but have to tolerate the interests of the many males that misuse us for their pleasures. But me, the Mad Maxx, well, I am pure homosexual. Sex with Leo and with Cary is the duty to me. I don't hate it but I don't enjoy it either. Noah is different. He is my only true love. In his arms and with his touching, I find my utter happiness and complete thrill."

I really did a second take when he said that as I replied, "But you said that one day I would get out of this basement and then neither of us would have to tolerate others having sex with us. Are you telling me that it isn't Jonas, Leo, or even Cary that I should be afraid will share our bed, but Noah? What the hell, Master." Mad Maxx took up the cane and let loose an uncharacteristically violent swat across my thigh.

He then growled out sounding beyond furious, "Meine Liebe, you know damned well I love you almost as much as my brother shards. But if you dare say another fucking insulting thing about my Noah, I will skin you, dammit. It is the truth that Mad Max tells you of our desire to have the monogamous marriage one day soon. That means you will never have sex with any other man and we will never take another woman to our bed either. However, you desire the girlfriend, that's up to you. It has long since been agreed that I have permission from Felicity to have Noah for my own. He is our only lover other than you. It is only fair that you can take a girlfriend to make us even. So, one day maybe you find a Nora, ja? Felicity will look the other way as long as it isn't another male you take to your heart."

I glared at him for a moment rubbing my angry welt then said, "You are fucking weird as hell, and I say that with respect, Master. I hate having sex with women, and you already know that. I don't want a Nora or a Jane or whatever. You are a happily married man, and you shouldn't be interested in taking outside lovers, especially Noah!"

Mad Maxx raised the cane above his head ready to lay me out with it. I cowered in his lap but suddenly his expression went blank. I watched as his gaze softened then in the voice I recognized as Christian when he spoke.

"Stop arguing with Mad Maxx, Meine Liebe. He is a schwuler and there isn't shit any of us can do about that or his obsession with Noah. You know better than to stir him up. He is disturbed beyond repair. Don't you remember I told you all about his, uhm, issues? It is best to just agree with him and be still. Next time, maybe I won't be able to knock him off the wheel before he really hurts you if you insist on arguing with him over this delicate matter. You know that Maxximillian influences his rage reactions, and that isn't safe to set off, right?"

I nodded then said with a huff, "Sure, whatever you say, Master Christian. Just know, I won't stand to have another obviously very confused man hanging out in my bed looking to fuck me the second crazy Master Mad Maxx is sleeping."

Christian chuckled in an evil tone then reached out and ruffled my hair as he replied, "Caught that bit about Noah being a straight man, did you? Well, just do as I ask you for now, Meine Liebe. I promise we will deal with this Noah situation if it becomes one in the future. Now, get back into position and pretend none of this happened. Max has erased Mad Maxx's memory of this exchange but if you bring it up, he'll remember he wants to beat your ass."

I nodded then turned around and snuggled back into my Master's chest. For a second Master Mad Maxx went limp, *then he cleared his throat and went on with his story right where he left off, not appearing to remember our tiff. Just as Christian said he would.*

Noah removed my vampire jacket, and dark blouse, but when his frisky hands attempted to unbutton my breeches I smacked them away. He didn't break from our mouthy adorations of each other's flesh but tried again to gain access to my manhood. I pulled out of our heavy petting and pushed him to his back and held him there using my weight to pin him down.

I glared into his overtly confused gaze and growled out, "Keep your dirty paws off my dick until I say you can touch it. You will do well to recall I am the one in charge during this risky male on male sex business. Piss me off again, and I will break that pretty face of yours."

The Dungeon Master stared at me appearing temporarily frightened again as he stammered out, "As you wish, Mad Maxx. I apologize for being the overzealous cad. You tell me what to do, and I do it."

With a nod I sneered then replied, "That's better. You lay there and take it like my good little bitch. My parts are in severe shape at this moment due to torture. However, the second they heal, I'll be coming to find you lover. Then I will give you instructions on how to please my violent interests. After that, you can claim your virginity no longer, because it will be mine. Do you understand me?"

He nodded with a smile starting to break across his face as he responded, "Ja, I do, Mad Maxx. I look forward to your favor with great eagerness. May you heal quickly." His eyes briefly focused on my crotch.

I swatted his cheek till his gaze returned to my own as I said in the harsh tone, "You will regret that thrill you show. It's in your best interest that I never regain my abilities, my little bitch. But there is no need to frighten you. Soon enough you'll be painfully aware that I offer no comfort in your misery but only brutality. I'm the twisted bastard, with an unquenchable thirst for your flesh. I intend to drill you into screams of mercy that will fall on my deaf ears. Now, what do you say to that, my pretty plaything?"

Noah's smile widened as he called out happily, "I say I thank you for the mercy of your cruel touching and brutal affections Master."

I laughed evilly then replied, "You sure you're a virgin, Noah? I think you play this game like the well-studied student of it."

He laughed along with me then said, "The walls of the Dungeon are thin, Mad Maxx. I have many years of dark, sleepless nights with an empty bed and perfect hearing. I suppose I've rehearsed for this role as your lover longer than I wish to admit it."

I nodded and began to run my hands along his chest while backing away from him as I replied, "Ah, then I shall have to move you from beginner's level to that of the novice in training. Let's see how prepared you are for doing more than the play acting to your reflection in the mirror, ja?"

With those words I reached his cock and took it into my mouth expertly.

Noah groaned and arched his back. His legs writhed next to my ears as I used my tongue to caress his engorged manhood. I thrilled upon this discovery that his limbs would respond dramatically each time I lightly licked his part. It was great fun to listen to his sounds of ecstasy as I moved from the teasing to full on oral adoration phase of the blow job.

At this point in my seduction, I let lose all my hard learned skills on my lover's cock. I moved effortlessly from deep throat to sucking, while tickling all his most sensitive areas. Noah was clearly nearing his apex almost before I got serious with this action.

Whenever I felt his muscles tensing in the telltale signs of impending climax, I calmly stopped all stimulation moves. I repeated this behavior at least five times in only seven minutes. By the eighth time he was ready to, uhm, blow, Noah was gripping his straining thighs with white knuckles, hahaha. Still I refused to permit his release.

Noah shuttered, shook and trembled as he wailed out in desperation, "Oh my God, Mad Maxx. I think I will die if you don't stop torturing me this way. Please, I beg of you, don't remove your beautiful mouth this time. I need to cum or my balls will turn bright blue and swell to painful levels."

I nuzzled his raging hard on with my nose as I cooed out in response, "I will torture you as much as I like, my little plaything. You'll cum when I decide not when you wish to.

Perhaps I'll bite off your dick instead of merely sucking it. Then you can become my truthful mare. You would like that wouldn't you?"

Noah moaned out sounding beyond thrilled, "Ja. Please bite me, fuck me, kill me, Mad Maxx. Just don't ever stop touching me. I am your willing bitch. Use me anyway you wish. I beg of you."

I let out a longing moan in response to his own, then said breathlessly, "Right answer, my little plaything. I suppose this time I will allow you to keep your schwanse, but maybe next time you don't get so lucky. Be still. When you cum you will call out my name, loud and clear or I will take you to the chains and remove an inch of your gorgeous flesh." I returned to blowing Noah but paid close attention to see if he remembered to obey my commands.

Noah's wild movements ceased and besides his groans of pleasure, he did manage to do as I told him. Sweat broke out all over his twitching thigh muscles from the strain of his forcing them to remain still. Then I felt him quickly approaching his limit.

He sat up suddenly. Before I could block him he snatched me by the hair and held me down onto his groin. I held on for dear life as he harshly bucked his cock into my mouth in orgasmic bliss.

I heard him yell out excitedly, "Oh, my God is Mad Maxx. I love you, Mad Maxx." He released me and fell to his back.

I rose from his lap and glared at him. Noah didn't move as he lay there chuckling under his breath with a huge smile, while staring at his ceiling with the glassy eyed look of satisfaction on his face.

His joy was interrupted when I crawled across his chest and forced his mouth to my own. In a single seamless move, I shoved the spent seed I had managed to capture into his head.

Then I broke from our kiss and growled out sounding angry, "You will not swallow that gift I give to you, little bitch. Instead you shall savor it and be grateful I've granted you mercy you haven't earned. The next time you dare to touch me like you just did, I will do far worse than make you eat your own cum. You'll be snacking on your cock, you understand me? Nod if you do." The subdued and frightened expression had returned to his face as he nodded slowly at me.

I reach up and Noah flinched as I petted his cheek, "That's a good, little bitch. You are still learning, ja? I'm the patient teacher, so don't you worry your pretty head over this minor correction. You may swallow in one hour and not one second before that. This way, you'll recall the lesson without further explanation. Now, I must go but I can promise you I will be seeing you very soon. Ah, don't look so sad, my plaything. This is the moment to rejoice. You already lost one virginity and there are only two left to go. I swore to soil you to completion and everyone knows I am a man of my word. Get up and give me proper dressing service. Then you will kiss me goodbye lover." I lightly kissed him on the forehead.

His eyes followed my every move as I caressed his cheek once more then returned to standing. Noah didn't hesitate to retrieve my tossed blouse and jacket. I stood there gazing at him lovingly as he replaced my clothing like only the well trained pleasure submissive can.

The moment he completed this task, he leaned in and brushed his lips to my own. He was unable to kiss me more deeply because he was being careful not to allow the contents of his mouth to spill out. I chuckled over his expression that seemed disappointed that I didn't release him from my command so that he could enjoy that last little pleasure more fully.

I stood there only a second more. I confess I wanted to hang out to bask in the vision of his beautifully formed, naked frame standing there appearing forlorn but the hour was getting late. I still had so many unresolved issues to deal with and not enough time to get to them all. I motioned Noah to take the key, which had been tossed onto his floor during our tryst, and to let me be on my way.

He obeyed the order with grace and speed. I started to leave but then recalled something I needed to ask him.

His expression became confused when I halted just within the crack of his door and asked, "Noah, when the Guard brought me to the dungeon, was I alone? I mean did you ever see any other boy that resembled me?"

The Dungeon Master shook his head and his eyes indicated he didn't understand the reason I would think such a thing possible.

I shrugged then said, "Did you ever hear tale that I was part of a set? Or perhaps, did you ever remove my silver manacle and see if anything was written on it?"

His expression went from confused to curious as he nodded.

That made me gasp as I leaned in and whispered, "Swallow, then tell me what you know, Noah."

Noah obeyed then looked around before he put his mouth next to my ear and said, "I once heard Ingrid saying it was the tragedy your brother didn't survive so they could tell the truth of your identity. Then one day, I was giving you the sponge bath and I removed your collar to cleanse the dirt away. I saw something scratched inside it."

I frowned at him and replied, "What did it say, Noah? Stop wasting my time by ending your answer before you give me all the details, dammit."

He looked to the floor then said, "Forgive me, Mad Maxx, but what it said is something I wished to never repeat."

I growled low in my throat, "Too bad for you, Noah. I command you to tell me what it said."

He sighed then without looking up said, "Brother of the corpse. That is what it said, Mad Maxx."

I sucked in my breath and felt faint as I replied, "Oh, well that's not a good thing to scratch into metal. I wonder what it meant?"

Noah shrugged as he responded, "I didn't dare to think on it when I read it, and I don't desire to ponder the meaning today either. I thank you for the mercy you given me, Mad Maxx. I will miss you until you return more than you can know." He pushed his mouth to mine and kissed me deeply.

I returned his adoration for a moment, then pulled away and rushed through the open crack in his door. Leaving him behind without looking back. His words of his discovery echoed in my mind, leaving me with the feeling that Claus wasn't being completely dishonest in his claims.

But for the moment, I had bigger problems to tackle than chasing after possible ghosts that didn't matter anymore. I hauled ass up the stone steps and burst into the first floor hallway determined to find Ruslan. I recalled he had wished to speak with me alone about some important matter just before Claus hijacked me into listening to his tales of woe.

Again all around me, the silvers, blacks and Dominants knelt in complete reverence as I passed them. While this behavior was the proper thing for them to do, it was starting to annoy me greatly. I decided to head for the back staircase in the effort to see Cary. I thought it best to send my Shadow King to find the burly head of the Guard rather than me using up my strength on this wild goose chasing.

However, to get to the place I was sure to find my Dark Bonded, I had no choice but to take the detour. I would have to pass that damned closet from hell, like it or not. This distaste that I have for that spot didn't change my mind in the plotting out of my journey.

I entered the untraveled corridor and could see the door of the closet clearly from several paces away. There didn't appear to be any other soul around, so I braced my resolve to continue without fear.

Nothing happened and no one jumped out to grab me as I briskly moved on by it. An unconscious but audible sound of relief escaped me the second that horrible place was far behind. I even chuckled a bit that I was the least bit worried about it. After that terror I unleased on everyone during the funeral, surely no one would be dumb enough to fuck with the Mortar King anymore, right?

It was at that moment I heard the DJ's voice call out from the closest wall, "Mad Maxx. Hey, Mad Maxx. Oh, thank God you are here. I thought you were killed I hadn't seen you around in so long. Listen, beware of the chocolate. The vampire bats fill it with rabies you know. If you would come with me, I brought you some soup if you are hungry. I even remembered to put it in the bowl this time."

I halted immediately and glared in the direction I'd heard his voice and growled out, "Go away, crazy motherfucker. You are not real. I don't have schizophrenia, so I cannot hear you."

The DJ scoffed loudly then replied, "Ja, you do hear me or else why do you answer? Superman is real and you fucking know that. Besides, you owe me services. Oh and a partridge in a pear tree."

I narrowed my eyes and did my best to spot him there in that darkened hall as I said, "Okay, so I did agree to this contract with you. Let's pretend that's true. I cannot complete the bargain if you never show yourself, idiot. Come out here where I can see you. Stop playing hide and seek, you coward."

He didn't respond to my attempt to call him out. Instead he rolled a chocolate donut down the hallway in my direction. I stood there staring at that treat unsure what to make of his offer. When for several minutes he still didn't say anything. I approached the sweet and picked it up.

The DJ whispered out, "Rabies, Mad Maxx. You'll get rabies if you eat that."

I laughed loudly and took a big bite of the donut as I replied with a mouth full of chocolate dough. "You must be bitten not bite to get that disease, fool. Did Florian send you to mess with my head? Hey, are you following me all the time? If so, tell me where I was coming from and where I was heading?" I was suddenly overcome with anxiety that the DJ had seen that private business with my Noah, you know.

I was also overcome with the sensation of sleepiness. That damned chocolate always makes me tired. I guess I should've put it in the pocket with my lamb to eat when I had time for the nap that I knew I needed immediately.

Chapter 16: Two Unexpected Kills
Master Mad Maxx and submissive Meine Liebe

I awoke on the floor in that empty hallway with a half-eaten chocolate donut next to me, and a terrible stomachache. I was groggy and confused as to where the hell I was for several minutes after I regained consciousness from that unplanned napping.

Once I had recalled that I had been on my way to visit with Cary, I attempted to take back to my boots. I was assaulted immediately with horrible pain from the bottom of the ribcage all the way down to the knees. With a loud groan I doubled over and retched up the contents of the little bit of the donut I had ingested.

That barfing made my tummy feel some better. But it didn't calm the horrible sharp pain sensation that was radiating all around my middle. I cast my weary eyes at the left-over chocolate sweet and decided I wasn't going to be eating anymore donuts for a while. I thought I may have developed an allergy to them.

I need not tell you, this discovery made my shitty day feel so much worse. My adoration for the chocolate was one of the very few things I could still find pleasure in. Given the horrible life I'd been enduring for years, the idea that I'd lost the ability to enjoy this tiny luxury caused me to feel suicidal for a second.

Maxximillian leaned over from his side of the wheel and growled into my ear, "Buck up Daddy O. Stop the drama will you? We got things to do, and the boy isn't on the list of those needing extermination to complete the mission, you dig?"

I turned my head that was heavy with the burden of the huge ram horns that had sprouted out on it and replied angrily, "Fuck off Maxximillian. The boy is not feeling well, and no doubt the wreck without any relief from this suffering coming anytime soon. I think it only makes sense that we consider ending this useless game before things get any worse."

Maxximillian snorted then said, "Look here Daddy O. I didn't say a thing about that nasty crap you pulled with Noah. I also said nothing about your need to fall asleep so close to that fucking closet. I realize you're the old man. Hahaha. However, consideration of taking the dirt nap isn't cool, man. Calm your jive ass down or I will be forced to push you out of command. I can run this bitch just fine without some gnarly loser always blocking my badass grooves."

I slowly returned to standing by using the wall to balance as I replied in the furious sounding tone, "You are lucky that you are my son or I'd murder you for speaking to me that way. As it is for the moment I don't desire to get into the battle with you. Stay on your side of the wheel and keep quiet. Later, when we have the time, you can take up your complaints with my fists. This you understand, ja?" I pulled my left claw into the ball and shook it at my handsome son.

He grinned with evil delight shimmering in his eyes as he responded, "Deal Daddy O. I'm more than happy to dance with you, you ugly motherfucker. Anytime, anyplace."

Die Brutal led out an angry bellow, then yelled out at the two of us, "Both of you shut the fuck up and get back to the action already in progress for fuck's sake. Your voices are not only annoying, but they are also being broadcast through the speakers. Do you wish for the DJ to gain more private information to use against the boy than he already possesses? We think not."

I let out a gasp, then turned my head in every direction trying to spy the location of that sneaky DJ. Die Brutale's warnings had reminded me that shady bastard was still following us around. It was obvious he was taking notes, and maybe even trying to get us murdered. Why else would he use the chocolate donut disguise to drug us into the helpless unconsciousness?

Honestly, I never had understood the reasons he hated us as much as he seemed to. Nor did I have any idea what he hoped to gain by always starting cruel rumors and stalking us as he'd always done. Though I had to assume it was likely he was patiently building the case against us to use in some dark blackmail plot with Gretta or perhaps Jonas.

When it became clear the DJ's hiding spot wasn't going to be easy to spot, I leaned into the wall. I stood dare trying to catching my breath as that horrific pain rolled down my spine.

Then I weakly called out, "Show yourself coward. Come out here and fight me like a man instead of acting like the fraidy cat you truly are. I swear to God if you don't stop playing games with me, I'm going to send your head to keep Florian company." I sucked in my air just as a sharp pain ripped down the back of my thighs.

The back of my breeches suddenly felt damp. A groan of misery escaped my throat as I realized I must have let loosen my bowels in the embarrassing accident. Uhggg, it wasn't fun to be survivor of multiple brutal gang rapes, ja?

Maxximillian chuckled as he said, "Oopsy daisy there pops. You need daily naps and now are ready for the adult diapers. It must suck to be the old man, ja? Looks like that meeting with Ruslan is going to have to wait while you run on home, so that Lucus can help you wipe your wrinkled ass."

I growled and replied, "I'm getting real tired of your insults, son. I am not old nor do I need baby swaddling, or that pervert to attend to my personal hygiene. You shut your mouth and keep your eyes out for that fucking DJ. I'll deal with this minor side effect of the rough handling I endured at the hands of the Stasi without your rude commentary, you dig?" Maxximillian laughed wildly at my attempt to mock his weird slang as I rushed off toward the first-floor apartment that belonged to Matz.

I had made the habit of keeping an extra pair of breeches in the bedroom closet of the place. I also assumed it would be the wise move to hop into the shower before I made this

307

necessary change of wardrobe, ja? The fear that my time of freedom from Mad Lucus's control was running out put the speed in my steps. I hadn't bothered to check the Haus clock but I assumed the hour of nine o'clock would arrive far sooner than I thought it would.

In case you had forgotten, Meine Liebe, I had made the agreement with Mad Lucus that he wouldn't interfere with my actions from nine in the morning until nine at night. After my daily hours of freedom from his interest I was to return to the fourth-floor apartment to play his loving spouse.

I say yuck and double yuck. My displeasure over this contract with the gross Mad Lucus was too bad for this idiot Master of yours. I no longer believed that my fate as the prisoner of the Mortar palace was unavoidable. Keeping him the happy man had become the necessity given my horrific fate as the foundation Monarch of Kaiser Haus. He was my only reasonable choice to name the regent able to speak for me the second I turned eighteen. This will happen in only five months from that day I tell you about now.

If I was unsuccessful at keeping his desire to possess me stoked, I was doomed, I was in no hurry to suffer the same horrific treatment from the Silk Queen I'd already endured during my last incarceration in the stoney cell. Like it or not, with each sunset my days of freedom, no matter how minor, were rapidly coming to an end.

This bitter knowledge was the fuel that kept me going despite the deplorable physical condition I was in at the time. I wanted to take to the bed and give myself time to heal, but as I said, the precious moments were ticking away. There wasn't a moment I could dare to waste in my efforts to prepare the best I could for what I thought was the inevitable.

It was my plan to force the residents of Kaiser Haus to respect my power over them in the few months I had left above ground. I'd already tried to gain dare allegiance by lobbying for better treatment of the subjugated and showing mercy toward those not completely loyal to me. I'd nearly been killed learning the hard way the population of the Haus didn't appreciate my efforts.

Well, this Mortar King had painfully discovered that Machiavelli was correct. It was far safer to be feared than loved. The collared of the Haus were mindless servants that only appreciated the one with a heavy boot on their necks. I needed all them to understand that the brutality that I was willing to level on them was more dangerous to their survival than even that of their Stasi Masters.

If I could manage to do this to perfection, I thought it could offer some protection once I was helpless in the Palace. Surely no one but Jonas, plus Byron and Peter, would dare think they could mistreat me ever again without facing dire consequences for their cruel actions.

Anyway, I rushed to Matz's old apartment without concern that I didn't have the key to it on me. I'm not sure what I was thinking. It's probably desperation to avoid anyone finding out about my dishonorable loss of bowel control that caused me to forget that important fact. The realization of my momentary lapse of good judgement came to my understanding just as his wooden door come into my view.

I rolled my eyes over my stupidity but decided to approach and give a try to enter anyway. Of course, I found the knob stubborn to my efforts to gain entry. With a growl I kicked the bottom of it with light fury while cursing it under my breath.

All around me, the traveling collars took off running appearing frightened over witnessing my mild fit of fury. I chuckled with humor as I watched them scatter off like roaches when you turn on the lights of the room. It goes without saying, I really started to believe that my dark plotting had already taken strong root within their dark hearts.

My momentary distraction of enjoying the demonstration of fear from the Haus residents was broken by a tapping on my right shoulder. I let out a yelp and jumped back into the apartment door, nearly blind with terror of my own. I barely recognized the owner of the hand that had brought me out of my dark mirth.

I saw Cary pull his arm away from my direction with an expression of surprise on his face. It was then that I realized Matz and Roland were standing next to him. The three of them didn't say a word while I panted and attempted to calm down my heart palpitations. It took several seconds for my fear reaction to calm down enough for me to regain the ability to speak.

The second I found my tongue again I yelled out, "God dammit. You scared the hell out of me, Cary. You better never sneak up on me like that ever again or I will kill you for it." With a groan of frustration and pain I reached down and picked up the walking cane I had dropped during my startle reaction.

Cary cast his eyes to the floor and the frown come across his face as he replied in a whiny tone, "I apologize Christian baby. I thought you saw us coming. We've been looking for you ever since we stopped by your apartment. Lucus told us you were wandering about the Haus. Where have you been hiding? Dammit, I've suffered being forced to stay away from you for over a week already. I just assumed you'd be as eager as me to enjoy each other's private company."

I glared at the Shadow King angrily as I responded angrily, "Oh you can be sure that while I laid around pretending to be sick, your touching was the only thing consuming my thoughts. As for being alone with me, if that was your desire then what the fuck did you bring your buddies along with you for?"

Matz's face took on the look of insult I'd come to know far to well as he yelped out, "Wait a fucking minute, Mad Maxx. I think you're forgetting we are partners, all of us, not just Cary here. His business with you is always ours too."

I nodded then said with a scowl, "I forget nothing Matz. Now are you fellows interested in getting around to this meeting with me or do you desire to stand here airing out our secrets for all the Haus to hear? If so, then would one of you

311

useless pricks be so kind as to unlock this motherfucking door."

Roland blew out his breath and moved toward the entry while digging for the key in his jeans as he replied, "Someone woke up on the wrong side of the bed this morning. Come on Mad Maxx, calm down. We are all friends here. There is no need to use insulting pet names when addressing the men that love you as much as each of us truly do." He opened the door and stepped aside so that I could enter.

I pushed him harshly as I walked past and said hatefully, "You love me until the dime runs out is what you mean, asshole. Move aside. You blocking my path with your big head and overblown ego." Roland's eyes went wide in surprise at my apparent irritation but he didn't offer to move as he watched me disappear into the darkened room.

Using the cane, I flipped on the light switch and nearly hit the floor from the shock over the sights my eyes reported to my brain. The normally empty living area had been completely redecorated with many pieces of high-end furniture. I almost left thinking I'd entered the wrong residence by accident. That is until I noticed Matz's ratty recliner still held its original spot in the middle of the room.

The three Wolf pack members streamed in behind me single file, each of them chuckling over my reaction of shock over the changes. I glanced at Matz briefly. He caught me looking at him and shrugged. Without saying a word I rushed to the bedroom both to find out if it had been rehauled and to check the closet for that pair of clean breeches I needed.

Cary didn't bother to ask my permission to follow but insisted on keeping pace behind me. I growled under my breath thinking it a burden that he couldn't take the hint I was in no mood for company.

As I suspected, the old bed that had been barely more than a lumpy mattress on a rusty frame had been replaced. A fine canopy one with lovely maroon curtains occupied the space now, with a dark wood sleeping table sitting next to it. I quickly counted it contained four heavy drawers. It didn't take the genius to know Matz thought having a place to keeping the items required to do my job as the whore close was a good investment. That bag of sexual themed things would still be needed whenever I worked inside the Catholic confessional, ja?

Without saying anything to my silent Shadow King, I hurriedly went to the closet. A sigh of relief escaping me as I saw that despite all this new stuff, Matz hadn't decided to chuck out everything. My spare pair of breeches hung there silently waiting for me to retrieve them. I did just that too, then headed for the bathroom with urgency in my steps.

To my dismay, Cary still didn't seem able to take the hint. He followed me into the small space and once clear of the door slammed it shut. I ignored his non-verbal attempts to alert me to his anger while trying to use my near useless hands to work the knobs for the shower.

After being unsuccessful in this task that would bring me mercy for a few moments, Cary cleared his throat and said with fury, "What the fuck did I do to piss you off at me this time, Christian? I demand you tell me right this Goddamned minute because I swear I've no idea how much more of this silence between us I can take."

I shot a look of frustration at him as I replied, "Why are you standing there yapping instead of helping me turn on the water? If you insist upon playing the voyeur to my situation of indignity I would think it is the least you can do."

Cary's expression melted from obvious fury to complete shock as he responded, "Have you gone deaf, Christian? I'm not filling the air with wasted words about the weather or worthless Haus gossiping. I asked you to tell me the reason you are acting like you're pissed off when I know I'm guilty of no crime against you."

I turned my head up to stare at the ceiling as I yelled out, "I've shit my pants, if you must know, Goddammit. I need to get this foulness off my open wounds before I end up with far worse than just the shameful memory of it."

Cary gasped and his expression softened to one of pity as he stammered out, "Oh my God. I'm so sorry, baby. I, uhm, didn't realize. Here allow me to help you get cleansed." He nearly knocked me to the floor as he rushed to turn on the facet.

I regained my balance and yelped out, "Be careful for fucks sake, you jive ass turkey. What is your damage, dude? Can you not see me taking up the space over here, man? You

314

nearly sent me to munching carpet. You know that's not allowed for this cocksucker."

Cary stopped his attempts to turn on the shower and turned his head to staring at me as he replied in the frightened sounding tone, "Huh? What is wrong with your voice, Christian? For that matter what the hell did you say? What does is a jive ass turkey and that thing you say, dude? Is that even a word?"

I snorted as I said, "These breeches aren't going to just crawl off me by themselves. How about you keep your trap shut and come over here to help a fellow out of a tight spot, ja?" I pointed at the floor in front of me.

The Shadow King worked the knobs until the water started then stood up to approach me as he replied, "Well now that's better. There is the Christian I have been missing. Of course I'm more than happy to help you get naked, baby. That is always been and always will be my pleasure." A lustful smile broke across his face.

Without any sign of aggression I responded, "Come and get it while it's hot then, lover boy."

When Cary got within my reach I lifted my cane with speed and swung it like the baseball bat. I let lose my blow into his oncoming frame about shoulder level. It collided with his left upper arm. An ear shattering crack and Cary's shocked wail of pain filled the air just as it broke into two pieces. The Shadow King fell to his knees at my feet almost before the sections of mangled wood hit the floor.

315

He ended his wail and yelled out in the confused sounding tone, "Holy hell. Why, Christian? Goddamn it that hurt."

I leaned down into his face so that I could stare into his eyes as I replied in barely restrained fury, "I told you that I'm in the most pitiful of situations. You know damned well this was caused by the rough affections of far too many eager cocks seeking there thrill without concern for the damage it caused me. Not only do you come in here as the witness to my dishonor. But Matz and Roland in the other room surely heard you loudly claim to love me and demand that I lick your imaginary wounds you say I've caused. Now, you can claim I am honestly furious at you because you think of nothing but of yourself in my moment of need. Since you don't respect my right to privacy nor my requests for aid, then you will be treated like everyone else in this fucking Haus. You shall kneel in the presence of your King and suffer punishment as I deem fit for your bad manners too."

Cary gasped and dropped his gaze to the floor rapidly as he responded in the raspy whisper, "Christian, please stop this. I hear you, my love. Again, I've judged your erratic behaviors incorrectly without calmly waiting for the proper explanations to be handed to me at your leisure. I beg your forgiveness. I thank you for the mercy of it."

I snorted then replied, "I've already given you far too much of that, Cary. Yet, you continue to push for more, even when you are fucking aware I'm far past my limits. That ends today, lover. Get up, help me clean up this mess I've made of myself, and keep your pretty mouth shut. Or, baby, I'm gonna staple your lips closed forever. You dig?"

He glanced up and I saw his expression of fear as he whispered, "Ja, ja I hear you, Master. I do as you command without further delay." With that he took to his boots and quickly began to remove my soiled clothing.

The air in the room grew damp with the rising steam of the flowing shower water while I endured Cary's clumsy work at dressing services. Though his skill was poor, he managed to get my vampire jacket, blouse and boots off in a short time. I was getting close to losing my temper again before he finally started unbuttoning my breeches. I wanted nothing more than to have the slimy cloth off my abused flesh faster than he was moving.

When at last, the Shadow King peeled the clingy cloth from my lower body. It wasn't the waste contents from my bowels that spilled out. The ceramic tiles were suddenly showered with crimson rain from the slow running river of blood flowing from my hindside.

Cary let out a gasp then yelped out sounding terrified, "My God, you're bleeding all over the place, baby. Matz. Matz. Hurry up and get in here. I think Christian is seriously injured somewhere. Roland, call the Haus doctor. We need help in here."

I backhanded Cary with suddenness and yelled loudly, "Ignore those commands, boys. Cary doesn't have the authority to speak for his King. He is being dramatic. I'm not harmed nor in need of Doctor Attila's skills. You just mind your business and keep watch on the door. If you do as you are told then I might let you live another day." I kept my angered gaze on the clearly upset Shadow King as I said that.

He held his reddening cheek and mumbled, "You need help, uhm, your Majesty. If you don't desire I get assistance for you from the doctor, fine. At least, tell me where does this blood come from? Please, believe me. I am only trying to serve you in the way that will bring you the best comfort, not trying to injure you further. Nor incite any more anger from you."

I stepped out of my disheveled breeches and hopped into the tub as I replied flatly, "That is your problem, Cary. You must be told everything twice. I already said I suffer from the insensitivity of those brutes that raped me near to death less than a fortnight ago. You are no better than Jonas to think your mare magically heals faster when badly used than any other being can claim. Bleeding and shitting without meaning to is the daily indignity I must bear. It is the sad fact I'm cursed to this horror with only the service return of false words of love and affection you keep giving to me. Now, go stand over by the door. I demand you give me a little privacy. I wish to attend to my personal pain and indignity without the burden of your nosey questions added to this nightmare." I pulled the shower curtain closed with a loud huff, making it damned clear I wasn't going to allow Cary to argue with me further.

The water flowed down my head like hands of a gentle mother. I stood under the showerhead allowing it to caress my aching flesh. This small comfort was quickly interrupted by my noticing of the concerning amount of bleeding I apparently was doing. With a nervousness building within I watched the river of departing fluid tinged to red head down the drain in the movement of the cyclone.

For a few moments, I wondered if Cary wasn't correct. There was far too much exiting my veins to say that the cause of it was nothing but a little left over blood from my original injuries. The thing I thought important to do is to discover the origin of the damage. I carefully examined my stitched wounds and found all of them free of any unexpected re-opening.

Then with a groan, I slowly realized the source of the blood was the very place I suspected from the start. It wasn't the nasty waste caste off by my gut that had gushed out of me when I stood up but the release of a heavy blood flow.

As you recall, Doctor Attila had just repaired my sphincter due to extreme tearing. He'd warned me and everyone else that he knew that had interest in my favors that I needed to heal. I was not to engaging in anal intercourse for six weeks or I would be at risk for serious and possibly irreparable damage.

Suddenly I realized the ripping sensations of pain in my middle, along with the tell-tale signs of blood, were dishonorably very familiar. Fury beyond comprehension burned in my chest as I finally understood that someone had fucked me within the last few hours. Worse than that, they had done this without my consent or even knowing it, and they did it with untampered violence.

319

My rage fueled thoughts switched to that meeting I'd had with Noah. While it was the truth our tryst gotten a bit rougher than I intended it to, he'd never touched me in anyway. Giving him the blow job certainly wouldn't open up the stitching in my sensitive area.

I let out an infuriated growl when I finally figured out the DJ had done this to me. No wonder he had offered me the drugged donut. He knew I love the chocolate and wouldn't turn down his offer to have it. No doubt he wanted to knock me out so he could have me anyway he wished without granting me the mercy to deny his cruel interests.

Well, that was the last straw. I'd had it with this creepy guy. Bad enough he had done all he could to sully my good reputation by announcing my mistake over the radio waves. But raping my already ravaged ass was going too far. I jumped from the shower, livid and determined to find the DJ without delay. It was my intentions to destroy him and his radio like I should have done the minute he targeted me many years before.

I cast my sights on Cary. He was loitering by the door, staring at his feet appearing sullen. I cleared my throat so that he'd realize I had exited the tub. Without delay he came rushing toward me and took up one of the fancy towels hanging on the decorative bathroom rack. I stood there silently fuming as my Shadow King began drying off my flesh.

Cary knew that I was very grouchy but despite my earlier attempt to teach him some polite manners he decided to test my nerves when he said, "So, is this the way it will be between us from now on? Do you really believe that I will be happy as your lover now that you tell me you intend to boss me around but I have no recourse other than to tolerate it?"

I rolled my eyes and sighed with frustration as I replied, "Cary, I'm getting real tired of constantly having to play both your mare and your nursemaid. You knew before we bonded that I was the King of the Collars. I seem to recall that is one of the reasons you desired to become my lover in the first place. Not that I'm saying you came to me seeking to associate with one that could raise you from the dirt into the sky, but that's what I did, isn't it? Now, this business with becoming the Mortar Monarch wasn't that much of a change in the power position I'm forced to play in the Haus. Yet, when it comes to realizing your duty to demonstrate ultimate trust and loyalty to my crowns, you continue to show public disrespect. Others in this place see that, my love. If you don't stop they will think me the weak Master that isn't worth obeying, ja? Why must I keep reminding you that our relationship is far more complex than that of the usual sort in more ways than I wish to count? Do you enjoy having to dress me because I have once again been nearly ripped to pieces?"

Cary shook his head and dropped his gaze appearing shamed as he responded, "You know damned well I don't, Christian. I know what you say is the truth of it, but I keep on feeling like somehow I will lose your affection. It drives me crazy thinking that one day you will love me no more."

With a groan I replied, "You keep on acting the jealous ass that prophecy is going to come true. Either because I kill you in a blind rage over your nasty insults or because the residents decide I'm the pushover and you are promptly made into the widower. Can't you see that the stakes in this game of power are too high to be bargained with? When we are around others you either are my ally or you are my enemy. Only when we are alone can I take the position as the subjugated to your affections. I thought we had come to this understanding already, but here we are, yet again dealing with it. You must decide if you wish to become exclusive with your commoner sex partners. Because if you wish to continue to spice up your love life by adding high value in your trysts by remaining my Shadow King, than you must obey me without hesitation. I've no more time to waste on this old business between us." I glared at him ready to throw him the fuck out of my life if he didn't respond properly to my demands of him.

He gasped, then with an expression of shock on his face stammered out, "I don't know what rumors you've been told but I haven't been slipping around behind you back."

I chuckled with evil humor as I replied, "Ah, so this is your answer to my question then? You sure you don't want to take a moment of time I don't have to rethink your words? Perhaps, the blood loss has made me groggy and I heard you incorrectly, ja? I asked you if you are going to start obeying my commands without constantly questioning me, or if you desire I send you away. I love you Cary, I honestly do. But I no longer feel guilty that without me you will be stuck in the unfulfilled marriage. I know that nowadays you could find your pleasures with your many black collar lovers and leave me the hell alone. Don't bother to try to lie about what I already know is the facts. You are the natural beauty, but when you attempt to put on the false face of indignation. It causes you to become the ugliest thing I've ever seen, lover."

Cary swallowed hard and I noticed sweat started to bead on his forehead as he said, "So, that's the reason you show indifference to my affections. You do believe that I have taken a lover or two and now you are jealous, ja?" That made me break out into wild laughter.

Once I calmed my mirth I replied in the solemn tone, "Do you really think I give a damn how many men you fuck, Cary? God knows this worthless man is in no position to caste a stone at your sexual indiscretions, no matter what I hear. I could care less who you sleeping with. I said that I love you and I mean that with all my heart. If fucking half the Haus would make you happy, than by all means enjoy yourself, lover. This problem between us isn't of the frivolous nature. I need to have faith in your ability to protect me and honestly wish to see me thrive. That means you must lay down your overblown ego to kneel at my feet anytime I demand you do it, no quarrel, and no hesitation. Otherwise, I think you and I must say goodbye. For the continued stable mental health of both of us."

The Shadow King nodded while still keeping his eyes to his boots said, "I think I underestimate your intelligence and wisdom far too often, Christian. I thank you for the mercy of your understanding, and your honest love. I am the lucky man to find favor with your beautiful heart. I no doubt don't deserve you but I will promise to try harder to be the man you need me to be."

I shook my head and replied in the angry growl, "Do better than try, Cary. You must do. The season for practice is over and the final game already has begun. I must not fail because there are no second chances. I'm grateful you've decided to remain at the side of the team that is the clear underdog in this race, but I meant everything I've said. We will never have this discussion again. Next time you get in my way toward the finish line, I will permanently remove you. Now, go to the cabinet under the sink and retrieve the box of the feminine napkins you find there. I need to borrow your pair of boxers because I didn't think to keep the extra pair here. This bleeding is heavy and Doctor Attila's office is a bit of a walk to reach. We wouldn't want this lovely clean up job go to waste, would we?"

Cary took to his feet and unbuttoned his jeans as he said in the curious tone, "Okay, sure thing, love. I happy loan my underwear to you. If it is permitted to say, I'm happy you've decided to see the doctor over this injury that's causing such a mess you are forced to put on the maxi-pads."

I tore my eyes from the disrobing Shadow King and looked upon the broken cane as I replied with a sigh, "Ja, I think the doctor won't be as thrilled to visit with me as you are that I am. I've got another problem that isn't so easily fixed with borrowed shorts and cotton barriers though. My left knee isn't functional as it once was. My mobility will be compromised without the aid of that useful walking tool."

Cary motioned me to lift my feet to step into his boxers as he started the dressing service and said, "Ah, well no worries, lover. You can lean on me and I will accompany you to the clinic, ja?"

I nodded. "That may work. I forgot to asking you, Cary. How was the labor for Roselina? I heard from Mad Lucus you are the proud papa of the beautiful baby boy. Being the father must be wonderful. I confess that I'm never jealous over your status as the lustful stud among the eager schwuler black collars but I am desperately envious of your place as the blessed patriarch." He sucked in his breath appearing as if I had punched him in the gut.

I realized that it wasn't my questions about his son but because I'd openly acknowledged his legendary status as the frisky promiscuous Shadow King. I swear that I honestly wasn't angry about the many rumors Mad Lucus had more than happily filled me in on about Cary's many conquests. I didn't expect him to stay monogamous to me, especially during all those months I'd been missing when Nestor nearly castrated me.

No doubt Cary had assumed like everyone else I was dead. I certainly didn't expect the man to deny his baser urges. Not after giving him his first taste of the pleasure he had craved since determining his sexual preference was for males. Plus, I'd not shown real interest in his affections prior to that lusty moment we shared in Roland's apartment the day I'd re-emerged from the care of the DJ within the walls of the Haus.

I guess I could've kept pretending I didn't know about his many ongoing torrid affairs, but that would put Cary in the bad position. If he didn't fess up on his own, knowing that many in the Haus were gossiping about it, I couldn't be sure he'd be honest about the important things between us. I'd desired to wait until a better moment to bring this silly business up with him. Thanks to his insistence to behave the needy bitch, I figured it may as well be dealt with so we could move past it.

Cary avoided my gaze as he responded, "Uhm, the baby and Roselina thrive. I'm indeed the man with many blessings to keep me smiling, that I agree. Christian, well, I, uhm, what do you want me to do? I cannot change the things that have happened, but I can correct the errors for the future. Say the word and I swear on my honor, I shall never show interest in anyone else for the rest of my life."

I shook my head as I leaned forward and kissed his forehead lightly then replied, "I already told you I wish only that you never feel neglected. I'm going to be removed from the sights of the world above shortly, my love. Making the pledge of monogamy isn't what I wish to gain from you. If you did that then you'd become condemned right along with me. A lonely man with only the hasty visits to your miserable lover encased in the heavy burden of stone and silver. That's not a fate I would wish on the one I love. Life was meant to be enjoyed. Please chase and capture all the pleasures possible until the reaper calls for your soul. I swear to you it will be the bliss I see in your eyes that will be my only light to drive away the bitter darkness coming to claim me. This you understand, ja?"

Cary's eyes suddenly fogged over with the threat of rain as he whimpered in response, "You speak as if you are about to be the dead man, Christian. I promise I will come to see you every day in the Palace. I won't allow anyone to stop me from holding you in my arms as often as you wish me to."

I chuckled bitterly then replied, "Don't make promises others in this Haus have the power to see you don't keep. You will soon be tempered in your ability to engage me with your lustful cuddles. Take your pick of villains, Cary. Mad Lucus, Jonas, or possibly that slippery Gretta will send you over the banister before they allow you to interfere with their full possession of my royal person. Don't be upset by this news, lover. You surely realized this terrible reality before this idiot lover of yours did. We must seize the moment and forget about the past or the future. Neither are of much use to us in avoiding our fate, ja? Now finish this dressing service and help me get to the clinic. I'm feeling woozy and this maxi pad isn't the sexy accessory to be sporting. Hahaha." The Shadow King sniffed back his burgeoning tears and chuckled mildly over my joke while he went back to finishing his task.

Cary wasn't the most graceful in his work to get my nakedness covered, but he managed to do it. Once I was sure none of the oozing blood could re-soil my breeches I motioned him that I was ready for the trip to visit with Doctor Attila. He wrapped his arm around my waist and I put my arm around his shoulders in the effort to gain balance. It took some effort but we managed to smoothly coordinate our movements. Then without any further discussion we exited the bathroom together.

We found Matz and Roland laying on the canopy bed in the spoon cuddle. The Wolves sat up, clearly concerned by the sight of Cary holding me like the cripple. Roland quickly rolled off the mattress and rushed toward us, appearing to be interested in becoming the unnecessary third wheel.

I growled out angrily just as the Wolf attempted to grab my free arm. "Get off me, Roland. Move aside and stop the fawning. Cary has this handled just fine."

Roland frowned and replied, "What has happened? Did Mad Maxx have a seizure?"

Cary grunted and shifted under my weight as he responded, "I don't have time for chattering. His Majesty is heavy as hell and in urgent need of medical assistance. If you desire to help, then clear the path in front of us as we journey toward the clinic. Otherwise I suggest you wait here till I return."

Matz let out a yelp and rolled from the bed as Roland had just as he exclaimed, "Wait, Cary. Is this something Mad Lucus will think we did to Mad Maxx? We don't need any trouble from that crazy bastard. If he forbids us to visit with the Mortar King how can we afford all this? The bills are already piling up as it is. Mad Maxx hasn't worked for weeks and the clients are getting antsy saying he isn't ever returning."

I glared at my pimp hatefully as I bellowed, "Is that all you think about is money, Matz? Look here you idiot. If I don't get to the doctor in short order, those greedy perverts are going to discover they speak the truth of it. If only to shut up your bitching, then I say to tell them I will return to most of my duties as the Haus whore in another few days. Only the penetration services are off the menu for a while yet. Everything else I think I can handle as long as for the next few weeks you don't overbook my talents."

Matz's eyes went wide as he breathed out, "Maxx I didn't mean, oh shit, I'm really sorry I said that brother. I know you barely survived God knows what. It's just that, well, Mad Lucus been saying that the Wolf pack is part of the reason you ended up in that mess with the Stasi. If you are to quit working then Roland's income isn't nearly enough to feed and house us or the silvers you painted black."

Cary nearly bust my eardrum as he yelled in response, "For fucks sake, Matz. Don't you pay any attention? The King is seriously injured and you dare to bring up this bullshit at this moment? This discussion can wait. If Mad Lucus dares to think he can lay the blame for this situation on us, I will personally deal with him. Now will you help me or nein?"

Matz hauled ass to open the bedroom door for us. Roland rushed ahead to clear the path of the traffic in the congested first-floor hallway. Cary grunted and puffed as he pulled me along next to him following his brother Wolves out of the apartment.

I did my best to carry myself by limping in unison with Cary's rapid stride. For a few moments, our trip went along without too many impediments. Roland and Matz's

329

reputation as fierce fighters, along with my own as a brutal Monarch, worked wonders at making everyone happy to leave the center and grab the nearest wall. Hahaha.

Then just as we turned a corner I saw one of the submissives wearing a black collar refuse to take to his knees. He stood in our way with the expression of defiance on his face and the mark of the Elders on his tunic. I recognized this young man immediately. He'd more than once been sent by the Vampire Jonas to seek me out to demand audience with me.

Th black collar put up his hand and cleared his throat then called out to us, "Halt. I've been assigned to retrieve the Mortar King for attendance to his husband, father, and guardian, the honorable Elder Jonas. Your Majesty. I must beg you to break from your present task and follow me, Sire."

Roland and Matz stopped dead in their tracks and turned around staring at me in apparent confusion as to what to do. Cary, on the other hand, began to growl low in his throat. No doubt he was about to blow up in full on fury at this servant that was helpless to refuse the orders of a crazy bat.

I gently squeezed him and replied to the black collar attendant, "Can you be a dear and return to your Master a message for me?"

The young man shook his head and said, "Nein, your Majesty. The honorable Elder told me you'd attempt to refuse his command you meet with him. He says if you deny him what he requests with politeness. He will not show manners when he punishes you for it. I beg you to forgive me for relaying those most harsh words, my Lord, but I am only the messenger." He then fell into the graceful kneel with his head pointed at the floor in a show of reverence.

I rolled my eyes then cast them about the hallway for a second. My sights set upon a small silver collar male not far from Roland's left flank. He appeared to be around the age of fifteen or sixteen, with dark auburn hair and very pale white skin.

Cary was trembling surely from both his efforts to haul my big frame and from holding back his fury.

I leaned into his ear and whispered, "That boy over there. Tell him to come here. I wish to speaking with him a second. You, Matz and Roland continue to the clinic to alert Doctor Attila I will be with him shortly to enjoy his skills, ja?"

The Shadow King gasped and shot me a look of fear as he replied, "Christian baby, I cannot just drop you here in the middle of the fucking hallway. If the Wolf pack leaves, you will be nearly helpless if any of these monsters decide to attack their King. Plus, you are unable to travel unaided to boot."

I sneered at him as I responded through clenched dentures, "You getting demented, Cary? What did we just agree only moments ago? I am your King, and you are my fucking servant, ja? Well, then serve me, damn you." I let go of him and pushed him away.

Cary's eyes demonstrated he was beyond frightened as he watched me maintain my stance despite his absence. Without daring to anger me further he put his finger into his mouth and let loose a loud whistle. All eyes of the many kneeling submissives and Dominants focused on the Shadow King immediately.

He bellowed out trying to sound official as possible, "You, boy, what is your name." he pointed at the kid I'd requested him to hail.

The silver collared boy shivered and stammered in response, "Liliam, Master." Cary glanced at me.

I calmly called to the silver child, "Liliam, your King commands you to fetch the Head Dungeon Master. Bring him with you ready to serve his Master. Do this quickly. I'm not the patient Monarch that has all day to wait for his attendance."

Liliam nodded, then jumped up and ran like the wind in the direction of the stone staircase of the Dungeons.

I watched him retreat then turned my attention back to Jonas's creature to say, "You will wait here with me for the return of my subjects. Cary, take these fellows and obey my orders. Noah will assure that I'm safely delivered to my original destination the moment I'm done swatting the bat out of my hair." I waved him away with the expression of stoic sureness on my face.

Cary nodded and hand gestured for Roland and Matz to come with him. All three of the Wolves looked back at me several times with overtly apprehensive expressions before they were finally beyond sight.

You could've heard a pin drop in the hallway while we waited for Liliam to return with Noah. Not even a cough or fart escaped from the crowd of witnesses cowering all around me and Jonas's black collar. I did all I could to stand as still as possible.

That pain in my middle was reaching near maddening levels. All I could do is wish that I'd managed to make it to the clinic before this motherfucker had managed to discover my whereabouts. I did do a quick scan of the faces within viewing distance, hoping for one of the only times in my life to see my shady brother Byron among them. Oh what I wouldn't have given for a shot of his magical pain killing mixture at that moment.

Only about fifteen minutes passed before my grateful eyes spotted Noah with Liliam fallowing close behind approaching with speed.

I glared at Jonas's collar as I growled out, "Get off your knees. You will lead the way the moment the Head Master has arrived to aid me in granting the honorable Elder his audience." The submissive did as I commanded without hesitation.

Noah approached and like all before him dropped into the graceful kneel, Liliam did this also, as he said in the reverent tone, "I am here at your request, your Majesty. Tell your worthless servant how I can be of service and see it done to perfection."

I nodded then with a groan replied, "I require you to help me get up to the sixth floor. My injuries prevent easy travel. You have my permission to carry my royal person. Do this in the most comfortable way possible to assure my fragile condition isn't further aggravated by this necessary journey. This you understand, ja?" I saw a small smile tug on Noah's lips as he nodded, he comprehended my orders.

Noah appeared to nearly float when he took to his boots. I stood there unflinchingly while the huge man scooped my ailing frame into his arms. He held me like I were the bride being joyfully taken across the threshold. The Dungeon Master didn't even appear to strain over the addition of my hefty flesh to his own. I snuck a quick glance at his beautiful face and felt my heart flutter when I caught him doing the same. He flashed a rapid grin at me and then put his eyes forward while taking on the expression of indifference.

I shook off that momentary experience of thrill and turned my attention back to my silver helper as I said, "Liliam, you're a credit to your class. Tell me, do I recognize you as the catamite of Master Kay?"

Liliam nodded but didn't look up from the floor as he replied, "Ja, you are correct, your Majesty. I thank you for your words of kindness that I surely don't deserve."

I chuckled then motioned the black collar messenger that we were to begin our journey upstairs as I replied, "You have indeed earned my affection, Liliam. On your feet child. You shall be my guest. Follow your King. Keep up and don't be concerned that your Master shall be upset to be without your talents for a bit. I'll explain the reasons for this hijacking of his precious collar once we finish with my official business." Liliam nodded then as commanded took up the rear of our strange procession heading for the Elder's back staircase.

We traveled in total silence until around the fourth floor. We ran into Ruslan and Sasha returning from a visit with the recuperating Gretta on the sixth floor. I motioned the burly Russian pair to pause their journey for the quick visit with me.

Ruslan eyed Noah with suspiciousness in his gaze as I said in the friendly sounding tone, "Ah, dearest comrade. It would appear that I've missed that appointment we had earlier today. I wonder could you find it within you to forgive me? It seems I'm not as healed as I'd first thought when we met earlier."

The Head of the Guard snorted then replied, "Apparently not,, your Majesty. I can spare Sasha for a bit if you need to be delivered back to the safety of your sick bed." He motioned for his partner to relieve Noah of his substantial burden.

I put up my hand to halt Sasha as I calmly said, "The Head Master's assistance is satisfactory but I thank you for the kind offer. You both are princes among men. However, if you really desire to be of use to your King, might I impose upon one of you worthy gentlemen to do a task of equal importance to my comfort?"

Sasha nodded then said gruffly, "Of course, Sire. I'd be happy to serve your needs. I'm not in the hurry to go anywhere at the moment."

With a chuckle I replied, "Ah, thank you, Sasha. I require the immediate attendance of both the Mortar regent to be Mad Lucus and the Mortar Dungeon Master Byron. Do you think it possible to find these two and demand their meet me at the honorable Elder Jonas's apartment with haste?"

Sasha bowed and responded, "As you wish, your Majesty. They are as good as at his door already." He turned around and practically ran up the steps to make sure his words were not the empty ones.

Ruslan watched him for a moment then turned his focus back on me as he said, "The Elder, the regent, the Head Master, the Mortar Dungeon Master and the Triple Crowned. Hmmm, that's a lot of important men all in one spot at the same time. Men that don't have much affection for the company of each other I add. I wonder is this a conversation the Head of the Guard should also attend, your Majesty?"

I chuckled with evil in my tone as I replied, "The more the merrier they say, Ruslan. Lead the way if you wish to come along. However, just remember, curiosity killed the cat, ja?"

Ruslan snorted and said, "Thankfully I'm not the pussy, your Majesty. I thank you for your invitation. I gratefully accept it." He bowed slightly, then like his brother Sasha rapidly ascended the staircase taking up the lead.

We reached Jonas's door in record time, given the circumstances. Ruslan offered to knock since Noah's hands were full. Hahaha. While the collared males took to the kneel at Noah's feet. I heard the footsteps of the fiend long before he opened up.

His initial expression of thrill quickly fell into one of absolute shock. I chuckled despite myself over the thought that in his darkest nightmares he never expected to be greeted by the sight that he saw that day.

Jonas, ever the asshole, appeared to quickly pull himself from surprise then gruffly called out, "What the hell is the meaning of this, Christian Axel? I sent Eichhörnchen to fetch you, not half the Goddamned Haus." I saw him shoot the glance of fury at Ruslan and then a far worse one at Noah as he said that.

I yawned then patted Noah on one of the huge arms that held me. "Do you always have to be dramatic, pops? I thought I'd bring a few friends along, just in case your party was lacking in interesting company."

Jonas's veins began to pop out on his forehead as he replied through clenched pointy teeth, "Don't piss with me, boy. Somebody better start explaining the meaning of this intrusion or so help me I'll torture each of you until I get the answer." He looked to Ruslan then to Noah but both men kept their heads down and tongues still despite his threats.

After I let the Vampire do his very best to intimidate my confused crew I tapped on Noah and said, "Okay Head Master, you may gently return me to my feet. Then you and

Ruslan shall remain out here in the Elder's hallway until my other guests arrive. Eichhörnchen, Liliam, you fellows come over here and aid your King. I cannot walk without help, Jonas. Not that you care, but I'm not feeling that well these days. Go ahead, lead the way, Herr Dracula. I've got my living crutches to assure that I can join you in the privacy of your lair." Jonas clicked his tongue appearing nearly ready to have the rage reaction but said nothing in response to my words.

Noah carefully put me to the floor. The collars rushed forward and took a place on each side of me. I allowed the young men to take my arms and using them for balance the three of us chased after the retreating vampire.

Once we were clear of his doorway, Jonas reached out and slammed it shut. He turned his furious glare at the collars. Both young men dropped to their knees rapidly, trembling in pure terror at the sight of his displeasure.

I stood there, no longer encumbered, and said with a humored tone, "Calm yourself, Jonas. You called and I came, didn't I? What is there to pissy about? Now, what the fuck is so important that you demand I miss my doctor's appointment?"

Jonas didn't break his fiery gaze from the frightened collars as he replied, "You were due to see Doctor Attila? I wasn't informed he had a meeting with you today."

With a shrug I said, "Neither was he. So? What do you want, dad? Spit it out will you. I have shit to do and standing here hoping that I don't fall down isn't at the top of my list, you know."

The Vampire shook off some of his irritation and turned his attention to me as he replied, "You haven't given me a transfusion in far too long, Christian Axel. Do you see these wrinkles? And my hair is sprouting snow. That is your fault. So, despite your unfortunate condition I must demand you do your job this minute before my bones start turning brittle."

I rolled my eyes and crossed my arms as I responded, "I have the doctor's note that says no penetration for at least the next five and a half weeks, lover. If you must suck my blood, that can be arranged with ease. You don't even need to get your fancy lancet in fact. Tell you what. I'll ask one of these lovely boys to pull down my breeches. Then I'll bend over and you can KISS my bloody ass." I yelled that last part. Hahaha.

Jonas let out a loud yell of fury and started to storm toward me. The two collars fell to their faces, yelping in terror. I stood there defiantly, refusing to attempt to escaping the backhand he was sure to be preparing to level on my head. I really couldn't retreat even if I had wanted to. That pain was threatening to send me to the floor crying like the helpless bitch by then. Yikes.

He stopped just inches from me and locked eyes with me as growled out, "You aren't getting out of this, Christian Axel. I refuse to allow you to bait me this time. I want what is mine and I will have it. I can be gentle or brutal about it. Up to you, boy."

With a sneer I replied, "Or perhaps you can take another route until I'm better suited to attend your rough needs. See these two beauties, that you've nearly scared to death? They are young, pretty, and the silver is the willing homosexual. You can drink blood from me if you must, but the sexual penetration of my flesh isn't possible. This isn't a lie I try to feed you. Christian Axel's shop is closed for renovations, lover. Choose one of them to stand in for the intercourse part of your feeding ritual, or I'm afraid I'll have to take you before the men I'm about to deputize as my council. They will find you guilty of attempting to kill the Mortar King with an action that I've offered suitable substitution for. I forget, but doesn't such a crime carry the death sentence?"

The Vampire stood there eyeing me doing his best to appear unafraid of my words for several moments. I could hear the boys at our feet whimpering over the thought that one of them was about to be brutally raped by the Vampire.

That made me want to laugh but thankfully I managed to quell my twisted sense of humor. This situation was serious. Levity at that point would work only to cause Jonas to think my words were a bluff. I was in a dire condition, and dealing with the historically insensitive brute, I'm grateful I was able keep quiet till he thought better of his unreasonable demands.

Finally Jonas backed up slightly and said, without breaking from my gaze, "This thing you suggest isn't possible. That isn't how the blood couple works and you know this. What the fuck am I to do? Five and a half weeks is far too long to wait. I age by the second, dammit." He was actually whining by the end of his statement.

I shook my head and replied, "Ah pops, which breaks my heart to hear you say. However, there isn't shit I can do about it. If you had wished to maintain our fucked up relationship as it was, then perhaps you should have muzzled your bitch Gretta, ja? So, am I to understand you don't wish to suck my blood and then finish the ritual using one of my subjects that I carefully selected for you?"

He waved me off and said in the frustrated tone, "Nein, I must decline your most generous offer, Christian Axel. I already told you the demons that hold off father time reside within you. The release I take with you after the feeding is the only way to filter out their power from the madness that rides along with them."

I let out a loud guffaw as I replied, "This poppycock you honestly believe? Well fuck me. You are more insane than me if you do, Jonas. Well never mind. You will never change, and I refuse to be misled by you twice in the same lifetime. I've told you time after time you age because that is what everything on earth does. There isn't a cure for old age within my veins, but I suspect that you know that. The horrible shit you do to me is because it feeds more than some crazy blood lust or fucked up superstition. The truth is that you love to see me suffer. Worse you steal my youth so that you can feel younger. That is beyond disgusting, and far worse than simply raping the unwilling."

Jonas shrugged then started to head back to his door as he called back to me, "Think whatever you like, Christian Axel. I don't require you to believe in it for the magic to work. If you cannot attend to my needs, then I suppose you are released. Go home to the prick Lucus. I command you to get back into bed and heal quickly. I won't force you to hold still for this today, but I also am not going to wait more than a fucking month either." He stopped and without looking back opened his entry wide.

I saw that Byron, Mad Lucus, Noah, Ruslan, Sasha, and strangely Fritz were hovering around in the hall just outside Jonas's door. The group of men were silently glaring at each other, appearing none too happy to be sharing company.

With a chuckle I motioned the collars at my feet to stand up. The young men did as ordered and each took up an arm. I didn't need to command them for the boys to realize that I desired their aid to help me leave with urgency. I kept my humored gaze locked onto Jonas's frustrated one as the three of us traveled toward the exit.

As we entered the narrow corridor Jonas approached his door and shot menacing glances at the audience that came to my call. I motioned my helpers to turn me around so that I could face Jonas. They performed this complex motion with perfection that made me proud to call them my subjects.

I cleared my throat and made sure that all eyes were on me as I said, "Oh, Jonas. one more thing. Do you see these fellow? I ordered them to come here without explanation for my motives. They came without argument nor hesitation. Do you see these pretty collars? One of each? They also obey their King without complaint. They didn't even try to run when a moment ago they assumed you would violate them like they were nothing more than the sex doll. I wonder why everyone else understands that I'm the Master of this Haus, but you continue to pretend you are above my power? You are only a little Prince, and not even likely to ever inherit the Fur Throne. Cora isn't too much older than you and she is the female. They live longer, ja?"

Jonas snarled in response, "I am very aware that you've become the Mortar and Collar King. I realize this rat bastard sneakily clothed you in the Golden Buckles too." He shot an angry glance at Noah. "But that is the point isn't it? They don't respect you any more than I do. This false display of obedience is merely the ploy to gain your favor. Each of them hope they can fool the biggest fool in the Haus into granting them favor. Once you do, they will ram it up your ass far deeper than I ever have, boy. That is the only power you really possess."

I laughed hard at his statement then replied in the vicious tone, "I am the Master of this Haus, Jonas. All must bow to me, and that includes deluded Vampires with a knack at appearing fierce but not a single kill. I am Power in the flesh. Oh, and Jonas, I am the law."

With that I turned with suddenness. I grabbed Liliam around his throat and before he had a moment to struggle leaned down and ripped out his throat with my teeth. Eichhörnchen stared unblinking at his brother collar that was wildly gripping at the gushing wound in his neck. He let out

343

a wail of horror and stepped back toward the banister. Almost in slow motion I turned and pushed Eichhörnchen over the banister.

His screams were still echoing in the distance as I pivoted and repeated that action on Liliam. The struggling youngster flew over the railing, hot on the tail of his black collar companion. I stood there glaring at the Vampire with Liliam's blood flowing in congealing rivers from my chin down my blouse.

Jonas's eyes were vide, unfocused and his expression dumbfounded. This look of stun was contagious among the gathered men standing as witness to the double murder I'd just committed against two of my own subjects.

I cannot express just how much it pleased me to see the terror in their eyes. I mean in the eyes of Eichhörnchen and Liliam. Though I confess watching the survivors struggle with uncomfortable emotions was pretty nice too.

Chapter 17: What A Catch.
Master Mad Maxx and submissive Meine Liebe

The frightened yelling and shouts of the residents rose up to the ears of all of us standing there on the sixth floor. There was no doubt that the witnessing of two collars flying off the banister was causing quite a bit of chaos.

I stood there saying nothing while the group of men I'd called together and Jonas continued to cast worried glances at each other. This silent confusion went on for far more time then I would have expected, given the usually take charge attitudes of these men.

Finally, Jonas appeared to recompose himself from that surprise ending I'd given those two boys as he said in the calm voice, "This is the reason we never gave you the toys to play with, Christian Axel. You always were far too rough with your things. Not that I honestly give a shit, but why did you feel the need to throw two perfectly good submissives over the edge, boy? It took me forever to train Eichhörnchen properly. Now I must replace him. Dat's gonna be the pain in the ass, you know."

Mad Lucus led out a yelp that sounded completely shocked over Jonas's insensitive words, then he yelled out, "Seriously, Jonas. That is all you worry about after seeing the horrific murders the Mortar King just committed? No wonder he is the brutal youth with the severe disturbance of mentality. He had only your bad judgement as the trainer for his way of viewing the world around him."

Jonas's expression turned furious as turned his attentions to the Mortar regent and growled in response, "He never ran around feeding people to the yard dogs nor tossing well trained submissives to their deaths when he was in my care, Lucus. You can attempt to point your perverted fingers at me but no one buys your empty accusations. Everyone knows it is your fault exclusively that there is suddenly many without heads around the Haus as of late. You took up with the cause of that hateful Silk Queen of ours and this calloused killer is the result of it. I dare you to deny it."

Mad Lucus took a step toward Jonas with hate glowing in his eyes as he replied, "I'm not the youngster with an easily suggestable mindset nor are any off these others around me, Jonas. Your accusations are not only rude, but an outrageous effort to spread lies that will not benefit you nor the Mortar King. I demand you give me the apology right this minute or I will be forced to see you punished for insulting the Mortar King's regent."

Jonas chuckled with the diabolical sound then said, "Oh, forgive me great one, for saying aloud what everyone whispers behind you back. You are right to demand that I remain silent and pretend you are honestly able to control the monster you've created. I beg your pardon. It is true that I am the cad to demonstrate my massive balls. Especially when you seem to hate the scrotum so much you wish to see them removed. Tell me something, Lucus, do you find that part of the male anatomy offensive because you are jealous that yours are miniscule or did it annoy you to have to keep moving the boy's massive pair out of the way while you rape him?"

Mad Lucus's face turned red with fast rising fury as he responded, "You are the twisted fiend suggest that my honest attempt to temper this boy's illness was for personal reasons. All the best authorities in the field of psychology recommend castration as the best cure to calm the violent schizophrenic. However, I know you already know that, Jonas. You are trying to win the Mortar King's favor by acting the ignorant asshole and nothing more. I refuse to engage any further with your low brow challenges to my rightful authority over the best treatment for the King's affliction."

I let out a loud bellow that caused all present to put their attention on me as I gruffly said, "Shut up, both of you. This noise is bothering my sensitive ears and neither of you were granted permission to speak. Noah, you come over here this minute and attend your king. I wish to be returned to the task that I was dishonestly interrupted from undertaking. Sasha, you and Bryon will go to the first floor and collect that garbage I've tossed. Take the corpses to the yard and rip them to pieces with your bare hands. Then feed my yard dogs the rotten flesh of those that have not earned the right to even feed the trees. The rest of you are to return to whatever deviltry you were engaged with before this idiot thought himself important enough to make demands of the Mortar King. You are dismissed." I waved them away while keeping an eye on the fast-approaching Head Dungeon Master.

Noah arrived and began to taken the position to lift me back into his arms when suddenly Jonas come running at the two of us. The Head Master halted his actions and without hesitation blocked the Vampire from his approach by placing his huge frame between us.

Jonas's face shown disbelief over this unexpected interference as he yelled out, "Get out of my way, Noah. How dare you think to prevent me from speaking with my husband, ward and son." He backhanded the Head Master with brutal force.

Noah took the blow without so much as a grunt. He shook his head and then with grace took to his knees before me and the Vampire.

In the calm voice he politely said, "I must beg your pardon honorable Elder, but his Majesty has given me the command that outranks your own. If you don't stand aside and allow me to obey my King's orders I will do what is necessary to remove your interference." With that Noah returned to his boots and once again attempted to pick me up.

Da Vampire let out a wail and kicked Noah in the backside with his pointy shoes as hard as he could. The Head Master winced and then shot me the look that appeared frustrated. To my surprise he turned around with speed and punched Jonas right in the nose. The Vampire wailed as blood poured from his nostrils like the hole in a water bucket. He quickly tried to stanch the rapid flow with his clawed hands, all the while cursing Noah with every crass word he possessed in his vocabulary.

I watched this humorous show for a second then called out in the angry tone, "I don't believe I stuttered fellows. You surely have better things to do then stand around cuddling your cocks in the hopes that I'll provide services to you. Get your asses back to work or find yourselves sharing space in the hounds bellies with the ones that found displeasing their King is fatal."

Jonas glared at me through his blood drenched hands as he mumbled, "Noah, you are the dead man. Ruslan, I demand you taken this bitch down to the dungeon and throw him into the pit for his crimes against a Prince of the Fur Throne."

Ruslan nodded then started to approach Noah, but I hand gestured him to halt as I replied, "You may send Noah to be punished for his crime after he completes the command I give to him first. The orders of the little Prince with limited power does not outrank that of the Master of this Haus and you know this Ruslan. Do not test me or I will see that you join the Head Master in the chains for worse than he has earned."

Ruslan took to his knees and said, "Understood, your Majesty. I ask your permission to follow you to your destination so that I may take possession of this criminal the moment you're satisfied with his service to you."

I nodded at the Captain of the Guard and replied, "Permission granted. Now, Noah? You already are going to lose an inch of flesh for daring to strike an Elder. Do you desire to taste the whip of your Mortar King as well? Do as I have commanded or that can be easily arranged."

Noah kept his eyes cast to his boots as he shook his head and responded, "Nein, your Majesty. I thank you for your mercy." He scooped me into his burly arms with speed and gentle poise immediately.

Jonas dropped his hands from cuddling his nose and flew at the two of us again. This time Noah could do nothing to prevent the Vampire from approaching his approach. Before I could demand that Ruslan, Byron, or Sasha end his assault on me, Jonas grabbed my head on each side and held me by the hair.

I opened my mouth to protest but no words escaping my throat as he pushed his blood drenched lips to my own sanguine coated ones. There wasn't a thing I could do but glare at the groping Vampire while he violated my mouth vigorously with his nasty tongue.

This embarrassing embrace continued for what seemed like forever. Jonas finally had to come up for air (thank God.). He refused to release my main from his hold while he stared into my enraged eyes. I noticed instead of his typical lustful interest the Vampire was fawning like the enamored schoolgirl.

I growled out, "Are you quite done pissing me off, Jonas? Or do you wish to test your ability to turn into the bat? Because if you don't get your fucking gross paws off of me, you will need to learn to fly pretty damned quick."

Jonas chuckled under his breath and then leaned into my ear to whisper, "You are beautiful to behold but that's not the only reason I love you like I do. Your lips are delicious with the taste of innocent blood on them. It is driving me insane that I cannot take you in the mount right here with everyone watching my place of good fortune. I demand you go see the doctor, then return to your sick bed, my darling. You were right to correct me for forgetting myself. I desire you return to your full health without impediment. In my defense, I find you so sexy every time I think of you I am nearly ready to rut with anything in the attempt to end the suffering of it." He pulled away with a huge grin breaking out across his gore covered face.

With a grunt I replied, "While I do enjoy the idea that you suffer, Jonas. I think in this case there is the easy fix for your distress. Next time you think of me, go fuck yourself. Noah, get me the hell out of here you slow motherfucker." The Head Master nodded and took off toward the back steps without waiting for Jonas to let loose his hold on me.

The Vampire took the hint for once and his hands opened before he snatched me baldheaded. I continued to glare at the deluded fiend for several moments while my human litter hauled me away with speed.

Bryon shot me hate filled looks as Noah passed by Sasha and him. I glared unblinkingly back at my shady brother. It cannot be known what he was thinking about this odd situation, but I assumed he was pissed I'd not managed to visit with him for the private discussion. It was true that the contract between us had changed substantially since he'd first tricked me into one with him. I knew he was beyond angry that he no longer held the powerful position over me as he once had. That said, I wasn't the fool to think this balance of control between us was set to remain in my favor. Not if I believed him the only hope I still had to escape my fate as the Mortar Palace prisoner.

That was the problem though. I honestly didn't think I could trust he was able to do as he had claimed. I was no longer ignorant of the terrible truth of my location within the world outside. The GDR and her Stasi rulers were not men that could be bargained with easily. I found it difficult to believe this brother of mine, which was also without proper papers of identity, could be clever enough to get me out of the Haus. and that was also the issue here. *Out of the Haus was no longer good enough for your Master, Meine Liebe. It came down to the choice of being held hostage in the Mortar Palace of Das Kaiser Haus versus the colorless life as the slave of the GDR.*

Despite that horrific truth, even if he couldn't produce the desired result, I still required his help. I'd found a new level of hell since my return to the Haus from the mental hospital. The beatings I'd been accustomed to as the Priceless collar had become far more brutal and numerous after I became the Dominant. Then there was the pain and suffering of the many sexual assault both from my hustling and from the unwanted attentions of Jonas, Peter, and Lucus. We will not bother to discuss in the repeat the other horrific situations I'd survived with the Stasi, Bartram, Sabastion, Tadeas, Noethan, and the yard dogs (yikes). I think you get the picture. Daily life for your Master was the nightmare.

Byron had access to the magical pain killing drugs that I'd come to appreciate far too much. He also was generous in his distribution of the cigarettes that brought me the tiny bit of pleasure in my dark world of chronic suffering. I'll not lie. I'd missed these most useful items more than you can imagine. That was the driving force behind my willingness to entertain renegotiations with my brute brother, if it became necessary. But for that moment, I wasn't free to speak with him. Given the expression I read on his face, the longer I waited to visit with him, the worse the outcome was going to be for me.

My deep thoughts of ways to curb Byron's fury were interrupted by the shrill voice of Mad Lucus when he yelled out to me, "I'm coming with you Christian Victor. Noah slow down, dammit. I cannot keep up if you run down the fucking steps. I don't want to trip and give Byron and Sasha the extra mess to clean up, you know." He took up a spot behind us, with Ruslan fallowing him.

I yelled back at that idiot, "You forget that until nine tonight you have no business sticking your nose in my affairs Lucus. Go home and I will be along before my carriage turns back into the pumpkin."

Mad Lucus snorted then replied, "I agreed to ignore your movements during the day light but that doesn't include your medical treatment, love. If you are so ill that you must be carried to the clinic to visit with your doctor I do believe your health poor enough that your Voice need be present, ja?"

A chuckle escaped me as I responded, "Ah, you think I go to see Doctor Attila because I am sick? Nein, I just stubbed my toe. I choose to be hauled around by this rough brute because I'm the lazy bastard too good to walk on my own power. Bugger off, Lucus. You bother me worse than those little fuckers I just swatted. Do you want to go home and relax or do you wish to know how the first floor carpet smells with your guts emptied onto it?"

Mad Lucus groaned then replied, "Christian Victor. You are out of control and that isn't good for your continued survival. You must realize you cannot just go around wildly murdering collars without just cause for it. I'm warning you. The residents won't tolerate you acting the brutal tyrant for long. They do their jobs with honor and trust that their leaders are forbidden to end their lives indiscriminately as you have done. Noah, I must beg you to speak in agreement with these honest things I'm telling his Majesty. If he won't hear my proper counsel, maybe he'll appreciate the added voice of one that was also injured by his mindless violence. You work too damned hard to train these collars properly to be indifferent when someone destroys all the years you've put into them, ja?"

Noah shook his head but didn't even glance back at Mad Lucus as he replied flatly, "I obey the wishes of his Majesty without question, my Lord Lucus. Even if I were permitted to offer my voice to his Majesty I wouldn't complain of the actions he took. I see no collars that I invested labor to train destroyed by his Royal Majesty this day."

Mad Lucus blew out his breath as if punched then said, "Then you are either blind or stupid, Noah. How dare you mind the King's flesh but refuse to heed the words of his tongue. Ruslan, you will add five extra lashes to the five this idiot already has coming by order of the Mortar Regent."

Ruslan sighed loudly then responded, "Your Majesties, I must beg you to rethink your unfair punishment of the Head Master. He was honorably defending his sovereign in both cases. It isn't my place to argue with men far above me in rank in this

353

Haus, I know this. However, I feel that I must alleviate my conscious by speaking on Noah's behalf since no one else seems to be willing to."

I snorted loudly then yelled out, "You speak another fucking thing, Ruslan, and I will relieve your conscious for good. Noah will accept the punishment ordered by the Elder Joans and the added lashes from my Regent without argument. Once he is broken from the whip, you will then take his spot in the chains to suffer the same sentence. I command you to fetch Ivan and see that these valid punishments are carried out without regard to any kindness. Now, you desire to complain further? Go ahead, Ruslan. I am all ears. If you are indeed done insulting my Regent then it is in your best interest to go find the man I've demanded see that you remember your fucking place in this pecking order without pissing me off worse than I am already."

Ruslan gasped but didn't say a thing as he broke off from trailing us. I heard him retreat toward the exit off the back steps apparently realizing, at last, that I meant business. Mad Lucus was silent for several moments while the three of us continued our rapid trip toward the first-floor doctor's clinic.

Finally, much to my dismay, he cleared his throat and said, "Thank you for, uhm, having my back, Christian Victor."

I guffawed loudly then replied, "Oh, if you ever think to betray me again Lucus, I promise I will do far more than that for you."

He sounded confused as he said, "What do you mean? I did no such a thing."

I motioned Noah to halt and turn around so I could face the Mortar Regent to be as I replied, "Do you think me too stupid to realize that Liliam sported the full silver around his neck but didn't answer to the name of the proper submissive? Yet Eichhörnchen, who wears black and comes to the common name of the pleasure class. I see neither of these young men were at the funeral for my beloved wife and son, but I ordered all my collared subjects to attend. I even sent out my Dungeon Masters to make sure my orders were obeyed. Liliam agreed he was the catamite property of the honorable Kay. You know one of the founding leaders of the FBL that you eagerly joined after you discovered Jacob nominated me for consideration as the new member. I found that interesting he claimed to be such a creature, because I happen to know Kay doesn't engage in the ritual of purchasing the silvers for his household."

Mad Lucus stood there staring at me appearing more confused than before as he responded, "So, you are saying that Liliam lied about the identity of his Master, and that Jonas has a sense of humor to demand the attendant of the second Fur throne be called by the pleasure submissive name. What the hell does this useless information have to do with that horrible accusation you make against me, your Regent."

I glared at him with venom practically dripping from my eyes as I replied, "You know Rudolph is an old friend of mine, and like Noah here loyal to his King above all in this Haus. He also is the man with the perfect view of everything that happened in the stables. The ones that used to belong to the Queens of the Fur and the Silk. He told me the bloody tale of two clumsy children. They were doomed to silver but were painted black by their loving Mortar King. The innocent boy was called Marc, and the girl his sweet sister, named Kloe. These two beautiful souls were attending their chores to the Queens' horses with honesty. But they had visitors that cared nothing for their skills. Two Dominants, a man and a woman, and one black collar that was dark bonded to the female of the three. It is interesting that neither child survived that unexpected and uncalled for meeting with these three criminals. Interesting because as of today, none of the bastards that killed those babies can claim the heartbeat either. Did you really think I wouldn't find out that Liliam was yet another Dominant working for Gretta in disguise, Lucus? I killed Casper already during the funeral for my Queen and Prince. He was also the Dominant pretending to be collared. It seems I haven't crush all the sneaky bastards running around pretending to be my subjects. These low Dominant are loyal only to their quest to rise in the ranks. Oh, and that motherfucker that's silver was so tarnished it turned black, wasn't renamed by the Vampire and you know this. Nein. I know every single one of the black collar staff of the fifth, sixth and seventh floors by first name and sight. I spent enough time suffering in those apartments of the rotten leaders of Kaiser Haus to remember them all. Eichhörnchen was not among them. I don't know what terrible thing he did to gain the amazing honor of coveted placement among the Elders but I can be sure that he more than earned the death I sentenced him to for it. Now, I say to you, Lucus, that bitch Liliam was employed by Gretta. You knew that but stand here and pretend you are ignorant of it. Noah just said he trained neither of those collared young men. He is the Head Dungeon Master and they were not old enough to be Hemmel's spawn. So, I must conclude that Eichhörnchen wasn't even the true tarnish silver I assumed him to be. I bet if I investigated the situation I'd discover Eichhörnchen worked for the bitch Queens too. You always make deals with Cora and Gretta behind my back, don't you? I tell you that makes me the nervous Monarch. I've often wondered if you had a hand in the plot of killing Kloe and Marc. After all it would be in your best interest to set off my rage and then pretend to be my friend by suggesting I seek out the murderers, ja? You've claimed to follow me for years, watching my every move. Always calculating the odds of my survival while guessing at the outcomes. You of all the people in this Haus had the deep insight into the things that would upset me. You think yourself so clever. I suddenly noticed you following me after never once spotting you tailing me before that day in the hallways. Ha, beware Lucus. I am not as insane nor as ignorant as you seem to hope that I am. Go ahead and do your damnest to warn all the dirty rats you and Gretta have set loose within the Haus. It will do them no good because I already discovered their secret hiding places. I swear to you I'm going to exterminate them with brutality unmatched in the realm of Hell itself. Oh, and Lucus. If anything were to happen to my beloved Rudolph. Well, then you, Cora and Gretta will not be granted any mercy as I skin you alive and send all you to the devil. As for the other person that leaked to me your part in the many conspiracies. If you wish to ask him why he turned on you, you can ask him yourself. He is easy to find these days. That fellow is busy in the Dungeon entertaining the hard working brutes down there. However, I think it will be hard for him to explain himself to you without the use of his tongue, ears or even arms and legs. I removed all that for him because his apologies for the damage he did in your name wasn't the equal service return. You know, a pound of flesh for the pound of flesh. Noah, I tire of this useless conversation. Proceed to Doctor Attila's office or I'll see that you suffer far worse than you already are going to get in those chains of the Pit." I smacked him on his big arm and he immediately took off down the steps without saying a ting.

Mad Lucus apparently was deeply disturbed by the things I'd confessed I knew. It was the truth that Bartram had felt the need to point the finger, that he no longer possessed by the way, at the ones he believed more guilty than himself over my predicament with him. He continued to follow us but didn't breath another word the rest of the trip.

As for Noah, despite his impending punishment, he served me with perfection, grace and above all no complaints. I was impressed the man didn't even utter a single sound begging me to release him from that unfair sentence handed to him. It was within my power to stop Ivan from seeing him suffer as Jonas and Mad Lucus wanted him to.

But I had good reason to allow those two idiots to have their way. It was important to me to watch Noah's resolve to obey my commands without begging favor he had not earned. After all, if he was the honest man, he knew those ten lashes wasn't even close to making us even over his cruelty toward me when I was the helpless boy. So, like it or not, I refused to call Ivan off from his brutal task.

Ruslan was not in any better position than Noah when it came to gaining my trust. He'd been thus far fair and minded his place without quarrel. His attempts to argue with my assumed regent was bothersome to witness. This behavior couldn't be left without a reminder that no matter how much he disliked the orders of the Mortar King, including the man assigned to speak for me, he had to mind them.

I confess to you that I honestly didn't enjoy knowing that these men that I called allies, and hopefully friends, were going to be tortured at my orders. That was just too bad for your Master, Meine Liebe. It often isn't fun to be the king and being the Mortar Monarch was proven to absolutely suck in almost every way indeed.

Anyway the rest of the journey went without incident. I was feeling very groggy and in almost unbearable agony before the three of us entered the clinic together. The moment we were safely inside Noah gently released me to standing.

I saw Doctor Attila standing in one of the patient rooms deep in hushed conversation with the Shadow King. Matz and Roland were lingering close to the reception desk. The two Wolves watched the Head Master as he bowed to me then moved swiftly to stand quietly the door. Noah didn't leave but instead placed himself where any visitors could see him easily.

I nodded my approval in his direction as I realized he was obeying my orders to perfection. He knew that Ivan would be along shortly seeking to arrest him. Noah's polite behavior assured that the Russian brute could extract him from the doctor's office without the need to cause undue drama.

I snickered to myself when I witnessed the pimp, the violinist, and the Mortar Regent glaring at Noah with expressions of suspiciousness on their faces. As I watched them prickling with unnecessary distrust for the Head Master, I noticed something about Matz I'd missed earlier in the apartment. I started to motion him to approach so I could speak with him about it but Doctor Attila had become aware of my presence by then.

He called out, "Herr Maxximillian. Don't attempt to move from that spot. Cary, assist me in getting, his Majesty into the examination room please."

I turned my head and shot a glance at Noah. He kept his eyes forward in the stoic stare without any expression on his face. Before I could move another muscle, the Shadow King had taken me around the waist. I gave him no quarrel while he and Doctor Attila hurriedly dragged me off for the medical inspection.

Mad Lucus, Matz, and Roland all took it upon themselves to tail us into the room. I wanted to tell them to back off but for that moment Cary's rough handling caused that pain in my middle to reach excruciating levels. I could barely catching my breath and was unable to keep from screaming in agony.

However, the minute I was safely perched on the exam table I roared in the furious tone, "Everyone but the doctor better get the fuck out of here. This is a one man show only. Don't make me repeat myself. I'm not in any mood to be ignored. I mean it."

Well, lucky for those four motherfuckers they decided not to test me. Doctor Attila and I watched the group of them leave the way they'd come. Of course Mad Lucus and Cary both appeared the sullen bitches that neither man had been permitted to stay with me. I wasn't the least bit concerned for what any of them thought or felt. I was determined to recoup the tiniest bit of dignity in this mess. Some things are just too private to share with anyone other than your physician, ja?

The moment the last man, Mad Lucus, was clear of the room Doctor Attila glared at me and said, "Okay, your Majesty we are alone. Cary told me he witnessed you bleeding heavily from the rectum. Before you say a word. I must ask you, did you engage in intercourse with him? Otherwise I must wonder how he was able to report this information to me." His expression was accusatory and he seemed barely able to contain anger over this misunderstanding.

I shook my head and said in the gasping voice, "Nein, I haven't slept with anyone willingly. I swear to you I minded your medical advice to the letter. However, Cary is correct. He was with me when I discovered heavy bleeding. Also there is horrible pain in my, uhm, damaged area." I groaned as another strong cramp gripped me in the middle.

The doctor raised an eyebrow appearing confused as he replied, "You said you haven't engaged with anyone willing. So, you are claiming you've been raped again?" He approached and placed his stethoscope to my chest to listen to my heartbeat.

I moaned then responded, "Honestly, I don't know what has happened doctor. All I can report to you with certainty is what I have said already. It feels like I've been penetrated, but I'm not sure that's what has happened. I was kind of hoping you could tell me."

Doctor Attila removed his medical tool abruptly and stared at me in disbelief as he replied, "How could you not be aware if anal sex has occurred or not? You have some memory loss? Wait, did you lift something heavier than ten pounds? I told you to mind that weight limit also. That could cause tearing of the stitches too."

I shook my head and said in with labored breathing, "Ja, I did breach your weight limit orders, but only briefly and not until after the heavy flow started. Don't ask about that. I think soon enough you will hear rumors of it in the Haus. As for the reason I don't recall. Well, I was drugged by the DJ. He left the chocolate donut in the hallway and I stupidly ate it. After that, I took a nap and when I awoke this pain came over me."

He blinked several times as if trying to clear his vision then replied, "Okay, so you claiming you ate a drugged donut given to you by a man named DJ? Who is this man. I wish to send someone to fetch him so he and I can discuss the reasons I gave strict orders that you are not to be having sex."

I rolled my eyes and then bellowed out nearly insane from the pain, "Nein, I didn't take fucking drugs. Not on purpose, dammit. This DJ says his name is Superman and he lives in the walls of the Haus. I called him the DJ for years because he owns the radio station. You know him. He's that guy that gossips about me during his annoying and never ending broadcasts. There, hear that? He's talking about me right now. Hush, listen. He's laughing about that nasty trick he's pulled on me. I think he wishes to have me ruined into wearing that colostomy bag. It is because I won't go live with him and his mummy woman, you know. He might be angry that I refused his pocket soup offer too. Please doctor. Make him stop. I cannot take the stress of it and run this fucking Haus as the rightful Mortar King."

Doctor Attila sucked in his breath and his expression melted from anger to one of deep concern as he very softly responded, "Ah, okay, I understand everything now, your Majesty. Please calm yourself. I believe you. If you are willing, I need to take the look at your injury in order to assess how much damage, uhm, the DJ has done. There is no reason to be upset. I'm certain I can repair you back to new, ja?"

I winced from the onslaught of pain as I whimpered, "I don't want to wear the colostomy bag, doctor. Please fix this without doing that to me. It wasn't my fault. I would have stopped him from doing this to me if I'd been able."

He nodded and said in the calm voice, "I know you would have, your Majesty. This isn't your fault, I know this. You need not be afraid. I can make it better without such a drastic cure but you must let me help you without fighting my efforts. Can you do that for me?"

Another loud groan escaped me as I did as he asked me to. I watched him rush over to his fancy medicine cabinet. Then he began to dig around in it until he found the bottle he was seeking. Terror rushed thru me when I saw him retrieve a syringe and push the needle to fill it with the medication. He noticed I was trembling and halted his actions with suddenness.

Then he smiled with peaceful expression taking over his face and said in the kindly tone, "Relax, your Majesty. This is the painkilling injection I'm preparing for you. I promise in a moment, that torment in your belly will end. Then we can speaking about how best to keep that DJ from taking advantage of you by drugging your food, okay?"

I let out a sigh of relief and replied, "Oh thank you for the mercy of it, doctor. I thought for a moment you intended to fill me with that mind altering crap that knocks me out cold. They did that all the time in the mental hospital. I'm not the schizophrenic but they worked for the Vampire. That bastard cares only about sucking my blood so he can steal the demons that live inside of me. Do you have to put the painkiller in the shot? Can I not just have the pills? I really hate getting jabbed." I watched him approaching me with a bit of apprehension.

Doctor Attila chuckled as he took a place next to me and held the syringe to the light. He knocked the air bubbles from the liquid then attempted to expose my left hip for his needle. I whimpered and blocked him from pulling my breeches down with my bandaged hand. The doctor backed off his task immediately.

He glanced at me for a moment then said softly, "Your Majesty, it is only a little stick and then you will feel so much better. I'm asking you nicely to let me treat you without your interference. If you don't do this willingly. I will be forced to call in those men to help get this done. You don't want them in here for this private business between us, and neither do I. So? You going to let me do this or not?"

I trembled slightly and then removed the hand that was obstructing his actions, "Okay doctor. I'm trusting you though. If you tell me lies, you will be sorry for it."

He nodded and then quickly administered his medication as he replied, "Your Majesty I am sorry every time I see you coming to visit with me. Sorry for the horrific situation you and others in this hell hole suffer all their short lives. Now, it is done. See that wasn't so bad, ja? There was no need for such a fuss."

I set my eyes on his kind face, and noticed the borders of it had become fuzzy. I yawned heavily but was unable to cover my mouth because my arms felt like lead weights. The room appeared to spin a bit but strangely it didn't frighten me. With a giggle I turned my head to watch the halos of light that seemed to emit from the walls.

Then I returned my groggy gaze back to Doctor Attila and said, "Doctor, you are the man of your word. The pain is gone. That is a miracle you have in your needles. I thank you for the mercy of it. Is it alright if I take a quick nap? It's been a hard day. I swear I don't snore."

Doctor Attila chuckled softly and replied, "You sleep all you wish Maxximillian. I will keep the DJ away so that you can get a long, peaceful rest." I started to thank him for offering to guard the door but the darkness of unconsciousness overtook me before I could.

When I awoke I found I'd been moved from that exam room into the patient bed. I groaned in groggy dismay upon the discovery that I was held hostage to the bed by the four-point restraints with the chest strap. This disturbed me because I thought Doctor Attila was making sure that I was unable to refuse the affections of any of the men that wanted to violate me at will.

I yelled out in the furious tone, "You lied to me, you motherfucker. I'm will kill you the second I get out of these restraints, Doctor Attila. Let me get out of this bed. Help me. Someone help me. I am the fucking Master of the Haus. My words are the law, Goddammit. I hate you. I hate all of you." With all the strength I could call upon I struggled and thrashed against the bondage devices.

The door of the room flew open and Doctor Attila and a huge nurse came rushing inside. I glared at them and gnashed my dentures threatening to bite either of them if their attempted to get close. Both medical professionals ignored my fit of rage while they hurriedly gathered the items to give me another of his 'nappy time' shots.

All I could do was curse them to hell as their worked together to hit me with their loaded needle. After that medication entered my flesh my antics went silent. The fast moving stuff stilled my tongue before it locked my lids closed tight. The last thing I could sense before I fell back into the dreamless void was the heavy smell of roses.

This scene repeated itself at least twice more over the next two weeks. I know how long this clinic visit lasted because Mad Lucus told me of it after the doctor thought me healed enough to be allowed to maintain solid consciousness.

Apparently, I'd suffered such heavy loss of blood I required one of the blood transfusions I'd become famous for needing. The obvious rape I had suspected and the hasty re-repair job on my sphincter were the culprits this time.

I was barely alert before I was further assaulted by a flurry of questions from Mad Lucus as to the identity of the criminal behind this horror. I still assumed it to be the DJ and told him so.

Of course, he didn't believe me anymore than Doctor Attila had. Both of them, and I was to find out Cary too, thought I had disobeyed with Jonas. Though I denied that vehemently, their refused to accept I would report that bat if he had been the bastard that raped me.

Then, I found out that Jonas had come by the clinic not long after Doctor Attila had admitted me as his long term patient. It did bring me a bit of thrill to hear Mad Lucus, along with the good doctor, had forced him to leave. They'd managed to keep him at bay during the entire time I'd been there by threatening to report his 'near fatal' behavior toward the Mortar King to King Claus. Which I found out not only continued to survive but seemed to have recovered his strength enough to travel about the Haus as he used to.

Well that sent the bat flying back to his belfry with speed. That didn't prevent him from making his presence known though. I was shocked to notice the entire sick room was filled from wall to wall with dozens of red roses. Mad Lucus told me with disgust in his voice tone that every day without fail Jonas had the flowers delivered to my room. He also said that initially he and the doctor had thrown them out, but eventually their gave up because as soon as their did, Jonas would send more.

It pissed me off that despite Doctor Attila allowing me to remain conscious, he still refused to release me from the restraints. His explanation for this was that I'd become severely psychotic and dangerous to myself and others. I supposed he was referring to my carrying out that death sentence to the criminals Liliam and Eichhörnchen but he never denied nor verified this as his reason to believe such bullshit about me.

So thanks to that Stasi business, then the week after it with the added two more, I'd lost almost the entire month of January. I was to turn eighteen in June. My short time left above ground, had woefully become even more precious than before.

As I laid there in that bed doing everything possible to appear the compliant patient. All I could do is worry the doctor intended to hold me prisoner until my clock ran out completely. It seemed this would be the solution that would suit many in the Haus. A restrained Mortar King couldn't put the Haus on notice that he was the force to be reckoned with. Nor could that Monarch hunt down the rest of the lurking monsters that had put him on this path to destruction in the first place, ja?

However, on the Tuesday of the beginning of my third week in his care, Doctor Attila came into my room that morning and began undoing the leather straps. I held completely still and remained silent while he did this. I feared he'd take any excuse to rethink his decision to let me free.

Just as he started to work on my right wrist he said without even glancing at me, "Before I finish I would like you to remember that I only do what I must to see that you are in your best health, your Majesty. If you are thinking of injuring me in any way, then there isn't a thing I could or would do to stop you. These men that hold power in this place are unyielding in their desire to cause you brutality. I did this because I feared if you were not given complete protection eventually one of them would damage you beyond my skills to see you made whole. I won't offer apology that I give a fuck what happens to you. Because I do care more than you know. So, do what you believe is the correct thing. Either get the hell out of here before that arrogant snot Lucus arrives to fawn over you, or you can waste that time killing me. Up to you, your Majesty. I say that with respect." He pulled the belt away and I sat up with slow deliberateness unsure if I would be in pain or not.

To my surprise I felt no burning nor ripping sensations as I replied softly, "I admit I did consider murdering you, doctor. However, you have been the life saver many times already. I suppose I owe you more than a few service returns. I thank you for your hard labors and kindness. Do you need me to return soon for the checkup or perhaps do you have further medical orders for me?" I glanced at him and saw that his face was breaking out in the small grin.

He shook his head and said, "No intercourse for at least under two to three weeks. I wish to say you should never engage in anal sex again, but I realize this isn't possible so I won't bother to waste words on it. As for the checkups. Come visit with me in seven days. I want to check on that latest repair. But before you go, your Majesty, forgive me for saying this, but I don't desire to have to pack your colon intestines back into your abdominal cavity ever again. If you see a donut laying around in the hallway floor. Leave it for the rats, okay?"

I chuckled lightly and took to my boots as I replied, "That is sound medical advice I am most happy to obey."

He reached over to the chair sitting next to the bed and handed me a fresh vampire outfit as he said, "Hurry up and dress, your Majesty. Lucus arrives every morning around eight thirty. It is now seven forty-five. He didn't bring a cane for you as I suggested but I have one that I loan out for the residents when their break a leg. You may use it until you can get the one he says is at your apartment. I will get it and give you a little privacy. That is unless you think you need help?"

I shook my head and said, "Nein, I can do this. Thank you for the cane. I promise to bring it back to you in one piece by tomorrow."

He laughed and headed out of the room as he replied, "It's made of the sturdy aluminum. It will maintain your weight but as the weapon I think you'll find it worthless. It happens to bend with ease if used for anything other than mobility." He glanced at me with a look of humored caution just as he exited and closed the door behind him.

Th moment I was presentable I limped out of there. I found Doctor Attila writing his medical notes at the desk in the reception area. He didn't even looked up from his scribbling as he pointed out the crutch next to one of the waiting chairs in the room. I quickly retrieved it and hauled ass out of the clinic as if the Russian army were chasing me. I knew Mad Lucus wasn't due to arrive for another fifteen or so minutes, but I wanted to put as much distance as possible between us, ja?

All through the hallways, as usual by this time, everyone I met fell into the reverent kneel. I didn't bother to acknowledge any of the many travelers around me. It was painfully clear that Mad Lucus was in the right to demand I attend to him until our agreed upon hour of nine. He'd surely be pissed I was attempting to scrimp on our deal.

The way I saw it he had already taken liberty by sitting daily by my side while I lay helpless to demand he leave me in peace. So, I decided to let him bitch about it later when I was forced to return to the apartment. Until I was certain he'd realize his time of holding me hostage to attend him had run out, I needed the place to hide.

The one place I knew he'd never dare to come seeking me was Matz's old first-floor apartment. I made the beeline right for it. Again, I forgot I didn't have the key to it on me. I arrived just as that occurred to me. With a sigh of frustration I reached out to try the knob expecting it to hold tight. To my surprise, it turned and the door groaned on its hinges as it slowly opened.

The room was dark, and there wasn't any sounds of life coming from within. I wondered for a moment which of those morons had forgotten to lock the apartment before leaving. I assumed this must have been the oversight that day the Wolves had hastily hauled me to the apartment. The idea that this important spot had been left unguarded and unprotected with so many expensive items contained within made me a bit angry.

I grumbled over their stupidity under my breath as I entered, closed the door behind me and flipped on the lights. Then I let out a yell of terror when my eyes come upon the silent figure of Matz sitting in his ratty recliner. He was still as the statue, staring at me appearing as stunned to see me as I was to be visiting with him.

I grabbed at my chest and yelled out in the breathless tone, "Goddammit Matz, what the fuck? Why are you sitting here in the dark with the door unlocked? You nearly scared me to death."

He gasped and shook his head slowly, "Ah, Mad Maxx. I, uhm, didn't expect to see you here. How are you feeling? Better I hope?"

With a groan I used the crutch to hobble toward the Wolf as I replied flatly, "No doubt you worried that I'll say I'm still under the weather. Well fear not Matz. I believe I'm mended enough to return to light duty work. Do you think you can get a few clients in this afternoon? Find out what they are interested in, and unless it is penetration services, I think I can oblige them." I stopped my trip across the room with a startle as I got close enough to view him clearly.

The two of us stared at each other for a few moments then I whispered, "Are you crying Matz? You are covered in bruises brother. Who has done this to you? What has happened."

Matz shook his head and sniffed loudly as he replied, "Oh, this? It's nothing, Maxx. I am the clumsy bastard, ja? I'm not weeping. It's allergies. I always did have the weak constitution." He grinned bitterly at me.

370

I shook my head and took to my knees before the wounded Wolf as I responded, "Matz, please stop trying to lie to me. We are old friends, ja? I come and find you hiding out in the dark deep in despair. You need not say another word. Come here and let me hold you. I think you need a little kindness after so much brutality. You get this pain off your chest. Then after that, if you wish, we can discuss dis."

His lips trembled with the threatening storm of grief as he replied, "Oh Maxx, what am I going to do? I love him so much." He came out of his recliner and practically fell into my lap, wailing like the lost soul he'd honestly become.

I wrapped my bandaged hands around his waist and petted his back while he sobbed loudly for many minutes. It was hard to hear the sorrow sounds that come out of him. No matter what had passed between Matz and I, no one had the right to abuse him as clearly had been done. I need not say this, but Roland had become the latest fellow on my list of assholes that had the corrective lesson coming.

Once Matz was able to get his depression under control he lifted from our embrace and said through his tears, "Thank you Maxx for, well, for always being the decent human being even when no one is to you." He wiped his eyes with the back of his hands.

With a chuckle I replied, "You certainly are one of the guiltiest of foul treatment towards me, Matz. Never mind that. You willing to tell me what happened or are you leaving me to guess?"

He closed his eyes then hid his face in my chest as he said, "It was all my fault, Maxx. I came home last night and found him in bed with someone. I threw the hissy fit over his constantly cheating on me and didn't know when to shut up. Roland doesn't need my bullshit added to the stress he already suffers. That job he has with the Haus orchestra gets to him, you know. and then there I go, acting the fish wife. You need not feel sorry for me I got what I deserved."

I pushed Matz off me and forced him to look into my face as I growled out to him, "Matz. Stop it. You didn't earn this beating Roland gave to you. People that love you don't beat you for telling them their actions hurt your feelings. Tell me, does he strike you often?"

Matz dropped his gaze to stare at my tear drenched shirt as he replied, "Uhm, not all the time, Maxx. Only whenever I piss him off. Look this isn't your problem, love. I just have to learn to keep him the happy man and stop bitching so much. He is the good provider and honestly, no one else would have me."

That made me snort loudly just before I said in the disbelieving tone, "Did Roland tell you that you are undesirable or do you merely assume that? I agree that you can be a handful to live with but Matz, sweetheart, this is the toxic love affair you have. There are many in this Haus that would adore to have your generous affections and eager attendance to their every whim. Leave this motherfucker and take up with someone that can appreciate you for the wonderful person you truly are."

He shook his head and his eyes filled with fear as he replied, "Nein, I tell you already that I love him. I don't want another lover, Maxx. I just want him to stop hitting me all the time. Maybe you could speak with him. Explain to him that I'm the ignorant bitch and sometimes he might need to just ignore my chronic complaints."

I reached out and caressed his cheek while gazing at him with awe as I responded, "Matz, you are too good for Roland, I wish you could see that. If there isn't anything I can say to get you to end it with him, then I swear I will have the discussion you request with him quickly as possible."

Matz smiled with sudden brightness and replied, "The only one that could steal me away from Roland is the only one I cannot have. You already know that. I thank you for doing this for me, Maxx. If you ever decide, oh never mind. I will not say the truth that you can clearly see in my eyes."

That made me groan as I said, "Matz, you are indeed the hopeless romantic you once told me Roland accused you of being. Look, you may be the little man, but your weight is killing my legs. would you be a dear and get the fuck off me." I pushed him with strength and he fell backward to his ass giggling the entire way.

Matz chuckled as he watched me struggle to stand then he said, "Goddamn you are more beautiful with every passing day, Maxx. I think if I were the religious man I'd believe you are the devil himself. They say he was the most gorgeous of all the angels and the unruliest too. I've even heard that he is the Master of all the sinful things that make life worthy of living."

I nodded as I cast a sour glance at the Wolf and replied, "Ja that sounds like me alright. So, are you able to get a few lusty perverts lined up by three this afternoon? As you told me, the bills aren't about to pay for themselves. Hey, have you eaten yet? Do you smell something delicious cooking? I'm starving."

Th huge grin broke out on Matz's face just as he lifted his right hip and suddenly the sound "Frrrrrraaaaaaaaap" echoed through the room.

He began to laugh wildly just as I pulled my damp blouse to cover my nose as he said, "Ja, you are smelling the refried eggs that I had for breakfast, Maxx. Oh, I'm sorry brother, but you totally stepped into that one."

I waved away the rancid smell of his gas emission as I replied in the pissy tone, "I'd better not step in anything that's come out of your ass, Matz. Damn you are fucking disgusting, do you know that? Can you be serious for a minute? Stop playing."

He stopped his mirth and took on the serious expression, took to his boots and bowed low while he said, "Oh, I apologize for making the offensive smells, your royal Majesty. I thank you for the mercy you grant your most unworthy servant. I beg that you allow me the most glorious task of accompanying you to the Great Hall. There I shall feed you with my low hands from the silver spoons off the golden plate, my King."

I reached out and swatted him lightly on the back of his lowered head as I chuckled in reply, "I must decline your most generous offer. I love my subjects and breakfast too much to expose either of them to death by Matz Mustard Gas."

Matz glanced up without rising to his full height and with the false offended expression responded, "Hey. I told you it was hen's bounty that caused this bloat. So, that is Matz Egg Farts, I thank you."

With a loud sigh I replied, "And that's what I tried to get you to understand. What's not to love about you, Herr Farts? I see you at three, Matz. I won't be late."

He nodded his agreement and I headed out the door, without further words between us. I had a lot to finish before that hour I was to return to the hustle. I had noticed on the fancy clock on the apartment wall, Mad Lucus was no longer capable of complaint

374

that I owed him attention. That was the good news. The bad, was that I'd already wasted more time than I'd intended in order to deal with a heart injured Wolf.

It wasn't fun to hear the facts of the thing that I'd suspected since seeing Matz that day I'd been violated by the DJ. He'd been sporting a black eye and busted lips but thanks to my state of distress I'd missed those tell tail signs. Matz had become the victim of domestic violence at the hands of his brutal lover, the abusive Roland. This was a mess that I was not too happy to become involved with. However, Matz's importance to the health and welfare of my black collar children made this private issue between them, my problem too. Ugh.

I limped along with speed down the congested hallways of the first floor. Everyone continued to engage in the demonstrations of reverence no matter how quickly I flew past them. Though I wanted to shout at the residents to end their chronic bowing and scraping, I realized this behavior was necessary. It had already been useful in making my job of 'rat hunting' a bit easier once. I thought maybe the superstition that lightning doesn't strike twice might be incorrect.

Each face in the kneeling crowd was scanned by my weary eyes. There was one in particular I desired to spot that morning but unfortunately, I didn't get lucky. With a sigh of frustration I headed for the Dungeon steps but halted just at the top of them. I was unsure if I could navigate them without falling to my death thanks to the bulky crutch I was using.

Though I was fearful, I decided the task I had to accomplish wasn't one I desired to share with the witness. I sucked in my breath, braced myself and slowly began to descend the stairs.

I was nearly to the bottom, without any tripping thank God, before I heard a familiar voice call out, "Your Majesty, please, I beg of you to stop your traveling. I'll be right there to see that you get to your destination safely."

I let out my breath that I'd been holding in relief as I replied, "You have my permission to see this service to you King is done. I thank you for the mercy of it Head Master." I watched Noah rush up from steps with the expression of worry on his face.

He arrived in moments and took me into his arms as he had before. I glanced at his face and noticed he had the small healing cut on his cheek. That caused the fury to rise within me immediately. I could tell even in the dim light this was the signature of the whip tail that missed its intended mark.

Noah carefully traveled the stoney terrain for a moment before I broke the silence between us by saying, "Are you angry with me for not protecting you from Jonas and Mad Lucus's wrath?"

He didn't even glance at me as he replied flatly, "Nein, your Majesty. I understood the punishment before I did the crime. I obey your commands without complaint or question."

I chuckled at that then said, "I could've granted you mercy, Noah. You honestly claim it doesn't piss you off a little that I not only didn't but punished your attempts to protect your King severely."

He reached the ground level just as he responded in the non-emotional tone, "I don't bear the heavy burden of the Mortar crown, your Majesty. I know nothing of it, nor do I desire to. Your will is my own." He gently returned me to my feet and dropped into the graceful kneel before me.

376

My eager eyes took in the sight of his perfect form for a moment before I hand gestured him that he could rise and said, "Is Ivan getting sloppy with his skills? This wound on your face. How'd that occur? Do not attempt to protect that Russian bastard nor lie to me, Noah. Speaking up dammit."

He kept his eyes cast to the floor as he replied, "I flinched, your Majesty."

With a sneer I responded, "Turn around Head Master and drop your pants. I wish to see just how much you 'struggled.' Do this now."

Noah shot me a glance of concern. Then quickly did as he was commanded baring his well-shaped buttocks at me right there where any passerby could see. His bottom was ravaged with healing welts, cuts and strips. I then saw that two of the signs of his thudding were outside the safety zones and far deeper than necessary too.

I growled out, "Enough. Make yourself presentable, Noah. You will follow me to your barracks. I think your being far too generous with your claims that these marks were caused by the unconscious response to avoid pain."

Noah rapidly pulled his leather breeches up and re-buckled his belt as he replied, "As you wish, Sire."

I took off towards his stone cell room without saying another thing. While we traveled in silence I thought of the terrible things I planned to do to Ivan for daring to scar up my beauty as he had. This was the insult that the old Russian wasn't going to be able to easily talk his way out of.

I was aware of the rivalry between the German Dungeon Masters and Russian Guardsmen. However, his taking out his aggression on the man that I knew never offended him in anyway, since Noah was condemned to remain in the Dungeon exclusively, was unforgivable.

Once we were safely behind his locked door and without chance of witness I glared at him furiously and said, "Noah, this is your last chance to tell me what I want to know with honesty. I warn you. I won't tolerate any further attempts by you to evade my command."

His eyes went wide and he fell to his knees at my feet as he whimpered, "Please believe me, Mad Maxx. It wasn't Ivan's fault. I confess that I wasn't capable of holding still while he took aim. His swing was wicked."

I nodded but maintained my angered gaze upon him as I replied, "So I have heard. However, struggling in the chains doesn't explain how his whip nearly took out one of your eyes, now does it?

Noah blew out his breath and dropped his head low as he responded, "Ivan showed mercy even though you ordered he grant none. He didn't clip either Ruslan nor I in the chains for his torture. His blow found my face because I stupidly turned my head to get a look at his position. He'd just let loose the first strike and I'd been unprepared for it. My knees buckled and I was heading toward the floor. Ivan was in the hurry to finish the sentence and released the second lash before realizing that I'd collapsed. He offered apology many times and gave excellent medical treatment."

With a snort I said, "Apology? Are words going to return your complexion to the flawless vision it was? I think not."

He shook his head then sighed as he responded, "Okay, he did say sorry but Ivan also gave me a small payment for the damage. I didn't wish to speak of it, but I always do as you command, Mad Maxx. He did adequately compensate me for the damage he did by accident."

That caused me to chuckle while I replied, "Oh, he paid you for your pain and suffering did he? So, what did you do with this fortune you were paid for with your flesh and blood, Noah? I suppose you bought a new harness or perhaps the girly magazines to masturbate to?" I glanced at his threadbare bed for a moment wondering if he had hidden it there. I kind of was hoping he had done that because I wanted to look at it too.

Noah stifled a laugh as he said, "Nein, Mad Maxx. I thought you already knew what I did with that money."

My startle and confusion was apparent as I growled out angrily, "How the fuck would I? Do you think I can read your mind? I'm the Mortar King, not God."

The Head Master looked up at me with suddenness and fear in his expression as he replied, "But I sent the roses every day at the same time you, uhm, you asked me to become your lover. I thought you would understand this silly gesture."

I suddenly recalled that Mad Lucus told me they stopped throwing out the roses Jonas sent each morning because by afternoon he'd send more. Neither he nor Doctor Attila realized the second batch was from Noah.

With a sudden stir of affection I motioned Noah to rise as I said lovingly, "I appreciated every single one of those beautiful flowers, my love. I was just making sure that no one harmed you seriously. If they had be assured I'd kill them for it. Now, I wonder, are you busy? If not I've got something I need to do and could use a strong, sexy back to aid me in it."

Noah's pretty face broke into the beautiful smile as he replied, "I'm always at your service. You tell me what you want and I will do it without question nor quarrel."

Laughter erupted from me as I said in the humored tone, "Ah, that is music to my ears to hear, lover. What do you know about the Mortar Palace? Have you ever visited it before?"

Noah shook his head and his eyes blazed with excitement as he said, "Oh, I've never seen it but I've heard it is glorious to behold. They say the entire place is made of pure silver and the Mortar throne is covered in jewels. No one is permitted to even know the location of your magical kingdom, Mad Maxx. I know you were there last summer. Could I dare to be so bold as to asking what it was like there? I bet it was as magnificent as the man that wears its crown."

My expression went dark immediately as I responded bitterly, "Come with me, Noah. I'm going to do far better than stoke your imagination with vivid descriptions. I'm going to take you on the personal tour, right this moment."

His face lit up with delight as he exclaimed, "Really? Oh Mad Maxx. You are too good to me. No wonder I love you like I do."

I raised my hand and gestured him to unlock his door then trail me in silence as I replied, "Do you, Noah? Well, I suppose it is time to determine if that is truth or the fantasy. Because shortly, you will find out why their leveled me Priceless"

**To be continued in book three in
The Most Brutal Man in Europe Series**

About the Author: Alexandria May Ausman

Alexandria May Ausman in her 16th year was diagnosed with Schizophrenia. She was quickly abandoned by her foster parents. While still only a teen, she was forced to battle this devastating illness alone.

Alexandria has struggled with lack of a support system, numerous psychotic episodes, exploitation, homelessness, and an uncaring mental health system.

Alexandria raised two healthy children. After obtaining her bachelor's degree in psychology she worked as a child abuse investigator and became a diagnostic psychologist while acquiring her Master's in psychology. Alexandria never forgot the experience of 'slipping through the cracks.' Her life's goal is to help people suffering abuse and/or mental illness have access to necessary services. By accident, she became a model of 'gothic attire' and the World Goth Queen.

She began writing a fictionalized account of her life experiences after a catastrophic return of psychotic symptoms. Today, Alexandria is retired, and homebound due to crippling symptoms of Schizophrenia. She currently lives in Tallahassee, Florida, with her loving husband and a loyal support dog.